****

Cherubim's Call

Book One of the Apollo's Arrows Series

By T.C. Manning and James Rosone

****

Illustration © Tom Edwards
Tom EdwardsDesign.com

Published in conjunction with Front Line Publishing, Inc.

Manuscript Copyright Notice

©2022, T.C. Manning and James Rosone, in conjunction with Front Line Publishing, Inc. Except as provided by the Copyright Act, no part of this publication may be reproduced, stored in a retrieval system or transmitted in any form or by any means without the prior written permission of the publisher.

ISBN: 978-1-957634-00-5
Sun City Center, Florida, USA
Library of Congress Control Number: 2022901245

Table of Contents

Prologue 5
Chapter 1: Kodiak 9
Chapter 2: Hall 21
Chapter 3: Moore 30
Chapter 4: Kodiak 37
Chapter 5: Hall 41
Chapter 6: Moore 48
Chapter 7: Kodiak 57
Chapter 8: Hall 62
Chapter 9: Moore 65
Chapter 10: Kodiak 70
Chapter 11: Hall 75
Chapter 12: Moore 82
Chapter 13: Kodiak 93
Chapter 14: Hall 102
Chapter 15: Moore 108
Chapter 16: Kodiak 111
Chapter 17: Hall 117
Chapter 18: Moore 126
Chapter 19: Kodiak 136
Chapter 20: Hall 142
Chapter 21: Moore 150
Chapter 22: Kodiak 156
Chapter 23: Hall 167
Chapter 24: Moore 175
Chapter 25: Kodiak 181
Chapter 26: Hall 187
Chapter 27: Moore 192
Chapter 28: Kodiak 196
Chapter 29: Hall 203
Chapter 30: Moore 209
Chapter 31: Kodiak 217
Chapter 32: Hall 225
Chapter 33: Kodiak 228
Chapter 34: Moore 233
Chapter 35: Kodiak 237

Chapter 36: Hall 246
Chapter 37: Kodiak 251
Chapter 38: Moore 261
Chapter 39: Kodiak 267
Chapter 40: Hall 270
Chapter 41: Moore 273
Chapter 42: Kodiak 277
Chapter 43: Hall 282
Chapter 44: Moore 286
Chapter 45: Hall 292
Chapter 46: Kodiak 295
Chapter 47: Hall 298
Chapter 48: Kodiak 301
Epilogue 306
From James Rosone 309
From the Author 310
Abbreviation Key 312

Prologue

Year 2093
Apollo Company, 1-331st Infantry Regiment
28 Kilometers from Combat Outpost Legion
New Eden, Rhea System

Observing the brownish water of the Lalibok River reminded Staff Sergeant Antinos of home—of Rosedale and the Mississippi River. The trees—were nothing like home. They could reach as high as two or three hundred meters in some places. They reminded him of banyan trees with the way their canopies expanded outwards—parts of the branches extended down into the soil below, almost like a house built on stilts. Even the species of birds, flying animals, and insects were so different, it was distracting. It was a harsh reminder…this wasn't home, and this wasn't the Mississippi. He was twelve light-years from Earth on a hostile planet he and his men were in the process of capturing. Somewhere across that river was an army…an army of horrifying beasts—an alien species so foreign in nature he still struggled to understand it.

Feeling a slight nudge to his right, Staff Sergeant Antinos turned slowly to look at Private First Class Domingo. "What is it?" he asked, barely above a whisper.

"Staff Sergeant, I'm gonna share my helmet's HUD view—I think I saw something," Domingo said sheepishly, pointing across the river while the two helmets' heads-up displays or HUDs connected.

Receiving the image, Antinos looked it over. The helmet HUDs were a game-changing tool being rapidly integrated into the infantry. The helmets provided grunts with an integrated night vision capability. They also incorporated a thermal view along with a FLIR or forward-looking infrared, giving them both thermal and IR ability. There was also a limited spectral scanner, especially useful for zero-g and situations like this planet. It wasn't to the same standards as the ones the Special Forces had, but it was better than nothing. Looking at the image, he tried to increase the magnification. It was clear whatever Domingo had seen was at the edge of the optical range of his helmet's visor. The dense underbrush made it hard to see too deep into the forest. They'd have to wait for it to get closer.

Looking in the direction Domingo had pointed, he waited to see if he saw it too. A minute or so went by, then he spotted something. The kid was right—there *was* something there. If he'd learned one thing during his eight years in reconnaissance, it was that there are no straight lines found in nature. He was about to say something to the kid when the line moved.

"Stay still," Sergeant Antinos whispered to Domingo and the other nearby private, Aldi. "No sudden movements. We aren't alone." The soldiers gripped their rifles a little tighter, continuing to watch across the river.

When Antinos looked for the object again, he'd lost it. He widened his search. Finally, he spotted movement again. This time he saw a figure. It was one of them—the sinister aliens hunting them, savagely attacking them whenever they had the chance.

Antinos reached for the talk button on the side of his helmet and called it in.

"Apollo Six, Romeo Four. How copy?"

Five long seconds passed; Antinos kept his eye on the figure the entire time. The giant four-armed blue beast seemed to be just standing there, hiding partially in the shadows.

"Romeo Four, Apollo Six. Send it."

"Apollo Six, I'm synching our helmet cams to you now. I've got positive ID on at least one enemy soldier. Adjust from my position, three hundred meters to my front, right twenty meters."

Each of the Romeo or recon units had a blue force geo tracker embedded on them. It allowed the tactical operations center back on Combat Outpost Legion to know exactly where they were in relationship to the COP and made calling for help or fire support quick and easy. They could adjust fire based on a soldier's location and what they were seeing. Once the TOC had synched their monitors to a scout's helmet cam, they could instantly see what the scout saw.

"Romeo Four, good copy. We're seeing what you're seeing. Are you aware of additional enemy activity?"

As the operator in the TOC spoke, the figure Antinos had been watching stepped forward, out of the shadows. A sliver of light cut through a gap in the tree canopy, dancing slightly with the wind. The light fully illuminated it, and a shiver of fear washed over him. The alien stood nearly three meters in height—ten feet. A thick braid of black hair, bound tightly with thin gold bands, flowed from the top of its head, down its shoulders and back.

The beast turned its head slightly, looking in his direction. Transfixed by what he saw, Antinos could swear the beast wasn't just looking his way, it was looking directly *at* him. The magnification on his visor allowed him to see its face clearly, noting the two standard eyes and a third eye positioned above the bridge of its nose, just below the center of its forehead. That third eye—it seemed to sense his presence. It narrowed slightly, then its other two eyes looked at him.

He can't see me from this far away…can he?

"Romeo Four, we see it. Recommend evac back to the COP. How copy?"

Antinos meant to speak but failed to. To either side of the alien, swarms of soldiers like it appeared. The beast he'd been looking at raised one of its four arms, pointing a short sword directly at him. Then it let out a guttural, primordial roar as it rushed toward the river—toward them. Running, it raised its two lower arms, firing a laser blaster from each of them.

Antinos depressed the talk button again as Domingo and Aldi opened fire on the charging horde. "Apollo Six, I hope you're seeing this! I count dozens—no, hundreds of these alien bastards. They're charging right for us. Rain a fire mission right on top of our current position. We'll do our best to run like hell for the COP. I'd advise you alert Muleskin and his unit as well. I think this is it."

He turned to his guys. "Arty's on the way. Let's get the hell out of here!"

Flashes of light zipped around them. Pieces of brush and branches clawed at them as they ran, attempting to hold them back. A couple of explosions erupted nearby. Domingo yelled out in pain as he went down.

"My leg, my leg!" he shouted in agony, writhing on the ground.

Antinos fired his rifle as he turned. He saw three quick shots hit one of the beasts, knocking it to the ground. He grabbed for a grenade, tossing it toward a group closing the distance on him faster than he'd thought possible.

"Start shooting, Domingo!" Antinos roared, hitting two more of the bastards.

A handful of blue beasts raced toward him, their blasters firing, their swords raised.

I'm not going to make it, Antinos accepted. Then he heard the familiar sound of incoming artillery. He smiled; he wasn't going to die alone. *I might be dead, but I'm taking you all with me.*

Chapter 1
Kodiak

Three Years Prior
2090
Texas
The Republic

Harrison Kodiak knew how the conversation with his parents would go. They obviously wouldn't be thrilled with the choice he had made, but they were always reasonable and would hear him out. His girlfriend, Tara, on the other hand, was a completely different story. She had dreams of them going to college together. He would play professional football, she would be the trophy wife, and together they would ride off into the sunset and live happily ever after. To him, it sounded like a terribly predictable and dull life.

Growing up in a small town outside of Austin, Texas, with parents who weren't farmers or breeders, he'd had a modest but easy life. Kodiak couldn't remember a moment when he hadn't had a football in his hands. It was a byproduct of his father trying to relive his high school glory days vicariously through his son, but he didn't mind. Football was fun for him. It allowed him to take out all his anger and frustrations from the day and leave it on a hundred-yard field. It wasn't until high school that Kodiak had been told he was good enough to play beyond that level.

He remembered the day when his coach had brought him pamphlets from all the different colleges that were interested in him. At first, he had been overwhelmed. After experiencing all the attention that came with being a star athlete, though, he had begun to enjoy it. He had the girl, he had the popularity, and he had a great opportunity to continue down the path he had been set on.

Then came some doubts, and with them, questions. The more he thought about this future, the more he questioned whether it was the path he'd chosen or one that was being chosen for him. That all changed one day when a Republic Army recruiter caught his eye.

Towards the end of the school year, the annual job and recruiting fair was announced. Knowing his life had essentially been planned out for him from the day he'd arrived at Marshall Whitman High, Kodiak hadn't seen the value in going. Deciding to ditch the event, Kodiak and a few friends had snuck off to the nearby woods behind the parking lot to joke around and kill time until the school day was technically over. When he looked over at the doors to the gymnasium, where the event was being held, someone caught his eye. Kodiak had seen him in the hallways before he'd graduated the year prior but couldn't initially remember his name.

"Isn't that Dig—ah, hell, what was his name again?" one of his friends asked.

"Oh, man, we used to call him Dingleberry. Damn, what was his name?" another asked, getting a roar of laughter from the others.

While his friends laughed, he didn't. Kodiak wasn't into making fun of people. It was something both his father and mother had taught him growing up. But something was different about the person walking into the gymnasium. The kid who used to openly pick his nose and eat it during class his senior year wasn't the same one walking across the blacktop. He was dressed in a sharp olive-colored dress uniform that made him look physically cut in all the right places. The kid who wouldn't even be picked during intermural sports looked a hundred pounds lighter, and strong. The transformation seemed lost on his friends as they focused on what his name used to be.

"Kyle Dingleman," Kodiak said, suddenly remembering.

"That's right, Kyle Dingleberry," was the retort as another wave of laughter filled the air.

They were laughing at old stories about the kid and hadn't picked up on Kodiak as he headed towards him.

"Hey, Kyle!" Kodiak called out as he was about to enter the gym.

"Oh, hey, Harrison, nice to see you," the once-awkward kid said, radiating confidence.

Kodiak smiled at the warm welcome and shook Kyle's outstretched hand. "Man, you look great. So, you really joined up last year?"

"I did. I finished senior year early and decided to enlist right away. You know, my dad's a career man in the Army, so it was only fitting I followed."

"Wow. I had no idea you finished school early, or that that was even an option, really," Kodiak thought out loud. "So, what? Have you left yet? Where are you going?"

Kyle laughed. "I'm just back for the next ten days. I graduated basic training and we get leave to come home. Next, I'm going to the moon." He looked up at the midday sky.

"You're going to the moon?" Kodiak almost shouted.

Space travel was pretty routine by 2090. There were bases on the moon and on Mars, and colonies stretched throughout the asteroid belt, where minerals and fuels were mined for use back on Earth. Tourism also existed, if you could afford it, but Harrison Kodiak could never dream of affording a trip into space or to one of the luxury resorts on the moon. That didn't stop him from daydreaming, though.

"Yeah, they do their orbital training portions in space and on the moon. It's wild—the recruiter told me it was going to be part of the training, but it doesn't really hit you until you get handed that boarding pass. One ticket for the moon, please."

Footsteps approached from behind Kyle as another uniform appeared by his side. Kodiak looked up towards the recruiter. His uniform, although the same color and fit as Kyle's, had rows of colorful ribbons above its breast pocket. A blue cord wrapped under his right arm, and on both on his upper sleeves were three stripes with a crescent swoop at the bottom. His face was harder than Kyle's, more stoic, and his eyes looked almost never-ending. Kyle still looked like he had something in him that hadn't been taken yet.

"Good to meet you. I'm Staff Sergeant Lopez."

Kodiak reached out to shake his hand. "Harrison Kodiak."

The recruiter had a softer voice than his face would suggest. It was inviting, like a friend about to ask you to grab some drinks and go to a party. Kodiak knew it was all an act to get you to let your guard down and relax while having a conversation that could alter the course of your life. He'd had those same conversations with scouts from different colleges that tried to recruit him. They would roll out the red carpet, tell you how much they needed you, promised the cars, girls, and fame that came with being a five-star blue-chip player. It wasn't offensive; he knew the game and the role they played in it.

"Ever give any thought to serving the Republic?" Lopez asked.

And here comes the sales pitch, Kodiak thought.

"Not really. I have nothing against it, I just really never felt the need to join," he replied.

"Well, the military isn't for everyone. You must make your own choices in life and there's no harm in that whatsoever. Do you mind if I ask what you plan on doing after school?" Lopez quizzed.

"I have a couple of scholarship offers for football. I think I'm going to pursue one of those." Kodiak stood a little straighter when he said that.

"That's a good route if you got the talent. Just remember, if you get that opportunity to go to college for sports, don't squander it. Professional sports are even harder to get into—the room for error is as close to zero as it can be. So, focus on a trade or a degree that can help you in the workforce afterwards."

Kodiak now felt as if he was going crazy. He'd fully expected to get the sales pitch on joining the Republic military shoved down his throat, but if anything, Lopez was giving him some pretty solid life advice. Kodiak wasn't naïve. He knew his chances of making it into professional football were slim to none. It was the scariest thing about taking one of the scholarships. He had no clue what he would do outside of football.

"Well, that's anywhere you go nowadays, right? It's basically a lottery to get into any substantial work with all the AIs and automation. You need to specialize and get the degree if you're going to have a shot at a six-figure career one day. I feel like football's my only choice at this point."

Lopez chuckled. "Well, Harrison, it's not your only choice."

He flicked up on his data pad and Kodiak felt his pocket vibrate.

He removed his own data pad and saw Lopez's number waiting to be accepted into his contact list. He hit the accept button and looked back to the recruiter. "Uh, thanks."

"You have other options, good options, and if you want to hear them, just give me a call or come by the recruiting depot."

Kodiak had looked at the newly received contact thoughtfully and then back to Lopez and nodded. "Yes, sir, I will."

A week had gone by since that conversation and Kodiak still hadn't taken him up on his offer to talk about options with the Army. He'd actually thought about the invitation a lot, but when it came to going through with a meeting, he'd felt nervous, almost anxious, so he'd made excuses and kept putting it off. As time ticked away, the deadline to choose a college was rapidly approaching. One way or another, he was going to have to commit. Then his path would be set. But was it really *his* path? Was this *really* what he wanted, or was his father still trying to live vicariously through him?

I need to talk to that Staff Sergeant Lopez or I'm always going to second-guess this decision, he finally realized.

One day during spring break, Kodiak told his parents he was going over to a friend's house and would be gone most of the day. With a day to himself, Kodiak headed to the hyperloop-train station to take the next bullet out to Austin. The hyperloop-train was amazing. He had taken it several times to the bigger cities around the country. A train from Austin, Texas, would make it to Chicago, Illinois, in under two hours, and the train he was taking would send him to Austin in just thirty seconds. That was why he had never taken the hyperloop-train to Austin before now. It was unnecessary and honestly a waste of money, but he didn't want his parents wondering where he was, and if they needed him home quickly, the best way would be with the train.

As he stood on the platform waiting for his bullet to arrive, he looked at all the different destinations the trains would be sending passengers today. Los Angeles, Orlando, New York City, Montreal, Mexico City, Cape Canaveral Launch Port. That last one made his mind wander. There was someone getting on a bullet train heading to a launchpad. Once there, that individual would be getting on a ship and launching into space to visit God knew where. To Harrison Kodiak, it seemed unbelievable. But to whoever was taking that train, it was a normal day.

The train came to a smooth stop and the doors opened. Kodiak held up his data pad to the scanner, receiving an approving tone as it confirmed his ticket. Others apparently shared his sentiment when it came to paying too much just to take a thirty-second trip to Austin, based on the number of empty seats. Sitting down, he connected the three-point restraints over his body so he wouldn't become a loose piece of cargo slamming about the cabin.

He sat back, and the train launched forward. He felt the blood pushing back in his veins from the intense acceleration. The butterflies in his stomach churned and he involuntarily laughed a little. When you took a train like this to one of the major cities around North America, the speed would regulate as it got going, allowing your body to adjust. For short little jumps like this, though, you felt the effects of the speed for most of the trip.

As quickly as the train got up to speed, it started a rapid deceleration until it came to a smooth stop. The doors opened as the AI announced they'd reached Austin. Removing his restraints, Kodiak stood up, finding his feet as he walked towards the exit. When he reached the station's underground, he found the grand stairs that headed up and into the outside world. The blazing-hot sun seemed to cook the air as the stairwell gave way to a cloudless sky. Kodiak turned around and looked at the dome of the Capitol Building. He always loved that sight.

****

The recruiting depot was located just outside of the gates that surrounded the state's Capitol Building. The dome stretched above all the other buildings in the area, giving the skyline behind it an unobstructed view of the heavens. Behind Kodiak was the incredible Austin skyline. Skyscrapers with sparkling windows reaching into the heavens were a sight to behold. Some of the buildings stretched upwards of two hundred stories tall. But behind the Capitol's dome, it was still blue skies. The downtown sprawl hadn't moved in this direction.

Kodiak made his way to the depot. When he found it, he had to double-check the address to make sure it was correct. The city was surrounded by gorgeously designed buildings, but the depot had to be the ugliest building he'd ever seen. It was made of dark gray concrete, with almost no windows, and looked more like a bunker than an inviting building filled with your future. Shaking his head, Kodiak crossed the street and entered the building.

A cold blast of air smacked him in the face as lights and sensors swirled around him. The faint glowing red light on the ceiling turned green and another set of doors opened for him to continue inside. The lobby was huge and the complete opposite of the outside aesthetics. Black, gray, and gold-painted marble made up most of the walls, floor, and pillars that stretched above. Looking up, he saw rows of balconies that stretched forty stories high and surrounded a tinted glass dome that kept the sun's rays from whiting out the entire building.

"Name?" a woman behind the desk asked.

Kodiak looked down and realized he had kept walking until he was standing in front of the desk. The lady sitting there had on a dress uniform like he'd seen Lopez wearing the previous week. She wore a black skirt, though, instead of pants.

"Um, I'm Harrison Kodiak," he managed to stammer out. *God, why am I so nervous?* he thought pensively.

She tapped away on the keys and smiled. "Ah, yes, Staff Sergeant Lopez put you into the system under his name. He's available right now if you'd like to speak with him."

"He put my name down?" Kodiak was confused.

"Yes. When a recruiter believes he or she may have found an acceptable candidate for the Republic armed services, they create a file on you. This allows a background check to be completed prior to you coming to the depot so you can be cleared to come in and talk further. It's the first part of getting your recruitment process started should you join."

Wow, a background check just to talk about the military. I'll bet it has something to do with all the space stuff, he thought.

"Wait, did you say recruitment process?" Kodiak asked, looking up at the offices.

"Oh, it's nothing too formal. You aren't joining yet. We have to perform a basic background check on you and make sure you aren't a security risk before we tell you more about what the Armed Forces has to offer. We can't have just anyone join. We only take the best. The fact that Staff Sergeant Lopez already opened a file on you says a lot. If you look over there, that's where the elevators are. His office is located on the thirty-eighth floor, room 382. He's expecting you."

Kodiak nodded, stammering again, "Thank you, I, ah, I guess I'll head on up."

What am I doing here? I'm no book-smart egghead like Kyle. She said they only take the best. I'm barely a B student. I'm only getting into college because of football, he lamented as he pressed the elevator button.

Standing in the elevator, Kodiak thought about the path before him. His dad and coach had a future already planned out for him. One they felt was set in stone. College football. He'd have the fame on campus, the girl, the glory, all of it. Yet here he was going up an elevator to speak to a recruiter and potentially go down a path in his life that would negate all of that.

Ding.

His thoughts were interrupted when the AI told him he'd arrived at his floor and the doors opened. *What am I doing...?*

Stepping into a wide corridor, Kodiak walked down the hall as it gradually turned to the right. The building was round on the outside, and inside, it was sort of like an egg. He looked at the numbers as they went down with each door he passed until finally, he stood in front of room 382. He knocked, waited a moment, and then stepped in.

Staff Sergeant Lopez sat behind his desk, gliding his fingers along his terminal. Whatever he was working on couldn't be seen from the back of the hologram with its privacy filter on. He'd seen the same type of privacy filter in his school's computer lab.

Staff Sergeant Lopez stopped typing. Looking up from his desk, he asked in a serious tone, "Harrison Kodiak, correct?"

"Eh, yeah," was all he managed to get out.

Kodiak was a little surprised the guy remembered him. He probably talked to hundreds of people every week, so it was pretty cool that he'd actually remembered him.

Lopez no doubt saw the surprise on his face and laughed. "I'd like to say I remembered your name from meeting you last week at the school, but whenever someone enters the depot, it biometrically scans them and lets me know who it is. That's not to say I don't remember your face, but names are a bit much. We get a lot of people going through the first steps of the process, you understand. Here, take a seat." He gestured to the chair that sat across from the table.

Smiling, Kodiak stepped forward and sat across from Lopez. On the wall behind him were old-school photographs that had been printed and put in a frame you could hang on the wall. He still saw those when he visited his grandparents in Lubbock. Nowadays, most families had the frames that cycled through several photos digitally saved to the cloud.

Lopez looked behind him and smiled. "Yeah, not a lot of people expect to see these anymore, but I'm a sentimental man." He removed one of the pictures from the wall and placed it on the table. "There's something more personal about a physical copy you can hold and feel in your hands. Take this picture, for instance. This is me and my buddy during orbital drop training."

The picture showed a much younger Lopez with his arm around another soldier. In the background was an open field of grass and a huge ship that had landed in it. His face was marked with sweat and some type of dark paint smeared all around. He looked like someone from the

16

military commercials Kodiak had seen, wearing some awesome-looking armor, and he even had a sheathed knife attached to the breast of it.

"What's orbital drop training?" Kodiak asked with a sudden curiosity.

"ODT is a phase within your training cycle. So, if you enlisted, you would be sent to one of the military bases in the Republic, depending on what specialty you choose. At that base is where you'll do your basic training, which we call phase one. Phase two, you'll be sent to Luna to train in low gravity and zero gravity. Once you reach phase three, you'll experience ODT. That's when they sit you inside an Osprey and it drops through the atmosphere at terminal velocity before swooping in and dropping you in the landing zone."

Kodiak stared wide-eyed at the description. "What's the point of doing that?"

"Well, that's a good question, Kodiak. You see, the Republic military has to be ready for any and all threats. One of the scenarios we regularly train for is landing an invasion force from orbit at a desired location, sometimes behind enemy lines. It sounds scarier than it is, trust me." Lopez sat back in his chair. "Back in the day, before we became the Republic, they would invade countries by driving what were basically waterborne tanks through the water to land on a hostile beach. Provided they didn't sink, of course. Another means of insertion was airplanes. Soldiers used to jump out of them with parachutes in mass formations, or they'd use helicopters to land soldiers behind enemy lines or to transport them long distances. Now we have the technology to maintain a force of soldiers in space that the President can readily deploy anywhere in the world in under an hour. The orbital assault soldiers are considered the Republic's 911 force in case of trouble. Pretty cool, huh?"

Kodiak didn't know what to say. He was blown away by the concept of soldiers assaulting from orbit. Sure, he'd seen it in movies, but that was Hollywood. Now he was being told *he* could do that kind of thing. Never in a million years had he thought it'd be possible to go to space, but here this guy was telling him he had not only gone to space but trained in the void. He had to hand it to Lopez—the man was a great recruiter. Who turned down a chance to tour the solar system or get stationed on Luna or even Mars? Still, Kodiak thought it sounded too good to be true.

Canting his head slightly, Kodiak asked, "OK, what's the catch? It's got to be a long training process, so how long would I have to enlist to do something that cool?"

"That's a good question—and, yes, the training is long, and very intense. If you're unsure, you can enlist for the shorter three-year contract. But keep in mind, if you only stay in for three years, you won't get the full benefits, like four years of free college. You'll most likely be stationed somewhere on Earth since you wouldn't have enough time on your contract to go through the orbital assault school. However, if you enlist for the standard eight-year contract, then if you choose not to make the military a career, you'll get full benefits so you can attend college on the Republic's dime. You'll also be able to attend orbital assault school, a requirement to be assigned to any of the off-world bases. This is where the cool opportunities are to be stationed among the stars. Luna, Mars, even a ship patrolling the Belt." Lopez motioned with his hand across a map of Republic installations outside of Earth. He was good.

"Um, you mentioned full benefits. What are the benefits beyond free college?"

"If you enlist on the eight-year contract, then when your term of service is up—again, should you decide not to make it a career—you leave the military with a multitude of really good benefits. How does a home in whatever state or province of the Republic you'd like sound? It also comes with a couple acres of land. If that doesn't scratch the itch, how about the best benefit—in my opinion, anyway—which is a paid job within whatever field you studied while serving in the military? If you decide to go into the medical corps, whether as a doctor or a medic, you'll leave training with a degree. The military will then take that degree and find you a job of equal or more pay once you get out."

"Equal or more pay? That honestly sounds too good to be true, not gonna lie," Kodiak almost laughed.

"I can understand that. The Republic values its military veterans and learned over time that if you want someone to serve your needs, you must serve theirs. It's hard to imagine, but there was a time when veterans were not held in high regard by the majority. The quality of hospital care was at an all-time low, unemployment among veterans was skyrocketing, and sadly veteran suicide was at an all-time high. Now, to be frank, we are asking more of our service members. We want them to fight our future wars not only here on Earth but also out in the Belt or on

Mars. Humanity has become a spacefaring people, and although we're relative infants in our race to the stars, the wolves are already at the door."

His last remark sent a cold shiver down Kodiak's back. "What if I didn't want to be a medic? What did you do?"

Lopez patted the blue cord that hung on his jacket behind him on the coatrack. "I was in the infantry. Boots on the ground. You see those ads before movies with the guys kicking in doors and taking the fight to the enemy? That's what I did—that's what all infantry does. To close with and destroy the enemy."

"What type of work benefits can you expect after the military with a job like that?" Kodiak asked.

"There are thousands of government contracts on Earth, the moon, Mars, the Belt—they all need security. The Republic military can't always be everywhere in the solar system, so to protect the Republic's assets, they have security forces. If that doesn't sound interesting, there are also options to join local, state, or federal law enforcement."

Kodiak thought about it but felt that was a limited future compared to being a doctor or a nurse. He looked over to a holo-poster on the wall that showed a bunch of different numbers and letters next to names. One stood out to him: Military Intelligence.

"What's military intelligence?"

"That's the super-secret squirrel stuff. They do all types of things within the Republic military, from counterespionage to hacking. Future jobs outside of the military can range from private consulting or working for the Republic Intelligence Agency."

Kodiak sat up straighter in his seat. "That sounds awesome."

"It does indeed. You must understand, though, if you choose to enlist, you'll go through a process of tests, both physical and mental. The scores you get will tell you what jobs you qualify for. You can want to be in military intelligence, but if you don't get the score that coincides with that job, you won't be able to get it."

Lopez must have seen the drop in Kodiak's shoulders. "I remember you telling me that you've been offered scholarships for football. That's amazing. Let me ask—with an opportunity like that, why would you want to join the military?"

At least Lopez wasn't trying to discourage him from his current path to enlist. "Recently I've started to get the feeling that I'm not doing this for myself. See, my father played football in high school, even played in college before he got hurt. Don't get me wrong, my father is a good man, doesn't beat me, doesn't treat me like crap or anything, but he pushes me when it comes to the sport. The dream of going to college to play ball—I mean, is it really *my* dream or is it his dream? I've heard the stats. Only the one percent of the one percent make it to professional football."

"Are you good?" Lopez asked.

"Yeah, of course. Am I professional-level good? I have no idea, and to be honest, I don't want to go through four years of that just to find out I'm not. Then what? I enter the workforce and hope my lottery number gets called for a job?" Kodiak was starting to feel like he was talking to a therapist rather than a stone-cold killer.

"I can understand that struggle. Harrison, your parents can't dictate what you want to do with your life. Mexico—that's where I come from—is far more prosperous nowadays than it was seventy years ago, but there will always be the sections of the world that the poor belong to. It's not their fault they were born into it, but it's their fault if they stay in it when they have a way out. The military was my way out. I now live really good. I have a stable income; I have a house that was given to me by the Republic while I finish up my career as a recruiter. I don't know what life has in store for you, Harrison, but I know that it's your choice. Not anyone else's."

Kodiak smiled and stood, reaching out his hand. "Thanks for the talk, sir. I really appreciate it."

Lopez reached across and shook his hand. "Anytime, Harrison. If you want to know more or even enlist, come on back and we'll get you all set up."

Chapter 2
Hall

Aiden Hall sat up quickly at the noise—or at least, he thought he'd heard a noise. Nights in Chicago were never quiet; the nights when he only dealt with car horns instead of gunshots were the nights Aiden longed for. He laid his head back down onto the pillow and stared up at the ceiling. The wallpaper was slowly peeling away after years of water damage from the summer storms and the winter snowmelts, but Hall didn't give a damn about repairing it.

Another sound resonated from outside his room. He wasn't going crazy. He was actually pretty proud of himself for waking up alert, but self-flattery would have to wait. He stood and removed the pistol from underneath his pillow, press-checking the upper receiver and noting that there was a bullet in the chamber, then leveled the gun at his door. He didn't need to worry about the safety; he preferred weapons that didn't have any.

As he neared the door, he pressed his back against the wall and waited. He couldn't remember what the noise that had woken him up had sounded like, but the second one had sounded like a window closing. The one in his living room creaked a little when it was closed. Using the barrel of his gun, he swung the door open, but he didn't account for zero resistance and the door slammed against the wall.

He stood as still as possible, aiming his pistol down the hallway. Whoever had come into his apartment would have to cross the hallway threshold no matter what, so he sat and waited. Something small and close to the ground flew by the hallway, scaring him, and he almost pulled the trigger. He felt the tiny amount of pressure release from his finger just in time. Putting the gun down, he laughed as the small orange-and-black cat came from around the corner.

He called her Tabby, despite the feline not being an actual tabby cat. "Come here, baby." He smiled, kissing his lips together. Tabby ran off just as he felt cold steel press against his head.

"You really gonna let a cat be your demise, Aiden?" the man laughed, pulling the gun away from his temple.

Hall's muscles relaxed and he turned to greet Eddy, an on-again, off-again associate of his. Eddy had helped teach Hall the way of the streets when he was younger and had run away from home. With Eddy, he'd pulled off numerous little jobs like hustling tourists in the park or knocking over a gas station at night. Small stuff. As of late, Eddy had gotten into the harder drugs that were starting to pour into Republic cities, coming from the Belt. It was exotic, it was new, and it was deadly.

Hall stayed away from that stuff. He didn't trust drugs. They made you numb and dumb, and in his line of work, you couldn't be either if you didn't want to get caught. Eddy still gave him good leads when he showed up after one of his monthlong benders. Looking at him now, Hall judged that either he'd just returned from one or he was currently on the sauce.

"What's the word, Eddy? Nothing better to do at three in the morning? You gotta come here and stick a gun in my head?" Hall asked.

"Oh, come on, man, I'm only playing with ya. Like old times."

"Just like old times—yeah, that's good."

"What's that supposed to mean?" Eddy took a seat on the only real piece of furniture in Hall's apartment, a couch.

"Take it easy, Eddy, I'm only joking."

"Ah, a joke for a joke," he chuckled. "I like that about you, Aiden. That's why I'm coming to you for this."

Hall anxiously waited to hear what was about to come out of Eddy's mouth. It could be another job, or he could be here to ask for money. You just never knew with Eddy Levine. Hall sat down on the floor across from him and set his gun on his lap, in easy reach.

"For what?" he asked.

"For the opportunity of a lifetime. New Musk Premium 2091 just came out. Only guy in the southside that has one and the moron keeps it unlocked on the street. I've cased it three times and all three times it's been unlocked. If we go now, we can have it in a chop shop before the sun comes up. Easy money and you can finally get the hell out of Chicago."

"So, this is a three a.m. courtesy call to tell me you have a life-changing opportunity for us, but I need to come now or it won't work. What's your plan, Eddy? Those cars are impossible to hot-wire."

Eddy held up a small black object that had a glowing red light on it. It looked like a computer chip from a processor.

"What is that?"

"It's a splicer. All we have to do is attach this to the computer and it's ours. Drives us to the drop point on autopilot and everything."

"Who gave you that?"

"Nobody. It's better you didn't know. All I need you to do is run lookout—it's literally the easiest ten grand you ever made."

"Ten grand?" Hall asked, shocked.

"Ten grand, baby, ten grand."

****

The night was a lot cooler than Hall had expected. He pulled the hood over his head and shoved his hands in his pockets as he and Eddy walked briskly down the sidewalk. The contrast between the poor and rich areas of Chicago became more striking with every passing year. One minute you were walking in slums with a liquor store on every corner, and the next you were surrounded by high-rises inhabited by the rich and famous. Eddy and Hall stuck out like a sore thumb here.

As they drew closer to the street Eddy was looking for, he began to crouch and walk along the wall. Hall almost laughed at how ridiculous he looked. They were in the open, streetlights on—if anything, crouching and walking like that made them look ten times more suspicious.

As they rounded the corner, the car in question was impossible to miss. Even in the midst of all the beautiful architecture, boutiques, and lavish restaurants, the car stood out as the most impressive. Its sleek red exterior sharpened and curved like a fighter jet. It was the newest electric car on the market, and it was beautiful. Just by looking at the vehicle, Hall knew his cut should be more, but ten grand was still ten grand.

"Now what?" Hall asked.

"Now we take this beautiful bastard and retire in the countryside or something."

"The countryside? Like farms? You won't survive that," Hall laughed.

Eddy gave him a sour look and turned to cross the street. Hall followed close behind and gave a reassuring tap to the grip of his pistol, ensuring it was still in his waistband. They bounded across the street, and when they reached the car, Eddy tugged on the door and it opened. The moment it did, someone lunged out of the driver's side and tackled Eddy to the ground.

Hall jumped back in surprise at the sudden violence unfolding on the street. The owner of the vehicle has been inside the entire time and now had the drop on Eddy. The driver's fists were coming down hard, but he didn't seem to notice that Hall was even there. With a quick kick, Hall caught the man in his temple with the heel of his shoe and sent him tumbling. Eddy got to his feet and opened his mouth to say something when the back of his head opened up and blood, skull fragments, and brain matter sprayed the morning air.

The gunfire caused Hall to trip over his feet as Eddy fell to the ground in a heap. Hall looked at Eddy's face one last time. Eddy's lifeless eyes bored through him as he slept in eternal peace. Hall's feet couldn't have moved any quicker. Getting up, he immediately ran down the street where he had come from. Two more gunshots rang out, the sound reaching him only after the bullets cracked past his head and impacted a parked car's window. A window on another parked car spiderwebbed from the impact and sent Aiden Hall scrambling down an alleyway.

It didn't occur to him at any point to take his own gun out and defend himself, and as he rounded another corner, he tossed the pistol into a sewer. He could always get another one, but would he need another one? As he continued to run through alleys, the reality of the situation set in. Eddy was dead, never coming back, and whoever had given him that device would be looking for it. And if the cops traced it to Eddy's contact, then Eddy's contact was all but certain to come looking for Hall. He was Eddy's longtime associate, after all. He needed to get out of the city.

****

After entering his apartment, Hall stripped off his bloodied clothes and jumped into the shower. As he washed the filth from his face, chunks of brain matter and skull fell into the drain and his stomach heaved violently. When he stopped vomiting to catch his breath, another wave would hit him, until finally, he lay curled up in a ball on the shower floor. The water was ice cold—always had been, so he was used to it, but the convulsing and retching sent him into cold sweats and his body shook.

As he got out of the shower and dried himself off, he began to think about his exit strategy. He barely had any clothes to pack, didn't have much cash on him, and didn't have a gun to worry about anymore at state-line checkpoints, but where exactly would he go? His brother's place in Michigan was out of the question. He was dead to his brother and his brother was dead to him. He had no other living relatives, though, and the prospect of trying to start another life as a low-level criminal in unknown territory wasn't appealing.

Hall decided that he would call his brother and ask him to send him some money once he got out of the city, maybe even pay him a visit in person to really put the knife into helping him. That would all have to wait, though. As he looked out the window at the rising dawn, he had to focus on how he was going to get out of the city undetected. By now the shooting was most likely being investigated, and with all the cameras around the city, they had to have seen something. How much, he didn't know.

Looking around his apartment, Hall took a deep breath and smiled a little. It had served him well for the time he'd lived there, even though it wasn't the most comfortable place he'd ever been. It was his, though, and he had taken pride in it. His backpack was light, with only a few days' worth of clothes inside and a couple of pairs of shoes he liked. Swinging it over his shoulder, he gave the apartment one last look and turned to the front door.

As he made his way to the door, a loud explosion knocked him back. The front door tore itself apart into wooden fragments as heavily armed men came storming inside with guns raised. They were on top of him before he could get to his feet, and his arms were yanked back behind him and placed in cuffs.

"Aiden Hall, you are under arrest for attempted auto theft and leaving the scene of a crime resulting in homicide," the cop that stood above him said.

****

The bright lights of the interrogation room made his head and eyes throb. They had kept him in there for what seemed like a couple of hours without anyone coming in to explain the situation. He knew he was screwed, but a little optimism in the back of his brain told him they might not be able to prove he had been there. If that was the case, though, they would've never brought him in. He didn't think so, at least.

He just hoped they didn't try and pin Eddy's death on him. He still couldn't believe the idiot was dead. He had seen it happen, had washed off the blood and crud that had come from him, yet it wasn't until the officer had mentioned the "homicide" that it had really sunk in. Maybe it was the fact that it had all happened so fast and he just couldn't register all that had happened. Most likely it was because, despite all of Eddy's flaws, he was the closest thing to a friend Hall had ever had.

The door opened and two detectives in suits walked in and took seats across from him at the table. The first one was young. Clean-shaven, neat haircut and spotless clothes that were all buttoned up. The second was older, balding, and his jacket had multiple food stains on it that obviously hadn't happened in the last twenty-four hours.

"I'm Detective Yates and this is Detective Holiday, Mr. Hall," the older man started. "We've brought you in on an arrest warrant for being involved in an auto burglary as well as witnessing a homicide and failing to report it."

Hall went to open his mouth to talk, but the older man held up his finger while continuing to read from his tablet. "You were witnessed in the act of these crimes by a camera in the car you intended to steal, the gun camera installed on the victim's firearm, and building security cameras down an alleyway between West Hubbard and Kinzie Street. Please take a look at the following footage."

The man spoke in a bored monotone as he turned his tablet around to play a series of videos for him. Hall looked at the two detectives and tried to get a read on their body language. It didn't look like they were fishing for anything. They seemed very confident that they had him dead to rights. The older detective was going through the motions, and the younger one sat silently as if observing the entire interaction.

The first video was from a camera installed somewhere on the left side of the vehicle. He could clearly see Eddy and himself approaching the car, and at first, he thought the hood over his head would mask his face in shadow. As they drew closer, his face came into plain view and the video stopped. Lines and dots appeared on his face, and a photo taken years ago when he was an inmate with the Department of Corrections came up next to the screen. It read "ninety-five percent positive match."

The next video was from the gun camera. It was an invention that had come out on the market years ago, but over the past decade it had become very popular. Usually, Hall was good about keeping clear of that problem. After all, Eddy had told him the car would be unattended. He'd been wrong. It was weird seeing an image of complete darkness and knowing that the gun was about to be retrieved any moment and used to kill his friend. He watched with morbid curiosity as the gun was unholstered and pointed at the door. In the next moment, the door swung open and chaos erupted. It happened much quicker on the video than what he remembered from earlier that morning. The scuffle on the ground was over, and before he knew it, the video paused.

In the foreground was Eddy's surprised face, moments from death. In the background, the lines and dots appeared again. This time it said they had an eighty-nine percent positive match. He didn't feel like he needed to see the last video. He had been down this road before, and with such a precise percentage, this was all just playing the game for them.

Hall shrugged. "I don't need to see any more. You guys got me, obviously."

The younger detective spoke this time. "Do you have any details you want to share before we bring you to a hearing?"

"Yes, I do." Hall sat up straighter knowing that what he said could maybe lessen the punishment for him. "I did go with Eddy to jack that car, but there was no plan for someone to be there. It was three in the morning. Why the hell would I think someone would be sitting in their car at three in the morning?"

"If you didn't plan on someone being there, why did you bring a gun? That third video shows you tossing one into the sewer drain, which we recovered, so why bring it?"

"Shoot, man, at that time? You always need to stay strapped. When that dude jumped out and started attacking Eddy, I didn't know what to do. Suddenly Eddy's dead and I'm running for my life."

"Why didn't you stay and try to help your friend?"

"'Cause his head exploded, dude. Not to mention the guy kept shooting at me as I ran away. What did you want me to do, stop and just die?"

"Could've called the police," the young detective said.

Hall laughed at that. "You're stupid, bro." He looked at the older detective. "Your boy is stupid as hell. Just take me to the hearing."

The older detective rolled his eyes and stood up. Hall turned around and let himself be cuffed again and then he was led down a hall to another tiny room with a large monitor and a camera. When he sat down, the monitor turned on and the light on the camera began to blink.

A judge pushing eighty years old sat behind his desk and looked through the files attached to Hall's case. Hall had never seen this judge before and had absolutely no idea how this interaction would go.

The judge looked up. "Aiden Hall, you are charged with attempted burglary of a vehicle, leaving the scene of a homicide, and having in your possession a firearm as a convicted felon. At this time, I have reviewed your recorded testimony and the files for the investigation. Usually this is the point where I ask you to enter a plea, but I must warn you about something first. This is a very cut-and-dried case. They have multiple pieces of video evidence linking you to these crimes, which would carry a minimum sentence of ten years in a Republic penitentiary. You have the right to plead not guilty, but in doing so, you will be handing your fate to the court, and I'll be honest, son, it doesn't look good. However, you also have the opportunity to plead guilty to these crimes. I have worked out a deal I would like you to hear before making your decision."

Hall looked at the judge in surprise. He had never been offered a plea deal before and had no idea what the old man was up to. "Yes, Your Honor, I would like that."

"I thought you would. If you plead guilty, you will be immediately released from the custody of the Chicago Police Department and into the custody of the Republic military, where you will serve a minimum of ten years in the Republic Armed Forces. If you are discharged from the military for any reason other than being wounded in combat, you will immediately be arrested and serve the remainder of the ten-year sentence you would have been given if you had gone to trial. Does that make sense to you?"

Hall found himself nodding involuntarily. He hadn't been expecting this. He had heard of people being put into military service instead of going to prison, but the rumors had all been from people in prison, so he hadn't taken them seriously. Now he was being given an opportunity at some sort of freedom. It ultimately came down to whether he wanted to sit in a prison for a decade or shoot some guns for the next ten years.

It didn't take long for him to give his answer. "I'll take the plea deal, Your Honor."

"Good choice," the judge said as he slammed his gavel down. "Aiden Hall, I order your immediate release from the Chicago Police Department to enter service with the Republic Armed Forces. I hope this journey leads you on a path of reform and you become a better person because of it."

The monitor went black and his handcuffs were unlocked and taken off his wrists. He smiled widely at the detective, who smiled just as widely back at him. It sent a shiver down his spine, and for a moment, he wondered if he had just made a mistake. When the door opened, he was led back into the hallway, where a man stood in uniform.

"I'm Sergeant First Class Cotto. Welcome to the Republic Army."

Cotto had a prominent scar that stretched over the right side of his face, from his cheek through his eyebrow, as if he'd been mauled by a lion that had just missed his eye. The sergeant was more ripped than any human he had ever seen, and when he talked, the veins on his neck pulsated.

Aiden Hall definitely felt like he had just made a horrible mistake.

Chapter 3
Moore

Oliver Moore had grown up in the high society of London, England, with his parents, Lord Archibald Moore and Lady Helena Moore…his father was an earl. His early childhood had consisted of elaborate parties and expensive toys. He was blessed and knew his young life was a lot easier than others', then and now. His parents' connections had landed him at Oxford, and after one semester, he was already over it. Everything had been handed to him from the day of his birth; he'd never had to work for anything. He knew a large majority of people would kill to have his life—it was the reason he had grown to hate it so much.

He refused to let people call him by any title or honorific beyond mister and cut anyone out of his life at university if he felt that they treated him differently because of his status, or rather his family's status. His father blamed his new rebellious tendencies on university and the "lowlifes" that had won the lottery to get in. It was that exact behavior that was driving Oliver to his decision now.

He had left university without telling his parents, gone to the Republic recruiting office, and enlisted. The benefits were enough to make him comfortable after he was discharged in however many years, especially since his parents would most likely disown him for the act. It was the duty involved that really captured his enthusiasm. He had gone to Oxford to learn the ways of becoming an earl and serving the community that flourished from the estate, but it wasn't at all what he was interested in.

When he had first brought up the idea of becoming a doctor to his parents, they'd immediately shut it down and put him down for even entertaining the idea of being less than what they expected. Being a doctor was an amazing prospect. You had the opportunity to save lives every single day and truly make a difference to the common man, not just sit in an ancient tower all day and pretend to care. The military would give him that life.

Moore had easily passed the physical exam and mental acuity tests when he had gone to the recruit depot. When he returned to his recruiter to discuss what job he wanted to select, the list was eight pages long. His idea was to become a doctor or a surgeon, but as he continued to flip through the list, it wasn't coming up for him.

He put the tablet down and looked at the recruiter. "I was hoping to do something advanced within the medical field, but all I'm seeing available is combat medic and physical therapist."

The recruiter smiled as if he had to have this conversation all the time. "It's impossible to just enter the military as a doctor. There is a lot of schooling you have to go through before even getting remotely close to that level. What the Republic military can do is give you the tools to work your way up. You can enter service as either a combat medic or a physical therapist, and from there you can work towards your goal. It's a long journey—it will take years, and I'm being honest with you when I say it will take multiple enlistments of five years to get that done. If you have the drive, which I can tell you do, and if you have the smarts, which, again, I think you do, then it's possible to go in as a PT or combat medic and retire as a doctor."

"So more than ten years to get to my goal." Moore felt a little defeated at that prospect.

"When you put it like that, it can seem daunting and even impossible, but becoming a doctor is never easy, whether in the civilian sector or the military. The key is to understand that the military can give you the necessary tools and schooling while also honing your skills. If you spend thousands of dollars, almost millions, on becoming a doctor at a university, the majority of your classes will be in a classroom setting, with very little hands-on training until the latter portion of your studies. If you join the military as a combat medic, you will learn advanced procedures and save lives. If you stay in for the necessary time and take advantage of the schooling we can give you, I promise you'll leave your military career more experienced than more than half of the residents at whatever hospital you end up at."

Moore sat back and looked at the "combat medic" occupation on the data pad. If he selected physical therapist, he could most likely learn at his own pace, and if war broke out again, he would be far from the combat. On the other hand, he'd most likely be stuck in some hospital on Earth, helping wounded soldiers get back to full health. It was an admirable job—there was no denying that—but the recruiter was right. If he chose combat medic, he would most likely be thrust into the thick of things and have to learn on the fly, in chaotic situations.

31

The prospect had him feeling drawn to the job as he watched his finger slowly edge closer to accepting the combat medic role. With a deep breath, he went for it and selected the role. He sat back, expecting something to happen, but the experience was anticlimactic as the recruiter took the data pad back and smiled. "Private Oliver Moore, welcome to the Republic military."
****

His orders told Moore that he needed to report to the recruit depot in twenty-four hours to begin his journey in the military. He had no intention of going back to Hoffshire Abbey and confronting his parents. He already knew they would be angry with him, and he didn't feel like celebrating his last day as a civilian by being told how much of a disappointment to his family he was.

Instead, he took a cab to nearby Hertfordshire to reconnect with someone from his past. Growing up at Hoffshire Abbey, he had the tendency to run off and party with the "common folk," as his parents so eloquently called them. He felt more at home with them. His parents loved to call the common folk "their people," but in the late twenty-first century, the age of lords and ladies was quickly fading. For a long time, the rest of the world had looked at the royal family as more of a mascot from the old days; now, even the English looked at them the same. Titles were still handed down within families. Until he'd joined the military, he had been destined for the same fate. Now it seemed he was making an escape at the perfect time.

He remembered heading into the countryside every holiday season, shirking his duties at the abbey to hang out with kids in the villages. As he grew older, his parents would send the household help out to round him up. One day, they'd sent out one of the baker's assistants to find him, and she had. Lillianna was a year younger than Moore and had been working for the family since they were both young children. He had grown close to her over that time, and when they'd made the mistake of sending her to look for him, she'd known right where to go.

They had stayed out all night under the stars as snow slowly fell around them. They'd wrapped themselves in blankets to keep warm as the temperature had dropped, and soon they'd drifted off to sleep in each other's arms. When they had awoken, the men of the house had discovered them, and he had never seen Lillianna again. That had been more than a decade ago, and it had taken him nearly that long to find out where she had gone.

Lillianna now lived on her parents' farm in the town of Bishop's Stortford. He didn't know if she was married or engaged and had no intention of winning her back in a day's time. What he did want to do was see her again and apologize for what had happened all those years before. If he was lucky, and he admitted he had to be for this to work out, he could get her to write to him when he left.

The cab rolled into the town square just as the church bells began to ring, and he paid the man a little extra for the long drive into town. He liked coming out to the smaller areas outside of London, which now stood as a sparkling gaggle of high-rises. All the major cities around the world had hit an economic boom when the countries had formed unified governments after the last great war. The result was towering skyscrapers that lit up the night skies across planet Earth. Where humanity had reached above and beyond into the stars, down on Earth they did the same.

A lot of the architecture in the cities seemed to be ripped out of the old movies and other forms of science fiction entertainment from the past. The smaller towns, like Bishop's Stortford, still held on to their roots, which Moore enjoyed a heck of a lot more than the newer steel and glass.

He removed his tablet and checked the address he had saved. A friend from his younger years had kept in touch with Lillianna and, after a little bit of convincing, had given Moore the address. It belonged to a small bookshop in the square he had been dropped off in. Bookstores had faded to near extinction by the 2030s but made a revival in the early 2070s, when it had become cool and hip to own a book. It was also more expensive for a paperback version than the digital formats used today, especially after books had stopped being printed in 2039.

The door chimed as he walked into the shop. The smell of paper permeated the air, and he felt a happy sensation prickle at his arms. Moore hadn't been in a bookstore in years, and he had forgotten the smell of printed books. It felt more like home than the actual abbey. He took the tablet in his pocket for granted, and nothing made that realization pop to the forefront like walking into a bookstore.

"Can I help you with something, lad?" came a deep voice from behind him.

Moore turned and saw a rather rotund man standing behind the counter, his meaty arms pressing down on it as he peered at Moore from behind half-moon glasses. His face was covered in a thick white beard with faint traces of red, indicating the color of his facial hair in younger years.

"Yes, sir, my name is Oliver Moore. I'm looking for a young woman by the name of Lillianna Peppers."

The older man squinted as he looked at Moore, who stepped closer so the man could get a better look at him. That seemed to help.

"Lillianna!" he shouted toward the back of the shop. "Some fancy boy is here to see you."

Moore couldn't tell if the man was being protective of Lillianna or if he was annoyed that Moore aimed to take the attention of one of his workers.

Lillianna walked in from the back and looked at the older man. "What is it, Harry?" she asked and then looked at Moore.

"Hello, Lilly." Moore smiled.

Lillianna stood there for a moment, looking him over from behind the counter. She didn't seem shocked to see him, didn't seem angry, yet she wasn't making her way over to him. Instead, she studied him, no doubt wondering what his intentions were.

"Harry, I'm gonna bugger off for a moment." She smiled at the older gentleman, placing her hand on his shoulder.

"Is he trouble?" Harry asked as if Moore wasn't standing a few meters away.

"We'll see." She squeezed his shoulder and walked around the counter, past Moore, and out the door.

"Be careful," Harry grunted.

"I promise I'm harmless, sir." Moore smiled, trying to set his mind at ease.

"I was talking to you, lad."

Moore followed Lillianna out the door into the cold, damp air. It was snowing now. As soon as the flakes touched the asphalt, they melted, but as the temperature dropped and the sun set, the snow would pile up.

Lillianna looked beautiful. Her golden-brown hair still reached to the middle of her back, and her brilliant blue eyes sparkled without the sun shining. She was no longer the pretty girl he had chased around the halls of the abbey but a gorgeous woman. He had a million things to say to her and he wanted to begin immediately, as if this were the last time he'd ever speak to her, but nothing came. His voice was caught in his throat and his eyes glazed over.

"There is so much I've wanted to say," he began, "but there's nothing more important than saying I'm sorry."

"Sorry for what?" she said flatly. "You're a soon-to-be lord and I was just a kitchen maid. It wasn't going to last forever, so there was no use in getting sick over it."

"That's not at all—" he tried, but she cut him off.

"Then what was it, Oliver? You were caught with me and I'm sure your father made sure you were rightly punished for it. As for me, I was tossed out of the only job I was supposed to have. I was raised from a small girl to be a damn kitchen maid. And oh! I could've one day been the cook. How lovely!" she laughed, but the words bit like poison. "So what are you sorry about, Oliver, and why the hell did you wait all this time to tell me? Is there some ancient family law that says you have to account for your sins before ascending to the throne?"

Moore knew she was saying those things to hurt him, and it worked, but he knew he deserved it. He quickly realized this visit wasn't going to go one of the ways he'd predicted, so he decided to go with the bullet points. "I left that. I rescinded my title in the family and joined the Republic Army. You know I never wanted that life for myself, and I'm not trying to come back here and win you over—"

"Good! 'Cause it'd never work."

"I know I—"

"So don't try it, Oliver."

"I wasn't going to—"

"You can't just make me feel the way that I feel and then walk away for all these years. Now you want to come back into my life all of a sudden? Why? You're throwing your title away and joining the military for what? Me?"

"Can you just let me explain, please?" Moore pleaded.

She stared at him, but she had stopped interrupting. He also noticed she said *feel*, not *felt*. Maybe she'd just been caught up in the moment and slipped, but maybe, just maybe, there was something still there.

"Lillianna, I didn't expect anything. I just wanted to see you one more time before I left."

"Oh, so you wanted to play the 'I'm going off to war' speech to try and get in my knickers. Well, that won't work either."

"Lilly, please. I don't want anything from you. I just needed to let you know that I was sorry, and I was hoping that you could write to me when I'm gone. My family won't talk to me. The people I was around in university are the same kinds of snobs my parents are. I have no one. It's selfish, but I was giving it a shot anyway."

Lillianna looked at him again as if to discern his true intentions. She finally let out a deep sigh and folded her arms. "I'm not ready to talk about this. You can't just show up out of the blue and disrupt my life, not after what you did."

Moore nodded in defeated understanding and stuck out his hand. "I'm sorry for bothering you, Lilly."

She walked past his outstretched hand and gave him a quick hug. "Yeah, I'm sorry too."

She turned and walked back into the bookstore. As the door closed and she walked out of sight, a knot grew in the pit of Moore's stomach. He understood why she'd walked away and didn't blame her, but it still hurt to see her go. It hurt that he wouldn't be able to talk to her for a while if ever, but he'd said what he'd wanted to say and that was that. As he hailed another cab and stepped out of the cold, he felt a weight leave his shoulders, only to be replaced by another.

Chapter 4
Kodiak

Fort Benning, Georgia, had been the home of the infantry for the United States Army since 1909. When the Republic was formed in 2053, a new military had to be created from the multiple different branches and specialties of the Republic's countries. Although many military bases in the United States had been decommissioned, Fort Benning still stood proud among the Georgia pines. What had once been 248 square miles of training grounds was now 600 square miles, making Fort Benning the largest military base in the Republic.

Private Harrison Kodiak found the history of the base fascinating, and as he continued to read about it on the bus, he grew more and more excited. His excitement faded when the bus pulled through the security gates and slowly drove toward the reception area. The main part of the base, the area they wanted the guests to see, was beautifully kept. Sculpted flower beds and plants lined the sidewalks and large trees towered over the roads. It was the welcomed sight they wanted the parents to see on graduation day. The area Kodiak saw as the bus took a hard right turn, the one he'd soon become accustomed to, was Sand Hill, one of the many basic training areas on the base.

Sand Hill used to be where only the infantry trained—it was the forge the country's sword had been made from. Now every occupation in the military came through there. The Republic had changed its basic training methods and now put every recruit through the same initial training. Communication soldiers and medics would train to fight just as hard as the infantry. Women and men were held to the same exact standard, and it was strictly maintained. After the basic training phase, the trainees would be given their next duty station for their advanced individual training, while the infantry would stay at Fort Benning and continue on to the more advanced tactics in future warfare.

Kodiak had found himself a part of Third Platoon, in a barracks bay that held thirty-six recruits on the second story of his training company's barracks. He managed to claim a top bunk. His bunkmate was a thin, darker-skinned man named Hall—at least, that was what the name tape on his uniform said.

"Hey, Hall, what was it you said your MOS was?" Kodiak asked.

"I don't remember tellin' ya," Hall answered, not opening his eyes.

37

"Ah, come on, man. I'm an Eleven Bang-Bang, infantry. What's yours?"

Hall was sort of the quiet type. Over the past couple weeks they had been here, Kodiak had never really heard him talk in paragraphs, just a couple sentences here and there. From what he could tell, Hall did his job and didn't slack, and when they were sucking, he was sucking right alongside them.

Kodiak tried again. "Come on, man, I got to know."

"You gotta know?" Hall asked, this time looking up at him.

"Yeah, man, I gotta know. If you're infantry, then, hell, we might be battle buddies for longer than just basic."

"If you don't ever call me that again and let me go to sleep, I'll tell you."

"All right, ba—bud," Kodiak stammered.

"Eleven Charlie. Indirect-fire infantry."

"You're a chuck? That's sick. Droppin' mortars and stuff. That's cool, man."

Hall continued to stare at him.

Kodiak chuckled. "All right, Sleepin' Beauty, I'll let you get your rest."

He rolled back over and looked at the clock above the front desk near the door. It was 2200 hours, and he couldn't get to sleep. In the morning they were going to get issued their rifles for the first time. Even though he came from Texas and was surrounded by firearms, he had never shot one in his entire life. He had no idea how he was going to react when he got to a range.

His eyes drifted to the soldier sitting behind the desk. He was on fire watch. Every night, for an hour, one of the soldiers in the platoon had to stay up and watch for anything out of the ordinary. It was supposed to teach you responsibility, but Kodiak thought it was just to make sure you never got a full night's sleep. His duty time was coming up in a couple of hours, and as he continued to look at the clock, he wondered if it was even worth trying to rest. He did, however, shut his eyes as he tried to watch the second hand tick away. Slowly, he drifted to sleep.

****

"When you stand at the position of attention, your eyes should be forward!" Drill Sergeant Yazzie Muleskin shouted.

He was a mean-looking man with scars down the left side of his face. His right eye was a light blue but his left had no color, only a black pupil. Rumors had run wild when they'd first arrived at their training company and seen who their senior drill sergeant would be. Kodiak tried not to give the rumors much thought and instead just focused on doing what Drill Sergeant Muleskin told him to do.

Kodiak stole a glance to his right to see who wasn't looking forward but didn't see anyone out of place. He then looked forward again and was greeted by Drill Sergeant Muleskin's face inches from his own.

"Private, are you stupid? Can you not comprehend a simple order of keeping your eyes forward?" Muleskin screamed. "Drop! Drop, Private Dumbass!"

Kodiak immediately dropped to the front-leaning rest position. His hands were placed fully on the ground and aligned with his shoulders, his back ramrod straight in the plank position.

"Now you want to listen to orders. Now you want to do what Daddy told you to do. Are you a glutton for punishment? Do you like that kinky crap, Private?" Muleskin continued to scream, bending down and getting in his face. "Push, Private! Push until you start moving the Earth beneath you!"

So, Kodiak pushed.

He had found out rather quickly that push-ups and sit-ups were his strong suit. He had tremendous upper-body strength, so doing push-ups didn't bother him too much. He of course put on an act as he continued to push. As Kodiak had found out quickly over the past couple of weeks, if you showed that a punishment wasn't affecting you the way the drill sergeants expected, you were in for a much more painful time.

His arms began to shake as he slowed the pushing. He felt that any moment, he would be brought back up to the position of attention as he pushed past forty-two push-ups, but instead he was greeted with a hard kick to his stomach. The impact lifted him a few inches into the air as he felt all the air escape from his lungs. Before he could get to his feet, he felt strong hands grip his uniform and drag him out of the formation. His back hit the pine-needle-covered ground and he stared up into the brilliantly blue autumn sky, trying as hard as he could to get air into his lungs.

Drill Sergeant Muleskin blocked his vision and stared down at him. "I don't like being sandbagged, Private. Get your ass up."

Kodiak struggled to get to his feet as air filled his lungs again. Muleskin had dragged him twenty meters into the woods, away from the rest of the formation. Kodiak brought his hands behind and to the small of his back and stood at parade rest.

They had ruck-marched five miles that morning to one of the many firing ranges that littered the military base. They were going to be issued their rifles, and Kodiak had been looking forward to it—that was, until this very moment.

"Private, you have big shoulders. You did well in your PT test when a lot of people fail the first test they have to take." Muleskin's face got closer. "You maxed out your push-ups, moron, so that whole arm-shaking nonsense you were just doing won't fly with me. Now get back in formation and don't disappoint me again."

"Yes, Drill Sergeant!" Kodiak yelled and ran back into formation next to Hall.

"You're an idiot," Hall muttered under his breath.

"Yeah, I heard," Kodiak responded.

He thought about what Drill Sergeant Muleskin had said. He was disappointed in him. That hurt way more than the boot to his stomach or the smoke sessions he had gotten since arriving. It was a weird phenomenon that these men and women drill sergeants could beat the absolute hell out of you and yet you continued to try and make them happy. Disappointing Muleskin felt like the ultimate sin and made Kodiak want to do better. Not even his coach had gotten that out of him.

Chapter 5
Hall

Private Aiden Hall's eyes lingered on Kodiak for a moment more and he shook his head. People like Kodiak only came around every so often in your life. Depending on when you met them, you'd see either a natural-born leader who has stepped into his role or a boy with so much potential but with no one to mold it into something special. Kodiak was in the learning stages, which was why Hall believed the drill sergeants were on him more. Drill Sergeant Muleskin hadn't even picked Kodiak to be the platoon guide when they'd first started training, despite the fact that he was one of the only soldiers actively trying to help others through the more difficult tasks.

The actual platoon guide was Private Tyler Skaggs, a wiry white kid from Minnesota. Hall hated him, at least at the moment. They were still only in the first few weeks of basic training, but Skaggs hadn't done anything to put himself above the rest. Hall figured he was the kind of guy who always got his way back home, and now that people pushed back, he had no other way to react but yell. Yet somehow, he still had a little clique of brownnosers that walked around him like personal bodyguards when they were in the bay.

Hall remembered back to the first week of basic. They had gotten their sleeping assignments, all their gear was stowed in lockers, and for a moment the drill sergeants were out of sight. It was a nice reprieve from the almost nonstop punishment the sergeants had been dishing out ever since they'd arrived. Skaggs had called him over and told him he needed to deliver a message to the female side of the barracks building. Hall admitted to himself that he had a hard time listening the first week there, but one of the rules he did remember was "no male is ever permitted in the female side of the barracks."

He remembered because that was one of the first thoughts he had. Here he was stuck in basic training for months on end, with no form of communication with the outside world and bunking with all males. The moment he'd seen some of the women when they got off the bus, he'd known he had to turn the game on. It was shortly afterward that he'd gotten the warning never to set foot over there. Hall knew what the drill sergeants would do to someone for the smallest mistake, like not making their bed properly. He didn't want to find out what would happen if they caught him near the female side of the barracks.

Nevertheless, Skaggs had a legitimate message, signed by the drill sergeant, stating that physical training had been changed from 0500 to 0400, so Hall took the message and made his way down the hallway. The female bay was just a couple feet down the hallway from the male bays and the entrance was always guarded by someone on fire guard duty, but after entering the hallway, he saw no one behind the desk. That caused him to pause, but after a moment he kept walking, this time with a little more urgency. Once that door was opened, he was just going to wordlessly hand the message over and be on his way. But when the door opened, he stopped dead.

Drill Sergeant Rodriguez had opened the door and was stepping back into the hallway when she locked eyes with Hall. "What the hell are you doing out here, Private?" she bellowed. Her voice bounced off the narrow hallway.

Hall had told the truth. "Delivering a message to the female bays stating that PT was changed from 0500 to 0400 hours, Drill Sergeant."

Rodriguez narrowed her eyes and reached out her hand. Hall stepped forward and placed the message into her hand and stood back. She read over it for only a few moments and then looked back at him. He didn't see anger or rage on her face. Usually, you knew when you were about to get smoked. Then again, you could never be sure.

"Who asked you to deliver this message?" she asked.

"My platoon guide, Private Skaggs, Drill Sergeant."

"And where is Private Skaggs now?"

"Inside our bay, Drill Sergeant."

That was all she needed to hear. The next moment, she was walking past Hall towards the male bay and storming in. He heard the yells of "at ease" and then watched as Skaggs was yanked out of the bay and into the hallway. She made him do push-ups, flutter kicks, and every other creative exercise she could possibly think of for the next hour. The entire time, Skaggs just stared at Hall with fire in his eyes. Of course, Hall knew he hadn't done anything wrong—but as far as Skaggs was concerned, he had left the bay and immediately gone to a drill sergeant.

"Eyes front, Privates!" Drill Sergeant Muleskin shouted, snapping Hall out of his memories.

The drill sergeant stood next to another sergeant who didn't have on the iconic brown drill sergeant hat. Instead, he wore the standard-issue camouflage patrol cap they all wore. In his hands was a large, bulky rifle with two barrels, one small and one large. Just behind the forward grip was a magazine that curved slightly, but on the back, under the butt of the rifle, was a small cylinder that glowed blue. Hall had fired a pistol before but had never handled rifles, and he had never seen that cylinder before.

"My name is Sergeant Forrester, and I'll be your instructor at this rifle range as well as other ranges during your stay at beautiful Fort Benning." The others in Hall's platoon gave nervous chuckles as if debating whether they were allowed to show that type of emotion. Forrester continued, "This baby is the M85 multipurpose rifle, the standard-issue rifle for all Republic military soldiers. It can fire a magazine-fed 5.56 magrail round as well as a concentrated bolt of energy. On the bottom is a third option for those hard-to-reach places. This tube on the underside of your barrel fires a 20mm smart munition that can seek out a target and obliterate it. Each magazine holds three hundred rounds of 5.56 tungsten. Your battery packs, which give your weapon the energy to fire a laser bolt, last for five hundred shots. Don't fear, though"—he turned the rifle so the barrel pointed skywards and showed the LED screen on the side—"this screen will tell you when it's about to run dry. Your helmet's heads-up display will also give you an accurate count of how many rounds are left in the magazine as well as how much charge is in the battery."

He removed the magazine, which looked kind of like a rectangular box, from the weapon and held it up for them all to see. "Unlike the weapons of old, the magrail technology ditches the brass casings to maximize the number of tungsten rounds a magazine can hold."

Sergeant Forrester placed the magazine back into the rifle, giving it a slight slap that appeared to lock it in place, then put the weapon across his chest and made his way over to one of the firing positions that looked out across a large, open field. The grass was still the color of ice as the cold air and dark clouds kept it from thawing in the early morning. The instructor shouldered the weapon, and Hall watched him flick a switch on the side.

"In the distance, about two hundred meters out, there's a cinder block structure. The round I'm about to fire is propelled by magnetic energy from the main barrel. On the side of this weapon is a selector switch. That switch needs to be turned to point at the M setting to fire the magrail round. M for magrail, for all those who only graduated elementary school."

He turned and took aim across the field from the standing position. The rifle boomed and dust kicked up from the wooden platform he stood on. Hall looked towards the building and watched a piece of the wall explode and break away. The sergeant then planted his feet, bent his knees slightly, and fired three more rounds. The wall exploded into tiny fragments, leaving broken sections and exposing the inside to the elements.

Forrester turned back to the gaggle of soldiers. "The next position I'm moving the selector switch to is 'semiautomatic.' Who knows what that means?"

Hall watched as a few seconds passed before Skaggs raised his hand. "Semiautomatic means the weapon will discharge every time the trigger is pulled."

"Correct. One trigger pull means one round is leaving the chamber. The rate of fire depends on how fast you depress the trigger."

Kodiak elbowed Hall. "You knew that answer—why didn't you raise your hand?"

Hall rolled his eyes. "You knew the answer too. Why didn't you ask?" he challenged.

"Was waiting on you, battle." Kodiak smiled.

He knew what he was doing calling Hall his battle, and it almost made Hall laugh. Almost. He did know what semiautomatic meant, but he didn't want to do anything that would single him out.

"Listen, man, I ain't tryin' to get noticed. Imma just do my job, do my time, and graduate."

Kodiak huffed. "If you know your stuff, make it known. You have the best PT score, you remember your battle drills—hell, you even completed the obstacle course in record time. I have no doubt you'll do good at shoo—"

Hall cut him off. "Listen, nothin' good comes out of getting noticed. If I do well, it may be great at first, but then the drill sergeants will expect that out of me every time and then what happens when I mess up?"

"Point taken." Kodiak nodded.

Sergeant Forrester walked back over to the platform and took a knee. He aimed the rifle again, clicking the selector switch over twice, and fired. A thin blue bolt of energy shot from the rifle and flew across the field so fast that you would've missed it if you blinked. When the energy bolt hit the cinder block wall, it splashed across the surface as if someone had thrown electrically charged water and then it dissipated. Left behind was a large black scorch mark.

"As you see," Forrester started as he stood and turned, "an energy bolt fired from this weapon can't penetrate thick objects like buildings. If fired at something softer, however, like a human with body armor, it will cut through it like a hot knife through butter."

The instructor removed something from his pocket that looked like an enlarged bullet. He placed the object into the bottom of the tube and slid it in like you would when reloading a shotgun. "This final round is our 20mm smart munition. It activates after leaving the barrel and will use blue force tracker data beaming from ships in orbit to find and eliminate targets that may otherwise be unseen to your eyes. Behind that cinder block building is a marked target. Say you've killed all of his friends and he doesn't feel like popping his head up anytime soon. You have to take him out before moving towards your objective, so what do you do?"

Turning, Forrester tucked the stock of the rifle under his right armpit and fired. The barrel gave a deep thunk as the round leapt into the air, arced, and fell towards the marked enemy. It found its target, and the resulting explosion shook the cinder block building, collapsing a few more pieces as smoke rose from behind.

"That's what you do," Forrester said, smiling as he walked back toward Hall and the rest of the platoon. "Now you will break off into your squads and will be issued your rifles. For the rest of the morning, you'll go over this weapon and how to properly operate it and clean it."

Hall stood next to Kodiak and a British guy named Moore who was also in his platoon. Moore had looked like a fish out of water when they had first arrived at their training platoon. If Hall was being honest, they'd all looked a little flustered, but Moore was struggling more than anyone else. It was almost as if he wasn't used to any sort of harsh treatment or hard labor. It had only been the first night when Skaggs and his cronies decided to give Moore a hard time. They cornered him and tried to push him around—after all, it was Moore that had been responsible for their first-ever smoke session of basic training. It wasn't his fault, though, and everyone knew it, even Skaggs. The drill sergeants were just looking for an excuse and Moore was, unfortunately, the first person to stand out. He had made the mistake of asking one of their drill sergeants a question without adding "Drill Sergeant" at the end. Then entire platoon had paid for it.

Skaggs had gone on and on about how Moore was a rich high-society boy in England and even hinted at him being royalty. Hall didn't exactly know if any of it was true, but it made Moore a more intriguing individual if he was. Hall had come from a rough life with little to no money. If he had been high society or even royalty, joining the military would've been last on his "things to do" list. For that, he gave the Brit props by breaking up the little powwow before it got out of control. Now he was stuck with Kodiak and Moore. If he was being honest with himself, though, the two weren't bad company.

Hall looked down at his weapon on the table in front of him and ran his fingers over it. The November chill bit at his fingers as he touched the cold metal, but he didn't mind. In his opinion, the rifle was a work of art. At first glance it looked bulky and hard to handle, but now that it was in front of him, he noticed its sleek curves. The first thing he had done when he'd gotten it was put the weapon into his shoulder, and he hadn't been disappointed. The rifle didn't feel too big in his hands, and with its curves it sat tight and comfortably in his arms.

"Pretty nice, yes?" an accented, higher-pitched voice said beside them.

Hall, Kodiak, and Moore all turned to see a woman with blond hair wrapped tightly in a bun. The name tape on her uniform said Moreau, and she held a knife. The three just stared at her for a few moments. Hall didn't know about the others, but he was nervous about the rules regarding this sort of thing. For every PT session and training session, the male soldiers and female soldiers had worked side by side, but up until now the training had been very formal and regimented.

"Is that a French accent?" Moore asked.

"I'm glad your ears work"—she looked down at his name tape— "Moore. It is a French accent. Yes, I was born in France. Yes, my mother and father are both French. When I was a teenager, we moved to the United Kingdom and took up permanent residence. In order to get citizenship for myself as well as my parents, I decided to join the

46

Republic military. Now if you don't mind, I would love to talk about this weapon because I'm sick and tired of having to answer the same damn question every time I talk."

Hall stood silent and Moore took a step back, but Kodiak took a step forward. "Well, hell, I'll talk about weapons with ya. The name's Harrison Kodiak." Kodiak stretched his hand out and shook Moreau's.

Hall smiled. "I'm Hall."

"Moore," the future medic introduced himself with a slightly redder face than before.

"Angeline Moreau. Pleasure to meet you boys. Shall we?" She lifted her weapon and placed it on the table with them.

Chapter 6
Moore

It turned out that Private Oliver Moore was not a crack shot after all. He'd had absolutely zero expectations going into rifle qualification, but he'd at least expected to pass. Drill Sergeant Rodriguez made him go through the course several times until he finally passed, and even then, he'd barely made the cut. It was humiliating to have to walk back to the platoon with his marksmanship badge. Others wore marksmanship badges as well instead of the sharpshooter or expert badges, but all in the platoon had passed on the first try except Moore.

Kodiak and Hall attempted to make him feel better about everything, and to their credit they were doing a pretty good job, but every time he started perking up, Skaggs would open his mouth. It started with little jokes about his inability to shoot straight or more crass remarks about shooting blanks, but when they arrived back at the company barracks, Skaggs's remarks took a more personal turn.

"Didn't your papa ever take you quail hunting? I thought that's what royalty did over in your part of the world," Skaggs taunted as he sat down on his bunk. "I mean, hell, Your Highness, can you do anything right?"

"Give it a rest, Skaggs," Kodiak groaned as he rose to his feet from the bunk he had been sitting on.

"I'll make you a deal, Kodiak. The moment he does anything right, I'll shut up. Until then, I'm gonna keep treating him like the stuck-up royal highness that he is."

"What gave you the idea that I was stuck-up? You don't know me, Skaggs. You don't know my background or where I came from. You just heard that I lived in a slightly larger home than your cottage in the woods and started drawing conclusions," Moore replied.

Moore would be lying to himself if he said Skaggs's insults didn't piss him off, but until now, he'd just let the guy walk all over him. He blamed it on the fact that he'd never needed to get into someone's face or snap back with a witty comeback. It was part of why he'd joined the military—not because he was a glutton for punishment but because he needed a taste of the real world—a world his parents had never shown him.

Skaggs now stood up, inspired by Moore's reply. "You were born into royalty. You're spoiled. Now you have someone that calls you out on your failings, someone who's holding you accountable for your fuckups, and I'm the asshole?"

It annoyed Moore that Skaggs repeatedly called him royalty when he obviously had absolutely no idea how nobility in the United Kingdom worked, but at the moment, correcting him on that was the last thing he was worried about.

"There's a distinct difference between giving constructive criticism and being an ass—so, yes, in this case, you are an arsehole," Moore replied. As soon as the words left his lips, he knew he'd gone too far.

There were some people who could be pushed constantly and just shrug off whatever was said, and then there were guys like Skaggs. He was obviously the type of person who thought fists spoke louder than words. Skaggs crossed the room in only a matter of seconds, and before Moore could do anything he was on top of him.

Skaggs's fist connected hard with Moore's nose, which sent Moore spinning backwards onto the floor. He kicked his legs and scrambled back but couldn't see clearly as tears obscured his vision. He wasn't going to cry—that was the furthest thing from his mind—but the blinding pain in his nose was making it harder and harder to focus. He felt his back press against one of the lockers and brought his arms up to block whatever came next, but nothing happened.

Taking the moment to clear his eyes, he looked back up and saw Kodiak with his hand over Skaggs's throat. He had lifted the scrawny man into the air and was holding him there while Skaggs flailed his legs frantically. Behind Kodiak, Hall was on top of one of Skaggs's goons, pummeling him with his own fists. The rest of the platoon just stood there and watched.

"At ease!" someone yelled from the gaggle of soldiers that had formed a semicircle around the others.

Without thinking, Moore got to his feet and went to parade rest. As he stood there, he felt blood falling from his nose and stole a moment to look down and see red droplets staining the white tiled floor.

Moore watched as Drill Sergeant Muleskin crossed the room to where Kodiak was still holding Skaggs up by his neck. "You must be deaf, Private, because I believe someone in here yelled 'at ease.'"

Kodiak hesitated for a moment before letting Skaggs go. He gasped on the floor, making the most inhuman of noises while trying to get to his feet. Muleskin looked down, grabbed Skaggs by the back of the neck and dragged him to his feet. The yelp that escaped Skaggs's lips made Moore smile. His smile faded as Drill Sergeant Muleskin's eyes crossed over him as he took in the room.

"Private Moore, why are you staining my floor with your unholy blood?" he barked.

"I was struck by Private Skaggs, Drill Sergeant," Moore replied.

Muleskin looked over to Skaggs. "Why did you damage Republic military property, Private Skaggs?"

"Private Moore is lying, Drill Sergeant."

Moore's mouth dropped open.

Muleskin's normally tan face grew ten shades darker, his expression strained as if he was about to explode. "So you're telling me that Private Moore, Private Kodiak, and Private Hall, three individuals I have not had a major problem with this entire cycle, just decided that today of all days was the day they were going to assault the most insufferable human being I have ever met? Is that what you're telling me?"

Skaggs looked at the drill sergeant, not knowing what to say. Moore wanted badly to laugh, but the fear of drawing the attention back to himself stopped that notion. Instead, he watched as Muleskin walked in circles around Skaggs like a shark on the hunt.

"When I was a know-nothing private in basic training, we had a bunch of people just like you, Skaggs. See, at the time, the military was taking everyone and anyone they could find. This was before the psychological profiles we do now on recruits—before we could ask the invasive yet necessary questions needed to clear you for recruitment. So, our drills decided the best way was through physical combat. Now back then we used our fists, feet—anything within arm's reach, really—to beat each other into submission. Through the pain, we learned to respect one another."

Muleskin now walked into the middle of the room and turned towards everyone. "We are more than halfway through your training and coming up on War Week, and yet you continue to fight amongst yourselves. Tomorrow, instead of physical training, we will have a duel. When it's all said and done, I expect the infighting to cease. If it continues, I will make sure the remainder of your training is the most painful and agonizing experience you've ever had—a pain that will drill so deep within you that if you are lucky enough to survive to the ripe old age of one hundred and thirty years, you'll still think about the pain you endured on Sand Hill. Do you all understand?"

"Yes, Drill Sergeant!" the entire platoon bellowed.

A lump formed in the pit of Moore's chest and rose into his throat. Although he'd expected to do poorly during rifle qualification, he'd thought he'd be better than he was, and he *knew* he was horrible at fighting. His father had paid for fencing lessons, which he had done well with, but when it came to throwing punches, he was a mess. It was another byproduct of not having to face the least bit of adversity in his youth.

"Private Skaggs will fight Private Moore tomorrow morning. Lights out in thirty minutes, so shit, shower, and shave."

****

The sharp morning alarm rang out in the platoon bay, jolting its occupants awake and sending them towards the showers. Oliver Moore continued to stare up towards the ceiling. He had woken up an hour earlier and hadn't been able to drift back to sleep. He had dreamt about taking a trip to the river with Lilliana at dusk and nestling underneath a blanket in the brisk fall air. When he had awoken, he had come back to the reality of what he had to do in the morning.

Moore was taller than Skaggs but lankier and not as built. Skaggs had come from a hardworking blue-collar family in the States and Moore had come from a posh background. It was what it was and there was no use hiding from that fact. All he wanted to do at this moment was talk to Lilliana. In fact, she hadn't left his mind since he'd seen her again all those months ago. All that yearning, yet he still hadn't written to her— but she hadn't written either, and he used that as an excuse.

"Are you ready?" Kodiak asked from the stall next to him.

Moore quickly rinsed his hair of shampoo. "You've asked me twenty-three times this morning and my answer has always been the same. No, I am not ready to get my face beat in. Yes, I am ready for it to be over."

The two turned off the water and exited the shower at the same time. Heading back into the bay with their towels, they dressed in their camouflage combat uniforms. Kodiak showed Moore ways he could defend himself against certain punches, how to counter punches thrown at him, and even how to check someone's leg kick. It was interesting to Moore how animated Kodiak was when talking about fighting. The rest of it went in one ear and out the other. He wasn't trying to be rude and not hear his buddy out, but at the same time he knew it would never help him in this short a time.

When they exited the platoon bay and made their way into the covered awning to form into squads, he felt the pit forming again. "You think they're gonna let him kill me?"

Moore felt hands on his shoulders from behind. "You need to relax, Moore, it'll be over so quick you won't even know it."

Moore turned to look at Moreau. "Gee, thanks. How the hell did you hear about this?"

"How do you think? Drill Sergeant Rodriguez came in and told us. Hell, we've been waiting for it all night." Moreau laughed. "I even got in on plus three hundred odds."

"You bet on him to win?" Hall asked.

"Win? Lord, no. Plus three hundred he'll be knocked out in the first minute."

Moore rolled his eyes and turned back around. "Love the faith, guys."

Kodiak nudged him. "Look on the bright side—that means the majority of people think you're tough enough to make it past a minute."

"Do you?" Moore asked.

"I don't gamble, battle." He nudged Moore again and smiled.

Moore had a lot of complaints when it came to the majority of his platoon, especially Skaggs and his goons, but there was no denying that over the past few months of basic he had formed a bond with Kodiak and Hall. Moreau was a wild card he'd only known for the past few weeks. She was nice when she wanted to be, but sometimes, she'd say the wildest things and you never knew if she said it to be mean or that was just who she was. Regardless, she'd fall into the realm of "friends" when he looked back on it one day. If he had that opportunity.

He looked down the line towards Skaggs, who was practically hopping from foot to foot with excitement. When he caught Moore's eye, he smiled and pressed his fist into his own cheek. Moore felt like he was going to throw up.

"Listen up, platoon. Private Skaggs and Private Moore got into a little disagreement last night. The tension and constant bickering have been plaguing the platoon for a while now, and although I had hopes that somehow those two idiots would figure it out by now, alas, they have not. So, we will be having a duel today. Private Skaggs, Private Moore, step forward."

Moore stepped out of line alongside Skaggs and marched to the front, where they did an about-face and looked towards the platoon. Drill Sergeant Muleskin walked around Moore and Skaggs before turning back to the platoon. "Duels are simple. Two individuals will put on combat suits and will be equipped with an energy baton. The first person to incapacitate the other wins. From that moment on, the fighting stops. And if it does not"—he grinned wickedly—"you all will pay. You are a unit, and you will either triumph together or die together. There is no in-between."

Moore watched as Drill Sergeant Rodriguez brought out two armored suits and two long metal rods. The batons were the length of his arm, and when one of them made forcible contact with something, it would send an electrical blast into whatever it was touching. He remembered watching them being used in the London riots.

After they'd donned the suits and been handed their batons, Moore looked across the floor towards Skaggs, who was still hopping up and down. Moore didn't feel that adrenaline rush. He instead twirled the baton to get a feel for its weight. It was shockingly light and flexible, to the point where any snap movement seemed faster. It reminded him of a thicker fencing sword.

One of the other recruits started a timer and Skaggs advanced, Moore made the snap decision to use his fencing techniques in the hope they would translate. Skaggs went first, swinging wildly, allowing Moore to sidestep the attack and counter.

He swung the baton at Skaggs's unguarded side and connected with his torso, sending him to the ground. Moore hesitated and looked over to Drill Sergeant Muleskin, who just smiled.

To Moore's right he heard Kodiak yell, "Finish him!"

It was too late.

Skaggs swept Moore's legs out from underneath him, and before he could get his footing, he found himself on his back. Taking the advantage, Skaggs rose to his feet and raised the baton above his head.

Moore rolled out of the way and heard the baton smack into the ground instead.

Getting to his feet, Moore positioned himself and raised his baton slightly in anticipation of Skaggs's next attack. He had made a critical error when he hadn't finished the fight. He had gotten Skaggs onto the ground, but only after he was on his back had Moore realized he needed to incapacitate him. The word alone sent chills down his arms.

What exactly is the drill sergeant's definition of incapacitate?

Skaggs didn't wait for Moore to make the next move and charged toward him again. At first, Moore had hoped his training would give him a slight advantage, even though the baton was thicker than an épée. But Moore was beginning to realize that the brute force Skaggs was applying easily outmatched his own fencing skills.

The first swing from Skaggs was heavy and inaccurate as he let rage take control of his body. The assault was sloppy, but even so, Moore found it hard to parry his strikes. After the third blow nearly took his own baton out of his hand, he decided to go on the offensive. Bending his right knee slightly and moving his body out of the way of the swing, he was able to bring his baton up and into Skaggs's wrist. His scream echoed through the metal enclosure where they fought but was drowned out by the cheers erupting from his platoon moments later.

Skaggs's baton had clattered to the concrete floor after he let go with the help of an electrified shock from Moore's own baton. Moore smiled; he couldn't help it. He wasn't a fighter. Back home, he'd avoided physical confrontation and instead used wit to defeat his aggressors. With the baton in his hand and the cheers behind him, he felt better than after any quick-witted stab he'd ever delivered. The pen might be mightier than the sword, but it wasn't as fun.

With a swift downward swing, he brought the baton down into the top of Skaggs's head. His opponent's body fell to the ground, stiff, but Moore didn't sense anyone coming in to stop the fight. Remembering the first time, when he'd been swept from his feet after stopping, Moore brought the baton down a second time and finally a third before Drill Sergeant Muleskin grabbed him from behind and pulled him off Skaggs, who still lay there motionless.

Oh my God, I killed him, Moore thought as the baton fell from his hand.

As if Muleskin had heard his inner thoughts, he turned to Drill Sergeant Rodriguez and nodded. "There's a pulse. Get him to medical."

The soldiers from Moore's platoon stood still, unwilling to carry Skaggs away. A few soldiers from another platoon rushed forward and unceremoniously dragged Skaggs out of the training arena to an awaiting medical vehicle.

Drill Sergeant Muleskin grabbed Moore's arm and raised it above his head. "Private Moore is the winner. Third Platoon may take an additional five minutes to celebrate, but then get upstairs and start laying out your rucksacks in preparation for War Week. Dismissed!"

When he let go of Moore's arm, Third Platoon bolted from their formation and cheered with Moore, giving him high fives and slaps on the back. Basic training had been an up-and-down experience for Moore. He'd loved some of the training but loathed the rest. That morning was the happiest he had been in months.

"Never lost the faith." Kodiak was smiling ear to ear and gave Moore a bear hug, lifting him off his feet.

Moreau was next to Kodiak. "Yeah, so much faith he bet the candy from his MRE you'd lose." She gave Moore a wink.

"After five minutes, Moreau! I'm not heartless. Listen, I had all the faith in the world you'd make it past five minutes after I saw some of the blocks you were pulling off. What was up with that?" Kodiak asked.

"I trained in fencing when I was younger. My father thought it'd be a good idea."

"He wasn't wrong, it seems." Moreau laughed.

"I doubt my father thought I'd be using those skills in the Republic military, Moreau, but thank you."

"Screw him, then, let's celebrate!" Hall cheered.

"For five minutes," Kodiak reminded him.

"Yes, for five glorious minutes," Moore agreed, and it was the best five minutes he'd have for a while.

****

That night, after the bay's lights were turned out and O'Connor had taken his spot for fire guard, Oliver Moore decided to send a video message to Lilliana. He swiped his hand across the console next to his bedside and typed in her name and address but paused before pressing the Record button.

He looked at his reflection and almost closed the video altogether. His eyes were sunken with exhaustion and dark rings appeared under them. His sandy-blond hair, which used to hang shaggy and curled near the top of his ears, was now buzzed almost to the scalp. He would be unrecognizable to those he'd left behind in England but hoped Lilliana would still see him.

He pressed Record. "Hi, it's me."

That was stupid, he thought.

With a deep sigh, he deleted the message and pressed Record again. "I don't really know how to start this to be honest. I hope you're doing well in the bookshop and, uh, in general. I'm already a few months into basic, and graduation is right around the corner. I'd ask you to come to graduation, but honestly it would probably be too much of a hassle and too much money for the trip. After that, I'm heading off to AIT—that stands for advanced individual training. The drill sergeants say it will be a lot calmer than basic, but they also said by this time it would become more calm. That was a lie. We still get smoked every day, and with War Week coming up the training has been ramping up.

"I fought someone today—not in a proper scrum but with batons and armor on. The guy's name is Skaggs and he's a dickhead, always blames his own horrible leadership skills on everyone else, and despite being in charge of the platoon, he's the farthest thing from a leader I've ever seen. He'd give my father a run for his money." He laughed at that. "I miss you. I miss home, but it's almost over and I can see the light at the end of the tunnel. I hope you video back, I really do. All right, I have to go. Hope to talk to you soon."

He ended the video and pressed Send, and a message in red blinked on the screen: *Automated Censorship found ten errors in your video that have been rectified. Message sent.*

He blinked at the screen and sighed. As he closed his eyes, he wondered if any of his message would be understood after the censors got their hands on it.

Chapter 7
Kodiak

War Week was upon the men and women of Third Platoon.

Private Harrison Kodiak looked up towards the darkening sky of the December morning and watched as the heavens opened with flurries of snow. His boots crunched on the dirt road, then veered off the main street towards one of the first areas of operation for the week. He had been up since three in the morning, checking over his packing list and rucksack, also taking the time to check the others'. That job was supposed to be Skaggs's, but after his ass whooping at the hands of Moore, he had become even less of a leader and that was saying something.

Third Platoon stepped off from the company barracks at 0500 hours to begin their twelve-mile march out to the training area. When they had left, Kodiak had been at the lead, but by the time they'd reached mile nine, he was walking up and down the line, trying to get the soldiers of Third Platoon motivated. Ruck marches were hard. Nothing was meant to be easy in basic training, as was well established by this time, but ruck marches were known to weed out the weak. In the last ten-mile the platoon had done, they'd had three people fall out. This morning he intended to make sure all crossed the line together.

"Private, you keep this up you might mess around and become the platoon leader," Drill Sergeant Muleskin barked.

Kodiak pretended to ignore the drill sergeant as he walked alongside Sims and fixed the shoulder straps on his ruck. Skaggs was still at the rear of the column and was slowly falling back. Kodiak looked him in the eyes and saw the struggle. He didn't want to go help him, if he was being honest with himself. If anyone in the platoon deserved to be weeded out, it was Skaggs.

The drill sergeants talked all the time about how the weakest link in the unit could end up getting someone—if not everyone—killed. There was no doubt in his mind that Skaggs was that guy. He was insubordinate, thought he knew better than anyone, and tried to take all the glory of being a platoon leader without doing the work—which fell on the others of the platoon.

Kodiak thought about what Drill Sergeant Muleskin had said about messing around and becoming a platoon leader. He didn't know what to make of that or if he'd even want that type of responsibility. It was a lot to take in, and becoming one so late in the training cycle would prove to be more difficult. He knew the others in the platoon respected him to a point but had no idea if they'd follow him. Not that they'd really followed Skaggs to begin with, but still, a leadership change this late in the game, especially in War Week, could prove disastrous.

Regardless of his feelings, Kodiak rolled his eyes in frustration and made his way back to Skaggs. "What's making it hard on you?"

"Who says anything is?" Skaggs snapped back.

"Well, something is unless you're just sandbagging it."

"I'm fine, Kodiak, get back in formation."

Kodiak gave a sigh and pulled his straps tighter as they had loosened during the march. "Well, one thing's for sure, Skaggs, you're a terrible leader and it's being noticed. You keep this up and the DS is liable to smoke your ass."

"Y'all will be smoked with me, Kodiak, so it's no skin off my back."

Anger rose in Kodiak and his neck turned crimson. "Get your ass in gear, Skaggs. You're being left behind."

Kodiak turned to walk away and march back up the line when Skaggs groaned, "It's my ankle."

Kodiak rolled his eyes. "What about it?"

"I think I rolled it on a rock a couple miles back and it's starting to hurt."

"We've all rolled our ankles on the march, Skaggs. Grow up."

"You wanted to help, right?"

Kodiak laughed. "And how can I help you, Skaggs? Want me to massage your ankle? If you want, I can stop the column and give us a little break for your weak ankles."

That last dig at Skaggs was probably not needed, but Kodiak was getting sick and tired of his BS. With basic training coming to a close at the end of War Week, he couldn't wait to get rid of the man and hated the fact that Skaggs could still get orders for his unit. The prospect of having to serve alongside him made Kodiak's skin crawl.

"Platoon, halt march and pull security," Kodiak called.

He watched as Third Platoon made their way off the road and pulled security. The men and women of the platoon removed their rucksacks, placed them on the ground, and took cover behind them. Their weapons all came to a rest on top of the rucksacks to give the weapons more stability in case they had to open fire. He smiled as he watched them do exactly what they had been trained to do, then he moved up and down the line, checking on the platoon's hydration levels and overall readiness. They were allowed three stops on the march, and this was their third and final one—with two miles left, he felt it was the right time.

He was aware of the watchful eyes of the drill sergeants, knowing all too well that if he overstepped any bounds, they were liable to smoke him right there and then. After all, he wasn't the current platoon guide, but the job had to be done and Skaggs wasn't doing it. What Kodiak was unaware of was that War Week had officially begun. The other platoons were spread out by miles on the march, and already First Platoon had made it to the objective and moved into position to begin ambushing.

War Week was the final test of a platoon's true combat readiness and effectiveness. They had fought through the sleep-deprived months of training and unit cohesion drills, and it was all going to culminate in a weeklong war scenario that pitted the platoons against one another. The rifles they held were the same ones they had been issued, but they didn't have any of the lethal ammunition in their combat load. It was the platoon guide's job to check for that, and Kodiak only hoped that Skaggs had at least done that job correctly. He thought about that for a moment and made a mental note to go over everyone's ammunition when they arrived at their destination.

"Contact front!" came a scream from down the line, and within moments, laser fire came sizzling from the forest toward the line pulling security.

Kodiak slung his rucksack off his shoulders and laid it on the ground next to Hall, diving behind it as bolts of laser fire slammed into the ground around him. The lasers looked like the real thing and were absolutely terrifying, but in the back of his mind, he knew if he was hit by one, it wouldn't kill him. The bolt was made of electricity instead of the lethal plasma they'd carry in combat. When a soldier was unlucky enough to be hit by a bolt, it would render his muscles immobile until a range officer came by and applied a stimulant.

Kodiak looked back down the line in between firing his weapon and saw Skaggs lying behind his own rucksack but not giving any orders. He remembered one of the lessons taught earlier in basic—if you were faced with overwhelming firepower in an ambush, the only move was to either tactically retreat or push through the objective. As he watched one of his soldiers down the line slump over their rucksack, he made the decision right then and there—they were going to assault through.

Kodiak keyed his mic. "All squad leaders, this is Kodiak. I'm taking command of Third Platoon. Pop smoke to our front, and on my order, we're going to assault through the ambush. Break." Kodiak looked up and down the line to get a read on where his squads were. Private Moreau and Third Squad were to the rear, pulling security, and hadn't received the bulk of fire from the ambush. "Third Squad, flank the ambush from your position and sweep right. First Squad, I want you to be the main force assaulting through. Second Squad, assist First. Weapons Squad, lay down suppressing fire to cover them while they move."

Confirmation lights blinked green on his tablet, showing that the squad leaders understood their orders—even Skaggs, who had no problem taking over Weapons Squad from Kodiak, acknowledged the order. Smoke grenades arched through the air to the front of the line and into the trees, enveloping the area in a thick screen. When Kodiak felt it was at peak concealment, he gave the order. "All units, execute."

He watched as First and Second Squads leaped from their area, leaving their rucksacks, and pushed into the smoke. Weapons Squad was doing a great job with their overwhelming suppressive fire, and he hoped Moreau and Third Squad were doing their best to get into position to flank.

From his vantage point behind the line, Kodiak couldn't see a thing. Blue lasers darted back and forth through the smoke, illuminating shadows of his soldiers, but whether they were getting the advantage or not he couldn't tell.

"First Squad, sitrep," Kodiak called.

Private Lacy Brown's voice came back to him. "We've assaulted through the objective but are being held up. We could use some help."

"I'm moving in now!" Moreau's voice cut in.

Kodiak knew if Weapons Squad didn't shift their fire, they would start to hit the flanking Third Squad. "Weapons, shift fire to your right. Shift fire!"

"We almost have them on the run!" Skaggs yelled back.

"I said shift fire! That's a damn order!" Kodiak yelled back.

60

The firing continued, and from the angle of laser fire, he could tell Weapons Squad hadn't shifted. Kodiak was immediately on his feet, moving to Skaggs's position, but halfway down the road, a laser bolt hit the dirt berm to his right and slammed into his side. His muscles tensed up immediately and his voice caught in his throat as he fell forward, stiff as a board, and slammed into the ground.

Chapter 8
Hall

Aiden Hall had been looking over toward Kodiak when motion in the forest had caught his eye. When he'd turned to investigate the shadows, he hadn't seen anything and had shaken his head, blaming his heightened senses on sleep deprivation. He should've gone with his gut. With the light dusting of snow covering the ground, he'd be hard-pressed to know if someone was sneaking up on the formation, but the snow hadn't yet been able to accumulate in the forest itself. A twig snapped and his breath caught in his throat.

The next moment, the man next to him shouted "Contact!" and laser fire was immediately hammering their position. Luckily, the road they had decided to take a break on had a dirt berm covered in brown pine needles, covering their position from the woods. Bolts of electricity sizzled and smacked against the ground in front of him, throwing dirt and dust into his face, but he squinted and returned fire. The first bolt from his rifle hit the ground in front of him and he cursed at the mistake as he tried to steady his aim and fire into the tree line.

The shadows were dense in the early-morning light that had not yet breached the canopies of the forest, making it difficult to find targets. More bolts danced in the darkness towards his position, and he decided to stop searching for figures and start firing at the locations the laser fire was coming from.

Kodiak's voice rang in his ears, and he heard the Texan giving orders to the different squad leaders, which made him smile. Apparently, Skaggs had once again shat the bed, and luckily Kodiak was picking up the slack. His squad, First Squad, had been ordered to assault through the ambush after concealing their position with smoke. He had only ever thrown a grenade once, during the earlier months of training, and he kind of liked the idea of being able to use one in a scenario like this, even if it was just a smoke grenade.

He removed the cylinder from its pouch on his armor and pulled the pin while still holding on to the spool. He waited for grenades to start flying, but none did. Was he supposed to wait for a signal? Another bolt slammed into the ground next to him and bounced into the air with a fizzle and crack.

"Screw this," he said to himself as he reached back and threw the grenade forward.

The cylinder arched through the air and into the forest, trailing smoke from the top, and within seconds, more followed from across the line. In minutes, the entire tree line had been engulfed in the thick white smoke. Grabbing tight to his rifle, he stood and followed his squad leader, Private Brown, toward the enemy fire.

Private Sato went stiff and fell onto his face next to Hall as he continued to push, taking note to stay in line and fire rhythmic bursts toward the enemy ahead of him. As he entered the smoke, his mind wandered to what it would feel like to be hit by one of the bolts. Would it be painful? Probably not as painful as a real plasma bolt, but painful enough that he didn't want to be hit. As more bolts lit up the smoke in a blue hue around him, he pictured one coming from the darkness and hitting him square in the chest, but the bolt never came.

He exited the smoke and immediately ran to the thick pine tree in front of him, pressing his shoulder into the wood. More soldiers from his squad and others exited the smoke and took similar fighting positions behind the trees. The enemy fire was letting up to a point, probably because they hadn't been expecting the platoon to push towards them, but once they had entered the forest, the movement had stopped.

Every couple of seconds, someone else would try to be brave and move forward but would be shot down quickly. "Stop moving forward!" he yelled over the gunfire as he peeked around his own tree and let off a burst of fire.

They were pinned down, and even though they had made up some ground on the ambushing unit, the advance had stalled and now they were in a pitched fight. The battery pack on his rifle blinked red and he realized he was out. That shocked him—he'd had no idea he had wasted so much ammunition in the first few minutes of the firefight. He removed another pack from his armor and slapped it into place on the rifle, taking two more shots towards the enemy.

"Where the hell is Moreau?" Brown asked Hall from an adjacent tree.

Hall just shrugged. He had no idea where Third Squad was, but he did know if they didn't flank around the enemy platoon soon, they would all be taken out.

A figure bounded out of the shadows and lunged at Hall. He had a red armband on his left shoulder, signifying that he was part of First Platoon, and Hall's eyes went wide in surprise. He raised his rifle to take a shot at the encroaching enemy but couldn't level it in time before the soldier from First Platoon yelled and collided with him. It was all a confusing mess. They had been pinned down by accurate laser fire after trying to assault through the initial ambush and the other platoon had them dead to rights—why did this one feel the need to charge at him? Were their lines getting that close?

The soldier who had collided with Hall grabbed him by his uniform and tried to roll him over onto his back. Hall locked his legs around the soldier's thighs to keep himself from being flipped over but paused when he was about to punch downward into the soldier's unblocked face. He knew War Week had begun but didn't know how far he could go without getting in trouble. Was punching another soldier in basic worse than shooting him with an electrical bolt from his rifle?

The hesitation allowed the soldier to swing upward and caught Hall under his chin. His eyes exploded in stars and tears as he took the blow and tried to hold on to his full mount. Apparently, there were no rules for combat during War Week, and although blinded by the involuntary tears, he knew where the soldier beneath him was. He struck downward and felt his elbow connect with the soldier's nose.

The soldier from First Platoon yelped in pain and released his grip on Hall, grabbing his face. Hall took advantage and spun away. Raising his rifle, he shot into the chest of the soldier and watched as he locked up. Turning, he watched more bolts splash into the trees and ground around him, forcing him back into cover.

His squad leader for War Week gave him a thumbs-up.

"Thanks for the help," Hall grunted.

"I'm a little busy over here, Hall. I saw you had him."

She did, huh? Hall rolled his eyes and fired off another burst.

64

Chapter 9
Moore

Oliver Moore could hear the fighting grow more intense as he moved with Moreau and Third Squad to flank the ambush. It was a weird feeling to hear the ongoing firefight happening a few meters away while his area was relatively silent. He even heard a bird chirp from the branches above him. When they'd moved into the forest from the side of the road, he'd expected to see laser bolts sizzling through the trees towards him, but they'd never come. As they rushed over fallen trees and thick brush towards the ambush, he checked his rifle to make sure it was ready to be fired.

Garza held up his fist and went to a knee, signaling for the rest of the squad to do the same. Moreau ran up the line to Garza. Moore tried to make out what they were saying, but between paying attention to his front and listening for any signs of the enemy, he was having a hard time hearing every other word. That was when Moreau approached his position.

"Take Redner, Griffin, and O'Connor with you up the left side. I'm going to move with the rest forward. When you hear we are in contact, I want you to assault from the left side. That will give you clear lines of sight to the enemy without catching us in the crossfire. Good?"

Moore blinked at her for a second and then nodded. "Uh, yeah, no problem."

"Good." Moreau winked and patted him on the shoulder.

"Redner, Griffin, O'Connor, on me," he ordered in a somewhat authoritative manner as he stood, making his way through the woods towards the ambush's rear.

He had no idea why Moreau had picked him to lead a team around to the back of the ambush. He wasn't the best shot she had in her squad and wasn't aware of any time he had shown leadership quality. In fact, he didn't like this one bit, and it began to feel a little overwhelming. Moore kept his eyes forward, slowing the pace of the others, as the sound of battle grew louder. He swallowed hard as his mouth grew dry with nervousness. Despite the brisk winter air freezing his lungs, sweat poured down his face.

The others in his team had done a fantastic job keeping themselves a good distance from one another. They moved at a slow but effective pace toward the ambush location, and Moore found he didn't need to correct any of the others while they moved. Having a good team made all the difference in a situation like the one he found himself in. The less he had to worry about the soldiers next to him, the more time he could spend working on formulating a plan for when they arrived. A knot formed in his stomach at the thought of having someone like Skaggs with him.

Moore took a knee and aimed his rifle towards the sound of gunfire. In the distance, he could make out soldiers jumping from behind trees and firing toward someone. He noticed the red bands on their shoulder and looked down at his own blue band, which marked him as Third Platoon.

"Moreau, we are set," Moore said into his headset.

Met with silence on the other end, he looked toward the enemy soldiers, who were still unaware of their presence, and keyed his mic again. "Moreau, we are set."

Static broke in over the line with Moreau screaming, "Tell them to shift fire, Kodiak!" before the comms went dead again.

Moore waited for a few more seconds and then turned to Redner. "We have to move. Follow me on line and open fire when I do."

Redner nodded, and Moore's team stood and began moving toward the enemy position. If they'd had grenades with them like in a real-world scenario, Moore would've used those to soften up the lines before assaulting through. Since they didn't, his team would have to try and overwhelm the position with laser fire in the hopes that in the confusion, the enemy couldn't react.

Moore raised his weapon and aimed at an enemy soldier kneeling from behind cover. Putting his sight's reticle on the soldier's back, he pulled the trigger and watched as a single bolt left his rifle and hit the tree next to the soldier. Moore cursed himself and fired off three more bursts as the rest of the team also fired on the enemy position. His burst of fire finally made impact on the soldier he'd tried to hit the first time, and they fell over.

Moore's team continued to move forward, and even in the chaos, his brain was able to note what was happening in front of him in the enemy lines. They were disorganized and confused about where the incoming fire was coming from. He smiled as he continued to take aim at the enemy soldiers, who were now running about like ants from a kicked mound. Moore took a knee and aimed once again toward the enemy position, but when he focused on a soldier jumping into the battle position, he noticed a blue armband on their uniform.

"Cease fire!" Moore yelled to his team, waving his open palm over his head.

His team did what they were told. "Brown, this is Moore, have you broken through the lines?"

"We're through!" Brown replied.

Moore smiled. "We're approaching from the north, hold your fire."

"Come on in, Moore, the water's fine."

****

The drill sergeants had ended the engagement and ambush attempt and brought both platoons together to do an after-action review. Third Platoon had successfully defeated the ambush but suffered a lot of casualties in doing so. Moore thought this was a failure, but Drill Sergeant Muleskin told the platoons that when dealing with a close ambush, casualties would be expected. They were getting the soldiers accustomed to dealing with loss, which made sense. They were training to fight for, and if need be, die for the Republic, and trying to maneuver around that harsh fact would only prove to hurt them in the end.

It was a weird feeling to dissect an engagement and talk about it as if you were playing advanced 3-D chess. You talked about the casualties in numbers, not faces. You tried to replay the scenario in your head to recreate a perfect picture of what had occurred and then afterward tore it all down with what had gone wrong. Despite winning the first engagement in War Week, Third Platoon tackled the AAR as if they had lost. Kodiak, despite not even being the platoon guide, was working tirelessly over the engagement with the other squad leaders while Skaggs bragged about his weapons team's efficiency. It made what came next that much sweeter.

"Private Kodiak, front and center!" Drill Sergeant Muleskin barked.

Moore watched Kodiak sling his rifle and run over to where the drill sergeant stood. The rest of Third Platoon turned to look at what was about to happen.

"You think Skaggs is getting the boot?" Hall nudged Moore in his ribs.

"That's what I'm thinking. He did nothing during that engagement—"

"Yeah, except get me and Moreau's squad killed by friendly fire. Kodiak told him to shift fire and he didn't. If I wasn't locked up from taking a hit, I would've gone over there and beat his ass myself."

Hall was fuming and Moore couldn't much blame him for that. "Well, let's hope the drill sergeants noticed it too, yeah?"

Hall nodded.

Since the beginning of basic training, Moore had watched Hall transform from a quiet, reclusive outcast to an outgoing and motivated soldier. Others went to him to see if their thoughts matched his because they cared about what he thought. He didn't overcomplicate his viewpoints—they were his and he stuck to them, which was more than the average soldier did. He wasn't insubordinate, he was starved for knowledge, and he used his questions wisely to get to the bottom of a problem, not to create one.

"Third Platoon," Drill Sergeant Muleskin barked, "you successfully defended against a complex ambush conducted by members of First Platoon. Your introduction to War Week has come with a victory. A costly victory. When you are ambushed, you can always expect to take casualties—that's what ambushes are good at. Sowing chaos and disorganization. With the help of Private Kodiak, you were able to become organized and fight back. During the engagement, however, one of your own disobeyed orders from the person taking control. Private Skaggs disobeyed a direct order to shift fire, which led to the deaths of multiple friendlies. That is unacceptable."

Drill Sergeant Muleskin walked over and ripped off the Velcro platoon leader patch from Skaggs's uniform, slapping it on Kodiak's. "Private Kodiak will be Third Platoon's platoon guide for the remainder of War Week. He is free to change up any of the squad leaders and team leaders."

Drill Sergeant Muleskin whispered something in Kodiak's ear and then dismissed the platoon. No one broke out in cheers, but the suppressed expressions on their faces told him they all wanted to. Instead, each member of the platoon patted Kodiak on the shoulder or congratulated him before he finally made his way over to Moore and Hall.

"Proud of you, platoon guide." Hall smiled, punching Kodiak in the shoulder.

Moore shook Kodiak's hand. "You deserve it, mate. What did, uh, Drill Sergeant say?"

Kodiak looked to Moore and Hall. "He just said good luck because if I fail now, I'll fail as a leader."

Moore stared blankly at Kodiak.

Hall let out a low whistle. "What a pep talk."

Chapter 10
Kodiak

Six Months Later
On Board the RNS *Currahee*

"You ready, Bear?" Private Alejandro Garza asked Kodiak, using the nickname that Hall had given him.

After graduating from basic training at the top of his class, Private First Class Harrison Kodiak had been promoted, then wasted ten days of leave going home, only to be broken up with by his girlfriend and take up boxing. Now he sat in one of the many seats that lined the walls of an Osprey dropship. He had taken the trip into space five months earlier to begin training in the low gravity on Mars and even lower g's on Luna, Earth's moon.

He remembered back to his conversation with Kyle Dingleman in Texas and how he'd asked him about leaving Earth and getting to experience space and other planets. It was a dream he never would've been able to attain if it wasn't for joining the Republic Army. When he'd taken the LAS or Light Atmospheric Shuttle from Space Port Canaveral to one of the many space stations orbiting his home planet, his breath had caught in his throat.

The bright sunny day over Florida had turned to pitch darkness. The stars were brighter than he had ever seen them in his life, brighter than any photograph he'd seen either. Kodiak marveled at the hundreds of transport shuttles, trading vessels, privately owned luxury vessels, and massive warships that moved harmoniously through the open lanes around them. He wanted to look to everyone else and confirm what he was seeing was actually there because it felt as if his brain wasn't quite believing it. He was in space, and he was in love with it.

He looked over to Garza and gave him a fist bump. "Ready as I'll ever be."

Kodiak wasn't ready at all. He had experienced excitement entering atmosphere both on Earth and on Mars, but not at the high level of g's he would be experiencing on a simulated combat drop. The armor he wore was the combat armor he'd been issued once he'd gotten to his actual unit after training. It had smart technology that changed with every environment the wearer encountered, from harsh weather on a planet's surface to the vacuum of space. As long as it did its job, it would be his lifeline in chaotic situations, but if the armor failed, it could become his coffin.

Kodiak checked his suit's diagnostics for the eighth time and watched as all the lights on his helmet's heads-up display blinked green. His suit was good to go. He should have known it was good to go from the other times he'd checked, but he was nervous.

"You ready?" Kodiak asked Garza back.

"Hell no, bro, I'm terrified," Garza laughed back as he patted down his restraints.

"Yes, let the fear flow through you, Garza," Moreau teased.

"*Silencio, bruja,*" Garza hissed.

"Speak English, *ese*," Skaggs snapped back.

Kodiak's face warmed as Skaggs spoke from across the Osprey. If he had been sitting next to him, he would have smacked him on the back of his helmet. Skaggs might have graduated basic training, but he'd left whatever dignity he had remaining back at Fort Benning. The man had grown more insufferable, which Kodiak hadn't thought was possible, and somehow, he was always able to get away with being a dirtbag.

"What did you just say, Private Skaggs?" Drill Sergeant Muleskin growled as he entered the Osprey.

The appearance of their drill sergeant sent the cabin into a hushed silence, but that didn't stop Skaggs from opening his mouth again. "I'm just saying, Drill Sergeant, the universal language of the Republic Army is English, and I was wanting Private Garza to acknowledge that."

Drill Sergeant Muleskin smacked the side of Skaggs's helmet, causing his head to ricochet against the back of the seat. "Don't disrespect a fellow soldier and then hide behind RA regulations, Private."

Skaggs didn't respond.

The rest of the soldiers laughed amongst themselves, including Kodiak. He could guarantee they were laughing to keep their minds off the drop ahead, and he didn't blame them one bit. Growing up, he'd visited numerous theme parks across Texas. He remembered one ride called the Rattler that would lift you high into the air on its tracks, and just as it got to the top, it would stop. The knot of anticipation that had formed in his stomach there was the same one he was feeling now, except at the end of the Rattler he would cheer. Kodiak had no idea what he would do once his feet were on Earth.

"Prepare to drop in thirty," came the voice of the pilot over the intercom.

Drill Sergeant Muleskin leaned forward and looked back toward his soldiers in their neat rows lining the walls. "This is it, Third Platoon. You chose to be infantry. Well, now it's time to experience their bread and butter. Combat drop!"

The dropship shuddered but then gave way to weightlessness. It was kind of a letdown if Kodiak was being honest. He had been expecting a drop like the roller coasters in Texas, but instead he felt his arms involuntarily lift as they entered the weightlessness of space. When he sat back and thought about it, though, it made sense. With space comes zero gravity, and without gravity there is no drop.

He felt his back press into the seat and shift to the left as the thrusters on the Osprey came to life. Now it was all beginning to make sense. This was just the staging phase. First the Osprey would detach from the Republic Navy ship and move towards their insertion point. Once they arrived at the IP, they would drop into Earth's atmosphere. From there, the ride would begin, and that made Kodiak's stomach knot back up.

"That wasn't such a big deal—" Skaggs was cut off by his own involuntary yelp as the dropship pierced Earth's atmosphere.

Kodiak laughed again but felt his voice getting caught in his throat just like it did on roller coasters. The Osprey vibrated and shook as it continued to burn through the thin blue atmosphere of his home world. It was like nothing Kodiak had ever experienced before in his life. His skin itched as his armored suit tried to compensate for the vibrations, but just as quickly as it had begun, it stopped.

The Osprey had entered a controlled glide as it finally broke through the atmosphere and entered the sky above Colorado. "Holy hell," Kodiak muttered.

"Ain't nothing like it in the world, Private," Drill Sergeant Muleskin said, patting Kodiak on the shoulder.

And he was right.

The Osprey pulled out of its controlled glide and activated its engines to bring the dropping soldiers towards their landing zone. The training mission for the day was to conduct four combat drops, and as the Osprey turned in a large arch before coming to a rest in a field of grass, Kodiak had finished his first.

The back hatch lowered, and the men and women of Third Platoon walked down onto the rolling fields of Colorado and gaggled together. Drill Sergeant Muleskin attached his rifle to the front of his armor and took a knee, and the rest of his training platoon followed suit.

"It's important to remember that you can never fully focus on the drop itself and how it feels. It's not supposed to be a warm and fuzzy experience—it will always sketch you out and make you uncomfortable. If it was easy, everyone would do it. Instead, try focusing your mind on the task ahead. What is your priority or job once you hit the ground? Is it an active combat zone you're dropping into? These are the types of questions you must ask yourself in order to be prepared for landing."

****

After an afternoon of land navigation courses, the men and women of Third Platoon made their way back to the landing zone where their Osprey was still sitting. The flight crew were sitting on the back hatch, eating some type of meal ready-to-eat, but began putting their bags away when they saw the infantry returning.

Training was way more relaxed now that Kodiak was out of basic training. In Georgia, it had been physically and emotionally draining. The drill sergeants had chewed you up and spat you out on an hourly basis. It had also helped Kodiak grow stronger. He had gained a lot of muscle, and although after years of playing football, he hadn't been weak before, he hadn't been as defined as he was now. He looked at the vein running down his arm and flexed, causing it to bulge a little bit more.

"That is just sad," Moreau's voice came from beside him.

Kodiak turned and his face flushed red. He knew what she was talking about but played dumb nonetheless. "What's sad?"

"You've been away from Tara for so long that right arm of yours is looking fit as the other," she laughed.

Kodiak rolled his eyes. "My arm looks fit because Tara broke it off."

Moreau sat down next to him in the field and put on a concerned face, but he read the sarcasm on it. "You poor thing. Little Tara has gone and run off. Now who are you going to settle down with on the great plains of Texas?"

Moreau had gotten pretty good at imitating Kodiak's Texan drawl. Whenever she broke the accent out, he always had to laugh. "Actually, she sent me a Dear John vid. Apparently, me going into the military didn't fit into her grand scheme of things. I guess Randy did."

Moreau put her arm around Kodiak and it felt different from her usual sarcastic replies. "Ahh, hell, I'm sorry to hear that, Bear. Truly, I am."

"Thanks, Moreau," was all he managed back.

"Hey, look at it this way—it's better you found out now rather than a year or two from now. Could you imagine buying a ring just to find out she was giving a handy to Randy behind the market?"

"Moreau!" Kodiak laughed.

She put her hands up in surrender. "I'm only playing with you, but you have to admit, I am right."

"That you are," he sighed. "That you are."

Chapter 11
Hall

Fort Cassidy, Luna

Aiden Hall had graduated basic training alongside a lot of men and women he would call friends, especially Kodiak, Moore, and Moreau. Now they were all gone, whisked away to other units for further training. Hall wasn't even being trained by Drill Sergeant Muleskin anymore, and if he was being honest with himself, he kind of missed the man. Hall had been the only mortarman in their training cycle and because of that, he'd gotten shipped off to another training unit on Luna.

Last he'd heard from Kodiak and Moreau, they'd continued advanced infantry training all over the place. He'd received videos from them on various different stations, but every time a new one came in, he had just missed them on either Luna or one of the many space stations that dotted the stars around the Sol System. He had heard from Moore as well, but rarely. It seemed every time a new video did come in, his hair had turned grayer and his eyes were a little more tired from the stresses of his medical training. Regardless, he talked about how much he loved it, which made up for the sleepless nights spent studying for the next exam.

As for Hall, he was having a blast, literally. He got the feeling from the others, at least Kodiak and Moreau, that training had become more lax since basic. For him, it definitely had. He was being trained not by a drill sergeant but by the NCO that would be his section leader when he was finally transferred to his first unit after completing his training.

Staff Sergeant Marcus Locke was a big, dark-skinned man with a bald head, zero body fat, and a hard demeanor. That was what Hall had seen in him when they'd first met; however, once he'd gotten to know Locke, he'd grown to like the man and his cool attitude toward almost everything. He'd also made some good friends in his mortar section. Kelly Fitzgerald was an Irish girl with fiery red hair that they affectionately, but not so imaginatively, called "Red." She acted as his gun crew's assistant gunner and would be the one who dropped the rounds in the mortar tube when he had leveled the sights, and she was fast.

The other member of his crew was a man from Kentucky named Gunner Jackson. The crass Southerner had a mouth to go with his wild attitude, but had already proven in maybe one too many bar fights that he was someone you wanted on your side, even if there wasn't much working between the ears. As Hall's ammunition bearer, he would prepare the rounds before handing them off to Red to be dropped into the tube. Together they were a crack team—so far, the best in training—and Hall, who was surprised to be named the gunner for the crew, wanted to make sure they carried that teamwork to their unit.

Privates Leslie Smart, Edoardo Giovanni, and Aurora Green made up the other gun crew and they were good in their own right, but even though they were in the same section, a healthy rivalry was beginning to form between them.

"Crews to the line," Staff Sergeant Locke bellowed as he prepared to start the timer on his data pad.

The heads-up display on Hall's helmet fed him information from Locke as well as the sight connected to the mortar system. The azimuth and directional information were blank, but soon they would be sent to him by the section leader when they began setting up the system. The moment the timer started, his crew would run to the setup points and begin putting the system together.

In many regards, the concept of the mortar systems hadn't changed that much since the Republic had become a spacefaring army. You still had an assistant gunner who carried the bipod, the ammunition bearer had the baseplate, and Hall would carry the tube itself. What had changed was the technology used to make the system work.

Hall was fascinated by the history of this tool of warfare and how it had evolved into what it was today. The mortars of the past weren't all that complicated. You had a standard elongated, bulbous shell that came in a few different varieties depending on the need. Near the base of the shell along the stem were the charges used to hurl the mortar towards its target. Adjusting the rounds consisted of modifying the elevation of the tube and adjusting the charges on the stem to give it more or less oomph in order to hit targets at various distances.

While the concept of the mortar was the same, the new system Hall and his team would use was a radical departure from the legacy systems. Where the old systems used steel tubes, the new one had tubes with walls consisting of magnetic coils, which acted as the charge that would hurl the round out of the tube once activated. The distance the round traveled was now controlled by the velocity at which it left the tube instead of explosive charges. What made the mortar systems of this age more deadly and accurate was the AI targeting module that turned what had previously been an untargetable dumb munition into an almost kamikaze-like micro drone.

Hall's instructor explained how when a round left the tube, a series of steering and stabilizer fins deployed. This allowed the round's AI targeting module to better utilize its velocity and adjust its downward trajectory to hit its intended target. What gave it the ability to function in different levels of gravity was the handful of tiny jets firing compressed gas. The use of steerable fins and micro jets made the weapon particularly useful in low or zero-gravity environments where you couldn't rely on a planet's gravity to achieve the arc trajectory profile that allowed a round to fall on top of a defender.

Having grown up in poverty on the streets of Chicago, Hall was mesmerized by the technology used in modern warfare—particularly how the military had found a way to allow a centuries-old weapon to function in the low to zero-g environments they might have to fight in. Hall found the use of the baseplate especially ingenious. Since the tube used magnetic coils to eject the mortars, a magnet at the base of the tube could be used to essentially pull the round down to the firing stud.

Hall's instructors explained how the firing stud performed two critical functions. Built into the baseplate, which also contained the power cells for the tube's magnetic coil system, was the fire control system or FCS. When a fire mission was received, the data was sent to the FCS, which synced the mission with the mortar team's HUDs. When the mortar connected with the trigger stud, the FCS transferred the targeting data to the round's AI module. Fractions of a second later, the coils activated and hurled the round out the tube towards its target.

While all this occurred, the AI module in the nose took control of the process. It deployed the fins along the sides of the shell first. As it arced through the atmosphere, or the low or zero-g environment, it used the fins and, if necessary, the jets to keep it on target.

Next came the evolution of the mortar rounds themselves and how they had transitioned from the dumb rounds of old to high-tech smart munitions. If they were targeting a bunker or building, the round would slam into the target and detonate once it penetrated the walls or roof.

There was also a smoke round variant able to lay down large clouds of IR and thermal inhibiting smoke should a ground unit need a cover and concealment mission. Similarly, like the dumb rounds, the HE or high-explosive round could detonate on impact with the ground or airburst for maximum shrapnel dispersion. What truly made this a smart round was its steering feature. Lastly, their instructors told them about a final feature that allowed them to turn the mortar round into an autonomous drone-like weapon. Once the round reached the kill zone assigned to it, the AI leveraged a programmable library of targets to scan the kill zone until it found a high-value target. If it couldn't locate an approved target, it self-detonated.

After months of classroom instruction and simulator training, Hall and the others graduated to live-fire training. During the training, they generally used inert rounds, meaning they still functioned like the real ones except that they didn't have the explosive charge built into them. As they neared the end of their training, they got to fire a few live rounds to demonstrate their knowledge of how to program and use the different features.

Once Hall's team graduated from the first phase of training, they transferred to Fort Cassidy for the final phase—learning how to use the rounds in low to zero-g environments.

It was here at Fort Cassidy that Hall's mortar team got good. Like a well-oiled machine, they each performed their duties with flawless precision and speed and quickly rose to become the best team in their training class. They were down to less than ten seconds to get their mortar system set up and ready to fire. The only thing that could hold them back was having to wait on the fire mission and coordinates to start dropping rounds.
****

Range 29

Standing on the lunar surface of Range 29, Hall's team waited with bated breath for their instructor to yell go. Once he did, the timer started.

The voice of their instructor spoke in their helmets. "All right, you've all done this training a few times. It's time to show me what you got. Go, go, go."

With the order given, Hall dug his heels into the ground and immediately read off the elevation and deflection data being sent to his heads-up display. The rest of his crew shouted acknowledgments and repeated the information back to ensure that what they heard was what he said.

Reaching the firing pit, Red and Jackson were perfect. They got the baseplate and bipod into position so when Hall arrived, all he had to do was snap the tube into place. While Red tightened the tube to the bipod, Hall manipulated the sight on the weapon itself until both the elevation and the deflection on his HUD blinked green and matched the fire control system on the baseplate.

"Hang it!" Hall shouted, and the others mirrored him.

Red took the mortar round in her hands and placed it into the tube, the bottoms of her palms hovering just over the metal.

"Fire!"

The mortar round fell into the tube as Red pushed her arms down and away and ducked below the muzzle. A blur spewed from the barrel as the round was hurled out and sent on its way. Some loose dust and moon rock near the baseplate shook briefly and floated all around them. In the absence of an explosive propellant, you didn't have to worry about the baseplate digging into the ground or kicking up dirt and muck around you. The new anchoring studs attached to the baseplate held the unit in place regardless of the gravity on a particular surface.

The no-gravity environment meant the mortar round had to rely a lot more on its onboard navigation system to find the target than on Earth. If you watched carefully, you could easily see the cylinder glint off the sun as it raced towards its objective.

Aiden Hall loved watching the rounds impact on the moon's surface. All you'd see was a puff of dust and tiny fragments glinting in the sunlight as they spiraled in different directions. He took a step back and looked over to Staff Sergeant Locke. His section leader continued to look at the clock, timing them. Hall realized the second gun's crew hadn't fired their round yet. Turning to look at what was taking them so long, he heard a shout that caused him to tense up.

"Misfire, misfire!"

Slowly, methodically, and without being told to, Hall observed them as they went through their misfire procedures. For whatever reason, the coils in the tube had failed to activate, leaving the round stuck at the bottom. When a round didn't fire, you had to remove it and bring it to a location on the range called a "dud pit." What made the job dangerous was the possibility of the round exploding. Once the FSC had transmitted its targeting information, the round became active and could not be remotely turned off. This was a built-in feature to make sure they couldn't be jammed on final approach to an enemy target. Placing the round in the dud pit until EOD arrived to handle things was the safest way to deal with a misfire.

While the other gun crews moved away from the team with the misfire, Hall watched in amazement as Staff Sergeant Locke showed no visible fear and walked towards the misfire. He calmly talked the crew through the misfire procedure. Demonstrating the procedure himself, he moved to the front of the tube as they detached it from the bipod and the baseplate, cupping his hands over the barrel. Two of the crewmen, Giovanni and Green, helped lower the tube flat and nervously held it in place.

Once the tube was flat, Locke pulled out a small magnetic device used for just this purpose. He placed the device down near the base and then slowly moved it along the length of the barrel. As he neared the edge of the barrel, he momentarily stopped. He handed the device to Giovanni, telling him to slowly move it past the barrel's exit.

With the device in Giovanni's hand, Locke placed another in front of the barrel. Moments later, the round emerged from the tube. Locke explained the importance of grabbing the round by the side and staying away from the top. It was a live round and any sudden pressure around the nose could trigger it. With the round in hand, Locke proceeded to carry it towards the dud pit.

"And that, kids, is how you handle and remove a misfire. Now I'm going to take it to the pit while we wait on EOD to come over and render it safe," Locke said with all the confidence in the world.

Hall had to marvel at his bravado. He was holding a live round in his hands as he talked with them. For all the benefits of a mortar tube using a magnetic coil, there were some downsides, namely the difficulty of removing a misfire from the tube. Watching Locke use the specially designed disk to pull it out was nerve-racking. He learned why it took a few minutes to do. It was a live round you were extracting. Hall suspected if it hadn't been for their armored suits, their limbs would've been burning as they held the tube flat like that.

Hall wondered if he could handle the situation the way Locke did. He was nearly to the dud pit at the fire side of the range. Hall felt it had to be an anxiety-inducing walk, which was likely why Locke insisted on doing it himself and not forcing the crew to handle their misfire. He was a soldier-first kind of leader, and Hall counted himself lucky to have someone like that as his first proper NCO.

Staff Sergeant Locke walked into the dud pit and slowly placed the round on the surface. As he was preparing to leave the pit, he called out, "All right. All clear. Let's call EOD."

Locke had taken a couple of steps away from the pit when something happened. A blast occurred. There was no concussive blast wave or sound wave that hit them, but they felt the ground beneath their boots reverberating from the blast.

Shouts of shock and horror erupted over his comms, but all Hall could do was stare helplessly at the spot where Staff Sergeant Locke had just been standing. One minute, his section leader had been telling them to call the explosive ordnance disposal team, and the next, a cloud of moon dust and red vapor covered the entire area. Hall blinked a couple of times to snap himself back to his senses. He looked at the site again, focusing on what he was seeing. An arm and piece of a leg floated near the pit. In a matter of seconds, Staff Sergeant Locke was gone and Hall didn't know what to do.

Chapter 12
Moore

Doss Station
In Orbit Around Earth

"My word. That's awful, Hall, I'm so sorry that happened."

That was all Oliver Moore could think to say at that moment. He had been about to head out for the training simulator when Hall had video messaged him. Despite being in orbit above the moon, there was a bit of a delay in their transmissions, so he just sat and waited to see if Hall wanted to talk about the incident more.

Even with a complete screwup like Skaggs in basic training, they hadn't had anyone die, let alone a seasoned soldier. Moore had heard the stories and rumors all throughout training about so-and-so dying on the range years ago, but none of it held any substance. Now he was hearing from someone he trusted who had witnessed someone getting killed—and not just someone, but his own section sergeant. He could see how badly Hall was taking it and he wished he could have been there or had the time to really talk to him, but every time he looked away from the screen, he found his roommate staring daggers at him.

"Listen, Hall, I'll either call or leave you a message when I get back from training and we will talk about this more"—he emphasized "will" to make sure he knew he was serious—"and we can work through this together, OK?"

Hall stared back at him for a few moments, his eyes finally dropping to the floor. "Of course, man, go save some virtual lives. I'll talk to you later."

The video feed ended, and Moore's eyes wandered from the now-empty screen to the window that looked down towards the moon's surface. He watched as the crater-filled landscape slowly drifted below the station he was on. Shift work in the military could create some strange schedules. Even though he floated just above where Hall was on the lunar surface, his day was just beginning, and Hall's was ending.

"I don't want to be late again because you were busy video messaging someone, Hall," his roommate, Private Dalton Hughes, stated flatly.

"Have some compassion, Hughes—the kid's sergeant got disintegrated in front of him."

"And if war really is brewing between the Republic and Asia, then he's going to experience a lot more of that. What's your point?"

"Why are you being such a callous jerk?" Moore snapped at him.

Hughes looked surprised at Moore's outburst. "I'm not. I'm being realistic, and you should be too. What are you going to do for him up here that his battle buddies can't do down there? Hell, you most likely won't even be in the same unit as him after our training is over, so maybe it's best you cut the cord now."

Moore shook his head in disgust. "Just because you have no social life doesn't mean I can't, Hughes."

"And just because you don't see me talk to anyone doesn't mean I don't have a social life, Moore," Hughes bit back.

Moore pushed past him and out the door of his room.

Doss Station was a large military facility that was primarily used for medical training. After going back to England and visiting with Lilliana, he had taken a shuttle into orbit for the first time and had remained on Doss Station. When it wasn't Hall, Kodiak, or Moreau on his video screen, it was Lilliana, and he cherished every moment of it.

It turned out she had received all his video messages from basic training, but they were so censored she could barely make any sense of them. She said it was her curiosity about the stories that made her want to talk to him again. He didn't know if he completely bought that story, but he would take it. Anything to talk to her again.

They'd had a wonderful time together when he'd gone back home. Lilliana had formally introduced him to the owners of the bookstore, who had taken her in and loved her as if she'd been their own daughter. They'd had dinner every night and he'd even tried to make a roast one night. They'd instead had leftover bangers and mash.

Moore had been only home for ten days, but in those ten days he had grown very close to Lilliana once more—as close as they had been when they were younger, and without the watchful eyes of his family handlers, there was no more hiding or worrying about being out together in public. They'd held hands, they'd hugged, they'd kissed, and they'd made love by the river under a blanket of stars. It was the perfect return home and a memory he would cherish for the rest of his life.

Now he was in space, walking down the long, winding corridors of Doss Station and dreaming of the moment he'd be able to hold Lilliana in his arms again. His schedule for the day consisted of more simulator training. He had trained in sims at Fort Benning and had been astonished at the realism they entailed. At the time, he hadn't thought it could get any more realistic. After only one training session on Doss Station, he realized he had been dead wrong.

The simulation room was lined with coffin-like white beds on which the soldiers would lie down and be closed inside. The lining was made of a mesh that swallowed the occupant's body, and neurological signals were then sent to their brain, transporting them to wherever the officer in charge wanted. Everything that the occupant experienced was made up of projected data streamed into their brain, but it all felt real. They could talk to one another, experience what the others experienced, and operate together. They felt pain, they felt fear, and they felt alive in a world created by a program. It was a terrifying marvel of technology.

First Lieutenant Rick Faraday, Moore's training officer, stood at his station on an elevated platform in the middle of the simulation room, waiting for Moore's medical team to arrive. Luckily, Staff Sergeant Cardinale hadn't joined them yet. Moore heaved a sigh of relief and took his place at his station.

Private Cara Nova turned to him and winked. "Nice of you to join us, Moore."

"He was talking to one of his buddies again," Hughes interjected.

"I wasn't talking to you, Hughes—or did you change your name to something more palatable?"

Moore snorted, trying to hold his laughter as Hughes groaned and walked to his station. "Thanks." He smiled.

"Oh, it's nothing. At least I don't have to room with him. Who was it this time? Did Lilliana call?" she asked with genuine curiosity.

"Hall. His sergeant was killed in a training accident on the moon."

Nova gasped. "Oh no, what happened?"

"I guess they had a training round that didn't fire, and when they removed it from the mortar, it exploded."

"That's horrible. Is he OK?"

"Yeah, no one else was hurt, but he was pretty shaken up about it."

Nova shook her head. "I have no doubt he would be. The things we see in this simulator are enough to make my stomach turn—I don't know what's going to happen when I see the real thing one day."

"Maybe you won't have to. We haven't been at war for a while."

"Peace never lasts, Moore, you know that. The Asians are pissed we backed out of the Space Exploration Treaty and now the drums of war are beating."

"You watch too much news, Cara," Private Jayne Campbell said from her station.

"I just don't watch *your* news, Campbell, that's the difference," Nova snapped back.

Cara Nova had been born on Earth but was the daughter of a transportation tycoon in the Belt. Having grown up among the stars, she had a soft spot for the Belters' plight and was more in tune with their news than any Earth-bound news organizations. Jayne Campbell was the exact opposite. Campbell had been born on Mars, while her father and mother were serving in the Republic Navy. Her father was now Commander Campbell of the scout ship RNS *Flashpoint*, and she was a fervent supporter of the Republic. The fact that the two hadn't come to blows yet over their differing political views was a surprise to Moore, who had no opinion on the matter at all.

"Do you wanna trade roommates?" Nova joked.

"Only if I get Jayne," he teased back.

She laughed. "Oh gods, no."

He was still not used to that terminology. *Gods*. Moore wasn't religious in the traditional sense but had grown up believing in the Christian God. He wasn't opposed to others' beliefs and found them more interesting than anything else. Nova had grown up to love the common religion of the Belters, who believed in multiple gods. Not all Belters were polytheistic, however. The asteroid belt was filled with all sorts of different cultures from Earth, but over time they had become a melting pot of cultures that clashed and stole from one another's history. It was all very interesting to Moore, and Nova's love for the subject made it that much more exciting to listen to.

"Sorry I'm late, sir," Staff Sergeant Cardinale started as he entered the simulation room. "I was meeting with—"

"With Captain Keene on the Andromeda report," Faraday cut him off. "I'm aware. Let's get started." He was clearly eager to begin training.

Lieutenant Faraday dragged his fingers into the air, and an image of a Republic Navy ship corridor appeared. "Today we will be training on what to do in the event of a space battle. If I were to fire a rifle in these hallways, even at one of the many windows on this station, the round would bounce around like a pinball before finding someplace to bury itself. That is not the case with the magrail and PDC cannon rounds that you may experience during space combat. It is true that this may be a rare occurrence for you all. We are ground forces and are meant to fight primarily on the ground, but battles in space can occur, and you're going to want to know how to deal with one if you're ever unfortunate enough to experience it."

Moore looked nervously over to Nova, who just shrugged.

"So go ahead and climb inside your coffins, kids, we got some training to do," Faraday announced as he stepped back to ready the training simulation.

****

It felt like a cold saline drip running through Moore's veins as his body drifted to a world between awareness and slumber. In the moment it took to blink his eyes, he left the confines of the simulation pod for the hallways of a generic Republic naval ship. In the first few minutes of a simulation, the occupants of the dream world knew it was fake, but as time ticked on, the line between simulation and reality became more blurred.

Moore, Nova, Hughes, and Campbell looked to Staff Sergeant Cardinale for an indication of what they would be doing next until several sailors silently walked down the hallway, weaving in between the medics. They didn't even acknowledge any of the medics as they went about whatever tasks they had been given. It was those little things that teased your mind, reminding you of the fact that you were in a simulation. Over time, it had become obvious that the brain could easily experience hyperstimulation within a simulation, which could ultimately lead to a stroke, so the programmers had learned to lighten the mental load by finding little ways of periodically reminding the dream occupants that what they were experiencing wasn't real.

The ship shuddered and red lights flashed as klaxons called the sailors to their battle stations. The ship was being attacked and a sinking pit opened in Moore's stomach. More explosions shook the behemoth, but the artificial gravity continued to hold. Moore knew that the bridge crew of the ship would be working tirelessly at this moment to divert different amounts of energy to systems throughout the ship. If artificial gravity was lost, their job would get a lot harder.

"We need to get to the medical bay right now!" Cardinale shouted over the klaxons, running towards the elevators that would take the medical squad down to the infirmary.

When battle broke out in space, individuals who weren't readily needed in the fight were tasked with collecting casualties and taking them to the medical bay. If medics and doctors ran throughout the ship in search of casualties, there would be no sense of order. Everything was calculated in these situations, and even though it looked like mayhem on the outside, it was organized chaos to the professionals.

As Moore and his squad rounded the corner, an explosion of sparks shot across the hallway, sending fire and debris in all directions. Moore felt his body lift weightlessly into the air and begin spinning slowly. He immediately checked the oxygen levels in the hallway—they seemed to be holding for the moment, but artificial gravity was dead.

Activating the magnets in his boots, Moore pushed himself back down to the deck and tried to regain his bearings and get a sense of what had happened. Before going to a casualty, you always had to take in your surroundings. If Moore was in immediate danger, he'd have to take care of the threat first before moving on to those who were wounded. If he was dead, they'd all be dead.

It looked as if a magrail round had found the soft armor on the ship's outer core and punched deep within the ship itself, most likely damaging the artificial gravity generators, which was why Moore found himself in his current predicament. When he looked around at the damage it had caused, though, his voice caught in his throat.

Several bodies of sailors and soldiers littered the space around them, floating lifelessly or on the verge of death in the hallway. The body closest to him was a blond sailor with gray eyes staring at the ceiling. He didn't need to plug into her medical port to know her condition but did so anyway to make sure. Her vitals were flatlined.

"Sound off!" came a shout from across the darkness, where headlamps were now illuminating what the emergency lights could not.

"I'm up," Moore shouted back, making his way over to the light.

It was Staff Sergeant Cardinale, who was trying to get a head count. As more headlamps winked to life, it became clear his squad had been lucky. Nova was pushing a floating body to the group out of the darkness and plugged in her medical device.

"Her vitals are just under acceptable parameters. It seems she has some internal bleeding, possibly a collapsed lung," Nova said, reading off the medical analysis from her device.

"She's urgent, then. What do you need to do to stabilize her for transport?" Cardinale asked in a measured voice.

Around them, dead and dying bodies floated about, and somehow his squad leader remained unbelievably calm. Moore found himself wondering if it was a gift Cardinale had been born with or if it came from experience. The thought that he could be so calm under pressure because he'd seen carnage like this before sent shivers down Moore's back.

Nova had frozen.

Moore looked over to her, waiting for the answer, but when it didn't come in a few seconds, Campbell broke in. "We can't do anything for her here except give her a cocktail to slow the rate of blood loss."

"Correct, Campbell." Cardinale nodded as Campbell attached her medical device and released the cocktail of medication into the wounded sailor's bloodstream.

The devices all Republic medical personnel carried were an all-in-one platform. When attached to one of the many ports on the wounded individual's armor, it would give the medic an accurate reading of the injuries the soldier had sustained. From there, they could diagnose and begin treatment to save the person's life.

The issue with losing blood in zero gravity was that the blood couldn't properly coagulate, meaning that even the smallest injury could be fatal. The normal synthetic coagulant gel could be injected into the soldier to stop the flow at the point of injury, but there was no telling just how bad the damage was inside until they were able to get the wounded individual to a medical bay.

Campbell removed the folded stretcher from her back and snapped it open, letting it float just below the wounded woman. Moore and Hughes helped strap the soldier to the stretcher, and without saying another word, Campbell began walking her down the hall to the medical bay.

Other explosions shook the hallway, which felt way worse to Moore with his feet magnetically connected to the deck. It grew quiet. Even the klaxons had stopped working, and the red light blinked out.

"What the hell is happening, Sergeant?" Hughes asked, his voice rising an octave higher than usual.

"I don't know," was all Cardinale responded.

Their helmet lights spotlighted around the room as they searched for more survivors, but the eerie calmness became unnerving. Moore heard a whistle, not from a human but from some sort of leak. It grew louder as he searched for the source, and finally his helmet's light came across a crack in the wall. Little rivulets of blood from a nearby floating corpse slowly drifted to the crack and entered it as if being sucked through a straw.

"I think we have a problem, Sergeant," Moore stated flatly.

Cardinale walked over to him and looked at the crack. "Yeah, that's not good."

Nova joined them. "Aren't there supposed to be hundreds of meters between us and the outside?"

"Supposed to be," Cardinale responded, still looking towards the crack.

"Then what the hell is doing that?" Nova asked.

"We need to get ou—" Cardinale was cut off as the wall ripped itself apart as if it were made of paper.

The crash of debris was instant as the hallway disappeared and gave way to the darkness of space. Moore felt his body spinning uncontrollably, and no matter how hard he tried to grab something, his fingers felt nothingness. Moore couldn't steady himself and stop his body from spinning. He knew he had to regain control of the situation and find out what was happening, but in the back of his mind, he knew what the answer was. He was spinning deeper and deeper into space, ejected from the ship he had just been on moments before.

Something collided with his head, throwing him back end over end, and although he couldn't focus on what was beyond his helmet, he could see that his visor had cracked. Alerts flashed on his heads-up display, showing that his oxygen was rapidly depleting and if he couldn't fix it in time he would suffocate.

It was too late.

His visor spiderwebbed and he knew that he only had a few seconds left before dying what he assumed was going to be a very painful death. He let out one more scream in an involuntary last-ditch effort to get someone's attention before his eyes opened and his body sat up straight.

His head collided with the top of the sim pod, and immediately he remembered that it was all just a simulation. Then the pain came.

"Damn it," he groaned as he swung the pod open and sat up unhindered.

The other pods opened around him as well as the simulation came to an end. Most of the squad did the usual head scratch and groan as they pulled themselves out of the machines, but Staff Sergeant Cardinale was red-faced and fuming.

"What the hell is that?" the sergeant yelled across the room to where Lieutenant Faraday sat at his console. "We were to experience a loss of artificial gravity and that was it! Where do you get off putting their minds into that type of scenario?"

Lieutenant Faraday stood and held up a finger. "Remember who you're talking to, Sergeant."

Sergeant Cardinale stopped in his tracks and glared at the young officer in challenge, but then he stood at attention.

"Not everything will go as planned. In a space battle, rapid decompression and ejection can occur—"

"Then you die. That's what happens. Even if you survive getting sucked out, even if you have a full supply of air and you're uninjured. You're dead. So what could you possibly think they could gain by going through one, sir?" Cardinale maintained his composure and military bearing, but his neck was still crimson.

"We shall discuss this in my office, Sergeant Cardinale." He turned to Moore and the others. "You're dismissed. You have classroom instruction at 1400 hours. Don't be late."

Moore snapped to attention and filed out of the simulation room with the others. It was nearing the time the mess would open for lunch and he figured he'd eat now and take a quick nap before class. The others must have had the same idea because they continued in a group towards the elevators.

"The sergeant was right. That simulation was absolutely pointless. We had only a few minutes to check on the wounded before we were decompressed," Nova said.

90

"You're just pissed you didn't actually save anyone," Campbell shot back.

"No, she's right," Hughes agreed. "I mean, sure, if it happens, then that's just horrible luck on our parts, but it's out of our hands. There's no reason to train for that because there's no possible outcome where you live."

"After battles, international law states that both sides are allowed to collect their dead or injured, and that applies in space as well," Campbell replied.

"Campbell, out of the dozens of space battles and incidents in space, only a handful of casualties have been recovered alive in space. It just doesn't happen. That simulation was absolutely ridiculous," Moore added.

Lieutenant Faraday wasn't a bad officer, but he wasn't a great one. He was as boringly normal as ever a person could be. He was fair but oblivious to most things, and several times, he had made the wrong call during combat simulations. Nevertheless, his expertise in medicine and combat medical application was fantastic; he had even taught Cardinale a thing or two.

"Lieutenant Faraday isn't a bad guy—he's just not the best officer when it comes to these sorts of scenarios," Moore commented. "He gets too carried away. I mean, hell—he triggered an avalanche in the Alps during one of the sims, remember?" Moore laughed.

"You have to always be ready for the unexpected." Nova mimicked Faraday's Canadian twang, which got the group laughing.

Oliver Moore knew he would most likely never see this squad again after training concluded. None of them had received their orders yet despite being halfway through their cycle, but the Republic military was huge. With that realization, he felt a little sad. He'd made a few very good friends in the short time he had been in the military, and already he was most likely going to have to see them go. Of course, maybe down the line they'd reconnect as their careers progressed, but who knew?

He'd miss Nova the most, he was sure of that, but only because Campbell and Hughes were so insufferable. There were the rare moments when they would all laugh and joke together, but it was almost as if they realized they were being nice and decided to pull back each time. He would still hold on to some of the memories, though. At the end of the day, they were brothers and sisters in arms.

Chapter 13
Kodiak

RNS *Currahee*
Orbital Training Platform R-34

A little over a year ago, Harrison Kodiak had been trying to get into Tara Livingston's pants behind the bleachers at his high school's football stadium. He had been planning on going to college to play football and, at the time, had seen himself playing professional ball one day. Now he was in a suit of combat armor, slowly using his thrusters to navigate outer space.

The orbital training platform outside of the RNS *Currahee* was where soldiers trained in zero gravity in the vacuum of space. They had several different platforms spread throughout the area, from close-quarters combat arenas to elaborate mockups of ship hulls to practice boarding. Orbital training platform R-34 was a training Osprey where soldiers learned to fix damaged vehicles.

The scenario Kodiak and his squad were working on today was fixing damaged fuel cells located on the outside of the Osprey. They always used some generic story to set the stage, and today they had become dead in space after a fuel cell failure left them stranded. They had an hour to fix the damaged system and replace the fuel cells before the Osprey fell into the Earth's atmosphere and burned up. Of course, it was just a scenario, and they were miles from any danger, but it paid not to fail under the watchful eyes of Drill Sergeant Muleskin.

"OK, Alpha Team, you have one hour to fix the damaged Osprey before you all burn up in Earth's atmo. Please try not to die," Drill Sergeant Muleskin's voice came over the internal communications in their helmets.

Kodiak looked across the Osprey's troop bay to Moreau and gave a thumbs-up, which she returned. "All right, Alpha, let's get this show on the road. Garza, Morgan, I want you to begin rerouting the power from the functional cells to keep the Osprey from getting off course. If those thrusters go down, we go down."

Morgan and Garza both gave him a thumbs-up.

"Skaggs, you'll be with me and Moreau. I need you to carry the replacement fuel cells so we can get them into place as fast as possible."

"I'm faster at rerouting the power than Garza—let me handle that," Skaggs interjected.

"I'm not asking for your opinion, Skaggs. I'm ordering you what to do," Kodiak snapped back.

"You're just a private like me, Kodiak—don't go on a power trip."

"He was made the team leader for a reason, Skaggs. Fall in line," Moreau said as she unbuckled her restraints and floated toward the rear of the troop compartment.

Garza and Morgan both floated over to the cockpit and began to open the panel that would start the rerouting process. Once they were done outside the ship, they could flip the switch from inside and complete the task.

Alpha Team had done this plenty of times before, and Skaggs was right—he was faster at rerouting the power. But Garza and Morgan needed the training and Kodiak knew that. They could get the job done, regardless of how long they took, and it was infuriating that Skaggs couldn't see the bigger picture. It was also why Kodiak knew Skaggs would never be a team leader. He was too focused on himself.

Kodiak made his way to the rear hatch with Moreau, and together they hand-cranked the hatch down once the inside had depressurized. As the hatch lowered, the expanse of deep space stretched out in front of him, blanketed by millions of stars. As he drifted out of the hatch and began making his way to the top of the Osprey, he wondered if there were others like him out there.

It was one reason why he was only partially religious. He couldn't imagine all those millions of stars denoting millions of different systems that potentially held life—life that could be as advanced as his own or even more so. Kodiak wondered what they would be like: if their buildings were the same, if they breathed the same air, and sometimes, if they even existed at all.

As he made his way to the fuel cell hatch, he worked the lever to open the box and begin his mission. The hatch popped open easily enough, and immediately he could tell which fuel cells had been damaged. Out of the four in there, three were burnt out.

"Just waiting on y'all now, Garza," Kodiak said into his mic.

"Rerouting now, wait one," Garza replied.

"I would've been done by now," Skaggs said.

Kodiak turned on his heel and snatched the bag of fuel cells from his hand. "It's not always about you, Skaggs. It's not about being the best, it's not about being the fastest. Sometimes others need time and training, and they will get there one day, but they'll never learn if you don't let them train."

"Great speech, Spartacus, but sometimes you need the best behind the wheel. You're only as strong as your weakest link."

"And that weakest link is you, Skaggs. You only care about yourself—"

"Enough!" Moreau shouted. "None of us are gonna pass if you two keep fighting like assholes."

Kodiak knew she was right and turned back to the fuel cell panel. "Twenty minutes, Alpha," he called.

"Twenty minutes," they all acknowledged.

"Power's rerouted, boss. It's good for you to pull the cells," Garza came over the comms.

Kodiak removed the three burnt cells and replaced them with the ones Skaggs had handed him. When they all snapped into place, he closed the hatch and turned back to make his way back inside.

"OK, fire it up," he called to Garza.

The Osprey vibrated and hummed as it powered on its internals and came to life. Kodiak gave a thumbs-up to Moreau when an explosion rocked the top of the Osprey, sending it into a spin. Kodiak grabbed onto the side of the Osprey as it began to rotate, and it felt like his arm was going to be ripped from his socket.

"Status report!" Kodiak shouted over the radio.

Garza and Morgan reported back that they were inside and fine but didn't know what had happened. Moreau was clinging to the side of the Osprey near the hatch, so Kodiak knew she was still with him. Skaggs, however, didn't reply.

"Skaggs, status!" Kodiak yelled again.

"I'm losing grip up here!" Skaggs shouted back.

"On my way!" Kodiak responded.

He looked to Moreau and used the magnets on his boots to push himself further down the Osprey to where she was holding on. With the armor's help, he maintained his grip, but the spinning was causing him to lose his bearings. When he reached Moreau, he grabbed on and began to help her towards the opening of the hatch. As the craft spun around again, the momentum carried Moreau through the opening and inside.

With a yelp, she confirmed to Kodiak that she was inside and out of immediate danger, which only left Skaggs dangling on top. For a split second, Kodiak felt like leaving him up there, but he knew he couldn't do that. Grabbing hold of the riggings, he was able to pull himself back alongside the craft and climb to the top.

Skaggs was flopping wildly against the Osprey, with only his tether keeping him in place. He was lucky to have thought to attach his tether to the Osprey when he had, because if he hadn't, he most definitely would've been miles away by now, spinning out into the great unknown.

"Don't you let me die out here, Kodiak," Skaggs yelped as his body continued to smack against the Osprey.

"I should be so lucky," Kodiak responded coldly as he continued to climb across the craft to where Skaggs was. The tether was taking a beating and looked like it only had a few more snaps before it broke free. Grabbing the tether, he looked up at Skaggs. "I have to unclip it."

"Don't you dare!" Skaggs snarled.

"I have to. It's going to snap either way—if I can detach it, then I can pull you to me and get you inside. If it snaps before I can get you to me, then you're a goner."

Skaggs looked into Kodiak's eyes, fear staring back at him. "Do it!"

Kodiak began to spin the clip to remove it when something slammed into the back of his head. His vision immediately blurred, and he felt his grip on the hull loosening. He didn't know what had hit him, probably a piece of debris that had come loose. Whatever it was, it knocked out his suit's systems, and his heads-ups display blinked out.

When his eyes cleared of the involuntary tears that had flooded them, he saw Skaggs holding on to one of the stabilizers in the rear of the Osprey. The tether had detached, or broken, and he was now inches away from being thrown into space.

Kodiak dug deep and began to climb the top of the Osprey towards the rear, his hands grabbing whatever he could to pull himself along its length. When he finally made it to the back, he looked up at Skaggs once more. Skaggs was only holding on to the fin stabilizer with one hand now, and Kodiak knew he had a few more seconds before he lost his grip.

He paused for a moment and stared into the eyes of the man he hated. His mother had always told him that *hate* was the strongest word you could use to describe your feelings about someone. Hate was all-encompassing, and it was very rare you could take that back. For the most part, he hadn't hated anyone in his life, even Tara after she'd sent him a Dear John letter in basic. Skaggs, however, was the exception because deep down, Kodiak knew he hated him. He knew at this very moment that if Skaggs lost his grip and was never seen again, Kodiak wouldn't care at all. He also knew that if he allowed him to die on a training mission, it would become his responsibility and open a whole can of worms he didn't want to deal with.

"I got you," Kodiak grunted as he reached out his hand, but he missed the one Skaggs outstretched by inches.

"Hurry, Kodiak!" Skaggs yelped.

Kodiak said nothing and stretched his arm out again, this time feeling Skaggs's armor glance across his grasp. He clamped down hard on the chest rigging that held his magazines and pulled hard, but nothing budged. He looked up towards Skaggs and saw he was still holding on.

"You need to let go, Skaggs!"

"Hell no!" he replied.

"How the hell can I save your ass if you won't let go?" Kodiak screamed, furious that even now, moments from death, Skaggs was being as difficult as he could be.

Movement to his right caught Kodiak's attention. He looked to see what was moving towards them that hadn't been there before and his eyes went wide. The Osprey's wing had begun to break away from its hull, and the uncontrolled spin was peeling it back towards the two soldiers outside.

"Let go!" Kodiak shouted as he let go of Skaggs's hand and pushed off the back of the Osprey.

If they had still been holding on to one another when the wing broke apart, it would've torn them to shreds. Instead, Kodiak was only hit by a piece of the debris. He was hurt, but he wasn't dead. Not yet, at least. He was spinning out of control like the Osprey was, but now he had nothing to grab on to, only the emptiness of space as it wrapped its cloak around him the further he spun out.

With his helmet not working, he couldn't tell if he had a leak or his armor was compromised in any way. He did, however, pull his emergency tab, which released several metal beacons that would send a distress signal to the training center. Now he just had to try and calm his breathing down and hope that he would be rescued.

Kodiak had zero clue whether Skaggs was still alive. He hadn't seen if the idiot had let go or not. Just as before, he reaffirmed to himself that if Skaggs did die, he probably wouldn't think anything about it, and that bothered him. Not in the way it would normally bother someone—it just made Kodiak sad that someone could be so awful as to cause others to hate them that much.

Kodiak yawned. He was getting tired, and his eyes drooped as his breathing slowed. He knew something was wrong—he knew he'd had a sufficient amount of sleep, and even so, he wouldn't just pass out during training—he'd learned that lesson in basic. This was something entirely different, and his heart beat faster as he tried to diagnose the problem. There had to be a leak of some sort. It wasn't coming from his visor—he would've seen the cracks—but somewhere on his armor there was a hole, and he had to try and plug it quickly.

Time was not on Kodiak's side, though, as he continued to struggle to stay awake and keep levelheaded. The blackness of space started to become the blackness in his mind as he drifted further and further away from consciousness.

As he forced his eyes open one more time to try and gather any sort of point of interest around him, a blinding light hit him. He heard a voice, but it was muffled, and felt something grabbing on to him. But the darkness still came and slowly his mind faded.

****

When Kodiak awoke, or rather felt like he did, he was lying in a field of wheat. It confused him at first because the last thing he remembered was blacking out in space. His eyes fixed on the white-and-red silo that sat behind his grandfather's house—it made him smile. It was a nice memory from his childhood. He used to play hide-and-seek in the tall wheat fields that surrounded his grandfather's farm and would always win because he would crawl inside the silo and hide.

One day the ground-up wheat had given way under him, and he'd become stuck. Even though Kodiak was only eleven, he hadn't screamed or yelled—at least, not at first. He had removed his belt and tried to lasso it around a piece of metal at the top to pull himself out, but after several tries, he had become tired. That was when he had begun to yell. He was most worried about getting into trouble. He knew how long it took his grandfather and his workers to fill the silo.

When someone finally came to get him, he looked up to see his grandfather peering down at him. He apologized, and his grandfather just laughed and helped pull him out. He even gave him a sandwich and some milk until his mom came to pick him up. He'd never told his parents about that day—it was a secret shared between a grandfather and his grandson. Like buying you a piece of apple pie at the café before Grandma served dinner. His grandfather had been the absolute best and spoiled him like that.

He had died peacefully in his sleep when Kodiak was fourteen. He remembered how large his funeral had been and how almost everyone in the community had come out to support his family. It was the first time he had realized just how important his grandfather had been to the town. That was why looking up at the silo was confusing him.

He sat up and then stood, his head now taller than the tops of the crop, and looked to where his grandfather's house would've been. There it stood, tin roof and all. Kodiak began to make his way through the field, and as he drew closer to the screened-in back porch, he paused.

"Harrison," his grandfather called to him.

He couldn't believe what he was hearing. His grandfather had been dead for years, but there was his voice, clear as day. He called out to the unseen man who'd helped raise him and made his way to the back door. When he stepped onto the back porch, his grandfather met him at the screen.

"It's good to see you, Harrison," he said with the same smile Kodiak remembered.

"It's good to see you too, Poppa." Kodiak smiled back.

He had thought seeing his grandfather again would bring sadness, but he was filled with nothing but joy. He wanted to walk closer to the door. He wanted to go inside.

His grandfather must have noticed this and held up his hand. "All in good time, Harrison, but not now."

This confused Kodiak further, and he went to grab the handle when his grandfather screamed, "Kodiak!"
****

Harrison Kodiak sat straight up in a bed and frantically looked around. To his right was an oval window that projected the image of inky black space. His insides churned at the sight.

He looked down and noticed he was in a hospital gown underneath a blanket. His arm was taped and had tubes running out of it, but what concerned him the most was the restraint attached to it. He gave a tug, but it wouldn't budge, and when he looked closer, he noticed it was the type military police carried. His heart rate increased as panic set in.

"What the hell is going on?" he shouted to anyone who could hear him.

The door opened and a nurse walked in. "Private Kodiak, you're awake," said a blond-haired second lieutenant.

"What is going on, ma'am?" he croaked.

"You've been in an accident during a training exercise, Private. The recovery team was able to retrieve you from space and bring you back on board, and it's a good thing they got to you when they did. Another couple of minutes and you would've been dead."

"I'm talking about this, ma'am." He gestured to his restrained arm.

"I'm sorry. I can't comment on that, Private," she said in a hushed tone as she checked his vitals.

Two more men, a colonel and a sergeant major, walked into the room and up to the front of his bed. The colonel removed a paper from his pocket and handed it to the sergeant major.

The sergeant major held up the paper and read, "Private Harrison Kodiak, you are being detained for questioning regarding the attempted murder of Private Tyler Skaggs during a training operation that occurred yesterday at 1900 hours station time. You are allowed legal counsel from the judge adjutant general if you so wish. You have up to twenty-four hours from the moment of notice, which is right now, if you decide to talk with us. If you do not wish to talk with us, you will be held for the attempted murder charges, and it will go to court. Do you understand your rights as a soldier of the Republic military?"

Kodiak just stared at him in disbelief. He hadn't tried to kill Skaggs. He'd tried to save him, and now he was finding out that the piece of shit not only hadn't died but was saying Kodiak had tried to kill him?

"Will you require the twenty-four hours? Yes or no?" the sergeant major spoke again.

"Um, yes, Sergeant Major, yes," Kodiak stammered.

The two men turned on their heels and left the room without another word.

Chapter 14
Hall

Fort Cassidy, Luna

"What a sad funeral," the man standing next to Aiden Hall whispered.

Staff Sergeant Marcus Locke's memorial ceremony was held in a tiny nondenominational chapel on Fort Cassidy. There was no funeral, no grand procession, and no wake; however, several training units, including Hall's, were in attendance for the small memorial to the fallen sergeant. Flowers of blue and red circled the altar, above which a picture of Locke in his dress uniform was projected. He was young in his picture, probably one that had been taken years ago when he was updating his Republic military profile. It was still Staff Sergeant Locke, though.

Hall had grown up rough, so death, even of someone close to him, was not uncommon. It had only been a little over a year since Eddy had been killed, and that had happened right in front of Hall. He wouldn't necessarily call Eddy a friend, not in the same way he'd call Kodiak a friend, but he had known him, had lived with him, and had been close to him. It still hurt to some degree knowing he would never see Eddy again, but not as much as losing Staff Sergeant Locke.

He had been told many times in his short military career how rare it was to get an NCO that wasn't completely full of themselves. Locke was a great leader and had taught him a lot since stepping foot on the moon. Now he was dead. The worst part was he couldn't be mad at anyone about the incident. It wasn't the fault of anyone in the squad. He hadn't been killed by enemy fire; he hadn't even been killed because of his own damn mistakes. If it were Giovanni or Green that had brought the misfired round to the pit, then they would be the ones gone. Instead, Hall had this raging anger deep inside of him that he couldn't release on the one responsible. It was a horrible accident, and now he'd have to deal with it.

Hall looked over to the man that had spoken to him. He had a bit of stubble on his face that darkened his pale white skin and dark hair that hung just below his black beret. The insignia on his shoulders told Hall that he was a staff sergeant like Locke had been, but he'd never seen the man before today.

"Isn't that how all funerals go, Sergeant?" Hall asked, still staring at the picture of Locke.

"Not all. Some ceremonies are more beautiful than others. This is about as bare-bones as it gets. Locke would've hated it."

"You knew Sergeant Locke?" Hall asked, interested.

"Marcus and I go way back—" He stopped and sighed. "We went way back," he corrected. "Basic training in Georgia, mortars at Fort Cassidy like yourself, and then served on the RNS *Blackpool* together. He was a great man."

"Well, I haven't had a lot of NCOs. I'm still in training, but Staff Sergeant Locke was a great leader. We all liked him very much and he taught us well."

"So I've heard."

The pale man smiled and turned to Hall, stretching out his hand. Hall took the man's hand in his and shook, his dark skin enveloping the sergeant's.

"I'm Private Hall, Sergeant—Aiden Hall from Chicago. Your accent, I knew a buddy in basic who kind of had one similar. He was from England."

"Well, I won't hold it against your friend, Private. I'm Staff Sergeant Kurt McHenry from Killarney, Ireland."

"Good to meet you, Sergeant." Hall nodded.

"Same. I wish it was under better circumstances, but what can you do?" Now that the ceremony was ending and the others began to mill about, Sergeant McHenry turned and faced Hall. "The question you've been asking yourself this entire time, or at least one of the questions, is 'will it ever get easier?' and the answer is no. Friends, comrades, whatever it is you call them, they can die. If we go to war, you can guarantee it. The best thing you can do is mourn in your own time, but only for the day, because whether you like it or not, you signed up for it. The military keeps moving with or without you, except the friends you got left still depend on you and you on them. If you let every death weigh you down, you won't be there for the ones that are alive."

Hall understood what the sergeant was saying, but it was coming from the mouth of a veteran. He had already experienced so much, and everything was still quite new to Hall. Nonetheless, the words stuck to him like the Velcro rank patch on his chest. He knew the death of Sergeant Locke would one day become a secondary thought, a distant

103

memory in the back of his mind. That was how he treated Eddy's death now. Every once in a while, something funny he used to say would make Hall smile, but it no was no longer followed by sadness. He thought about the memories he still had and moved on, and Locke would become the same. It still didn't help him in the here and now.
****

After the memorial service, Hall and the rest of his mortar squad went back to their training barracks and prepared to lie down for the night. There was no more fire guard, no more getting woken up at three in the morning to run five miles, and no more drill sergeants looking over their shoulders every five seconds. They were still considered recruits but were treated more like the regular soldiers milling about Fort Cassidy.

The barracks became laxer as well. Females and males both shared a barracks bay if they were in the same squad. Showers were also shared between the two genders, and it wasn't treated as some kind of taboo. They were expected to arrive in formation at a precise time every morning and to be at each training session fifteen minutes early. They were always thirty minutes early to be good. They recognized as a unit that if they did what was expected and kept a low profile in every other respect, they would retain the freedom they currently had.

"You think we'll get a new training sergeant in the morning?" Kelly "Red" Fitzgerald asked as she closed her locker and walked to her bed, which was situated between Aiden Hall's and Gunner Jackson's.

Jackson placed his book on his chest and looked over to Fitzgerald, his reading glasses sliding down his nose. "We can't train without a training sergeant, and they expect us to train every day. Ipso facto, we'll have a new sergeant."

"It just seems wrong, I guess." She lowered her head onto her pillow and looked at the ceiling.

Hall looked at his personal device and checked for messages. He hadn't heard from Kodiak or Moore in a few days and was wondering what they were up to. Part of him wanted someone to vent to about Locke's death and discuss who their next section leader would be. His hand hovered over Kodiak's name, but he decided not to send a message and instead closed his device and placed it back on the table next to his bed.

He rolled over and looked toward Red and Jackson. "Life moves on even if we don't want it to. The best we can do is keep Locke in our memories and focus on the training ahead. It's gonna happen whether we like it or not, so we might as well be prepared."

"Are you saying this sits right with you?" Red continued.

"Doesn't matter if it does or it doesn't—the facts remain the same. I'd rather show up tomorrow ready to show our new section leader how good we are as opposed to showing up feeling sorry for ourselves."

Red closed her eyes and set her head back on her pillow with a sigh. "I suppose you're right."

The room fell silent as the others still milling about began to find their way back to their bunks. Hall was looking forward to getting back into training. The past few days had been filled with too much sadness, and what Sergeant McHenry had told him earlier that day was still lingering in his mind. Locke was most likely only the first person he would have to mourn while he served his time in the military. How many more would die?

War had been the furthest thing from his mind when he had been pressed into service. Earth had been at peace, albeit a strained one, for decades. Of course, he hadn't been as up-to-date on current world events at the time of his arrest, so he hadn't really known what he was getting into. Now that he had a better understanding, it seemed a new cold war was beginning. The Republic seemed keen on expanding into the outer reaches of space without the constraints of a treaty with the other nations. He now wondered if he would be present for the first battle of a new war.

"Where do you wanna get stationed?" Red asked, breaking the silence.

Hall turned and saw she was staring at him. "I haven't really given it much thought to be honest. The moon's gravity takes some getting used to, but the view is nice."

Red smiled. "I want to be stationed on a Republic Navy ship. It would be exciting. Like, what if I happened to be on a ship that goes to discover a new world?"

"What are the odds you'd be so lucky as to get stationed with a unit going on the voyage?" asked Private Edoardo Giovanni from across the bay.

"A girl can dream, Gio," Red shot back.

105

"Keep dreaming. One in a million, that's the odds," Giovanni laughed.

"Well, I heard the Republic is sending ships to other worlds that the other nations don't know about," said Private Leslie Smart from her bed. She had flipped herself around and lay on her stomach with her arms holding up her head.

"Now you're dreaming," Jackson laughed.

"Am not!" Smart snapped back. "I happen to have a relative serving on a ship that's not headed for the same worlds as the treaty nations. They're headed somewhere else, somewhere no one else knows about except for us. He even says it could be habitable, with its own ecosystem."

"What are you smokin', Smart? Who's this relative?" asked Private Aurora Green as she sat up on her bed and crossed her legs.

"He's close to me; I trust him when he tells me this stuff. I shouldn't even be telling you, but Red got me thinking. What if we all get stationed together and end up on a ship heading out there? Why would they have us train so hard together and then not keep us together?"

"You can't keep this person a mystery, Smart. How the hell can we believe you if you don't tell us who it is?" Jackson asked.

"You guys can't say anything," Green warned.

"Why the hell would we go to anyone about this?" Gio asked.

He had a point. They might have their friendly rivalry when competing against one another in gun qual, but at the end of the day, they were close. They had become somewhat of a family.

"I told you about my past," Hall chimed in. "I could've just lied—it would've been much simpler—but I didn't. I told you all about my messed-up life."

Smart's eyes softened and she smiled. "It's my brother. He works on the bridge of a ship heading out on a long-haul voyage—packed with Deltas, fighters, Ospreys, you name it. He says they're gonna try and find a world they can colonize."

Hall and the rest sat up straighter. Giovanni was one to tell exaggerated stories, but not Smart, and she had told them before that she had family in the military. Now Hall's mind wandered to what it would be like to step foot on another world. He could have a new life, a new path. Joining the military, which had once seemed like a curse, might give him the best life yet. It was a bit overwhelming, and he had to put his emotions in check. Even if what Smart was saying was true, the odds of him ending up on one of those ships were slim to none.

"Hot damn," Jackson exclaimed.

That pretty much summed it up for the rest of them as well.

Chapter 15
Moore

Doss Station

"Today you will be receiving your personal access code or PAC. With your PAC you will be able to plug into a wounded soldier's armor and administer the necessary dosage of medicine. These codes must be known to you and only you. If someone else has your code, they can use it to abuse the drugs. It happens and it will continue to happen, but if you remain vigilant and professional, it won't happen to you. If someone *does* manage to get your PAC and medical device, or you yourself abuse your MD14s for a quick high, you'll find yourself brought up on charges, stripped of your rank, and likely serving a prison sentence before you're dishonorably discharged. Moore, are you listening to me?"

Oliver Moore had been listening to Lieutenant Faraday, but his mind had wandered to his friend Kodiak. He hadn't received a video message from him in a couple weeks, which was very out of character—so out of character that the others in his squad had begun asking questions.

His eyes went from the stars outside the faux window back to his platoon leader. "Yes, sir, I'm listening to you. If we abuse our PACs or let another soldier use our code to abuse the drugs in our armor, we will be brought up on charges and imprisoned, sir," he replied sharply with a nod.

"Good. These codes are not only your lifeline but also the soldier's lifeline when they are wounded. You have been trained and tested on how to properly apply medicine to a soldier whose armor is either damaged or not equipped, and you all passed. At that I am pleased, but the majority of the time, you will be utilizing your MD14s to get the job done." Faraday moved across the formation over to the window and looked out.

Moore couldn't help but roll his eyes, and Nova hit his ribs with her elbow and giggled. Lieutenant Faraday always had a flair for dramatics, and looking out of a fake window projecting the image of space from outside the ship was up there on the dramatics list. Now that Moore's medical platoon was close to graduating, he realized he'd probably miss Faraday's cheesy antics.

****

Later That Night

There were no more final tests and they had been issued their PACs and their MD14s upon the completion of their training earlier that day. All that was left was their graduation ceremony, which would take place on the moon later that week. With their classes completed and nothing left to do before graduation, Moore and his squadmates looked forward to the much-needed opportunity to blow off some steam.

The enlisted bar they always went to on Doss Station was called Flanders' Landing. The rotating bar near the top of the station slowly turned as its massive impact windows displayed the stars, Earth, and the moon below—the real deal, not the fake images on video screens that were all over their barracks and training rooms around the station. Tonight was also Nova's twentieth birthday, and although the squad didn't need a reason to go out most nights, this gave them a good excuse. The Republic had changed the drinking age to be the same as the universal legal age a while ago, so they were all able to partake.

After entering the bar, they took their normal seats at a table in the back, adjacent to one of the large windows. In minutes, they all had drinks in their hands and were conversing jovially about graduation and where they might end up. Their orders would come in any day now as the clock ticked towards the end of the journey they had been on ever since arriving at the station.

"I heard they got the damage when they jumped to the other system and had to turn around," Moore overheard Hughes say.

Moore looked over at him. "Sorry, what?"

"One of the ships that went on the Republic voyage to the other system came back and it was all torn up. Obviously, the Republic wants to keep it under wraps, but with all the cameras floating around space, there was no way a massive warship was going to sneak by without pictures leaking to the media."

Moore knew he didn't keep up with all of the media networks floating around space as much as the others did, but he still thought he would've heard about a damaged Republic ship. "How bad was the damage?"

Campbell whistled. "It looked awful. Huge holes and gashes all along the sides. They had to have lost hundreds on board."

Moore was stunned. "And that can happen to a ship that has a bad jump?"

"That's the official story right now," Nova added.

"Why would they lie?" Campbell shot back.

"Why wouldn't they?" Nova calmly replied. "Peace between the other nations is thin, even more thin with Belters. No one claimed responsibility for an attack on the Republic ship, and the balloon hasn't gone up here, so the Republic claims it happened when they jumped." She pulled out her personal device and brought up a picture. "But do you really think a jump could destroy a ship like that?"

Moore took the device and inspected the photo. "Whoa," he muttered, taking in the scene.

He moved his fingers apart, and the photo zoomed towards a large hole on the starboard side. Its edges of twisted metal pushed deep inside the ship. Whatever had made that hole was big. Moore had heard stories of antennas being disintegrated while in transit or the occasional electronics being fried, but the Republic was prepared for things like that. When a ship arrived at its destination, it attached a new antenna, or the engineers went to work repairing the damage. This was much different.

"There's no way that was caused by jumping the ship," Moore exclaimed, pointing to the gaping hole. "Look at that hole—it's massive. It's easily punching through, what? Thirteen decks? That must be hundreds dead, if not thousands."

Hughes took a sip of his beer. "Well, if it wasn't the jump and it wasn't one of the other nations, then what was it?"

Nova slammed her hands on the table, making everyone jump. "Aliens!" she shouted, and the entire table erupted in laughter.

As the others continued to drink, the thoughts of the wounded ship slowly faded from their minds. At the end of the day, it wasn't their problem. Space and the military were so large that you had the benefit of not really paying much mind to others' troubles, wherever they might be. Moore still felt uneasy, though, and despite the occasional smile, his mind continued to go back to that picture. He didn't know what had created those holes, but something had, and not knowing made him uneasy.

Chapter 16
Kodiak

RNS *Currahee*

Private Harrison Kodiak stood in his dress uniform at rigid attention in front of his training unit's company commander. After being discharged from the medical bay and cleared for duty, he had immediately been detained and brought before the company commander to be read up on charges he was facing from the training accident.

He was still confused about exactly why he was being charged with anything. When the explosion had happened on the training Osprey, it had taken him by surprise, and he didn't think he was the reason behind the accident. Moreover, he was the one who had tried to save Skaggs, and now he was being blamed for trying to kill him. Deep down inside, he wished he had let the scumbag die—at least then, all this would have been warranted.

Captain Andre Wesley continued to scroll through the data pad in front of him, his glasses hanging near the bottom of his nose. With a snort, he placed the pad down and stared at Kodiak, who was also accompanied by Staff Sergeant Muleskin. "Private Kodiak, it is alleged you sabotaged the Osprey during your training exercise with the intent to kill Private Tyler Skaggs. This is a serious crime for someone to allege, and if formally charged and found guilty, you will be shot for treason. We are having this meeting now to hear your side of the story as is required by Republic military law. If I do not find an adequate reason to throw out this charge, it will go to court, and by that point it will be out of my hands. Do you understand this?"

Kodiak looked over at Muleskin, but Muleskin didn't make eye contact and continued to stare straight ahead. Kodiak looked back at Captain Wesley and nodded. "Yes, sir, I understand."

"Good. So, tell me, what happened during the training exercise from your perspective?"

"Yes, sir. My squad and I were training on how to properly fix damaged fuel cells on the outside of an Osprey during a critical emergency. While half my squad stayed inside to reroute the power, Private Skaggs, Private Moreau and I conducted a spacewalk to replace the damaged fuel cells with the newer ones."

"Who was in charge of transporting the replacement fuel cells during the spacewalk portion of the exercise?" Captain Wesley asked.

"That was Private Skaggs's duty, sir. He carried the case that held the replacement fuel cells. Everything went just as planned. We had done this same exact exercise multiple times before, and honestly it had become second nature at this point. Private Skaggs complained about the fact he had been stuck with the fuel cells and wanted to be a part of the team that stayed inside the Osprey to reroute power."

"What was his reasoning for staying inside?"

"I believe he was scared, sir," Kodiak replied.

"I didn't ask for your personal opinion, Private Kodiak, I asked what his reasoning for staying inside was," Captain Wesley countered.

"Sorry, sir. He stated that he felt the others left inside wouldn't reroute the power fast enough to replace the fuel cells in the time provided, sir. I disagreed, and I was right—we were able to reroute the power and replace the fuel cells in the given time and had completed the mission."

"Hardly," Captain Wesley scoffed. "The Osprey had a catastrophic failure due to the fuel cells that almost led to the deaths of you and your team. How is that completing the mission?"

"With all due respect, sir—"

Captain Wesley cut Kodiak off. "You watch too many movies, son. When a lower enlisted says 'with all due respect' to an officer, whatever follows usually has no respect at all. You understand?"

"I have never had an issue with Private Kodiak, sir," Muleskin interjected. "Private Skaggs is another story, sir." It was Muleskin's first time speaking up since coming into the company commander's office with Kodiak.

"And I have no doubt you'll tell me all about it when Private Kodiak has been excused. For now, I want to know what happened after the explosion, Private." Captain Wesley's gaze turned back to Kodiak.

"After the explosion, I assessed the damage and saw that whatever happened sent the Osprey into an uncontrolled spin. I was able to magnetically attach myself to the ship with my gauntlets and boots but saw that both Private Moreau and Private Skaggs were unable to get a proper grip on the Osprey itself. Angeline...Private Moreau, that is, was in a more critical state than Skaggs was, so I made the decision to get to her first, sir."

"What did you see that caused you to make that kind of command decision?" the captain asked.

"Skaggs had managed to attach his tether to the Osprey whereas Private Moreau was not able to do so. If she'd lost her grip on the Osprey, she would've been thrown from the wreckage, sir."

Captain Wesley typed something on his data pad. "Did Private Skaggs attach his armor's tether before or after the explosion?"

"I don't recall, sir. He was behind Private Moreau and myself when the explosion occurred, but I doubt he could've done it after the explosion."

"Based on what?" Wesley pushed.

"Well, it happened so quickly, sir. When the explosion occurred, it threw Moreau and me off our feet before we had a chance to react, let alone attach our tether to one of the holds on the side."

"Doesn't training doctrine state that you must have your tether secured at all times during spacewalks? Why wasn't yours or Private Moreau's attached at the time of the explosion?"

Staff Sergeant Muleskin cut in, "During a training exercise such as this, I have my men and women train without tethers, sir. In a real-life situation, you won't have the luxury of attaching yourself with a tether as time is of the essence. I cleared this new SOP with First Sergeant Tipton a few months ago before this training cycle began."

Captain Wesley stared at Muleskin for a moment. "I will review this new training SOP and have it further evaluated after an incident like this." He turned back to Kodiak. "So. You've decided to go for Private Moreau. Then what?"

"I was able to recover Private Moreau and get her inside the Osprey, sir. At that point, I then moved along the Osprey's hull towards Private Skaggs's position. I saw that debris had damaged his tether and that, in order to pull him in, I was going to have to detach the tether from the ship. Just above the tether's lock, the line had been damaged. If it snapped before I could reel him in, he would've been gone."

"And yet you both still ended up as floaters and had to be fished out. Why?"

"More debris came loose from the Osprey and collided with us, sir. I didn't even know Private Skaggs had survived until I was approached in the medical bay about these charges, sir."

"In your opinion, Private Kodiak, why did the explosion occur?"

Harrison Kodiak thought back to the fuel cells he'd replaced in the Osprey. From what he remembered, they hadn't looked any different than the ones they had trained on several times before. His team had gone through the same training so many times that they could have done it with their eyes closed by that point. It was all muscle memory at that point, so he couldn't possibly fathom what had been different this time around.

"I don't know, sir. We did everything exactly how we had done before. There was no change whatsoever to how we approached the scenario."

Captain Wesley sat back and flicked his fingers up. The image of a damaged fuel cell lifted into the air above his desk and rotated slowly. "This is the fuel cell recovered from the wreckage. Does anything on it look out of place?"

Kodiak thought he heard Staff Sergeant Muleskin make a noise, but looking at the image, he couldn't see anything different. "No, sir. It looks like a fuel cell." Kodiak looked at Captain Wesley in honest confusion.

"After the incident we had salvage crews recover the debris and bring it back to the station so our investigators could take a look. They were able to create a digital composite of the fuel cell." Captain Wesley rotated the image and zoomed in to a device on the endcap. "This is a time-controlled shaped charge used for destroying airlocks. It was to cause the explosion that nearly killed you and your team." He closed the image and stared at Kodiak, leaning forward in his seat. "Now you see why charges have been filed. Now you see why we're all in this mess."

"I-I didn't—" Kodiak stammered in disbelief.

"Go sit out in the hallway, Private Kodiak, while I talk with Staff Sergeant Muleskin."

Kodiak slowly stood and gave a salute, which Captain Wesley returned. He spun on his heel and then made his way out of the commander's office and took a seat next to the door. He was in complete shock. He had only learned about that kind of explosive device in a one-day class. He'd never handled one in his life, let alone knowing how to use one. He hadn't checked the fuel cell when it had been given to them for the training op, but he also hadn't thought he needed to.

He was so angry he wanted to punch something but clenched his fists and gritted his teeth till his face turned red. Skaggs had to have been the one who'd placed that charge on the cell and the idiot probably had no way to know what the outcome would be. Then again, why on Earth would Skaggs try to kill him? Sure, they had their differences—hell, they even hated one another, but enough to commit murder? And for what? The guy could've died with them. Something clicked in his head. That was probably why Skaggs had tethered himself before the explosion when on every training exercise beforehand he hadn't bothered. It was also why he'd been so adamant about wanting to be inside, rerouting the power, instead of outside, where the danger was.

A head turned the corner down the hall and Kodiak stared into the eyes of Angeline Moreau. She hurriedly moved down the hall to where Kodiak was and turned to look at a digital painting on the wall, so her back was turned to him.

"What's the word, Bear?" she asked.

"They found that the training cell had a shaped charge placed on it, like the ones they use to destroy airlocks. I don't know if the idiot didn't think it'd be that big of an explosion or what, but, damn it, he could have killed us all. Moreau, I'm gonna be put up against a firing squad for this mess if we don't somehow find evidence to show that he did it."

Moreau looked at the ground but still didn't turn. She was biting her lower lip, something Kodiak knew she did when she was deep in thought. "I'll get some of the others to see if we can find out anything."

"Don't do anything stupid," Kodiak said sternly.

"Like what?" Moreau almost laughed.

"Like beat the shit out of him. Not now anyway. That'll definitely make me look guilty."

"I'm not an idiot, Bear. We'll find something out." Moreau turned and gave a small smile before heading back down the hallway and out of sight.

Soon after, the door opened and Muleskin poked his head out and motioned Kodiak inside. When he entered, he moved to the front of the table and remained at attention. Captain Wesley was busy scrolling and typing in his data pad before finally looking up.

"Staff Sergeant Muleskin is going to bat for you in a big way, Private. See, I look at situations like this as pretty cut and dried. In this instance, you placed a training cell with an explosive device attached to it, which resulted in the destruction of military property and almost killed your entire team. In my opinion, you should be tried and put up against a firing squad. Staff Sergeant Muleskin here says there's more to this.

He has brought up your rather short military history and your leadership qualities. And despite what you may think, I hold Staff Sergeant Muleskin's opinion in high regard.

"Because of that, I am postponing your official hearing another twenty-four hours to allow the criminal investigation agents to conclude their reports. You will, however, remain in custody under the watchful eye of a military police guard. If no evidence turns up to justify throwing this case out or changing its direction, then a trial will go ahead, and you will formally be placed under arrest. Does this all make sense to you, Private?"

"Yes, sir," Kodiak responded.

"Good. Then get out of my sight."

As Kodiak walked out alongside Staff Sergeant Muleskin, a small feeling of hope crept in. Moreau and the ones he trusted were looking for anything to show that Skaggs was behind this, and Staff Sergeant Muleskin had gone to bat for him. Even though he was having restraints put on his wrists, he smiled.

Chapter 17
Hall

Fort Cassidy, Luna

Aiden Hall and his squad woke up earlier than they needed to. They had waited more than a week to get their new section leader, and finally the day had come. Hall didn't bother worrying over why it had taken so long. All he cared about was that he and his squad made a good impression now that the day had arrived. Over the past few weeks, they had trained with another mortar section, and he had no doubt the section sergeant for that team was glad to see them finally go. Staff Sergeant Locke had taught them all well. They were faster at setting the guns up, faster at laying in their targets, and faster at getting their rounds on target. The other section hated them for it because every time they were beaten, which was pretty much every time, they would get smoked.

It wasn't smooth sailing for Hall's section, though. The other mortar section's NCO wasn't unfair by any means, but when Hall's team made a mistake, the sergeant was there to see it and would punish them accordingly. It was just how it went. Hall and his section weren't angry about it—they didn't even hold a grudge—but to say they were glad to be rid of that section and finally meeting their new NCO would be an understatement.

After donning their uniforms, grabbing their rucksacks and checking their rifles out of the arms room, Hall and his mortar section made their way to the vehicle bays on the lower levels. The new section sergeant wanted to meet them at 0800 local time, so naturally, his section arrived at 0730 hours. During the half-hour wait, they checked their gear and rifles and milled about the large area. Inside were several armored personnel carriers and infantry fighting vehicles, vehicles they had trained on before. Hall wondered if their new section sergeant had something in mind for training they hadn't worked on before.

Every NCO had their own way of training. Drill Sergeant Muleskin had his, Staff Sergeant Locke had had his, and no doubt their new leader would have his own, and so on and so forth through the rest of his time in the service. He had been sentenced to ten years in jail or ten years in the military. When he'd accepted the plea deal, he'd done it knowing he'd have more freedom in the military than behind bars, but even still,

117

he hadn't known what to expect from the experience. Now, as his training was winding down and he'd soon be sent to his own unit, he found that he was beginning to like the Armed Forces.

Hall had learned skills he otherwise would've never discovered and met individuals he thought of as friends along the way—the good kind of friends. He'd thought of Eddy as a friend but had known how that story was inevitably going to end. Of course, he hadn't expected Eddy to meet his demise at the end of a gun—more like hard prison time—but his death hadn't come as much of a shock. On the other side of the proverbial coin, he had met people like Kodiak, Moore, and Moreau—friends he cared deeply for and whose friendship had not only helped him get through basic training but also shaped him into a better person.

Hall wasn't naive. He knew he still had a long way to go when it came to bettering himself. If he was granted freedom right now and went back to Chicago, he knew he'd fall right back into his old ways, but that was the major change he'd seen so far in himself. He no longer wanted to go back to Chicago. The Republic was giving him three meals a day and a place to lay his head and had sent him to space and the moon. Yes, it was only part of his training, but it was still the moon.

"What do you think he's gonna want to do?" Kelly Fitzgerald asked, snapping Hall out of his thoughts.

He looked over at her. "I have no idea. For all I know, he just wants to introduce himself, but"—he patted the buttstock of his rifle—"if he wants to train today, we'll be ready."

Giovanni spoke up. "I bet he's gonna flex how badass he is and run us through gun drills—but, you know, his way of doing it."

"Remedial gun drills. That sounds new and exciting," Jackson said sarcastically.

"Why does he have to be an asshole in your scenario?" Smart asked Giovanni.

"The odds aren't in our favor. It's rare to get someone like Sergeant Locke. There's no way we get someone like him a second time," Giovanni responded.

"Doesn't mean he has to be a dick," Green shot back.

"NCOs are either great leaders you'd die for or dickheads that just want you to suffer while they flex all over you. There is no in-between," Giovanni insisted.

"Who hurt you?" Green asked Giovanni, laughing.

Hall saw movement to his left and looked over. He did a double take as he realized it was Staff Sergeant McHenry, the sergeant he had spoken to at Locke's memorial. He was walking with purpose towards his mortar section, and as he approached, Hall realized he was coming to talk to them.

"At ease!" Hall bellowed as he stood and went to parade rest, his hands placed together at the small of his back.

The rest of his section instinctually jumped to their feet and did the same, placing their hands at the small of their backs. That was an ongoing gag in basic training. It had become ingrained in their heads that whenever an NCO entered the room, you yelled "at ease" and stood at parade rest. If you didn't, there would be hell to pay. Because of that, soldiers got into the habit of yelling "at ease" when an NCO hadn't walked in. Everyone in the platoon would immediately stand ramrod straight at parade rest, only for fits of laughter to break out from the one who'd yelled it. Hall always thought about that when he shouted the two words, and he smiled.

"Thank you for that boisterous introduction, Private Hall," McHenry said, slapping Hall's shoulder.

Fitzgerald looked over at Hall and raised her eyebrows, but he only shrugged in return. Could Staff Sergeant McHenry be their new NCO? If he was, why hadn't he told Hall that at the memorial? He now hoped that McHenry was their new section sergeant because from what he could tell from their brief conversation, McHenry was a good guy.

"I'm Staff Sergeant Kurt McHenry. I've been a mortarman in the Republic Army for eight years. I knew your last NCO, Staff Sergeant Locke, way back at Fort Benning. Served in the same unit for a while. We were good friends. I can never try to replace him and what he has instilled in you all, but I can do my best to make sure you continue training and working hard so one day you can look back and know he approved. Today, we're going for a march on the moon's surface. If you don't have MREs, you can go and retrieve a box to hand out. We'll take lunch at one of the outposts." Sergeant McHenry looked around at everyone. "Who's the senior team leader?"

Giovanni stood forward. "Technically Hall and I entered basic at the same time—"

"It's Private Hall, Sergeant," Fitzgerald cut him off.

McHenry turned to Hall. "Private Hall, check everyone's armor and make sure it's sealed properly for the surface and ensure they have one MRE apiece. Once that's done, meet me by airlock thirty-four. Roger?"

"Trackin', Sergeant," Hall responded. He then turned on his heel and spoke to the others. "If you don't have an MRE on you, go and retrieve one. If you do, let me get eyes on it and then I'll check your armor seals. We have about fifteen to get this done, so hustle, please."

Everything that needed to get done in the military came down to a strict time. If you were supposed to be in formation by 0500, you better damn well be in formation by 0430. If you were on time, then you were late. Hall also knew from his minimal experience that it took about fifteen minutes to get everything done that he was asking of them. He just hoped they wouldn't mess around and make him into a liar.

Staff Sergeant McHenry was already walking out of sight when Jackson snapped his heels together and saluted Hall sarcastically.

"Putting on the soldier boy act a little too much, Hall," Fitzgerald laughed.

"Where does he get off saying he's in charge?" Giovanni asked.

Fitzgerald rolled her eyes. "I said he was, Gio. You got a problem with it?"

Giovanni looked at her for a moment and then shrugged. "I'm just sayin', we went to basic at the same time."

****

When Hall had checked that all the others' armor was sealed and they had an MRE, they met Staff Sergeant McHenry by the airlock. He looked over Hall and the others before turning and pressing the button to open the door. They all stepped into the airlock and Hall's attention went out the window to the bright gray surface of the moon.

Taking his helmet, he placed it over his head and down until he heard the clicks of the locks snapping in place. Once his visor's HUD acknowledged that he had a good seal, he gave a thumbs-up. Soon the entire squad held up their thumbs to show they were good to depressurize. The lights turned off and the red glow of the airlock warning lights illuminated them.

McHenry's voice crackled in their ears. "When we exit, just follow behind me in a staggered formation. Don't separate yourself from the group and don't be overexcited. We're just going for a casual walk."

The doors slowly opened once the room finished depressurizing, and in only a few steps, Hall was walking on the surface of the moon again. His armor worked to fight the minimal gravity on the surface, and although he wasn't ready to run sprints in record time, he also wasn't bouncing all over the place. Republic military armor came in various forms, some more high-tech than others, but those were mostly for the special operation groups. Grunts like Hall received armor that was a few steps up from the training armor they'd used in basic. The armor was smart enough to compensate for the gravity of whatever planet or moon you walked on, but it had its limitations. If you were to step foot on a planet the size of Jupiter, you'd be pancaked like a bug on a sidewalk.

The armor also worked to compensate for any recoil their rifles or other weapons created by dispersing the force through the nanotech weaving that lined the inner layers. If Hall was being honest with himself, the suit was perfectly fine. The gravity change was noticeable but not enough to throw off his equilibrium, his heads-up display never glitched, and the internal comms worked perfectly.

"What's your read on him?" Fitzgerald asked Hall using their internal communication channel.

"Sergeant McHenry? He's a good guy. He's the one who came up to me at Sergeant Locke's memorial."

"Yeah, but he wasn't our NCO at the time."

"What do you want from me? You asked what my read on him was and I told you, Red. As for him being our NCO, I know as much as you do. He didn't act any different when he gave his speech compared to how he talked to me at the chapel, so there's my answer."

"Hey, Smart, have you heard from your brother at all?" Jackson asked.

Smart was further up in the formation, but because they were all on the same comm channel, she answered as if she were right next to them. "No, and to be honest it's beginning to bother me."

"Why?" Giovanni asked. "If he truly is going to another star system, it would take a long time to receive word from him."

"He's got a point," Green added. "They also might've been told not to contact anyone during the transit, so the other nations don't get word about it."

"I doubt they kept it a secret," Jackson broke in.

"Why do you think that?" Hall asked.

"The minute the Republic chose not to join the others in their expedition, it had to have thrown up red flags. From that moment on, you bet your ass the EU and Asians had every satellite they owned pointed at our ships. It's hard to keep any secrets in this age."

Hall agreed with Jackson on that one. Even if the Republic managed to get to another star system and even if they found a new world to colonize, how long would it be before the other nations came knocking to ask for their share of "humanity's prize"?

They continued their march across the barren landscape of the moon. Back on Earth, you could waste your time on long ruck marches staring at the trees and animals that scurried about, but on the moon, you had nothing. The horizon was split between the blinding bright gray of the moon's surface and the pitch black of space above. In the distance you could make out the hundreds of habitable domes. Inside were civilians and military alike, cohabitating as they went about their duties. Outside there was nothing between you and death except for the armor you wore on your body.

Ahead of the column was one of the hills that climbed upward before falling deep into a crater below. The soldiers all stopped and took a knee while waiting for their next orders. Hall looked around and couldn't make heads or tails of where he was. The weapon and vehicle ranges were in the other direction from where they'd stepped off and Locke had never taken them out this way.

"Squad, gaggle around me," Sergeant McHenry said in comms.

Hall and the rest made their way over to where Sergeant McHenry stood at the bottom of the hill. McHenry then took his rifle and placed it across his chest, the magnetic clamps locking it to his chest armor. He turned and looked towards the rest of the squad, but Hall couldn't see his face because of the gold tint of his visor that protected his eyes from the harsh sun.

"Good, we didn't lose anyone. Stow your rifles and come with me," McHenry said as he turned and began to walk up the hill.

Hall took his rifle and attached it to his chest armor and headed up the hill behind Sergeant McHenry. He had no idea what was going on, and by the looks of the others, they didn't know either. Fitzgerald turned and gave a shrug, which Hall returned. When the squad had all made it to the top of the hill and stood shoulder to shoulder beside Sergeant McHenry, Hall looked up and gasped.

In front of them was a vast plateau that stretched for miles. Several launchpads covered the area, some with rockets standing tall and some empty. It was a relic from a long-ago time that now stood as a memorial to the ones who had come before. Hall had heard about this place when he'd first arrived on the moon. Musk Flats had been the very first landing zone for humanity when they'd come to the moon to colonize and set up bases. The rockets that stretched high above the horizon were some of the first shuttles that had brought people to live on the moon, and they had been kept just as they were after humanity had moved on to bigger things.

The sight that made Hall gasp, however, was above the memorial. The gray moonscape stretched as far as his eyes could see until it touched the blackness of space, and in the middle of the darkness was the big blue-and-green ball of his home world, Earth.

"Take it in, squad. Forget about the bars and fancy restaurants in the domes. Forget about what you've seen in the movies and shows. This right here is what I love the most. That is our home, and somewhere down there, some kid is looking up at us without even knowing that we're doing the same. He's standing there wondering, hoping that he'll one day get to do exactly what you're doing right now, standing on the moon. What you get to do is a privilege, an honor, that should never be taken lightly. It doesn't matter where you've come from, who your family is, or how you ended up in the military. What matters is the woman or man next to you. As long as you serve under me, in my squad, I will always have your back just like you will have each other's backs. You may have a family back on Earth still or even in the Republic military, but the people standing next to you? They're the only family that matters now."

Hall stared toward Earth and listened to the words Sergeant McHenry was saying. He felt that the comment about how you ended up in the military had been aimed at him, but then again, it could be the same speech McHenry gave everyone. It was a good speech. Hall liked it a lot and even thought about using it someday if he ever got into a position like McHenry's. That was a long way away, though, and he knew that.

Sergeant McHenry turned and held up his wrist pad in front of him. He pressed a few buttons out of view of the squad and then flicked his fingers up, sending the information to everyone. A message popped up

123

on Hall's HUD and he opened it and viewed his orders. He smiled—his training was over, and the last piece of this experience was the orders he was receiving for his first unit in what would be at least ten years of service.

To: Hall, Aiden PVT
Orders:
Private Aiden Hall 438291034 is hereby assigned to Apollo Company, 1st Battalion, 331st Infantry Regiment. 1st Battalion of the 331st Infantry Regiment is stationed on board the Republic Navy Ship Boxer.

As Hall read his orders, a flood of emotions washed over him. He was being stationed on a Republic Navy ship. He wouldn't be returning to Earth anytime soon and would be spending his time traversing the stars and…well, he didn't know exactly what he would be doing. His job was to rain hell from above on the Republic's enemy, but as of right now, they weren't at war. Despite the numerous rumors filtering through what recruits called the private news network, he didn't believe they'd be at war with anyone anytime soon. Time, of course, would tell.

He turned to Fitzgerald to ask where her orders were sending her when she spoke first.

"You're right. He's good in my books," Fitzgerald said into Hall's comms.

"That was a pretty damn good speech," Jackson replied.

"Can you not butt into our comm channel, Jacks?" Fitzgerald snapped.

"Never. I'm always gonna—"

An alarm rang in their helmets as a red "Incoming Alert" message blinked on their HUDs. Hall tried to click on the message, but it didn't play anything. After trying a few times, he exited out of the alert as the ringing and flashing were beginning to give him a headache. He turned to look at Sergeant McHenry, who was standing still, most likely listening to the priority message in his own helmet.

McHenry turned and keyed his comms. "We need to head back to the base immediately."

"What's going on, Sarge?" Giovanni asked.

"I don't know, but it's a priority alert recalling all units for a general assembly. That's pretty damn important," McHenry replied.

They made their way down the hill at a quickened pace and started toward the base. Hall's feet picked up their pace to stay in line with the others, but they could only move so fast on the moon's surface. If they ran too fast, their feet would lift off the ground and they'd have to try and restabilize themselves or embarrassingly start bouncing around until the armor regulated.

"What's going on, Aiden?" Fitzgerald asked, a little worry in her voice.

"I have no idea, Red, but it doesn't sound good," Hall replied.

Chapter 18
Moore

Doss Station

"I swear to my gods it's true," Nova pleaded as Moore's medical training squad made their way from the training simulators back to their quarters.

Oliver Moore and his training squad had just gotten done with their final medical exams before graduating advanced individual training and were now headed back to their quarters to receive their orders. On the way, Private Cara Nova was explaining that there was a leaked Republic video circulating through Belter news. Jayne Campbell, who wasn't so subtle about her wariness of Belter culture, wouldn't listen. Moore was intrigued enough, though—if anything, because he liked and trusted Nova.

"OK, say you're telling the truth—can you pull up that video? Last I checked, all Belter news was banned from our newsfeeds," Dalton Hughes huffed as he jumped onto his bed and lay back.

"My sister, Andromeda, sent me the video, and if you ask nicely, I'll show you." Nova stuck her tongue out.

"Nova, Andromeda—what names you Belters have," Campbell laughed.

"Another word about my family and I'll show you that creative names aren't the only things Belters are good at."

Campbell stood up and dropped her bag. "Oh yeah?"

Moore stood between the two and held up his hands. "Both of you, knock it off. I didn't come this far just for you two to muck it all up. We're supposed to get our orders today—can you just chill?"

"She needs to apologize, Moore. I don't ridicule her religion or culture no matter how weird I think it is," Nova snapped.

Moore looked over at Campbell and shrugged. "She's kind of right, Jayne."

"Kind of? I am right, Moore. Ever since we got to Doss Station, she's been up my ass about my family and our way of life. Has she tried to understand it? No. All she's done is criticize me and my people since the drop. I don't deserve it."

Moore's arms lowered. "I know," he sighed and turned to Campbell. "Apologize."

Campbell laughed. "Or what?"

Before Moore could react, Nova pushed past him and landed a straight punch to Campbell's nose. Her head whipped back, and blood sprayed across her face as her nose made a sickening crack. Hughes jumped off his bed and knelt beside Campbell, who was kneeling on the ground, grabbing her face, blood dripping onto the floor.

"Holy shit, Cara," Moore exclaimed.

"You broke my nose!" Campbell cried out, tears filling her eyes.

"Oh, I'm sorry, princess. Did I mess up your pretty little face? Hope your pretty blond hair doesn't get ruined."

"That was a bit much, don't you think, Nova?" Hughes asked, helping Campbell to her feet.

"I don't think it was enough," Nova spat.

Moore took Nova by the arm and pulled her over to her bed, pushing her onto it. "Enough!" He turned to Campbell, who was now sitting on her own bed and tilting her head back to stop the bleeding. "You deserved it, and you're lucky she only hit you once."

"To hell with this, I'm getting Sergeant Cardinale!" Campbell belted out before running out of the quarters.

Hughes looked over at Moore and Nova, and a half smile came across his lips. "That was a pretty solid hit to be honest."

"She deserved it," Nova reiterated.

"She did," Hughes agreed. "But was it worth what Cardinale is gonna do now? You're probably looking at an Article 15. Hell, they might even charge you."

"I don't give a damn. She had it coming."

"You need to think more clearly, Nova. We were about to get our orders. Hell, you might not have even gone to the same ship, let alone the same company. You couldn't have waited a day or two?"

"Why? So she can go be a bitch to some other poor kid? Maybe now she'll rethink how she treats people."

"I doubt it," Hughes laughed. "Now, before the MPs come to take you away, do you mind showing us this video you got all worked up about?"

Nova looked at her personal device for a moment as if thinking about showing them. After all that drama, Moore would've found it criminal if they hadn't gotten a chance to actually see anything. Thankfully, she picked up her device and sent the video over to her workstation. The screen lit up with a paused video, and Moore and Hughes gathered around it.

"They're saying it's helmet cam footage from a Republic soldier on that pathfinding mission to another world," Nova explained.

Moore looked over at her in surprise. "You're kidding. How the hell did they get that?"

Nova shrugged. "I don't know, but they have it. Here, look."

She pressed the screen, and the video began to play. Three Republic soldiers were running through what looked like a forest back on Earth as gunfire rang out all around them. They were shouting and seemed to be retreating from something. The sound of the soldier's breathing drowned out a lot of the noise around them and raised the hair on the back of Moore's neck.

"Who's shooting? Why is there shooting?" Hughes asked.

Nova shushed him as the video continued to play. The soldier's helmet camera turned as he found a very large tree trunk to kneel behind, and Nova pressed Pause. Hughes and Moore both let out an involuntary gasp. The forest on the screen was nothing like on Earth. The towering trees were larger than any tree that could be found on Earth, but that wasn't what took their breath away. Surrounding the area were bioluminescent mushrooms and plants that clung to every inch of the ground.

"Where the hell is that?" Moore asked flatly.

"Not Earth," Nova replied.

"Obviously not Earth, so where the hell is it?" Hughes asked again.

"I don't know. Nothing in the video tells you where they are."

"Well, if it's not Earth, then it has to be another planet," Moore exclaimed.

The full weight of what he'd just said hit him in the gut like a ton of bricks. In a span of a minute, his entire view on life and the universe had changed. Humanity had somehow reached out into the stars and landed on another planet. A planet that sustained life—a planet that could sustain human life, as evidenced by one of the soldiers running nearby without a helmet. Oliver Moore's world changed in that moment, and suddenly he felt very small as he briefly looked out the faux window at the cluster of stars sparkling in space.

"Nova, this is dangerous to have. You have to delete it," Hughes warned. His voice had now turned very serious, and Moore thought he detected a tinge of fear too.

"Not yet. Keep watching," she replied and pressed Play again.

The helmet cam's owner raised his rifle and fired. Streaks of lasers shot out into the growing darkness under the trees' canopy, illuminating the surroundings. An alien-looking deer with three sets of antlers and six eyes ran past the camera in a flash, which made all three of the soldiers recoil in shock. The presence of the animal didn't explain the gunfire, though, because the soldier ignored the animal and kept shooting into the darkness.

More screams came from the soldier's right as they finally heard a voice speak. "This is Lima Squad. We're pinned down in the north sector of AO Aardvark. I say again, we are—"

Whoever had been talking was suddenly cut off. The soldier looked to his right, where another soldier—most likely the one who had just been talking—now lay on his back. A large smoking hole covered his chest. The soldier looked to his front again, and the video went dark with a final, horrifying scream.

Nova rewound the video and paused it just before it went black. Moore and Hughes took a step back from the monitor and Moore shook his head. On screen was a blurry image of what Moore could only describe as a monster bearing down on the camera. It had blue skin, long black braided hair that hung down toward its lower back, and daggerlike teeth. The image was blurry, but in one of its four hands, Moore could make out a large sword. One of the creature's four arms was extended, and its outstretched hand had sharp claws on the end.

The three sat in silence as Moore continued to look at the screen. Hughes was now pacing back and forth behind them, and Nova looked at the two, waiting for them to say something, anything. Moore didn't have the words.

"What the hell is—" Moore began.

Nova cut him off. "It's alien life, Moore."

"Delete it," Hughes stated flatly.

"What? Why?" Nova protested.

"Cara, this isn't a power trip. This isn't me trying to tell you what to do with your property and this isn't me taking a cheap shot at Belters. I am saying this to save your ass: delete that damn video. If you don't, you'll be arrested and who the hell knows what else? They might even make you disappear."

"Don't be absurd," Nova began, but this time Moore cut her off.

"He's right. I'm saying this as a friend, Cara—delete that video. You're not even supposed to have been able to obtain it, and now? Jesus. What if this gets out to Earth or Mars? It's already gonna spread through the Belt, but do you really want to start a panic on Earth? Think for a moment. You didn't think before you coldcocked Campbell, but I'm telling you now, *think* about this!"

Nova swiped her hand across the screen and hovered over the Delete button. At this moment, she had the ability to share this video virally across the network and introduce humanity to alien life. She paused as she considered the ramifications.

The door behind them opened, and thankfully, Nova quickly pressed the Delete key. The three turned as Sergeant Cardinale walked into their quarters. Nova stood and raised her hands, about to explain why she had assaulted Campbell, but the look on his face made all of them check their reactions. Moore felt a lump grow in his chest. Had Cardinale seen what was on the computer screen?

"There's been an emergency called by the base commander. Everyone on Doss Station is being directed to go to the nearest conference room. I need you to come with me immediately," Cardinale ordered before turning and heading out of the room.

Moore, Nova, and Hughes all left their stuff piled on their beds and by their racks and headed out of the quarters behind Cardinale into the long halls of the station. They moved at a very fast pace, almost running toward the nearest conference room. Moore glanced at Nova, who looked worried that all this could be about her hitting Campbell, but with the way Cardinale had reacted, it had to have been something bigger.

He moved up alongside Cardinale. "What's going on, Sergeant?"

"I don't know, Moore, but it's serious. Nothing like this has been called since I've been in the military. They're literally recalling every unit and this address is being read to everyone across the system."

"Holy shit. Are we at war?" Hughes asked.

Cardinale turned to look at them and shook his head nervously. Hughes and Moore looked at each other and then at Nova. They were all thinking the same exact thing. Were they about to be alerted to what they already knew—that alien life had been found?

130

The four entered the conference room on their deck and found Campbell sitting next to Lieutenant Faraday. She stared daggers at Nova but said nothing at the moment. The four who had entered took their seats in front of a large projector, waiting for whatever was to come. Floating above the room in front of them was a revolving image of the seal of the Republic Armed Forces. It was reserved for press conferences and announcements made by admirals and generals.

The screen flashed and the Republic military anthem began to play, but it was cut short as the image of an admiral appeared in front of them. Moore didn't know who the man was or if Moore even fell underneath his umbrella, but the medals and ribbons that covered his uniform confirmed he was someone very important.

The balding man's eyes were tired from days of no sleep. He was pale, and his glasses slipped low on his nose. He pushed them up and tried to sit up straighter than he had been and finally spoke. "Women and men of the Republic Armed Forces—I come to you at this moment not as your superior but as your equal. Equal in status as a human being. Humanity, as we have come to know it, has changed forever. In the coming hours, newsfeeds across the Sol System will begin to play footage that was obtained illegally by Belter hackers but nonetheless is confirmed to be real and unaltered. As you all might be aware, the Republic chose not to renew the SET Treaty. Instead, we chose to traverse the stars alone on our own adventure to find humanity a home outside of our system. I am here to confirm to you that we have done just that."

A holographic image of an Earth-like planet came onto the screen and began to rotate slowly, so the viewer would eventually see all sides. It had wisps of white clouds within its atmosphere, and although the continents were arranged differently than on Earth, it looked almost like an exact copy of their home world, albeit with much smaller oceans.

The admiral continued, "This is the planet we found: New Eden, a planet like Earth found in a faraway system. We landed on this planet and discovered more than just life in the form of tiny organisms and cells. We discovered new types of plant life, animals, and even intelligent beings. For millennia, humanity has wondered if we really were the only intelligent life among the stars. We made movies, novels, songs, and poems about alien life. Now we have confirmation. Republic soldiers landed on New Eden and encountered an alien race calling themselves the Zodarks. Although humanity came in peace, the Zodarks wanted no part in it."

An image of the blue beasts popped up onto the screens, clearer than the one they'd seen in Nova's video. The four-armed beasts looked terrifying and massive. One of the pictures showed a deceased Zodark with more laser burns on its entire body than Moore could imagine would be required to take something down. Next to the body was a Republic soldier, his face hidden by a helmet, but obviously dead. The human was referenced by graphs to be standing at six foot tall. The Zodark was every bit of that and more as the graph calculated its height near ten feet. Moore felt the air escape his lungs as he looked over to Lieutenant Faraday and Staff Sergeant Cardinale to see their reaction. The veteran soldiers sat with their mouths agape in horror. He looked to Campbell, who also sat in shock. All of them had the same expression of disbelief. Although Moore, Nova, and Hughes had seen a video of a Zodark minutes earlier, they still looked on in shock as the gravity of the situation set in.

The admiral removed his glasses and sighed. "The Zodarks are an intelligent race who use their strength and weaponry to put a stranglehold on others. They make slaves of the powerless and kill anything that tries to stand in their way. Our Republic military has fought bravely, they continue to fight bravely, and even at this very moment, humanity is fighting on the planet of New Eden, light-years away from here, in the hopes that they can pacify this alien threat. Warriors of the Republic, we are at war. I have been authorized to activate and will be activating every unit within the Republic military to train and take the fight to the alien threat known as Zodarks, and together humanity will be victorious!"

The screen cut to black and was immediately replaced with the image of General Riverside, the commanding officer of Doss Station. "Warriors of Doss Station, I understand the information you have just received can be hard to believe. I myself was stunned into silence for a long while after being told. None of this changes the facts that lie before us. It doesn't matter how it started or why. What matters is that humanity has been attacked by an alien race and we are currently in a fight for our lives. From this moment on, nothing else matters but the preservation of our human race—because make no mistake, warriors, if the Zodark threat finds Earth..." He let that last part hang in the air.

"Those of you that have completed your training will receive your orders following this message. If the unit you have been assigned to is being deployed to New Eden, you will also receive those orders. At this time, whether you are spiritual, monotheistic, polytheistic, or not religious at all, I ask for you to pray for your fellow humans. We are no longer a species divided by cultural, religious, or racial differences. We are no longer a nation of borders and conflict within. We are now one. We are humanity and are all in this together."

The video cut off and everyone's device in the room chimed an alert.

Moore retrieved his from his pocket and looked at the urgent message that held his orders. Without thinking, he read them out loud. "Private Oliver Moore, 281675930, is hereby assigned to Apollo Company, 1st Battalion, 331st Infantry Regiment. 1st Battalion of the 331st Infantry Regiment is stationed on board the Republic Navy Ship *Boxer*. You are to report to your company no later than one week from now and will prepare for deployment to New Eden. Do not tell anyone of your orders or—" He paused and his face flushed red.

He looked up towards Lieutenant Faraday to see if he was in trouble for reading it out loud, but his lieutenant was staring at his as well. He looked around the room and noticed everyone was staring at their devices, reading to themselves.

"Mine says the same." Nova was the first to speak.

"Mine too," Hughes added.

"Yep, same here," Cardinale sighed.

"Holy shit, are we all deploying to New Eden?" Moore asked, surprised.

"Yes, we are, Private Moore. I have also been assigned to Apollo Company and you all will be under me," Faraday announced as he stood and placed his device in his pocket. "I want every single one of you packed and ready to leave for the *Boxer* at 0800 hours local time tomorrow. Make all of your calls to family tonight, but *do not* mention anything about aliens or where you will be deploying. Tell them you were stationed out in the Belt and won't be able to reach them for some time. After a while, the news is gonna reach Earth and the inner planets and your family will most likely realize what has happened. I'm sure in due time you will be allowed to tell them what's happening, but for now, for operational security reasons, don't say anything. If you do, I will shoot you under authorization of the Republic UCMJ articles of war. Is that clear?"

133

Moore didn't know if he was being serious but replied, "Yes, sir," like everyone else.

****

Oliver Moore tried for the third time to call Lilliana, but the call didn't go through. Tears blurred his vision as desperation to talk to her began to fill him with anxiety. He didn't want his last communication with her before he left to be a video message. He tried a fourth time, and when her face appeared in front of him, the tears poured down his cheeks and he laughed.

She had a look of worry on her face, but he could see that she was still wearing the uniform apron she wore in the bookshop. With all the excitement around him, he had lost track of what time it was back on Earth.

"What's wrong?" she asked, worry enveloping her words.

Moore didn't know where to start now that the moment was here. How did you tell the woman you were in love with that she was probably not going to see you again for a very long time—possibly years?

"Oliver, what's wrong?" she asked again, insistent this time on getting an answer.

"I've been assigned to my unit. Apollo Company on the RNS *Boxer*," he explained.

She sat back in her chair and smiled. "Wow. You're being assigned to a unit on an actual ship. That's amazing—that's what you wanted, right?" Her excitement for him made the video call that much worse for him.

"Yeah," he choked. "Yeah, it is."

"But?" she added, knowing that something was wrong.

"Listen, Lilliana." He sat back and wiped the tears that were beginning to itch his eyes. "Listen."

"I'm listening," she responded anxiously.

"Something has come up. Something big and I can't tell you. I'm so sorry and I want nothing more than to tell you what's happening, but I literally can't. I don't know what to do about it."

"Then just tell me what you can, Oliver, and get it off your chest."

She was so amazing and understanding, and tears filled his eyes again. "We're being deployed. I can't say where I'm going or for how long, but it may be for a very long time."

"Years?" she asked.

"Could be." He struggled to answer because he didn't know for sure, but if it was years, he didn't know how they'd survive that.

"Will they let you come home first? To settle things?"

"No. We're leaving for the ship in the next forty-eight hours."

"OK. Well, you'll be able to call me regularly, right? Or at least, I won't go months without hearing from you, right?"

Moore saw the worry slowly creeping onto her face. "It might be a while before you hear from me, but the moment they let us contact home, you'll be the first one I call."

Her eyes whipped up to meet his on her screen. "You better, Oliver Moore." Silence filled the air for a few moments before she continued, "Will you be in any sort of danger or...?" She let the last word trail off.

"I honestly can't tell you, sweetheart. I'm sorry."

Lilliana was a tough woman—that was a huge part of why Moore had fallen in love with her or was falling in love with her. Realistically, they had spent only a small amount of time together after reconnecting, a chore unto itself, but every call was worth it. He only hoped she felt the same.

"Well, as soon as you get some sort of timetable, please let me know." She sighed, resigned to her powerlessness in this instance.

"Don't go running off with some other loser while I'm off, yeah?" he laughed.

Her expression soured. "I have a perfectly good loser staring at me."

"I love you, Lilliana."

She blinked at the screen for a few moments. "I love you too, Oliver."

"Why the pause?"

"It just seemed too final. I didn't like it. I do love you, Oliver, and I can't wait for your next call, whenever it is. Just...I don't want this moment to end."

So, he didn't let it end. She got excused from work and they talked for another hour and then left the screen on as he fell asleep. She sat there for another hour watching him snore before finally kissing her screen and going to bed herself.

Chapter 19
Kodiak

RNS *Currahee*

"I don't understand, sir," Harrison Kodiak remarked, in complete shock.

Kodiak had been retrieved from the brig only an hour before to stand before his company commander and receive word on whether they would be charging him or not. The meeting had started out in his favor—Moreau had come through and retrieved evidence that proved his innocence and had given it to Muleskin. A training fuel cell now sat on the desk of Captain Wesley that had the same shaped charge device attached to the end cap, but before he could examine them, an alert came across his console.

Together, the three of them stood in stunned silence as Admiral Kincade and General Riverside debriefed all Republic soldiers in the area of operations in a joint sector-wide address. Humanity was at war, and not with another nation but with an alien race. Kodiak's head pounded as he tried to wrap his head around that fact. Even in a time when humans patrolled, worked, and lived in space, the thought of aliens was reserved for movies. Now he was being told by commanding officers that they were real, humanity had made first contact, and apparently it had not gone well.

"What don't you understand, Private? That we are at war or that we have discovered an alien race?" Captain Wesley replied, taking a large gulp from his coffee mug.

The company commander set the mug down and then picked up the modified fuel cell. He handled the inert cell and tossed it up and down in his palm. Kodiak noticed the cell took a fraction of a second longer to fall back into his hand in the one-third gravity, not too much but noticeable. He looked at the captain and wondered if, even after this revelation, he would still be brought up on charges.

"All charges against you are dismissed, Private Kodiak. Considering the evidence brought forward and the Republic's new problem, I see no reason to put you in the brig and throw away the key. You are to report to your quarters immediately and are released to the charge of Drill Sergeant Muleskin. You'll have received your orders and will report to your new company per those orders, got it?"

Kodiak let out a huge sigh, the relief cascading off his shoulders. "Yes, sir. Thank you, sir."

"What of Private Skaggs, sir?" Muleskin asked.

"In light of recent events, this matter is closed, Sergeant. Gather your men and make sure their orders are executed properly."

Sergeant Muleskin saluted, and Kodiak followed suit as they turned on their heels and left the room. The two of them walked in silence down the corridor that held the command structure for the RNS *Currahee* towards the banks of elevators that transported sailors and soldiers to different areas around the massive ship.

When the elevator doors closed, Kodiak spoke. "So, what exactly just happened, Drill Sergeant?"

Muleskin stood in silence for a moment and then turned to face him. "The Republic is at war, Private. Therefore, we are going to war."

Although Kodiak was curious to know more about that subject, he had something else on his mind. "I mean with my charges, Drill Sergeant."

"The charges were dropped, Private, or were you not listening?"

The doors to the elevator opened to one of the many training decks and they stepped off, continuing towards his squad's sleeping quarters. He hadn't seen or spoken to his squad since being arrested, except for those few moments when Moreau had come to see him.

"I was listening, Drill Sergeant, but I don't understand why. Even if we are at war, I was being charged with attempted murder. I doubt the Republic is struggling for bodies so much that they'd keep me around without a better reason."

They came to a stop in front of his squad's sleeping quarters and Muleskin turned to face him. "Private Moreau came to me with a tip on where I could find another training cell that had been tampered with like the ones used on the Osprey. My hands are tied when it comes to giving you more information—the military is a political bureaucracy as much as a fighting force. It would behoove you to remember that if you have friends in high places, you sometimes cannot be touched. Now I'm saying too much." Muleskin sighed and shook his head. "The only thing this war business did was take the pomp and circumstance out of dismissing the charges. Be grateful and use this miracle to the best of your ability."

Kodiak thought he saw a faint smile cross Muleskin's lips as he stared ahead and let the retinal scanner flash across his eyes. The doors separated and Muleskin stepped inside, with Kodiak following behind him.

"At ease," came the unmistakable shout of Moreau from across the bay. As Kodiak's eyes adjusted to the light, he saw his squad all standing with their hands behind their back.

Morgan, Garza, and Moreau's eyes lit up when they saw Kodiak standing next to Muleskin. The drill sergeant turned and motioned his head for Kodiak to go join the others. When he walked over, he received high fives, fist bumps, and a hug from Moreau.

"I owe you one," Kodiak said to her.

"Yes, you do." She winked back.

"Listen up, Privates. You all saw the sector-wide transmission. The Republic, as of this moment, is at war. You've also received your orders, except Kodiak here, who I was breaking out of prison, and you probably noticed something similar. You are all being transferred to the RNS *Boxer*, a Republic warship that is home to Apollo Company of the 331st Infantry Regiment. I have received those orders as well and will be your squad leader."

They all looked at each other for a moment and then back to Muleskin. They didn't know how to react to the news. Not in the sense that they felt it was awful, but more that they feared if they all started cheering, he'd probably drop them into the front-leaning rest position.

Kodiak smacked his hands together and began a slow clap that Garza and Moreau joined in on, but after a few claps, Muleskin snapped, "Drop."

So, Kodiak and his squad all dropped to their hands and began to do push-ups, but for the first time he didn't mind it. Training was over, they were officially soldiers in the Republic military, he wasn't going to be shot for attempted murder, and they were all sticking together. The happiness of the moment faded almost as quickly as it had entered his mind. All those things were true, and for that he was happy at his good fortune, but now they were headed for something totally different, something he hadn't expected when he'd joined. They were headed to war. Where, he didn't know. Against whom, he had no clue. But he

would have Moreau, Garza, Morgan, and now Sergeant Muleskin, and that gave him some comfort.
****

The video call had only lasted for an hour. Kodiak didn't want to drag out the goodbyes any longer than that. His father and mother were proud of him and what he had accomplished. He had to admit, he looked pretty damn good in his dress uniform. The others in the squad quarters had laughed when he'd kept it on for the video call, but he didn't care. Realistically, he had no idea when he was going to wear it again, so he might as well make the call to his parents memorable. They had sent over some Republic dollars to him as a graduation gift, which was a really nice gesture that he appreciated, even if he didn't have the heart to tell them there was nowhere to use them where he was going.

The private news network was already buzzing throughout the other squad quarters, and it was only a matter of time until they reached his. Someone had started a wild rumor that the aliens were headed for Earth and they'd be part of its defense. That thought scared the hell out of Kodiak if he was being honest with himself. He had to admit it would be easier fighting on his own home turf, but that would mean a lot of civilian casualties across Earth. Not only that, but the nations of Earth were still divided, even in the face of this new extraterrestrial threat. The prospect of having to mount a defense on humanity's home world when humans couldn't even agree with one another was a depressing one.

The other side of the coin came from a place of selfishness. He had seen Earth, had grown up in its gravity. He wanted the opportunity to go to another world, see another planet. That was where another rumor came from, one that held a little more credibility. Apparently, there was another planet just like Earth that the Republic was fighting over at this very moment. The same story was being told over and over again, but the name of the planet always changed. That was where the rumor became muddied with half-truths.

"Where do you think they sent Skaggs?" Garza asked from across the quarters.

"Ugh," Moreau groaned. "I just got done getting his name out of my mouth."

Kodiak swiped across his terminal and the screen disappeared. "What do you mean, where did they send him? I thought they arrested him?" he asked incredulously.

Moreau looked over towards Garza with a disapproving look and he shrugged.

"They didn't arrest him? He tried to kill us! He tried to get me shot for treason!" Kodiak roared and stood up from his table.

Garza stood and raised his hands. "Whoa, Bear—don't shoot the messenger."

Kodiak relaxed his shoulders and sat back down. "Sorry, Garza."

"It's OK, bud. I understand. It's not the cards you wanted dealt, but it is what it is."

Everyone in the quarters repeated, "It is what it is," even Kodiak.

"Yeah, well"—Kodiak stood again—"wherever he goes, he's gonna get someone else killed. Why the hell was he able to get away with that? I said the same thing to Sergeant Muleskin about myself—the Republic has enough bodies for this war. He's dangerous, and they know it."

Morgan was now the one to talk as she turned in her seat. "By the time this is over, we're gonna need all the bodies we can get."

"That's depressing," Moreau said.

"Well, it's the truth. You've seen the video. Those were Deltas, the best of the best of the best, and those big blue bastards tore through them like a wet paper bag."

"Deltas roll in smaller units, Gwen," Garza said. "We're mobilizing the entire Republic military, and pretty soon the other nations will join, you'll see."

"Yeah, keep dreaming," Morgan countered.

"You'll see," Garza said again in a singsong tone.

"Well, I feel better with Muleskin leading us. That counts for something," Moreau said.

They all made very good points, Kodiak thought. Then again, other than the Deltas, conventional Republic armies hadn't fought in a war in a very long time—certainly not on this level. Muleskin had the chest candy to show he wasn't someone to mess around with, but Kodiak knew he'd never fought an enemy like the one they were going up against.

"You think the *Boxer* will be nicer than this?" Garza asked, changing the subject.

"Oh, hell yeah," Morgan responded. "That's a proper warship. This hunk of junk has been orbiting Earth, tossing out the likes of us, for decades. It's held together by spare parts and bubble gum."

"Man, I could go for some bubble gum about now," Garza said to himself.

Kodiak walked towards one of the faux windows that projected the outside of the ship and stared down at Earth. He could just make out Texas through the clouds that swirled above where Austin would be, and he felt a sinking feeling in his chest.

"You think we'll ever see it again?" he asked.

"You know you look really dumb basically staring at a wall, right?" Moreau laughed.

Kodiak grunted. "I'm being serious. Do you think we'll ever see Earth again?"

Silence fell across the room. He could tell they were all pondering the same question, and from the growing silence, he could tell their answer. The fact was, a lot of them wouldn't see their home world again. A lot of them, maybe even the ones in that room, would die on a distant planet no one from Earth would ever hear about and that would be that. Sure, they'd get a nice military funeral, maybe even a parade to help sell bonds, or whatever other gimmick the government would think up, but the fact remained.

"So that's what we'll fight for," Kodiak said, breaking the silence. He turned and made his way to the others, who were now huddled around the same area. He put out his fist. "We won't fight for the Republic or any hokey slogan they come up with. We'll fight for us. We'll fight so one day we can step foot back on Earth and say that we made it, we survived. Yeah?"

The others, one by one, put their fists in the middle together. It seemed silly, even in the moment, but they all did it. "For Earth," Kodiak said.

"For Earth," they agreed.

Chapter 20
Hall

On Board the RNS *Boxer*
En Route to New Eden

Aiden Hall remembered the first time he'd caught sight of the Republic Navy Ship *Boxer*. It was a massive beast that dwarfed the other ships he had seen traversing the space around Earth. It also looked unbelievably well kept. The guns were massive, and the ship itself looked deadly. Its dark gray paint disguised it perfectly against the blackness of space, but when you got close, you could see a blood-red stripe painted along its side. To Hall, it was a marvel, even if the other soldiers around him whined and complained about being stuck on the "slow boat to hell." The *Boxer* might not be as fast as the other Republic ships, but they wouldn't be suffering on board, either. It sure beat his crappy apartment in Chicago.

The transport shuttle used to ferry him and the other recruits to the ship gave its occupants a tour of the outside as it passed underneath the hull and over the top before trailing behind to begin docking in one of its massive hangars. The *Boxer* was home to the 1st Battalion of the 331st Infantry Regiment of the Republic Armed Forces and, more importantly, to Apollo Company. When the Republic had declared war, new units had been born within the military, and the 331st Infantry Regiment was one of those units. The regimental commander, Lieutenant Colonel Waddington, had been a historian at the war college before being given the 331st. His former occupation had shown clearly when he'd decided to name every battalion and company within the regiment after ancient mythological gods from Earth's past. In 1st Battalion there were Apollo, Belus, Chaos, and Dolo. The names became a joke within the command structure of the Armed Forces, but Kodiak actually liked the name Apollo. When he arrived, he and the others were given a tour of its decks, at least the ones they were allowed on, and a brief history of Apollo Company. From there, he was introduced to his company commander, Captain William Striker, his executive officer, First Lieutenant Julie Gallagher, and his platoon leader, Second Lieutenant Samantha Cooley.

First Platoon, nicknamed Apollo's Arrows, was touted by Lieutenant Cooley as the premier platoon of the company. Hall had a feeling he hadn't gotten slotted into First Platoon because they considered him the best at his job, but it was nice to know they expected everyone to be the best. He only assumed that was what he'd want around him when the shit inevitably hit the fan. The laser-etched design on his newly issued armor was awesome as well.

On his left shoulder plate was the designation "A-1" for Apollo Company, First Platoon, but beneath that was an arrow clenched in a fist with a lightning bolt as the arrow's shaft. That was First Platoon's emblem, and he had a patch to go on his uniform sleeve as well. It wasn't long into his stay on the *Boxer* before he noticed that others stared at him when they saw the patches, with a mixture of silent respect from those new to the unit and mournful knowing from the older ones. The first meeting with his platoon leader made him realize why.

In Lieutenant Cooley's own words, "Apollo's Arrows are the tip of the assault force. You will be the first patrol, the first ones to engage, and the first in the door. There is an expectation for all of you to do your job not only to the best of your ability but better than anyone else in the entire company. The lives of you, your comrades, and those on Earth rely on what you do on the field of battle."

At the time, Hall had almost rolled his eyes. To him, that was what every platoon, company, battalion, and regiment should strive for. If you didn't train to be better than everyone else, then what was the point in training? But after only a few training simulations, he began to realize that the expectations were higher than any he'd experienced before. Their days and nights were longer than every other platoon's, their training was harder than every other platoon's, they were outfitted with the best equipment on the *Boxer*, and they were issued brand-new armor while the others were given a variety of hand-me-downs.

Now, after traveling through slip space for over a year, he and the rest of his mortar squad were growing restless. Simulator training had wound down as infantry squads took priority over indirect-fire infantry. That pissed Hall off, if he was being honest. He'd had to endure the same basic training as the regular infantry, but his basic had gone on longer than theirs. He was expected not only to know the job of the basic grunt but also to drop rounds better than any other mortarman in the unit. Yet here they were, sitting in on another boring slideshow and being told what to do and what not to do on their three-day weekend.

He almost snorted with laughter at the thought of a "three-day weekend." They were confined to a Republic warship traveling faster than the speed of light through slip space. The *Boxer* was huge but light on extracurricular activities. The enlisted men and women had a bar they could go to and relax with a cold beer, but that was all they had, and it was watered-down beer that barely gave you a buzz. Meanwhile, the officers had a fully stocked bar with the best liquor the Republic could buy. They had recreational simulators where they could play sports against one another, theaters and lounge areas to watch movies or shows, and even a military athenaeum where they could research military history in great detail. The idea of having a three-day weekend like back on Earth was as alien now as the creatures they were going to fight.

It was quickly approaching the one-year mark since their journey had begun, and all he'd done in that time was wake up, train, and go to sleep. The occasional holiday was thrown in to shake up the monotony, like this three-day weekend, but for the most part it all remained the same. Of course, he was now stronger, faster, and better at shooting and firing the mortars, but if he hadn't been by now, after twelve months in slip space travel, they would've thrown him out the airlock.

"Yoo-hoo, sunshine." Sergeant McHenry snapped his fingers from in front of the room and Hall shook his head and looked at him. "I'm sorry, is this boring for you, Hall?"

"Um, no, Sergeant," he answered quickly.

"Good, because it's very important that you know not to kill anyone during this three-day weekend—because if you do"—he clicked a button on his data pad and the next slide appeared, floating above the room—"you'll be in big, big trouble."

An edited photo of Hall behind bars floated above the projector and everyone laughed. Sergeant McHenry had turned out to be a good guy and fit in perfectly with the rest of the squad. He had said from the very first day on board *Boxer* that they were going to treat each other differently. The respect of rank had to still be there, and nobody had a problem with that, but instead of always snapping to parade rest when they talked, it was more laid-back, like friends having a chat. Life was different in the military when you were on your way to war.

"Listen, killers," McHenry continued, "you've seen the damn slideshow a million times. Don't do anything stupid this weekend, all right? Don't kill anyone, don't kill yourself, and please don't get anyone pregnant. I'm looking at you, Richards."

The sergeant sitting at the front of the small room laughed. "Don't worry about me, bud."

Sergeant Caleb Richards was a Canadian from the Vancouver Natural Containment zone, where he'd worked as a park ranger before joining the Republic military. He was on the shorter side but had the jawline and features of a model, which got him into more trouble than he knew how to handle. He also paraded himself around like he knew he was the shit. Hall didn't mind the guy. He was quick to anger when you didn't listen to his orders immediately, and unlike McHenry, he required all privates to stand at parade rest, but other than that, Hall thought he was OK.

"Hey, cherry—you gonna bust yours tonight on this three-day?" Richards asked, looking back.

"You're gonna have to be more specific about which cherry you're talking about, Sergeant," Jackson replied.

"Definitely not you, Private. I'm talking to Hall," Richards replied. A couple of the others laughed at the joke, mostly so they didn't get smoked for not laughing.

Hall looked over to him. "Rule number three, Sergeant. Always remember rule number three."

Richards looked confused for a moment until he remembered what McHenry had just said. "Right. Just testing ya, cherry."

"Cherry" was the designation given to fresh recruits who had never seen combat before. In the years of peacetime, it had become synonymous with every new recruit that came in, since the majority of NCOs hadn't seen combat either. That fact wasn't lost on Hall and most likely not on Richards, but Hall wasn't about to test that theory out.

"Last time I checked, we're all cherries, Richards," Sergeant Julia Wells broke in.

Wells was Bravo Team's leader and was from somewhere in the United Kingdom region of the Republic. She didn't share too much about herself with the others, and Hall, not having been around too many people from the UK, didn't want to guess where exactly she came from. Moore had a very uppity-sounding accent that didn't reflect his personality. Hall knew that Moore came from England but had also found out from Moore that England itself had too many regional accents to count. So, his guess was as good as anyone's as to where Sergeant Wells came from.

She was fair, far more fair than Richards was when it came to NCOs, and he felt a tinge of jealousy that Smart, Giovanni, and Green had her as their team leader. Whenever Wells and Richards were around each other, though, he tended to go a little easier on Alpha Team. Hall figured that Wells was the leash that held Richards back in most cases, which was another reason to like her more than the Canadian.

"Hey, you can get your biscuits and tea all soggy. Just don't rain on my parade." He smirked.

"And you can shove your maple syrup up your ass for all I care, eh?" she snapped back.

Richards looked around the room to see if anyone was laughing. Hall did the same and saw Giovanni almost busting at the seams trying not to let out a noise. This in turn made Hall begin to shake as he kept his laughter from coming up as well, and thankfully Sergeant McHenry came to the rescue.

"Hey, lovebirds, not around the children."

"Yes, Dad," Wells replied.

"On a more serious note," McHenry continued, "we will be dropping out of slip space after the three-day. Once we get into system, we will begin moving to get into orbit over New Eden. From that point on, this shit gets serious. The planet is hostile, this is war. It's not going to be like the cool sci-fi vids you probably drooled over back on Earth. You need to understand that it is a very real possibility that some of you in this room might not make it back on the ship once we leave. Take that understanding and get your mind right because it'll be the difference between making it home or dying on a planet no one's ever heard of."

"Way to bring the mood down, Big Sarge," Sergeant Wells replied.

"Someone's gotta be the bad guy, Wells, and I prefer it's me over your candy ass." That did get a laugh from the rest of the room. "So you're dismissed. Have a good weekend and stay out of damn trouble, will you?"

****

Later that evening, Hall sat in his bunk in the squad's sleeping quarters. The room was spacious enough for nine people and far nicer than anything he'd had at Fort Benning or Fort Cassidy. That being said, he wished the sleeping arrangements weren't so cramped. Then again, it allowed more space in the room itself. The bunks were stacked one on top of the other, four pods on the left side of the room and four on the right. Red carpet extended down the hallway and opened into a wide space that had two couches around a small knee-high table, a video screen on the wall, and a table with a U-shaped bench that stretched around it.

At the far end of the sleep hall were two doors. One of the doors had Staff Sergeant McHenry's name etched on a silver plaque and led to his private quarters, one of the benefits of being a squad leader. The other door led to the communal showers. The showerheads lined the wall and at the end was a separate area that held the toilets. The entire setup was very intimate, and over the past year, the squad, both male and female, had grown to accept it for what it was.

Now they walked around the area freely in their towels and dressed in front of one another like it was no big deal because it wasn't for them. When Hall was younger, he would've had a rough time hiding himself whenever Green or one of the other females walked across the floor stark naked, but now it was as normal as seeing someone clothed do the same. You grew accustomed to the close quarters and worked around it. No one objectified one another or even thought about stealing a glance or two. It also helped that any of the women could've easily taken Hall or Jackson or even McHenry in a one-on-one fight. At the end of the day, it was what the Republic had given them, and the men and women of the mortar section accepted it as the way things were.

Fitzgerald poked her head into Hall's bunk from above. "So what's the plan for this three-day?"

Hall shrugged as he kept scrolling through the newsfeeds on the screen projected on the bottom of the bunk above his head. "I don't know. I was just gonna chill here to be honest."

"Ugh, boring!" she groaned.

"OK, what was your plan, then, Red?" Jackson asked from his bunk above Fitzgerald.

"Well, not sit around here like a loser." She stuck her tongue out at Hall and her head disappeared from sight. "Maybe we can put something together for the platoon."

Smart laughed. "Like what? What could we possibly do that we haven't done already?"

"We haven't had a party," Fitzgerald continued.

Hall closed the newsfeeds and stared blankly at the bunk above. "All right, I'll bite. Whatya got in mind?"

"Why not put a party together for the platoon? Send out feelers to see if any of the other squads are down and put something together. A last get-together before we go planetside."

"Yeah, like command would go for that," Giovanni said.

"Who says command has to know?" Fitzgerald shot back.

"Right. Command knows everything that we do—you think they wouldn't hear about a party being thrown?" Giovanni retorted.

"Not if you kept your big mouth shut, Gio," Green added from one of the couches.

"If you have this idea in your head, Red, you need to articulate better how you're gonna pull it off," Hall continued. He was truly interested in what she had in mind.

"I was thinking—we get some of the others to see if people are interested. We snag a conference room on our deck, get some alcohol from the bar, put on some type of show, and just have one last hurrah."

"One last hurrah?" Jackson responded flatly.

"Oh, you know what I meant, Jacks, shut up," Fitzgerald said. "Seriously, it could work."

"You've piqued my interest, I'll say that," Hall said. He then thought of something. "What if we put on a fight? Ask a couple of guys—"

"Or gals," Green added.

"Or gals," Hall agreed, "and ask if they wanna fight for some cash. We take bets from the rest and we have ourselves an actual fight night."

"A fight night?" Smart said skeptically.

"Yeah, a fight night," Hall responded in a mocking tone. "No one's gonna come just to have some watered-down beer—they could just go to the bar for that. They'll need a reason."

"What if we jacked some liquor from the officers' bar? That'll bring some people in," Jackson added.

"Yeah, genius, steal from the officers. That's smart," Green laughed.

"That's not a bad idea. Didn't Sergeant Richards try to bang that quartermaster lieutenant a few months ago?" Giovanni asked.

"The one who gave him a black eye?" Smart said.

"No, that was the mechanic chick from engineering. The quartermaster is the one with the funky eye," Jackson replied.

"Her eye isn't funky," Smart replied.

"You're right. She meant to be staring at the wall when she was talking to me," Jackson laughed.

Smart threw a pillow from the couch at him and he continued to laugh. "I'm just saying, if you can get Sergeant Richards on board, he could easily get us that alcohol. You get that alcohol, you get your party."

"And if all else fails, I know just the guy to fight," Hall added.

"Kodiak?" Fitzgerald asked.

"Yeah, the big bear himself," Hall confirmed.

"Holy shit, are we really doing this?" Green asked.

"I think we are," Hall replied.

Chapter 21
Moore

Traveling through slip space was an incredible experience. If you had told Moore a couple of years before that he would be on a top-of-the-line Republic warship traveling through space towards an alien planet, he probably would've tried to have you committed to the loony bin. Now he stood on the observation deck reserved for the enlisted on board and stared out the window with wonder in his eyes. It looked like the northern lights on Earth but was a mixture of wisping blues and reds. It was far more beautiful to him than space itself, which was filled with darkness and speckled with dots of light millions of light-years away.

It was these memories that he would capture and hold in his mind to tell Lilliana about one day. She was a curious girl and would most likely ask him about the other things, the more horrible things, he would undoubtedly experience—but those were going to be reserved for when he was ready. He just hoped that he would make it that far. A year ago, when the *Boxer* had gotten underway, Moore hadn't thought too much about the impending conflict. It was still too far away to be real. Instead, he'd put his head into training in the simulators or working with the training cadavers the *Boxer* had. Now they would be coming out of slip space soon and they'd be able to see New Eden with their own eyes. Now it started to become real.

When he wasn't sending messages back home to Lilliana, he was either training or spending his downtime with the other medics in the enlisted bar. It was a nice setting during his off-hours. When the grunts showed up, it became a little more rambunctious, but by that time, he would take his leave and head back to his sleeping quarters. He was upset with the selection of alcohol or lack thereof. Back on Earth, Moore had been more of a whiskey drinker, and although the occasional pint would pass his lips from time to time, he usually stayed away from beer. The beer served in the enlisted bar was nothing but water with some flavor in his mind. He could drink three or four pints and not feel a single thing.

He understood the reasoning behind keeping the good stuff out of the hands of the enlisted. There was less chance for a drunken brawl to break out when no one was actually getting drunk—but the occasional fights did break out. Moore figured that, rather than being caused by inebriation, the fights occurred over frustrations built up because the beer didn't cause intoxication.

"What I wouldn't give for three fingers of good Irish whiskey," he said to Private Cara Nova, who sat in the same booth as him.

"Is Irish whiskey rare on Earth?" she asked.

"Not necessarily, but good whiskey is. It was never a problem for me, though," Moore admitted.

"Ah, right, privileged royalty and all," she joked.

Moore was used to the teasing and didn't mind it because he knew Nova only said it to poke fun. It was the ones who used his past as a personal jab that bothered him, but none of his fellow medics had crossed that line as of yet. Dalton Hughes and Jayne Campbell had joined them on the *Boxer* but had been transferred to Belus Company halfway through their journey. The holes that left in First and Second Squads had been filled by two more experienced medics in Sergeant Kellen Alexander and Corporal Leanne Martin.

The two NCOs that had joined Moore and Nova kept to themselves and didn't give the two a hard time. When training, they passed on some great knowledge to the two young medics, including tricks to expedite certain procedures in a safe manner. The four medics worked well together during simulations, and the two senior members were the stable cornerstone of it all.

"Irish whiskey is abundant in the Belt, and I mean the good stuff," Nova said.

Moore looked surprised. "Really? How the hell did that happen?"

"A lot of the first settlers out in the Belt were Irish. Now it's a melting pot of cultures and people, but they were some of the first big pioneers out there."

Moore thought about that for a moment. "Huh, that's pretty interesting. They were some of the first pirates too?"

"Them and the Nords, but they prefer the term space Viking," she said, taking a swig of her beer.

"You're kidding?" he asked incredulously.

"I am. There's no space Vikings," she laughed.

"Damn, that actually makes me kind of upset. Space Vikings sounded pretty cool."

She laughed. "It does, doesn't it?"

Nova was already easier to talk to than the others he'd trained with, but with Hughes and Campbell gone, he leaned on her more than usual when it came to remaining social. She didn't have that problem from what he could see. Nova would spend the majority of her free time in the bar, picking the brains of the more intellectual folks and pushing buttons when it came to talking politics. She knew how to get under someone's skin.

"How's Lilliana holding up?" she asked.

"Good. The messages I send her take almost a month to get there and about the same for me, so we send each other videos almost every day and have different conversations each time. That way we can have about ten conversations at once without it seeming like there's nothing to talk about."

"That's smart," Nova said, surprised.

"Yeah, 'cause it was all her idea. Today's topic is about children."

"Oh, gods. She wants kids?" Nova asked, almost horrified.

"We both do, Nova. Nothing wrong with that, especially since my service can pay for a future," Moore explained.

"Yeah, but are you really sure you want to bring a kid into this world now?"

"It's not like our parents' generation, Nova. Humanity is finding planets we can breathe and live on. They used to worry about overpopulation, running out of resources. When that happened, people escaped to the Belt, then the moon, then Mars. It's our destiny to keep pushing further and further—but now? Now we have the opportunity to start colonies on breathable planets. Now there's enough room to go around."

Nova's face never changed. "That's a pretty speech, but you forgot one major problem."

"What's that?"

"Humanity just declared war on an alien race we know very little about. We traveled light-years to discover a new world, only to find it claimed by someone else, and what did we do? We started a war over it. That is what you'll be bringing your kid up in. That will be their future."

She'd made a point, but Moore wasn't one to relent. "That's as good a reason to fight as any. Besides, I'm gonna be stuck out here for who knows how long. It's not like I'm gonna get to baby making anytime soon. Not only that, who knows if I'll ever make it home anyway." He sighed. "Listen, talking about our future together helps us. It definitely makes it easier on Lilliana. I know I might never make it back, but then again, I might."

Nova polished off her pint and pushed back from the table. "You're right. It's none of my business anyway. I'm gonna take a piss."

She got up from the booth and walked off.

Moore looked down at his half-full pint and pushed it to the side before taking another drink. Before they had launched and in the following months, Nova had been the same as always, but as the time to fall from slip space had drawn closer, she had grown distant, more confrontational. He shrugged it off as nerves getting to her—they all got them—but maybe something else was bothering her.

He looked around the bar and watched the off-duty soldiers and sailors milling about for the moment. Some were in their civilian clothes, others wore different variants of their uniforms. His eyes crossed over a familiar face who happened to look his way and he smiled. Dalton Hughes had his camouflage fatigue pants on and black undershirt tucked inside. He had most likely come from some sort of training and was washing the stresses of the sim pods away with some watered-down alcohol.

The fellow medic got up from his barstool with his pint and headed over to Moore's table. "Well, well, well. Fancy seeing you here, Moore."

"Cheers, mate. How've you been?" Moore asked.

"Good, brother, good. Belus Company is a little less wound up than Apollo, which is a nice change of pace. The NCOs have worked us hard, but nothing Campbell and I haven't dealt with before."

"Enjoying it more?"

"Much more, thanks for asking," Hughes laughed and took a swig of beer. "How about you and Nova? Still kicking ass?"

"When we can. The simulation rooms have been filled up by the grunts recently and that's really hurt our time in there. We're hoping to work with them in the next session, but there's some politics going on."

"How you mean?" Hughes asked.

"The grunts think we just get in the way. They want to get their updated battle drills down before adding us into a simulation."

"Wonder if they'll feel the same when one of them actually gets their legs blown off," Nova broke in as she returned to the table and took a seat next to Hughes.

"There's the spitfire. How ya been, Nova?" Hughes asked, giving her a hug.

She returned it. "As good as it can be. Sounds like Moore filled you in on the sim problem."

"He did. I just hope that if I get my legs blown off, you're there to pull me out of the fire," Hughes replied.

"Wish they held the same sentiment," Nova laughed, taking another sip of her refilled pint.

"Campbell and I talked about this the other day, and I want to get your thoughts," Hughes said. "When we get into a real firefight, you think you'll be able to save your friends? I'm not talking about the squadmates you don't really know—I'm talking about the ones you went to basic with." Hughes was looking at Moore, and Moore felt Nova's eyes on him as well.

"That's what my job is. I mean, I can't know for sure, obviously, until it happens. I hope it doesn't happen, but if it does, then I have to believe I'll do the best I can."

"It'll be hard, that's for sure," Nova said.

"Who'd you rather be fixing you if you do go down? A random medic you don't know or your friend?" Moore asked. He had the feeling they were trying to gang up on him.

"Whoever can do the job the best," Hughes responded.

Moore looked over at Nova. "You've seen me in the simulator. Am I up to snuff? Would you trust me if you got a hole in your chest?"

Nova's eyes looked away from him but she answered, "Yes, Moore. No one's saying you aren't good at your job. You're just friendlier with the grunts than we are. You can't blame us for asking."

"No, but I can get upset when it calls into question how well I can do my job. I don't give a damn if it's you or Hughes or Kodiak or whoever. If someone is injured, I'll try my best to save them and that's all anyone can ask of me."

"He's right," a voice came from behind them.

Moore looked up and saw Sergeant Alexander standing behind Nova. "You're good in the simulator. It's obviously nothing like real life, but it's good enough, and that should be good enough for all of you."

"Yes, Sergeant," Nova and Hughes responded.

"Moore, can I have a word?" Sergeant Alexander asked as he began walking away from the table.

Moore got up and moved around Nova as he headed for the door behind Alexander. In the brightly lit corridor, his eyes adjusted, and he saw Sergeant Alexander standing in front of him with his arms behind his back.

"Yes, Sergeant?" Moore asked.

"Over the past month, you've done exceptionally well—one of the best cherry medics I've seen in a long time, if I'm being honest. Lieutenant Hodges even likes what she sees in the simulator data. You keep this up, and you'll be fast-tracked for a promotion. See, it works different when you're deployed. Most soldiers have to wait for their time in grade, but NCOs can recommend a few soldiers every quarter for rapid promotion. Keep doing what you're doing, and it'll work out."

"I appreciate that, Sergeant, thank you," Moore replied, not really knowing what to say.

Alexander looked at him for a minute and then nodded. "Just want to make sure the people who are doing well know it. Carry on."

Sergeant Alexander turned and walked around the corner and out of sight. He was a man of very few words, but this time, the very few words left Moore smiling. It was nice to get recognition that he was doing a good job, especially after having doubt pushed into his mind by Nova and Hughes. Now he knew he could stay the course, continue doing what he had been doing—and now he had another story to tell Lilliana.

Chapter 22
Kodiak

The Republic intelligence branch did some of the most amazing work for the Armed Forces as a whole. Shortly after first contact with this alien species, they had begun uploading data to create a simulation around training to fight what the Republic was calling the Zodarks. Halfway through his journey, Kodiak began fighting the Zodarks with his squad in the simulators. At first, they were fighting building to building on simulation grounds based on Earth, the moon, and Mars, but in the last six months, the biggest updates had come.

Military intelligence had built a perfect environment to simulate life and combat on New Eden. The weather, the foliage, and the animals down to the smallest ant were all perfectly recreated within the simulation. This was a massive breakthrough that saw the simulations being booked up by different squads, platoons, and companies. Now whenever their squad booked slots, they booked massive twelve-hour stints.

At first, Kodiak and his squad were livid about working nonstop in a simulator for twelve hours. The simulation was strenuous enough on the human body, but prolonged usage could take you out mentally for a whole twenty-four hours. Because of this, his company began training twelve hours on and seventy-two hours off. This helped the morale a little bit, but it was still exhausting work. Kodiak spent more of his time off duty working out and sleeping just to catch up with the training.

He had to admit, though, it was paying off. When they'd first battled the Zodarks, it had been easy. They were fighting in familiar environments, and a lot of the Zodarks' tactics were based on guesswork. As the Republic had learned more about them and how they fought, the simulators had grown harder and harder. At one point, his squad hadn't lasted thirty seconds in a well-placed ambush. Now they could fight back with ease.

The earlier training operations were where they'd learned from their mistakes. The Zodarks were ferocious warriors that took a lot of damage before going down. They were savage fighters. If they lost a gun, they would unsheathe what looked like those old Roman short swords and cut you down. When they could overwhelm you, they would, no matter how many they lost. If you outnumbered them, even in the slightest, they would become stalkers. They'd set up ambushes at night and pick you off one by one on patrol. They would lure you where they wanted you to go without you even knowing. They were cunning, and they scared the ever-living hell out of him. That was why his squad trained so hard. That was why they were in the simulator at that very moment.

He was slotted into First Squad's Alpha Team under Sergeant Mark Woods. Staff Sergeant Muleskin had known Woods from earlier in his career and handpicked him to join Apollo Company when everyone was being shuffled around. Kodiak liked Woods. Between the casual banter he engaged in with his men and his seriousness in the simulators, he was one of the best young NCOs in the platoon. The others from Kodiak's basic found their way not only to Apollo Company but to First Platoon as well.

His team from the RNS *Currahee* training cycle stayed with him, minus Skaggs, who was still in the company but in a different platoon. Garza, Morgan, and Moreau flanked Kodiak as they stood next to a large DC-10 Puma infantry fighting vehicle near the spot the simulator dropped them in. Their mission that day was to patrol from their current location to a small mining facility ten kilometers north. It had the same set of parameters almost every training scenario came with—the Zodarks were hiding somewhere along their route and would ambush them at some point.

Command had drilled it into the platoon's head that the Zodarks loved to ambush and that it was their favorite method of attack. They were effective and had the firepower to decimate a squad and their vehicles in seconds. To combat that, the Republic had invented new standard operating procedures to give any patrolling unit the edge against ambushes. Every Puma that went out on patrol with a unit came equipped with a folding quadcopter drone compact enough to transport in a grunt's standard-issue backpack along with ammunition, explosives, and whatever else was required for a mission.

Morgan was their team's drone operator, and she was a damn good pilot. The controls were easy enough, and if Kodiak needed to, he could operate it—but not like Morgan. She would train for hours on her own time in one of the vast vehicle bays with a real drone and had gotten so good at it that she could traverse the corridors of the *Boxer* without hitting a wall.

"When we get underway, I want that drone up as quickly as possible. Take it out about a thousand meters ahead of the column and tag our route. If you see anyth—"

"Tag 'em and place them on our blue force tracker—I know the deal, Sergeant." She winked.

"Don't get cute, Private," Sergeant Woods warned. "Now mount up."

Alpha Team walked up the large ramp into the belly of the Puma and took their seats. Sergeant Woods jumped into the command seat behind the driver and set up his computer with their route, checking the location of other units in the simulation and the weapons' ammunition logs. Behind him and to the right, Private Sims from Bravo Team, who manned the weapons systems on top of the Puma, checked to make sure all the readings were in the green. Sometimes Bravo Team and Alpha Team would help with each other's training operations, taking turns driving the vehicles and manning their weapons. Up front, in the driver's seat, Private Griffin sat behind the wheel and fired up the engine.

The Puma roared to life as the back ramp slowly closed, shutting the Alpha Team in momentary darkness before the interior lights kicked on. There was always going to be the threat of not even getting into the fight when traveling in vehicles. One moment they could be moving along down a road and the next, they'd be specks of dust. That was something they just couldn't train for. However, unless they were doing platoon simulations or had a sadistic person manning the simulation scenario, they wouldn't have to worry about being vaporized by a missile. So, Kodiak checked the navigational GPS on his helmet's heads-up display and then relaxed.

"As we enter the area of operations, I need your head on a swivel, Sims," Sergeant Woods ordered, still tapping away at his station's console.

"Don't have to worry about me, Sergeant. I got the system online and loaded," Sims replied.

Kodiak could hear the big weapons on top of the Puma moving in different directions as Sims gathered his bearings. The weapons system's camera fed directly into Sims's HUD, and what he saw could be seen by anyone else who decided to tap in and watch. Kodiak watched from time to time during operations, not only to get a better understanding of where the vehicle was when they dismounted but also to study the planet.

He knew it wasn't the real thing, but the spooks had done a fantastic job recreating the planet they'd soon land on, and Kodiak wanted to be prepared. He brought up the weapon system's camera and watched as Sims traversed around the vehicle. The planet was beautiful and relatively untouched by civilization. It was being reported that the Zodarks only used the planet to mine its rich resources, using slave labor from all across their own territory in the cosmos. Other than the mining facilities and small towns that sprung up around them, Kodiak hadn't seen many other structures. Instead, he watched as the colorful trees and plants rushed past the vehicle as it continued down a dirt road towards their dismount point.

"Enemy contacts spotted north of our position about eight hundred meters out," Morgan reported as she flew the drone ahead of the patrol.

Five red "foe" indicators popped up on the blue force tracker, marking the enemy positions down the road. The Zodarks had the high ground in the trees, looking down at the road down which Kodiak's Puma would be traveling. Sergeant Woods confirmed the enemy locations and ordered the vehicle to halt.

"Sims and Griffin will stay with the vehicle while Alpha Team maneuvers to flank the enemy element. Once completed, we'll call for the Puma to continue on its route and we'll link back up on the road."

Kodiak hit his restraints' release and stood, grabbing his weapon and checking to make sure it was ready to fire. The ramp in the back of the Puma dropped, and Alpha Team filed out and began to pull security along the road. Kodiak recognized they were very much in the open. There wasn't a lot of cover for them on the side of the road and wouldn't be until they took off into the forest. At the moment, they were sitting ducks, and a sinking feeling hit Kodiak in the stomach.

"Kodiak, take the team off the road and into the tree line," Woods ordered over his shoulder as he walked back into the Puma.

Kodiak rose from his knee and swept his arm up and over his head. "Follow me, Alpha."

Garza, Morgan, and Moreau followed Kodiak across the dirt road and into the ankle-high grass as they moved towards the tree line. When they ducked under the boulder-sized leaves of New Eden's massive trees, Kodiak took a knee as the others made a circle around him.

He took a moment to take in the planet's dense and colorful foliage. Massive bioluminescent fungi caused the tree trunks to glow orange and green, which gave the forest a haunting yet beautiful hue. You always wondered what it was going to be like when you went to another planet, but until you got to actually experience it, you had no idea. Even now, he wasn't actually on the planet, but his brain took its chances when trying to blend simulation and reality.

Sergeant Woods came bounding through the foliage and took a knee next to everyone else. "The enemy is up the ridge a little ways but still concealed under the treetops. Morgan, get your drone to begin recon on the area."

Morgan looked at her wrist tablet that controlled the drone and began clicking away. Another feature of the drone was that you could set up flight patterns so you could forget about it while moving. Morgan gave a wordless thumbs-up to alert their team leader that the drone was on its way, and they set off.

Alpha Team separated themselves by more than ten meters on either side as they moved up the slope in a file formation, trying to stay within each other's footprints so as not to set off any explosives that might have been placed. When the distance between themselves and the enemy fell to only a hundred meters, they took a knee. An aerial view of the enemy rotated overhead from the drone, and each target was getting marked by Morgan. Kodiak watched as four, five, and now six targets popped up on his HUD, a red glow emphasizing the enemy's outline.

Kodiak lowered his head below the bulbous top of a mushroom and peered out toward the location where the ambush was waiting for them. He could make out the outline of one of the marked Zodarks and immediately tagged that one as his. More tags appeared over Zodark bodies that were concealed from view. When all six were accounted for, they waited for the signal.

"On me, open fire," Woods ordered through their internal communications.

Kodiak moved his finger into the trigger well of his rifle and slowly placed his finger lightly on the curved trigger. He tried to slow his breathing and fight the adrenaline rising in his bloodstream. It was imperative to hit his target quickly and effectively in order to make sure the enemy couldn't reorganize and take the fight back to them.

"Slow is smooth, smooth is fast," Kodiak muttered softly to himself.

Woods's gunshot barked, his railgun only muffled by the dense foliage. Half the soldiers had their rifles set on blaster mode while the others used their railgun setting. The railguns had a way of decimating the underbrush around them, clearing the area for the blasters to land more accurate shots.

With the first shots fired, the area around Kodiak erupted with the sounds of battle. He squeezed the trigger, zeroing his own rifle center mass on the large beast. Dropping the first Zodark, he pivoted to fire his laser fire into the area from which the enemy was charging. He watched as one of the beasts rose to its feet, taking three more rounds in the back before turning and trying to level its weapon towards the team. Kodiak squeezed the trigger three more times and watched as the final laser split the Zodark's skull in half as its lifeless corpse slipped below the bushes.

He moved his weapon to acquire another target as gunfire continued to bounce around the area. The green-and-orange hue of the fungi now mixed with the bright blue plasma of laser fire from both the Zodarks and Alpha Team. With the Zodarks firing back, it became easier for Kodiak to see where they were hiding. The lasers leaving their weapons' barrels acted like a beacon to Alpha Team, but Kodiak knew his weapon was doing the same. It was imperative they maintain the advantage of the ambush by shifting positions every couple of shots so the enemy didn't zero in on them.

Kodiak flinched as he saw two lasers leaping up from the same tree to his right and fired back, watching the bark split and break away in a shower of blue. It was ineffective. The Zodarks' laser fire continued from behind the tree as they utilized the slight defilade of the sloping ground for cover. Kodiak ducked behind cover—laser bolts slapping the three he was shooting behind. He reached down and grabbed the baseball-sized grenade from his armor and depressed the red button on top, activating it. Once he released the button, the grenade would be armed and he'd have about six seconds before it exploded.

He reached his arm back and yelled, "Grenade out!"

The ball spun in the air towards the tree and detonated at the base of the trunk. The concussive blast enveloped the bottom of the tree and shattered the thick trunk. When the smoke dissipated, Kodiak glared at the spot the Zodarks had been firing from and didn't see any more movement.

"Cease fire!" Kodiak yelled, waving his hand palm out in front of his helmet. The others echoed the orders down the line. "Garza, Moreau, on me."

Kodiak and the two others got to their feet and slowly moved towards the area where the Zodarks had been concealed, their weapons raised towards the lingering smoke. When Kodiak reached the spot where the grenade had detonated, he peered behind the tree and saw the mangled bodies of two Zodarks.

He fired two more times into both their heads and turned towards the others. "Get Sergeant Woods over here—" Kodiak was cut off.

"Ahh shit, we got a problem," Morgan called from the rear.

Kodiak, Garza, and Moreau bounded back up the ridge to where Morgan was standing and stopped at the feet of Sergeant Woods. He was lying on his back, his rifle still gripped in his right hand but his helmet destroyed. They couldn't see the devastation inside the helmet, but Kodiak didn't need to in order to know he was dead.

"That's annoying," Garza said.

Morgan smacked him in the shoulder with the back of her hand and stifled a laugh. "Stop."

"It's not like he's really dead. Dude's probably watching us right now on the monitor and getting mad as hell we haven't moved to secure the road," Garza continued.

Kodiak looked back down the hill toward the dirt road, which he could just make out through the leaves and tree trunks. If Woods died in actual combat, it was Kodiak's job to step up as interim team leader, but in the twelve months they'd been training in the simulator, Woods had never died.

"What happened?" Kodiak asked.

"He died," Garza responded. Garza couldn't see Kodiak's eyes through the visor of his helmet, but the slight tilt of Kodiak's head was all he needed to add, "I don't know, I wasn't with him. When he fired, we all fired until it was over. You gave the order to cease fire, not him."

Kodiak looked back down the hill and thought for a moment, then realized they were exposed standing in the open. "Start pulling security while I think about this real quick."

The others spread out and disappeared into the undergrowth as Kodiak turned back to look at his possible choices. He knew they needed to secure the road below and call up the Puma, which he now realized hadn't arrived because Woods had been killed. He should've been monitoring the team's built-in EKG readings in his helmet's HUD and made a mental note to fix that when he got out of the simulator.

He switched to the comm channel linked with the Puma and keyed his mic. "One-Alpha Delta, this is One-Alpha Actual, how copy?" The "one" stood for First Platoon, "Alpha" stood for Alpha Team, and "Delta" was for "driver" to alert Griffin that Kodiak was talking directly to him on the radio.

"Bear, is that you?" Griffin responded.

"Yeah, Sergeant Woods is KIA, I need you to move up to the next rally point, where we will Oscar Mike to the objective."

"On the move," Griffin responded.

Kodiak switched back to his interteam comms. "Alpha Team, let's move to RP Bravo and secure the road for the Puma. Moreau, you're on point. Morgan, I need you to take up the rear and get that drone over the RP."

"Drone is down and not responding, Kodiak," Morgan responded.

Kodiak sighed. "What took it out?"

"I don't know; I wasn't monitoring it when it went off-line. Could've been atmospheric interference, the trees' canopy, or Zodarks. I have no clue."

Kodiak checked his weapon's battery pack charge—it was still in the green, so he shouldered his rifle. "All right. Move out and stay alert."

The team stepped off and advanced down the easy decline of the hill towards the road below. With the drone out, Kodiak had no idea what was waiting for them below. If there was another enemy team on the other side of the road ready for an ambush, they'd have to deal with them first. It was rare that Zodarks would be out with only six or fewer soldiers. Usually, they wanted to fight with heavier numbers than their opponents; however, it all depended on what scenario the person controlling the simulation had built.

When they moved into a line on the edge of the road, still concealed in the foliage, Kodiak scanned for movement on the other side. He couldn't see anything, which didn't mean the enemy wasn't there, but with limited information, he was pressed to make a hard decision.

"Anyone have a marking disk?" Kodiak asked the team.

"I only brought one," Moreau called.

"Well, make it count. Try to get it on the other side of the road, deep enough to penetrate the trees," Kodiak ordered.

Moreau removed a small disk from her armor and activated it. The marking disk was a tool used by Republic soldiers to mark enemies while on the ground when drones weren't available. When it landed, it would send out pulses that would identify organic life within its radius and send the information to the soldier's HUD. The disk spun through the air and disappeared on the other side of the road. The pulses radiated throughout the area on the other side of the road, but no markers were popping up on Kodiak's HUD. For the moment, there didn't seem to be any enemies on the other side of the road.

The rumble of the Puma's engine vibrated the ground as it rolled down the road toward their area, and Kodiak stood to begin securing the other side of the road. "Garza, on me."

The two soldiers stood and bounded across the road and into the bushes on the other side. When Kodiak broke through, he saw an open area surrounded by trees that looked as if they had been cleared out by nonnatural means. The hairs on the back of his neck stood up, and a horrible feeling sank into the pit of his stomach. He turned to tell Garza to get into cover but was hit in the chest and thrown backwards. When his back hit the ground, all sound faded immediately. He had a moment to look down at what had hit him and saw a gaping, smoking, charred hole in his chest armor. He had been killed.

The simulation was hyperrealistic and helped soldiers prepare for a true combat scenario, but the one thing it never got right was death. When a soldier was killed in the simulation, everyone knew they weren't actually dead. The same went for when you were killed. There was no pain, just a heaviness that slowed your ability to think until darkness enveloped you. It was as painless as falling asleep.

When he woke, he flipped open his simulation pod and pulled himself out. He looked over and saw Garza crawling out of his pod as well and gave a deep sigh, realizing he hadn't been able to get Garza out of the danger zone. Moreau, Morgan, Sims, and Griffin were still in their pods and therefore still in the battle, but for Kodiak, the fight was over.

He looked over and saw Woods with his hands behind his back, talking to Staff Sergeant Muleskin. He nodded and then made his way over to Kodiak. "Sergeant Muleskin wants to talk to you."

"Yes, Sergeant," Kodiak replied.

As he headed over to the platform that Muleskin was standing on in front of the monitoring consoles, he heard Woods speak from behind him. "Garza, you had to have known I was listening to you. Come on, drop. There ya go," Woods said as he began to run Garza through some corrective training consisting of push-ups and mountain climbers.

"You wanted to see me, Sergeant?" Kodiak said as he approached Muleskin and went to parade rest.

"Relax, Kodiak," Muleskin responded, still watching the monitors. "After Sergeant Woods was killed, why did you wait so long to continue to the next objective?"

"I was thinking, Sergeant. If I moved too quickly, I could lead us into another ambush, and I knew if I took too long, I would give the enemy too much time to coordinate if they were out there watching."

Muleskin held up his hand. "Calm down. You're overthinking it. It won't be the waiting too long or jumping off too soon that will kill you in the end, it's the overthinking it all. Remember, the right thing to do won't always result in a victory. Slow down, take a moment—but only a moment—assess and act. I'm assuming you went with your gut when you did step off?"

"Yes, Sergeant. I realized the Puma was still coming no matter what, and we needed to secure the road. We didn't have the drone online anymore for some reason, so we decided to use a marking disk, but it didn't work." Kodiak's shoulders sank.

"Moreau simply didn't throw it far enough. It happens. That's what the simulator is for. So keep your head up and don't take the loss so heavily. Learn from it so when the real shit hits the fan you're prepared.

"You're doing a good job, Kodiak, especially when leading the team in Woods's absence. There's another lesson I want you to think about. In the absence of orders—attack without mercy! Remember, violence of action almost always wins out in the end. You've got this, Kodiak. I also wanted to let you know I'm recommending you for an immediate promotion to private first class. It's just an increase in pay, but I'm also giving it to you because I recognize your leadership potential, so don't let me down."

Kodiak stared blankly at him for a moment and then smiled. "Thank you, Sergeant."

"All right, wipe the smile off your face and hit the showers. We'll debrief in an hour and then you can begin this three-day the brass has gifted you for some reason."

Kodiak nodded, turned, and left the simulation room with his head held a little higher than normal. When he arrived back at his sleeping quarters, he saw the private first class rank insignia sitting on his bunk. With pride, he removed the single chevron from his uniform and placed the new rank on his chest. He couldn't wait to tell his parents.

Chapter 23
Hall

The plan was set in motion. Operation Big-Ass Party was underway. Hall was indifferent about the name, Fitz thought it was stupid, and Jackson was the one who had come up with it. Hall had been tasked with talking to Sergeant Richards about getting liquor, but first, he needed to try and talk Kodiak into fighting. They still needed to find a way to procure a conference room for the party, but Jackson and Red said they could find one and he trusted they would.

The mortars were bunked on the starboard side of the *Boxer*, so Hall had to take the long way around to get to Kodiak's squad on the port side, but he didn't mind the walk. He took the time to figure out exactly how he was going to talk Kodiak into fighting. Kodiak had done well in combatives in basic training and was built like one of the blue aliens they were going to war with, but Hall didn't know if he'd ever fought before. A twinge of guilt bit at him when he realized he probably should've known that if he considered Kodiak a close friend, which he did.

As the doors opened up to First Squad's sleeping corridor, he saw the piercing eyes of Angeline Moreau staring back at him. "Oh, hey, Moreau," he stammered.

"Hello to you as well, Hall," she replied in her thick French-accented English. "What brings you to these parts?"

"I'm actually looking for Bear—have you seen him?" Hall asked.

"He's in his quarters, two down on the left." She pointed.

"Thanks, I appreciate it. Good seeing you, Moreau."

"Good seeing you too—might even see you at your little party," she teased.

His heart sank. "How'd you hear about that?" he asked nervously. The last thing he needed was for their plans to be found out.

"Calm down. A couple of the people in our squad were talking about it. Even the NCOs are excited for it."

"Well, please don't go getting this thing shut down before it even kicks off," he pleaded.

"No one important will find out, Hall. Relax." The doors behind him opened and she walked past. "And don't be a stranger, OK?"

"Mortars are only a hop-skip away, Moreau," he said as the doors closed.

167

He turned and made his way to the room Moreau had pointed out and walked in. He had never been in the grunts' sleeping quarters, but they weren't any different than the mortars'. Same layout, same paint, same lights, same everything. He stood in the door and looked around for a moment until he spotted Kodiak sitting in his bunk.

He made his way over and slapped him on the back. "Hello, Private Kodiak, nice to see you again." He tried to put on his best Muleskin impression.

"That's Private First Class Kodiak to you." He smiled, showing his new rank.

Hall smiled. "Damn, that's awesome, bro! Congrats. How'd you manage to pull that off?"

"Sergeant Muleskin put me in for it today—said I had leadership potential."

"Hell, Bear, we all knew you had leadership potential in basic. It's lucky ol' Muleskin transferred with you guys. How's that working out?" Hall asked.

"Good, actually. Muleskin's the real deal, man. He just sees the battlefield different than others. He's coached us for a long while and now lets us do our own thing and watches from the simulator consoles."

"Yeah, I had a good feeling about the guy in basic. He was rough, don't get me wrong, but he was fair, and honestly that was enough for me compared to the rest of the drill sergeants."

"No kidding," Kodiak replied. "So how about you? How's the mortar life?"

"Could be worse, man. Sergeant McHenry took over after we lost our last sergeant in training, but he's a good guy. Fair but rough, like Muleskin—a little bit less rough, but I'll take it," he laughed.

"Can't be much rougher than the old man, that's for sure. Has he got you in the simulator much?"

"You guys take up most of the time, but we get our fair share. Every once in a while, McHenry gets us in with some grunts and we can work on providing indirect fire for them, but that's about it. Haven't even been killed yet."

"Well, I don't know how to tell you this, Hall, but that's a good thing," Kodiak laughed.

"I know it's a good thing, asshole. I'm just saying we don't really get into the shit like you guys. We just receive some coordinates, drop rounds, and endex. Listen, when it comes to the real thing, I'll be happy if I never fire my damn rifle, but in the meantime, it'd be nice to get into a situation so I can prepare better."

"Well, hopefully us grunts will get the job done first so you don't have to," Kodiak replied.

"I'm a grunt too, Kodiak, just like you."

Kodiak held up his hands in surrender. "Whoa. I know, buddy—relax. You know what I meant."

Hall nodded his head. "I know, my bad. Just, mortars get a bad rap is all. I'm kind of getting tired of it."

"When the lasers start flyin' and we need some high-angle hell rained down on the enemy, they'll appreciate you."

"Well, hopefully after tonight they'll appreciate us a little more," Hall said.

"You talking about your party? Are you really doing it? Moreau was talking about it, but I didn't know if it was serious."

"Oh, yeah, buddy. We're doing it. That's actually why I'm here."

"Oh, if you're having it, I'll be there," Kodiak replied.

Hall paused for a moment to find the right words. "Actually, I was hoping you could help with something."

"Shoot," Kodiak replied, "what's on your mind?"

"Well, I'm gonna try and get Sergeant Richards to sneak us some liquor from the officers' bar, but on the off chance he can't, I want to have people bet on some fights."

"I thought the *Boxer* couldn't get live vids?"

"They can't." Hall let that hang in the air for a moment.

Kodiak's face went from confusion to realization quickly. "You want me to fight someone?" he asked.

"Exactly!"

"Hall, I've never fought anyone outside of like combatives or football—what the hell?"

"I know," he lied. "But there's not much to it to be honest. You're big, you're strong, and it's not like you're gonna have to hang in for twelve rounds. Just swing one of those tree trunk arms once, and you'll knock 'em out."

Kodiak sat back and sighed. "Oh, I don't know, man. I just got promoted and I don't wanna have to deal with getting into any more trouble."

"Dude, it's the military; they know how it goes. Hell, a bunch of NCOs are coming to the party anyway. You'll be fine."

Hall had no idea if Kodiak was actually going to agree. He'd felt a lot more confident about it before stepping into the sleeping quarters. Now he was scrambling to persuade him. "What if I let you pick who you fight?"

Kodiak sat up and stared at Hall. "Who?" he said flatly.

A wide smile crossed Hall's lips. "Skaggs."

That was all Kodiak needed to hear as he smiled back. "You get Skaggs, then you get me. Deal?"

Hall's hand shot out and shook Kodiak's. "You got yourself a deal, my guy."

****

Finding Skaggs was a bigger issue than Hall had thought it would be. It turned out his new platoon didn't like him much either. He'd been transferred out of Apollo Company before they'd even deployed to the *Boxer*. Luckily, he had stayed within the battalion and was stationed on another deck with Belus Company. When he had approached Moreau about finding Skaggs, Moreau had been visibly angry. She'd filled him in on the finer details of what had happened—how Skaggs had framed Kodiak on purpose and how they'd caught him by finding fuel cells rigged to explode in his locker. Moreau had gotten lucky that Skaggs was such an idiot as to leave the evidence right there under their noses.

"All Kodiak said was Skaggs framed him for something, but I never knew it got to the level where they were going to try him for attempted murder." Hall shook his head.

"Now you see why he might want to fight him." Moreau shrugged.

"Yeah, or kill him. You need to talk to Kodiak and make sure he doesn't go too far—I'm serious. He got beyond lucky with them throwing out charges the first time. Take it from me, there's usually a catch involved."

Moreau put her hand on Hall's shoulder. "I'll talk to him, Hall. Don't worry about it."

"Good, 'cause he'll only listen to you if he gets in that zone," Hall said.

"Don't I know it," she said, patting him on the shoulder and turning to walk away. She turned again. "On second thought, Hall, I don't know."

Oh, here we go.

"He'll listen to you, Angie."

Moreau's shoulders quivered. "I know you said 'Angie' to try and make me feel better and make it seem like you care, but don't ever call me that again."

Hall held up his hands in surrender. "Won't happen again, but I'm being serious. Talk to him, tell him not to tear the kid's head off, make him promise and that's that. If you have a feeling he won't withstand the impulse to actually commit murder, then we'll call it off."

Moreau stared at Hall for a moment, her eyes piercing through him as if she were trying to solve a riddle. "Skaggs is in Belus Company, one deck up. But I swear to the Republic that if you still bring him, even if I tell you not to, I'll be the one up for attempted murder."

Hall looked down at the finger pointing into his chest and smiled. "Yeah, I already plan on getting iced by the Zodarks, so I'll have to pencil you in."

Moreau's face relaxed and she stuck her tongue out and laughed. "Good luck," she said as the doors closed behind her.

When she'd wished him good luck in finding Skaggs, he'd thought it was going to be a lot harder than it actually was. Hall took the elevator up to the next deck above and began his search by asking anyone he saw with a Belus Company patch if they'd seen him. He got a lot of sneers and snide remarks in return—it seemed Skaggs had already made a few enemies in his new company.

Hall entered the deck's mess hall and found the once wiry but now pudgy man called Skaggs, eating alone at one of the corner tables. With a smile of victory, Hall headed over and took a seat across from him. It took a moment for Skaggs to recognize Hall. They might have been in the same platoon in basic, but they hadn't seen each other since.

"Hall, right?" Skaggs asked in between bites of rehydrated beans and rice.

"Good memory, Skaggs. How've you been?" Hall tried to be as polite as possible but found it hard to regulate his voice through the anger.

"Well, let's see. We're traveling through slip space, light-years from Earth, toward an alien planet where we'll most likely die. So, all things considered, pretty good," Skaggs replied, taking another bite.

Hall was finding it harder to give Skaggs the time of day and decided to get to the point. "That's why I'm here, bud. Apollo Company is putting on a little party in the lower decks to blow off some steam before we head planetside. One of the events is a combatives fight. Now, I can get you into the party even though it's Apollo Company only, but—"

"Just get to the point, Hall," Skaggs sighed, taking another bite of his food.

Hall was tired of beating around the bush. "The only way you can gain entry is if you fight in the match. You held your own in combatives in basic," he lied, "so I thought it'd be a great show if you took to the ring in an actual fight."

Skaggs put his spork down and looked at Hall for a moment, thinking it over. "What do I get if I win?"

Hall almost laughed but kept himself composed. "Half the winnings, bro. Almost all of Apollo Company will be there and will be betting on the fight. Winner takes half and the other half goes toward the company and more parties in the future."

"Who would I be fighting?"

Hall was almost there. "Your old pal…Kodiak."

Skaggs's eyes dropped for a moment. "I don't know."

"Come on, man—you absolutely demolished people in combatives," Hall lied again, leaning closer, "and I heard you were able to get the drop on him in AIT."

A grin came across Skaggs's lips and Hall knew he had him. Skaggs's ego just couldn't let it go, and Hall had him hook, line, and sinker. "OK, when and where?"

"It's going to be tonight. I'll send you the location on your personal data pad." Hall raised his palm-sized data pad up and Skaggs tapped his against Hall's, transferring his information to him.

"You won't regret this, Skaggs. We're gonna make out like bandits." Hall stood and began to walk away.

"Aren't you gonna take your tray?" Skaggs asked, looking at the tray of untouched food.

"Naw, man, that's yours. Eat up, you're gonna need your strength." Hall smiled, but it wasn't friendly—more like a cat who knew it was about to topple the Christmas tree when its owners were asleep.
****

"So, what did he say?" Red asked as Hall returned to Apollo Company's deck.

"Kodiak and Skaggs are both in and are gonna fight tonight," Hall said with a smile.

"Are you sure that's a good idea? Didn't Skaggs try to kill him?" Jackson asked.

"And tried to frame him afterward," Hall said.

"Right. You don't see how it's probably a bad idea to get Kodiak to fight him?" Red replied.

"I've already talked to Kodiak about it and a friend of ours is also gonna talk to him. It'll be all right, and to be honest, maybe this is exactly what Skaggs needs to fall in line."

Fitzgerald and Jackson looked nervously at each other and back to Hall. He could sense they were unsure, which he completely understood, but he knew Kodiak would keep his cool. He hoped Kodiak could keep his cool. Those two being so worried began to become infectious as doubt creeped into Hall's mind now, but Moreau had said she'd talk to him. She would put Kodiak on the straight and narrow and keep him calm.

"How are we looking for a conference room tonight?" Hall asked the two.

Jackson smiled wide. "Red here put on some charm and flirted with the dude in charge of security for that section."

Fitzgerald shook her head. "I gave him three hundred Republic dollars to leave that corridor vacant. He said he'd even guard the entrance and act as a bouncer."

"I appreciate it, Red," Hall said gratefully. "Now all that's left is getting Sergeant Richards to snipe some liquor for us from the officers' bar and we got ourselves a party. Word is already spreading about it."

"That's why I had to give the guy three hundred bucks; he was upset he was going to have to miss the party, so he wanted some compensation for it," Red said.

"Don't worry, I'll pay you back with the profits tonight," Hall assured her.

"Oh, I know you will," Red shot back with a smile that said, "you better."

Hall was beside himself with excitement. He couldn't have imagined the plan coming together any better. He thought for sure the plan had come to a dead halt once he'd had to ask Skaggs to fight. Luckily, he had done a pretty good job convincing him that it was going to be an easy win. Some people's egos were also their demise.

"There is one slight problem," Jackson said.

"What?" was all Hall was managed to ask. He was riding high on perfection up until now.

"Richards said he can't get us the liquor," Jackson said, confirming Hall's biggest fear.

"What the hell happened?" Hall asked.

Jackson looked down towards the ground. "I guess he and that officer chick aren't together anymore. I don't know. He said it wasn't possible."

"He said it wasn't possible?" Hall asked.

"Well, what he actually said was, 'Why the hell are you asking me to steal you liquor from the officers' lounge? Are you insane?'—so take from that what you will," Jackson replied.

"Well, no big deal. We have the fight lined up, so all we have to do is grab a couple of kegs from the enlisted bar and we'll be fine. Can you manage that?" Hall asked.

"Yeah, I can manage a few kegs, no problem." Jackson nodded.

Hall put his hand on Jackson's shoulder. "Hey, no stress, tonight is gonna be amazing."

"Hell yes," Jackson replied with a smile.

Chapter 24
Moore

The rumors of a party for Apollo Company being put on by Hall and the rest of the mortars had been making the rounds all day within the sleeping quarters. Oliver Moore had no idea if he was going to attend such a thing—the chances of it being discovered by the officers rose every time someone opened their mouths. Cara Nova had already decided she was going and had attempted to pressure Moore to go as well, but so far, he'd resisted. There were just so many things that could go wrong, and with planetside coming up, he really didn't want to risk it.

"You're boring," Nova teased from one of the couches in their sleeping quarters.

Moore rolled his eyes and tried to ignore the comment. He was at his private terminal, trying to send out a reply to Lilliana's last message, and was getting annoyed at being distracted every two minutes. Lilliana was dealing with her own issues back home, and he was trying his best to stay involved. She had been offered a chance to take over the antiquarian bookstore she had been working at for years. Over time, she had developed a familial relationship with the owners, and before he'd left, she had told Moore this could happen. He didn't see any problem with it—if she was passionate about it, then why not?

So that was what he said. "If you're passionate about keeping the shop running, then you should do it. We could live above the shop just like they did. When they leave, of course," he added, staring at his own image in the screen. "I'll support you through whatever you choose to do."

He finished his message and sent it back to Earth. He had hoped to receive a reply about the situation before they inevitably left for New Eden's solid ground, but hope and the deliverance of it were growing hard to come by. He could use a drink. He could use that party, but whether he would go or not still hung in the air.

Almost as if the question were answered by a higher power, the doors to his sleeping quarters opened and in walked Harrison Kodiak, sporting his brand-new rank on his uniform's chest. Moore looked over from his terminal and closed it out, smiling wide at his old friend. He got up and gave the big man a hug.

"How are you doing, mate?" Moore asked.

"I'm doing well, Doc. Can't complain to be honest. I actually came by to see if we could talk about tonight."

"You don't have to call me Doc, mate."

"I know, it's just become a habit as of late when working with the other medics."

"How do you like your medic?"

"Sergeant Alexander? Yeah, he's good. Knows his stuff. A little on the strange side—kind of keeps to himself the majority of the time before simulations, but inside the sim, he's fantastic. How's your squad?"

Moore was the medic for Fourth Squad, which was led by Staff Sergeant Hamilton. He was from England, too, in the north, near Durham, but that was where the similarities ended. Where Moore was tall and lanky, Hamilton was short but large in the shoulders. Hamilton was someone you'd want to go pub crawling with, whereas Moore wanted to be pulled up to a fire reading a classic twentieth-century novel. The others in the squad either were fresh out of basic or had been in for a couple of years, but they all treated him with respect. Other than having to eventually deal with soldiers you had grown fond of dying, being a medic was one of the nicest positions. Everyone treated you nicely in your squad because at the end of the day, you were going to be the one that saved them.

That was why Moore had no problems when it came to the thought of having to save Kodiak or Hall's life. He was just a friendly person and got along well with most people, and he felt having that trait would serve him in the field when it came time to save lives.

"The whole squad's fine. They treat me better than they treat themselves sometimes," Moore replied.

"The benefits of being the one to save them," Kodiak chuckled.

"So other than sims, what have you been up to? Message the family?"

"I do sometimes, but honestly, there isn't much to say other than how much I love them and miss them. And all that does is make me sad." Kodiak shrugged.

"Yeah, I feel the same way with Lillianna sometimes, but then again, we have a lot to catch up on that we didn't have time for before I shipped out. Why not go to the party Hall is throwing tonight? Maybe let off some steam, find yourself in the arms of someone, perhaps?"

Kodiak just smiled. "I was actually going tonight. I'm headlining."

"Headlining what?" The smile faded from Moore's face.

"The fight," Kodiak replied, oblivious to Moore's worry.

"Against Skaggs? Are you insane?" Moore blurted out.

"Thanks for the confidence, buddy," Kodiak said.

"Oh, I have all the confidence in the universe you can kick his ass, Harrison. What I'm worried about is what will happen to you."

"Shoot, he don't hit that hard, Moore," Kodiak laughed.

"But you do, Harrison. *You* do. What if you disable him, or worse, kill him?"

"It ain't gonna get that far, Oliver."

"How do you know? Who will stop you if it does? Hall? I love the guy, but he's anything but someone who will step up to stop you from making a mistake."

"And who can? You?" Kodiak challenged.

"Who do you think made it possible to find those fuel cells on the *Currahee*?" Moore smiled.

"Moreau did, Doc. You were off floating around your moon station."

Moore ignored the harsh tone. "And who do you think gave Moreau the idea?"

Kodiak stared blankly at him, not understanding what he meant. Moore had kept in touch with almost everyone he liked from basic. It was true he'd mostly video messaged Hall and Kodiak during their time in advanced individual training, but he'd also messaged Moreau from time to time. When Kodiak hadn't been answering his calls for a few days, Moore had called Moreau to touch base, only to find out that Kodiak was in the brig for attempted murder. Moreau was smart—she knew there had to be some way to show that Kodiak was innocent, but she couldn't connect the dots, so Moore had helped. He'd told her to look through Skaggs's footlocker for the fuel cells. He was just lucky the idiot actually had hidden them there.

"It's true. I was in the room when he was videoing Moreau," Nova spoke up from the top of her bunk.

Kodiak looked up for a moment, not having realized she was there, and shook his head. "Damn, I had no idea," he finally said. "Why didn't you tell me?"

177

"You honestly had enough going on—I didn't want you getting concerned about outside help and me getting into trouble. I was just happy I could help."

Kodiak reached over with his large arms and wrapped Moore into a hug. He counted these moments as the big takeaways from joining the military. The initial goal had been to distance himself from his family, piss them off, and save as many lives as he could while doing it, but in doing so, he'd reconnected with the love of his life and made some of the best friends he could've asked for.

"So will you do it again?" Kodiak asked.

"Save your ass from killing Skaggs?" Moore sighed, giving in. "Yeah, I could help you with that. It'd probably be a lot easier in person than from behind a video terminal."

Kodiak gave him a playful punch in the chest and cheered. "Thanks, bud!"

Moore rubbed his chest—he knew have a bruise there in the morning, but he smiled. "Sure thing, mate."

Nova's feet landed next to them after she dropped down from her bunk. Her face was lit up with a huge smile. "So, you're going?" she asked, looking at Moore.

"Yeah, Nova. I'll go," Moore replied.

Nova squealed with happiness and ran off to the shower with a towel. "Yay!"

Kodiak looked over at Nova as she went out of sight and then turned back to Moore. "What was that?"

"She gets a little excited. Cara's been wanting me to go to this party all day and I've been brushing her off."

"Is there something there, or…?"

"Oh God, no. I'm happy with Lillianna and Nova knows that," Moore replied.

"Does she, though?" he asked, cocking his eye.

"Yes, mate, she does," Moore replied, but a little bit of doubt passed into his mind.

"All right. Well, you be careful. The girl looks lovestruck and you'd be smart to let her down quickly rather than draw things out."

"Wise words? Coming from a place you're familiar with?" Moore asked.

178

"Well, you know I had that girl Tara who sent me the Dear John letter while we were in basic. The thing is, she had all these dreams and aspirations built around what she had created in her head. It was a fantasy world that she wanted to live in. She saw me going into professional football, becoming a millionaire, living in a big house with a big family and some dogs. Man, it was a lot to take in, and I realized pretty quickly I didn't want any of that. When I told her I'd joined the military, she didn't take that well at all, but she went along with it. I knew right then and there it wasn't going to last, and I should've ended it before I left. Then when I got her letter in basic, it actually hurt ten times worse. I don't know why—I still didn't want to be with her and I know now that it was for the best—but at the time I was torn up. So, like I said, just rip the band-aid off, brother. Life will be easier."

Moore thought about it and nodded. He knew Kodiak was right, and if he took his blinders off, he might realize from time to time she acted differently with him. He surmised it to be a schoolgirl crush. Nova was a few years younger than him, still a little on the naive side, but that was all he made of it. She was always the one who brought up Lillianna, which could have brought his guard down some, but he always treated Nova like a kid sister, not a lover.

Kodiak stood and patted Moore on the shoulder as he walked by. "I appreciate you helping me out, Ollie. I'm gonna need that leash tonight, and it's a little better knowing you'll be the one holding it."

The door opened and Kodiak walked out as Nova came out of the shower, hair dripping wet, in only a towel. "Did he just say something about you holding him on a leash?"

Moore rolled his eyes.

"'Cause, like, I totally understand if you have a kink for that—I'm not judging."

Moore tossed a pillow from his bed at her and she did a turn, gracefully dodging the projectile. "You're gonna need to try a little harder if you wanna take me out, Moore."

"Is that a challenge?" Moore laughed.

"Is that a threat?" She smiled back.

Moore checked himself. He didn't know if it was because of the talk he'd just had with Kodiak, but it sat differently with him when she said that. "Hey, you know I love you like a sister, right?"

Nova rolled her eyes. "Is this an 'I love you but not like that' speech? Because if it is, I don't want to hear it. I know you and Lillianna are together, despite the distance, and I'm not gonna be the one to get in the way of that."

Relief washed over Moore. "Good to hear, Nova. Good to hear."

Chapter 25
Kodiak

Hall and the mortars had outdone themselves. The conference room was huge, most likely one that was used for larger briefings by the battalion commander and his staff. The prospect of throwing a party in such an area should have scared people away, but it ended up being one of the more secluded areas on the ship. The guard standing outside the corridor's access didn't so much as look up as First Platoon began filing in one squad at a time. Inside the room, music blared from ten personal speakers provided by some of the soldiers in attendance.

The bar was set up at the end of the long conference table with ten large kegs underneath. That was where Kodiak found himself first. He had seen Skaggs as he'd entered the party, and an awful taste had found its way into his mouth. The beer was the same watered-down bullshit from the enlisted bar, but it still worked great to calm him down. Hall was busy trying to serve drinks and make sure everything was in order, and his chaotic movements made Kodiak laugh.

Hall very rarely got invested in something, but when he did, he went all out. He was happiest when he was doing something he loved to do. Throwing a party must have been a little taste of home for him. Kodiak looked into his empty cup and shot more beer into it from one of the keg spouts, then looked back toward the ring in the middle of the room. The ropes around the four pillars that made up the ring were an entanglement of 550 cord and Velcro strap. On the ground were a few of the thin foam mattresses from the sleeping quarters. It wasn't pretty, but it would serve its purpose.

Already, bets were being placed on the fight, and although he tried to ignore the different names being called, he couldn't stop himself from counting. Very few of the bets were going for Skaggs, which caused him to smile, but the fact remained, he didn't know how to actually fight. He had done well in combatives, but only because he could take people to the ground and use his muscles to his advantage. He could throw strikes and could even send a heavy kick to someone's chest if he needed, but there were absolutely no mechanics to it.

Meanwhile, Skaggs was in a corner, shadowboxing a wall. He had good form and was striking very fast, and a thought formed in Kodiak's mind—what if Skaggs got him? He was confident that one of his blows could knock Skaggs to the ground, and from there he'd easily overpower him, but Skaggs was fast. He'd need to prioritize getting him onto the ground as fast as possible.

"Nervous?" someone asked beside him.

Kodiak turned to see Moreau standing next to him. "Anxious," he replied.

"Good. Just do me a favor and don't kill the guy. Don't get me wrong, I wouldn't shed a single tear, but they'd lock you up and throw away the key. I've grown rather fond of your face—I'd hate to lose it this soon."

Kodiak did a double take and almost choked on his beer. "What?"

"Calm down, soldier. Win the fight first. Then we'll talk." Moreau winked and walked off into the crowd.

Kodiak pressed off from the bar to go after her when Hall grabbed him by the shoulder. "Yo, Bear. It's time!"

Kodiak looked over to Hall and noticed everyone crowding around the ring. "Now?"

"Yeah, dude. We can't be in here all night—we could get caught. Your fight's on, so let's do this!" Hall laughed as he pushed Kodiak toward the ring.

When Kodiak got alongside the ropes, Hall helped tape up his fingers and wrists. On the other side of the ring, Skaggs was taping his own. It was painfully obvious who the favored fighter was and who had no one in their corner. If Kodiak wasn't so damn angry at the kid, he might have felt bad, but Skaggs had gone too far, and Kodiak had to settle it.

With his fingers and wrists taped, he ducked underneath the ropes and walked into the ring. The foam mattresses were horrible to stand on and very unstable. He wanted to turn and ask Hall if they could get rid of the mattresses, but the music had turned off. Using a microphone connected to the speakers, Hall introduced the two fighters. If the conference room hadn't included a noise dampener, Kodiak would've been freaking out because Hall's voice was booming.

"Fighting in this corner," Hall shouted, pointing at Kodiak, "standing at six feet and six inches, weighing in at two hundred and ten pounds of solid muscle, hailing from the ranches of Texas, Harrison Kodiak!"

Kodiak raised his fist into the air but was laughing as the crowd hooted and hollered. In truth, Kodiak was six feet four inches and only weighed two hundred pounds, but Hall had gotten pretty close seeing as he hadn't even asked Kodiak what the right information was.

Hall turned and looked towards Skaggs, who stood alone on the other side. "The opposing fighter, standing at five foot whatever, one hundred and something pounds, and hailing from who cares, Tyler 'The Quagmire' Skaggs!"

Cheers erupted around the ring, and despite the lackluster introduction, Skaggs put his fist into the air as well. Kodiak could hear some boos, and although he tried not to, he had to give Skaggs credit for ignoring a crowd that was heavily against him. The referee for the fight was a sergeant from Third Squad who now stood in the middle of the ring, waving for the two fighters to approach.

Skaggs put his fist out to bump it with Kodiak's. "Somehow you keep finding a way to get out of trouble. But that ends tonight, Bear." Skaggs smiled.

Kodiak gave his own fierce smile back. "You keep smiling, Skaggs, 'cause you ain't gonna have any teeth left when I get done with you," Kodiak replied as he bumped his fist against Skaggs's and walked back to his corner.

Skaggs's smile faded as he backed up toward his corner, never taking his eyes off Kodiak. Harrison Kodiak kept smiling and wondered if, at the last moment, Skaggs would withdraw from the fight, but he remained in his own corner, alone, with his fists up in front of him.

When the bell rang, Kodiak walked forward and met Skaggs in the middle. His head bobbed back and forth, but he didn't want to be the first one to take a shot. He felt that he could easily take Skaggs and would probably have the advantage if he just swarmed him, but something was telling him to bide his time. Staff Sergeant Muleskin had told Kodiak at one point to slow everything down and let his enemy make the first mistake. From that mistake, he'd find a weakness, and from that weakness he'd find victory. At the time he had been talking about Zodarks and combat, but Kodiak felt it applied to this scenario just as much.

Skaggs made the first move. He cheated left but struck with his right hand toward Kodiak's head, but Kodiak was able to step back and watch the punch miss. Skaggs was fast, something he had noticed before the fight when Skaggs had been shadowboxing the wall, but he could use that to his advantage. Skaggs was desperate to land a decisive blow, which was evident in the way he'd thrown his entire weight into that punch.

Kodiak now stepped forward. With every step he took, Skaggs moved back, wanting to keep the distance between the two. Kodiak had the reach on him and quickly realized that all the cards were in his favor. He let loose with a two-punch combination that connected with Skaggs, who stepped back and shook his head.

He was surprised at how Skaggs had taken the hits. They weren't thrown with all of his power, but they weren't soft, and Skaggs just shrugged them off, so Kodiak pressed on. Moving forward again, he set himself up to throw another punch straight into Skaggs's nose, but the shorter man planted his back foot and struck out with a kick to Kodiak's stomach. The top of Skaggs's foot connected hard, and Kodiak felt the air leave his lungs as he stumbled back.

He could now hear the crowd roaring behind him as he felt the ropes against his back. Hall was screaming something at him, but Kodiak did his best to tune out all the noise as he gathered himself. He had no interest in hearing any tips from his friend—all it would do was confuse him. He had the height advantage, the weight advantage, and the wingspan on Skaggs. Now it was up to him to figure out how to expose him.

It didn't take long as Skaggs, who'd grown more confident after his first kick, tried to land another one. This time Kodiak caught his leg, letting his stomach absorb the hit, and lifted. Skaggs lost his balance and fell onto his back, but as Kodiak dropped his body to get on top, Skaggs pushed himself out of danger and back to his feet. Without time to react, Kodiak watched as another kick came towards his head. He tossed himself to the side with little grace, just to get away from the attack. Quickly getting to his feet, he reset himself, but Skaggs continued forward, the smaller man's confidence growing.

Kodiak had had enough. It was his turn to go on the attack. Planting his foot and swinging, he struck out with his own kick and made contact with Skaggs's leg, causing him to stumble. Not wanting to be lured into another trap, Kodiak struck with his leg again, once again making contact with the same leg. Skaggs was stumbling now, finding it hard to put pressure on the leg, and Kodiak used his lack of maneuverability to his advantage. He moved forward, shortening the ground between them until he was right on top.

His first punch caught Skaggs in the left cheek. The next punch was an uppercut to the jaw and Skaggs was on his back. The advantage was fully on Kodiak's side as he dropped on top of the smaller man and sent his fist down toward the man's head. Once again, Skaggs, despite being at a disadvantage, made the most out of it. He grabbed onto the back of Kodiak's neck and, with a strength Kodiak hadn't expected, pulled him down.

"Didn't see that coming, did you, Kodiak?" Skaggs hissed as he drove his forehead into Kodiak's.

The blow glanced off Kodiak's eyebrow and did little to faze him. "Just loosening you up, Skaggs."

Kodiak delivered his own headbutt, which connected perfectly with Skaggs's forehead. The blow also sent stars into Kodiak's vision as he stood and stepped back, wanting to put a little bit of distance between himself and Skaggs in case the blow wasn't as bad for him. Skaggs was still lying there, and when Kodiak's vision focused, he saw that Skaggs's eyes were all over the place.

That was the advantage he needed to finish the fight. Not wanting it to go on any longer, Kodiak felt a bloodlust rush inside his veins. Skaggs had not only tried to kill him and their team but had then tried to frame Kodiak for murder. Even after he'd been found responsible, nothing had happened to him, and that was beyond unfair. Kodiak's mother always said that the world wasn't fair, and he'd do well to remember it. His grandfather, however, had said something that stuck with him more than anything his parents had said. On a cold winter night, he'd sat on his grandfather's lap on the back porch of his home as he'd said, "Your mom is right, Harrison—the world isn't fair and it is indeed important to remember that, but it's also important to remember that if there is injustice, it will take hard men to bring about justice."

Kodiak fell into a blind rage.

He dropped on top of Skaggs and pinned his legs and arms to his side. "You deserve more than this, but it'll have to do."

Now he heard the cheers, a year's worth of pent-up aggression from his platoon as they reveled in the carnal blood sport of man. Kodiak dropped punch after punch, feeling Skaggs's face bounce against his knuckles. The more he struck, the more the skin broke, the more the blood sprayed, the more Kodiak felt that justice was being served.

Chapter 26
Hall

Aiden Hall felt good about his announcing before the match. Cheers had erupted from the crowd when both fighters had been introduced, and he'd even gotten a few laughs when he'd announced Skaggs. The moment he'd stepped from the ring and grabbed himself another beer, the fight had begun. The first thing he'd noticed was how prepared Skaggs had looked. If he was being honest, he'd thought the annoying little rat was going to get pounded into the ground right off the bat, but at the start of the match, he was making some solid contact.

The party itself was turning out to be a major success, but it was beyond stressful. Between getting everyone into the conference room without raising any alarms and smuggling in kegs of beer, his stress levels were at an all-time high. Every time bright light flooded the doorway, he'd feel his breath catch in his throat, only to see some private late to the party. If any of the command staff found them—or God forbid, someone from the ship's command—heads would roll. This wasn't an invasion force where they'd need all hands on deck—the higher-ups could easily sacrifice one or two nobody privates to set an example. Hall knew he'd be at the top of the list.

"Hell of a party, Hall. I'll give ya that," Sergeant Richards said, taking a pull from a silver flask.

He had been surprised to see Richards walk into the party earlier that night. At first, he'd thought for sure he was there to spy for Staff Sergeant McHenry, or worse, the platoon's lieutenant, but after seeing him chase beer down with the contents of his flask for the last hour and a half, he was sure it was kosher. Hall looked at the flask as Richards put it back in his pocket. The silver container was about palm-size and had the Apollo Company crest on the front.

"Coming from you, that's one hell of a compliment," Hall replied.

"You bet your ass it is," Richards replied.

"You bet on the fight? My boy Kodiak is the big fella in there."

"I'm not a gambler. Life's enough of a gamble."

Hall nodded. "Pretty deep statement there, Sergeant."

"I can be deep when I want to, cherry. I just don't need to around you," Richards replied.

"What do you mean?" Hall asked, turning to face his team leader.

"Well, let me put it this way. When someone who normally doesn't come off as a Shakespearean with a heart of gold and the brain of a poet all of a sudden wows you, it means they want something from you. In my case, I'm just trying to find the next piece of ass I can tear up. If that means I have to quote Chaucer or Angelou, then so be it."

"You lost me at Chaucer, Sergeant," Hall replied. He had never been much for reading, especially poetry.

"I don't doubt that, Private. Regardless, good party, but you might want to stop the fight. It looks like your buddy over there is about to kill whoever the other kid is."

Hall looked up from the table and saw Kodiak on top of Skaggs, dropping one punch after another into the other's face. He immediately bounced up from the table and tore through the crowd.

"Kodiak, stop!" he yelled as he jumped over the ropes.

Moreau was now there at his side in a flash, tearing Kodiak off Skaggs.

"I got him," Moreau said as she led Kodiak to the corner.

Hall turned to the sergeant from Third Squad who was refereeing the match. "You could've stopped the fight, asshole. What's wrong with you?"

He didn't wait for an answer and turned to look at Skaggs, who was still lying motionless on the mat. He wanted to go over and check on Kodiak, but if Skaggs died, they'd all be screwed. The drill sergeants had always said "do what your rank can afford" when talking to their recruits about all the different ways one could screw up. He was pretty sure throwing a party for an entire platoon, with alcohol and a fight amongst service members that also included gambling, was probably grounds for some bad punishment. Nothing like getting put up against a wall and shot, but hard labor would suck. In hindsight, it was pretty dumb for him to have thrown this party when the outcome could have been the exact same thing he'd joined the military to avoid.

"Is he dead?" Oliver Moore's voice came from behind Hall.

Hall turned and saw his friend. "I hope not. Might be a little difficult to explain this one away."

"You're right about that, mate," Moore replied and knelt down next to Skaggs.

Hall followed suit and checked for a pulse. Luckily, he felt the rhythmic thumping of Skaggs's artery pushing back against his fingers and let out a sigh of relief. "Well, he's not dead."

Moore put his fingers to Skaggs's throat and nodded. "Yeah, very much alive. It's a shame, though." Moore looked over to Hall. "It would've been proper fun throwing him down a staircase and pretending he fell."

Hall let out a howling laugh. "You're damn sure right about that."

Hall had only heard Moore crack a joke once or twice since meeting him. They always came unexpectedly and at times that maybe weren't so appropriate, but when they did come, it always got a laugh out of him. Hall thought it might be because Moore was usually so reserved and proper. He admired the man for that—and not just that, but the many other things Moore had done in his life. Hall had had no choice—it was either prison or the military. At the time, the Republic hadn't even known what Zodarks were, let alone been at war with them, so he'd felt pretty confident in taking military service over being stuck in a seven-by-seven-foot cell. Oliver Moore, on the other hand, was practically royalty. His family owned a mansion, lived on a massive plot of land, and even had butlers, cooks, and maids. He could have been home right now with his feet propped up on the couch, lounging in his softest of bathrobes. Instead, he was kneeling beside Hall, checking to make sure their friend hadn't just killed someone.

Hall laughed again and shook his head. "What a life."

Moore laughed as well. "What a life is right, mate." He stood and moved to where Skaggs's head was. "Well, let's get this sack of space rocks to the medical bay so I can fix him up."

"We can do that? Won't we get caught?" Hall asked.

"Oh yeah. There's a service elevator to be used in the case of a mass casualty event that leads directly to the med bay floor. I also happen to be friends with the person on duty tonight." Moore winked.

"Who?" Hall asked.

"Nova," Moore replied.

Hall grabbed Skaggs's legs and began walking with Moore towards the door. "I thought she was coming out to the fights with you."

Moore pointed with his head towards the bar, where Corporal Martin, Second Squad's medic, sat. "Corporal Martin over there found out about the party. As punishment, she made Nova take her shift at the clinic while she came to investigate."

"Investigate?" Hall almost dropped Skaggs.

"Calm down, mate, she only said that to make it sound good. In reality, she's been drinking half the grunts under the table all night," Moore replied.

The two exited the conference room and entered the brightly lit corridor that stretched in both directions until it curved seamlessly out of view. They waddled down the hall towards the service elevator, finally approaching the door the guard was standing behind. Hall held his breath as the doors opened and the guard continued to sit there with his feet kicked up on the counter, staring at them.

"What happened to him?" the guard asked.

"He lost the fight," Hall answered.

"OK." The guard shrugged. "Just make sure I get my cut by the end of the night."

Hall dropped Skaggs's legs with a loud thud and walked over to the table. Removing his personal device, he opened his bank account and selected the amount owed to the guard. The guard smiled and removed his and held it out. Hall tapped his device to the guard's and transferred the funds.

"Pleasure doing business, gentlemen," the guard replied and went back to reading his book.

Hall picked the unconscious man's legs back up, and they continued down the hall and into the service elevator. Moore plugged in his code, and the lift took off through the bowels of the ship. When the doors dinged and opened, they lugged Skaggs into the first open room and dropped him on the table. Moore attached electrodes to Skaggs's body and a bunch of information crossed the screen connected to the nodes. It might as well have been Martian slang for all Hall knew, but Moore seemed to understand.

"All vitals look good. Just knocked out," Moore confirmed.

"You sure he's not gonna have any brain damage or something? Kodiak was taking it to him—I mean, I hate the guy and even I was feeling a little bit bad."

"I'm sure. Other than bruises and swelling, he'll be all right," Moore reassured him.

The door to the room opened and Hall turned, expecting the worst. Instead, he saw the medic, Cara Nova, standing in the doorway. She wasn't wearing the usual civilian attire he'd seen her in at the bar but instead white medical scrubs.

She scratched the shaved side of her head and smiled. "What happened to this guy?"

"Kodiak got a little bit of payback in the ring," Moore replied.

Nova's face dropped. "Oh. How was it?"

"The fight?" Hall asked, ready to go into all the details.

"The party," Nova corrected.

"It was a blast!" Hall answered. "We couldn't get any liquor, but—"

"Hall, don't you need to get back there and run everybody out before someone important shows up?" Moore cut him off.

He was confused. He could've spent the next hour talking all about the party and how awesome it was. Even Moore had had an absolute blast. No brawls had broken out, besides the scheduled one, and everyone was jamming out to the music. It was absolutely perfect. Hall looked at Nova and then back to Moore as he realized what was happening. Looking at Nova a little closer, he could see she was more disappointed than excited.

"Oh shit, I'm sorry, I wasn't thinking about—" Hall tried to explain.

"It's all good, go clear the party out," Moore said.

He was right—Hall did need to get back to the party and clear everyone out before the next guard shift, and he didn't want to upset Nova any more than he already had. Nodding, he took his leave and left the clinic floor. On the way back down the elevator, he thought about how he was going to get everyone out of that conference room, clean everything up, and get back to quarters before curfew. It was going to be a long damn night.

Chapter 27
Moore

Oliver Moore watched his friend Aiden Hall walk out of the clinic and into the elevator. He hadn't had any idea that Nova couldn't stop talking about the party for the past few days. Still, Moore didn't need Hall going on a rant about how amazing the party was. Nova wouldn't want to hear about it, and Moore didn't need to. All he wanted to do now was wake Skaggs up and go to bed.

The room they were in was where soldiers and sailors came for sick call or to get prescriptions filled. The other wings on the deck housed several medical units from admin to intensive care and could handle almost any mass casualty event both on the ship and on the surface of a planet. He had worked shifts in the clinic all the time and practically lived on the medical deck during his platoon's work rotation, but he still hadn't seen half the areas.

Nova walked over to the bed. "So what are we gonna do about him?"

"Well, first," Moore said, removing a medical injector from a bin, "we're gonna wake him up."

He stabbed the injector into Skaggs's thigh and dispensed a cocktail that would wake the unconscious man up while keeping the pain down. The last thing he needed was for Skaggs to wake up, feel all the pain Kodiak had inflicted, and then die from shock.

The man's eyes fluttered open as the drugs began working their magic. Slowly Skaggs stirred and sat up, his eyes focusing on the two figures in the room. "Where am I?" he asked.

"You're at the clinic. I'm just gonna dress up some of these cuts, apply some Skin-Rejuv gel and get you on your way," Moore replied.

"How bad is it?"

"It's honestly nothing—I've dealt with worse injuries during training sessions. Just a few cuts from the punches. But because of modern medicine"—Moore shook a small cylindrical device in his hand—"we'll have you patched up in a few minutes."

Moore cleaned the few cuts Skaggs had on his face and stopped the bleeding with the same coagulant gel medics used to seal wounds on a battlefield. Once the gel entered any open wound, it would begin to cauterize and stop any external and even internal blood flow. That would, in theory, buy the casualty more time while they were moved to a field hospital or back to a ship. In a medical clinic, they kept tiny pouches of the gel for situations just like this.

After stopping the bleeding, Moore applied a skin-healing antibiotic cream that would clean the wound and rejuvenate the skin cells. Within a few hours, the scars would be gone. It only worked on smaller cuts or shallow wounds—for larger lacerations, the solution was worthless, but even if it wasn't, he was sure most soldiers would like to keep battle scars.

"Did I win?" Skaggs asked.

Moore stopped himself short of laughing and glanced around the room. "Does it look like you won?"

"True. Hey, why are you doing this?" he asked.

"Why am I doing what?" Moore asked.

"Fixing me up. You're Kodiak's pal, so why are you fixing me up?" Although Skaggs didn't touch him, Moore felt like he was poking him in the chest with each word he pronounced.

"It's my job," Moore said. If he was being honest with himself, he just wanted Skaggs to shut up.

"No. Don't play that card, Moore. You might have been the quiet one in the back while Kodiak and Hall bounced around like a couple of clowns, but you're still all friendly with them, so why help me? Pity?"

"Not pity," Moore answered back rather quickly. "I'm doing this because tomorrow, when you're limping around and your sergeant asks what happened, you can say you slept wrong, and he'll be none the wiser. Your cuts will be healed, your bruises faded, and no one will know why you're hurting so much on the inside."

"What's stopping me from telling my sergeant what happened?" Skaggs asked, his face turning a shade of crimson.

"Nothing at all," Moore answered truthfully. "But no one will believe you."

Moore ignored his open mouth and finished applying a liberal amount of coagulant gel into the cut over Skaggs's left eye. "From what I've heard, you've made just about as many friends here as you did when you were in basic. Your new platoon despises you like we did. I'd go into a whole speech about how you could use this as a teaching moment, change your ways, and become a better member of this unit, but I doubt that'll ever happen."

Skaggs leapt to his feet and stood as tall as he could, pushing his chest out and clenching his fists. Moore admitted that he might have gone a little too far with the insults, especially because it had gotten Skaggs all riled up and he was now threatening physical violence.

Moore looked down at the clenched fists, took a slow breath to calm the spike of adrenaline that pumped into his veins, and smiled. "You're good to go, Private Skaggs. I hope I never see you again in this clinic."

Skaggs just stared at him for a minute and Moore began to think he really was going to throw a punch, but after a few more tense moments, he turned and headed toward the door. Before he could walk out, Nova stepped in his way. Moore had forgotten she was there for a moment, especially during his heated discussion with Skaggs, but now the medic made herself known by moving her face inches from Skaggs.

She raised a surgical knife up to the man's throat and hissed, "If I sniff out even the faintest of rumors that you went and started blabbering to your unit about tonight, I'll slit your throat and call it a suicide. Got it?"

Skaggs once-crimson face turned pale white, and his shoulders sank. He only nodded in defeat and sulked out of the clinic. Nova turned to Moore and shrugged, giving him a wide smile as she placed the surgical tool back onto a tray.

"A little much," Moore said, but he smiled to show he wasn't upset.

"Screw him. After what you said he did to Kodiak, to his own squad, and for what? Because he squandered his chance at being platoon leader in basic training? He deserves worse than what he got."

Moore admired Nova's loyalty to her friends and the Republic military. She had come from a place that traditionally despised the Republic or in the less severe case was indifferent. That fact alone had made it hard for her to fit in when she and Moore had first met, but over time, every soldier she'd encountered had grown to appreciate her in some way or another. Moore knew he did.

"I know he does," Moore sighed, "but he of all people is not worth getting thrown into a cell for the rest of your life. I think we got our point across, and honestly, I don't think we'll have to wait very long to see the results we deserve."

"Why do you say that?" she asked.

Moore forgot how innocent she could be at times and smiled. "We go planetside in less than a month. No matter how slippery he is, he won't be able to stay out of the fight, and when that time comes, he'll either die as the Zodarks tear him apart or get fragged by one of the dozens of people he's pissed off along the way."

"Damn. We've been floating around on this space turd for so long I forgot just how close planetside actually was." She shifted her weight and leaned against the wall. "Do you think we'll be able to do it?" she asked.

"Do what?"

"Our job," she responded seriously.

"Yes, Cara. We've trained as hard as we possibly can over the past year. We'll be ready," Moore answered confidently.

She still didn't seem convinced. "Will *I* be ready?"

Moore took the chance to give her a hug. It was platonic, brotherly, loving. "I've seen you stabilize patients in the simulator with your eyes closed. You can do it, and our training will kick in. Just focus on the job, everything else is noise."

"That's easy for you to say. I've never once seen you get scared, but even in a simulator, those blue things terrify me."

"I'm scared, Nova. Terrified to my core, but I have a job to do. If I don't do what's expected of me and do it right, people will die, and if I don't do it at all, even more will die. For better or for worse, we have no choice. We are in another solar system; in a couple of weeks, we'll look up at a sun that we've never seen before. God knows this is not what I signed up for, but it's the hand we've been dealt."

Nova looked at him for a moment and seemed to shake the sudden nerves away. She smiled. "Got any aces up your sleeve, perhaps?"

Chapter 28
Kodiak

RNS *Boxer*
In Orbit Above New Eden

The RNS *Boxer* had dropped out of slip space a month earlier. All of Apollo Company had expected to be planetside by now, but they were quickly learning the rules of space travel, along with everyone else. Harrison Kodiak remembered first laying eyes on New Eden as the days had clicked closer towards planetside. The large blue planet mirrored Earth in a lot of ways, so much so that until you were close enough to make out the continents, your brain tricked you into thinking you were back in the Sol System. Once you were in orbit, the perspective changed.

When night fell across the planet, there was no light pollution dotting the darkness from space to remind those above that there were cities below. Kodiak had spent his entire life looking up at the moon every night, seeing lines of lights etched into its surface. When he'd trained on the *Currahee*, he'd seen the same exact thing down on Earth if not tenfold what was on the moon, but on New Eden there was nothing but darkness.

He knew from the briefings that there were several mining villages that covered the sector of the continent they'd be landing on, along with several military installations and spaceports. Even with all that activity, you couldn't see their light from space. At first it had been peaceful, but as they drew closer, radio traffic from the planet was picked up. He began sitting in his platoon's conference room for hours with the rest as they listened to patrols and other operations taking place on the planet's surface. At first, it was morbid curiosity that kept him glued to his seat for hours on end, but over time, he used the sessions as a training tool. From the radio traffic below, one thing was certain: fighting the Zodarks was pure chaos.

"This is the last time I'm gonna say this. First Squad, if your weapons and rucksacks are not properly stowed in the correct positions, you're gonna have a bad time. Imagine the message I'd have to send to Mommy and Daddy, explaining that it wasn't the Zodarks who claimed their child's life in the heat of battle but an unsecured rifle that decided to make your face its new home on entry." Staff Sergeant Yazzie

Muleskin walked up and down the length of the Osprey dropship, checking to make sure all of his soldiers' weapons were locked into their magnetic lock plates.

"I ain't got no momma, Sergeant Muleskin!" Garza shouted from his seat next to Kodiak.

"Good! One less person to inevitably disappoint, Garza. Congratulations."

Muleskin's response got a roar of laughter from the others, and even Garza chuckled and shook his head. "Thank you, Sergeant," he responded.

Apollo Company was officially about to become the first boots on the planet for the 331st Infantry Regiment, and Kodiak's squad was anxious to finally leave the confines of the *Boxer* and roam. Their first stop was going to be Forward Operating Base Edwards, named after the first Republic soldier killed in the conflict against the Zodarks, where they'd become acclimated to the planet's environment and its wildlife.

Kodiak tugged on his rifle next to him to make sure the magnetic locks held it firmly in place, and when he was confident it'd stay put on the ride down, he focused on the rucksack strapped above. The name tape stitched onto the fabric of the rucksack stared back at him, and he nodded to himself that the pack was secured correctly. In basic training, they'd trained in crash drills that had seen them strapped inside a hollowed-out Osprey and spun in circles. Of course, nothing had been strapped down inside, so the entire time, Kodiak had been getting pelted by anything and everything the drill sergeants could fit inside the craft. They said it was to teach them the importance of securing their gear. At the time, he'd thought it was just another excuse for them to haze recruits. But now, as he checked for a third time, he realized the message had sunk in.

"Well, now if your rucksack comes down and kills someone, you'll be really embarrassed," Moreau teased him from the other seat next to him.

Kodiak laughed. "It's always good to double-check."

"I agree, but a fourth, fifth, sixth time? Calm down, we aren't dropping into a hot landing zone." Moreau patted his leg and slipped on her helmet. The visor was still transparent, and he could see the soft blue eyes staring back at him.

"I heard that an Osprey got hit on the way down for a supply run. Zodark anti-aircraft knocked it right out of the sky," Sergeant Woods chuckled as he stowed his weapon and took his seat across from Kodiak.

"Zodarks only light up the sky with anti-aircraft when it's an invasion force or they're trying to take out bombing runs. Troop transports aren't normally targeted," Muleskin broke in. "Luckily for us, the initial invasion went to plan while you were all pussy-footin' around on the *Boxer*. Many of the continents on New Eden are under Republic control, but since Apollo Company asked politely, we will be setting up shop on a contested continent. This is gonna be a fight on their turf and by their rules. They like to fight on the ground, so it's a damn good thing we do too. Now stow it and let's get to the dance."

The lights in the cabin dimmed until only the red glow from the vacuum warning light shone. The Osprey had been pressurized and the massive shuttle bay doors opened to the black void of space. Kodiak had grown to love drops as the training had gone on, but even then, it was no match for the feeling of weightlessness one experienced before hitting a planet's atmosphere. Aboard the *Currahee*, he'd participated in numerous drops, but always formal ones as part of training. They had hundreds of drops a day and they weren't going to take the time to let you enjoy your surroundings on the way planetside. As soon as the dropship left the *Currahee*, it would accelerate toward Earth's atmosphere and the show was on. When it came to an actual planet insertion into a war zone, the insertion method had to be precise.

The Osprey lifted off the deck of the shuttle bay and was expertly flown by the Republic pilots in formation until all the dropships had launched. Flying in a loose formation, the twenty Osprey dropships carrying Apollo Company and all their supplies for their three-month planetside rotation, or PLANRO, moved in concert towards New Eden.

Deployments worked differently than what he had learned while at Benning. He had always been told that units were called to war zones on nine-to-twelve-month deployments back on Earth. After that, they would rotate back home. That unit would then be lucky if they deployed again in the next two years. While Apollo Company was in transit to New Eden, a lot of rules had been changed and Kodiak had had to re-sign his enlistment contract midflight. Deployments could now last upwards of two years, not counting travel to and from the systems. Once deployed planetside, an infantry company would then take part in multiple

PLANROs, spending a year on New Eden and then one to two months back on board their home ship.

Apparently, after only six months into the war, the Republic Operational Command of New Eden had decided to implement a lottery system. If you had more than three months' planetside time, you were eligible for an R&R back on Earth. One soldier from each company was selected by the company commander and that name would be put into the lottery. The name of the one lucky soldier was then picked by Republic Operational Command of New Eden or ROCNE and would receive a ticket home, with a return ticket to match. They only selected one soldier every four months, and out of hundreds of thousands of names, your chance of being selected was virtually zero. For all the others, there were only three other options: survive your deployment, get horrifically wounded to the point where even modern medicine couldn't fix you, or die. From the rumors, dying was the easiest option.

The dropship buffeted and bounced as sound returned and the Osprey broke the sound barrier, busting through New Eden's atmosphere. The drop was as intense as Kodiak had remembered. His stomach seemed to climb into his chest, and it took everything in him not to scream or yelp. Instead, he did what everyone else did, and that was clench and make a face that looked like he was severely constipated.

Soon, the transport leveled out and began to glide smoothly in the sky above what would be their home for the next three months. Immediately, First Squad all clambered to connect to the camera attached to the outside of the dropship to get their first look at the planet. Kodiak was no exception as he turned his visor's transparency off and connected to the video feed on his HUD. The color was absolutely brilliant and took his breath away. He had always thought Earth was beautiful—sure, when you got to the cities and their suburbs, it was cluttered, but when you experienced the expansive countrysides, you could find real beauty. But even the snowcapped San Juan mountains were no match for the sprawling green fields of New Eden.

The ground was a mismatch of rolling emerald fields that covered miles into deep rocky mountain valleys covered in colorful trees and plants. The forests were dense and covered whitecapped rapids on expansive rivers that snaked through the landscape like coursing veins. As the Osprey drew closer, Kodiak could make out herds of galloping animals that were unlike anything he'd ever seen before. The movements looked like those of a gazelle, but the heads were topped by three razor-sharp bones shaped like curved blades. Birds soared in formation below, and at first, they looked like eagles to Harrison, but as the Osprey drew closer, he realized they were only a little smaller than the craft he was riding in. Their beaks hooked down and their talons were massive. Their feathers changed color as they crossed the landscape below, no doubt acting as a natural camouflage to mask their approach to prey.

As the dropship angled its way into a valley, the ground suddenly dropped away into a deep canyon covered in rolling fields of emerald grass. Open ground spread out around them for miles and at the canyon's center stood a large military installation. Radar communication towers marked the open fields to the base's east, and to its west were rows upon rows of solar panels. The base held landing pads, guard towers, and hundreds of buildings cramped within the high walls that surrounded the massive compound. If Kodiak was being honest, it looked like a massive stain on a beautiful canvas.

At first when they had learned about the forward operating base's location, a lot of the more experienced soldiers had thought they'd hate the spot. It was billed as having large cliff faces on every side. Seeing the area from a bird's-eye view, they noticed just how much space was between the FOB and the canyon walls, which put their minds at ease. The Zodarks would not be able to shoot down into the base, and attempts to flank the area would be met by heavy resistance from the several outposts placed around the area.

When it was their Osprey's turn to land, Kodiak disconnected the camera link and made sure he was ready to disembark. Once on the deck, First Squad stood and grabbed their rucksacks and weapons as the back hatch of the Osprey dropped. One by one, they filed out in their teams and stood in line as officers shouted directions on where to go. In all the commotion, he noticed Sergeant Muleskin signaling for his squad to move in the direction where other fresh arrivals were headed, so Kodiak shouldered his bag and fell in line.

The barracks were large three-story steel buildings that housed the rotating companies coming from up the well. The dropships that had dispensed Kodiak's company were now loading the last company of the 92nd Infantry Regiment from the RNS *Glasgow*. Apollo Company were their replacements. They were now the lucky ones who would be headed back to Earth. Kodiak had to admit, the thought made him immediately jealous.

Each section was marked with four buildings standing in two-by-two square configurations. One building housed an entire platoon, with one squad of three teams having a floor to themselves. The buildings were so close that the company before them had tied large sheets of camouflage material to each building, creating a shaded overhang above the walkways where tables and chairs sat. It was oddly familiar for Kodiak, who immediately had thoughts of nightly cookouts when not on duty.

As they walked into Building 1141, Kodiak's platoon leader, Second Lieutenant Samantha Cooley, began giving out living assignments. First Squad would be housed on the first floor along with the command staff, which almost made Kodiak groan out loud. It wasn't like he was already planning on doing something stupid; he just didn't like the idea that he could accidentally bump into his squad leader, platoon sergeant, or platoon leader at any moment during the day.

Alpha Team took the aptly named A wing that stretched down a long hallway with rooms on either side of the wall. As they entered the hallway, Kodiak began counting doors and a smile crossed his face when he got above three. Each soldier had his or her own room.

Kodiak stopped in front of the second door on the right and stared at his name displayed on the digital scanner in front of him. He tried waving his hand in front of the scanner, but nothing happened. He hadn't received a key when he'd arrived, so he looked at the others to see if they had the same issue. He smiled when he realized they did. He then looked down the hallway, past the building lobby, toward the other wing. Sergeant Casper of Bravo Team had removed his personal device and tapped it onto the scanner. Kodiak frowned when he watched the door slide open for Casper and shook his head at how painfully obvious it was.

Removing his own device, he tapped it against the scanner and the door slid open. "Good afternoon, Private First Class Kodiak," came a synthesized female voice from the scanner.

"Thank you?" Kodiak replied.

"It's an automated response, idiot," Sergeant Woods called from down the hall as he tapped his own device and walked into his room.

Kodiak closed his eyes and sighed as he walked into his own room and waved the door closed. The lights came on as he entered and then dimmed to an optimal setting for his eyes to adjust. It was a plain room with a small kitchen, bed, couch, terminal station, and vid screen on the wall. The walls were painted light blue with white wooden trim lining the floor and ceiling. It was cozy, roomier than his quarters on the *Boxer*, and Kodiak found himself settling in almost too easily.

"Private Angeline Moreau is at the door," came the disembodied voice from the terminal station.

Kodiak dropped his rucksack on the bed and stowed his rifle on the magnetic strip next to it. "Open."

The door slid open, and Moreau walked in. "How do you like our new home?"

"It seems almost too good to be true, right?" Kodiak replied.

Moreau took a seat on the couch and lay back. "Well, our life expectancy just plummeted exponentially since we arrived. Maybe they want us to live in comfort before kicking the bucket."

"Charming, but not wrong," Kodiak agreed. "I wonder if the others got it this good."

Chapter 29
Hall

Forward Operating Base Edwards
ROCNE-South, New Eden

"Hey, yo, we got dicked over hard, guys!" Aiden Hall exclaimed as he took in his mortar team's sleeping arrangements.

"That's what she said!" Sergeant Richards roared back, drawing laughter at Hall's outburst.

After landing at FOB Edwards, Hall had followed his section leader, Staff Sergeant McHenry, to where they would be sleeping for much of their three-month rotation. When they had passed the three-story apartments the infantry was filing into, he'd had hope. As they'd continued walking past the infantry billets and towards the far side of the compound, his hope had wavered. When they had come to a stop in front of a single-story structure that looked more like a communication hut than a barracks, his hope had died.

"We're mortars, cherry. No one gives a damn about us until they call for fire," Sergeant Richards replied as he pushed past the group and walked inside.

"Legs get the penthouse, chucks get the outhouse, Hall. That's how it is, and that's how it will be." Staff Sergeant McHenry patted him on the shoulder and walked inside as well.

If Hall was being honest, he had lived in worse, and the quarters weren't horrible. The front door didn't have a card scanner and instead relied on motion sensors to open and close. When he entered with the others, he stared down a long hallway with rooms on either side. At first, he thought all the doors were open, but when he got to his, he noticed there was no door at all. Inside were a large bed, a dresser, a closet, a bedside table, and a terminal station. Other than having no privacy, the room was nice.

He laid his rucksack down on the bed, secured his weapon in the magnetic rack that could only be disengaged with his fingerprint, and then ventured back into the hallway. At the end of the hallway, the wall opened to a larger room that had a massive vid screen, couches, and a few holographic gaming tables against the wall. On the opposite side was a large kitchen that had an oven and a refrigerator.

"Communal showers, no doors on our rooms, and if I want to watch anything I have to do it with everyone," Jackson groaned as he came up next to Hall.

"Could be worse," Hall said with a shrug.

"It could be a lot worse," Sergeant McHenry confirmed. He turned his head and shouted down the hall, "Mortars, meet in the living room!"

One by one, the soldiers of Alpha and Bravo Teams slowly filed into the room and sat down on the couches or leaned up against the wall. Hall took a seat next to Red and looked toward his section leader.

"We are no longer aboard the *Boxer* or in the lavish living quarters of Fort Cassidy. We are deployed on an alien planet where somewhere outside the wire"—he pointed out the window behind them—"big blue scary monsters with guns are waiting for us. This isn't a vacation, so stop acting like it's one. I know you may not view these quarters as ideal compared to the bravos, but there is a reason for everything. As a mortar section, we oversee this sector's defense, and in a few minutes, I'll take you around to the different areas you'll grow quite comfortable with during your time here. You know from your training that a fire mission can come in at any moment—we need to be ready when that happens. You'll know it's the real deal when the red lights in your room flash and scream at you. Every obstacle that delays your reaction time getting to the guns and getting some high-angle hell into the air will be the deciding factor on who lives and dies outside the wire. If having no door going into your room bothers you, then take some five-fifty cord and hang a sheet over it."

Staff Sergeant McHenry wasn't being harsh with his explanations. In fact, he was laying it all out for them in a very understandable way. On reflection, the mortars were always going to be on call whereas the grunts were not, so ensuring they could be ready to react had to be top priority. It was another thing that Hall liked about McHenry—he never talked down to you or tried to make you feel inferior while explaining things.

"Now, let's take a trip over to our mortar pits and get reacquainted with our boom sticks." He smiled.

The mortar firing positions or "pits" were located a hundred meters from their sleeping quarters. Two 120mm mortar systems were already seated into their bipods and baseplates, ready and waiting to bring the rain. They stood twenty meters apart in smooth craters formed by the

204

heavy recoil of the large weapons, surrounded by a wall of sandbags for added crew protection. Fifty meters behind them was a steel bunker that led underground to where the actual mortar shells were held. Inside were thousands of smart rounds packed tightly in ammunition boxes and labeled specifically according to the different types of rounds. This bunker was where the ammunition bearers for the section would be, waiting to bring additional rounds to the pits if the gun teams needed them.

Hall would be in one of the pits with his team leader, Sergeant Richards, and his assistant gunner, Red, while Jackson ferried the rounds to and from the ammunition bunker. Hall closed his eyes and imagined what he would do when they eventually did get a call for fire. He was Alpha Team's gunner, and it was his job to listen for the deflection and elevation they received from the tactical operations center or TOC and input the data into the system's computer. He would then make sure the system was leveled on its bipod and give the OK for a round to be dropped down the tube.

The TOC was a single-story square building made of the same material as all the others were in the center of the FOB. That was where Staff Sergeant McHenry would be for much of his time on deployment as he rotated through shifts with Apollo Company's other mortar NCOs. It was the nerve center for all military operations taking place across the ROCNE AO. Whether he liked it or not, this was where Sergeant McHenry received his calls for fire.

"In here, they monitor all comm traffic across the area of operations," McHenry explained to his squad. "When troops get in contact, they may request a fire mission for any number of reasons. They may want high explosives to destroy or soften the enemy, white phosphorous for cover and concealment, or if it's a night mission, they may request illumination. That last one might not come around too often, what with our helmets' heads-up displays, but you never know."

As the squad made their way back toward the sleeping quarters, Hall turned and watched some of the last Ospreys take flight. Sergeant McHenry had given them the rest of the day off before they officially assumed duties on the gun line the next day, and he wanted to take a chance to appreciate this new planet they had landed on. He watched as the last dropship faded out of view, heading through the clouds toward the ships waiting in orbit just out of sight.

The sun was setting in the east, and a mixture of purple and orange replaced the blue sky that had welcomed them earlier. Over in the three-story barracks buildings, laughter and music carried itself across the warm dusk toward Hall and pushed farther north until it was barely audible. Soldiers in different states of dress milled about vehicles and walked to and from the dining facility and other buildings that seemed to spread out in that section of the base, and an unoccupied metal guard tower called to him.

Hall climbed up the ladder and was greeted by a beautiful sight. The tower overlooked the grass-filled valley to his front, flanked on either side by large rock walls that stretched hundreds of meters into the air. Waterfalls flowed over the edges and spilled into rivers that crisscrossed the valley, leading to a large lake south of the base where wild-looking animals bathed. In the sky, he watched as another flock of the massive birds he'd seen on the ride in flew in a diamond formation toward the setting sun.

New Eden was not only a long way from Earth but also a far cry from the loud, claustrophobic streets of Chicago, and the silence was more refreshing than he could've ever imagined. It struck him how such a peaceful-looking world could be at the center of an interstellar conflict. Then again, wars had been started over much less. The thin veil of calm was pulled back as loud thumps of explosions echoed somewhere in the distance. He looked over to the darkening horizon to try and pinpoint a flash that could give away the position of whatever was happening, but he couldn't find any.

Then he saw it.

Flashes of light flickered in the distance in front of him. His heart raced as they drew closer to the valley, his nerves settling when he realized the flashes of light were not from enemy or friendly fire but from lightning that was skipping across the ground and sky. He had thought the rapidly growing darkness was because the sun had already set, but it was actually a large storm gathering on the horizon. He watched as the lightning danced across the black clouds and struck the ground—more lightning than he'd ever seen in his life.

Soon rain slowly fell onto the base, and he realized it was time to head back to his barracks. The rain was cool as it landed in big drops around him, drenching him from head to toe as the warm day turned to a frigid night. He remembered the storms they had in Chicago and thought how different they were from this one. In the Midwest, there might be a nice lightning show up within the clouds, but very rarely did it hit something. New Eden's lightning stretched from the grass to the heavens across the valley. Hall counted thirteen strikes in the minute he took his eyes off the sidewalk as he made his way down an embankment towards the pits and his barracks.

As he slipped into the building, Hall shook the excess rain from his uniform and made his way to his room. The storm had begun to roll in harder, and the building vibrated with the thunder as it cracked the air outside. Listening closely, he heard the patter of the rain slamming into the side of the steel structure and smiled. The sound of rain remained the same no matter where he was. Hall remembered that same sound that had helped him fall asleep so many nights back on Earth; it was calming.

"Sergeant McHenry said the storms are pretty violent on New Eden, at least in this area. Wind comes down through the valley, and the cliffs on either side act as a wind tunnel," Jackson said.

Hall ran his hand over his shaved head and wiped the water off on his pants. "Makes you wonder why they picked this place."

"Easily defendable is my guess. Plus this is pretty deep in Republic territory. All of the guys I've talked to said they've never been hit by the Zodarks," Giovanni offered.

"Who have you talked to?" Jackson asked incredulously.

"Chefs at the DFAC. They've been here for damn near the whole thing. They said if anything, FOB Edwards is like the safest place in ROCNE-South."

"They're chefs, Gio," Jackson laughed, "they got one job in the whole Army and that's to cook. And would you believe it? They still mess that up."

"The spaghetti was good." Giovanni shrugged.

"Gio, my God, it's rehydrated plant-based noodles and chopped-up tomatoes. As someone with an Italian name, you should be insulted," Jackson scoffed.

"Only thing Italian about me is my name, dude. I'm like tenth-generation Italian American."

"You're about as Italian as the spaghetti in the DFAC," Hall said.

"Sounds about right," Giovanni laughed.

"Hey, we were gonna try and catch a game on the vid-net, wanna join?" Jackson asked Hall.

"They have sports all the way out here?" Hall asked skeptically.

"They're a year or more behind, but they come out with packages of them every month. Not like it matters when it happened—it's new to us," Giovanni replied.

Hall nodded in agreement but then shook his head. "I'm actually gonna turn in for the night. Tomorrow's gonna be a long day."

Jackson and Giovanni headed off down the hall, leaving Hall standing outside the still-uncovered door. He'd fix it in the morning. His mind and body were exhausted from the day he'd just experienced. Dropping into natural gravity after a year adrift was strenuous on the human body even with the muscle and bone meds they gave you. His body ached as he undressed and crawled into the tightly tucked blanket and sheets, laying his head on the pillow. It was a good ache; it was a reminder that he was back on solid ground.

As the rain continued to methodically rap at the walls of the barracks, Hall closed his eyes and allowed the rhythmic taps to sweep him off to sleep. He went to bed that night excited for this new chapter on this strange new planet, not knowing it would be the last good night's sleep he'd get for a long time.

Chapter 30
Moore

Forward Operating Base Edwards
ROCNE-South, New Eden

The joint troop medical facility was only a short distance from the landing pads in the heart of FOB Edwards. After getting settled in his barracks building, Oliver Moore took a tour of the large field hospital that serviced the area of operations. The facility was run by doctors from almost every branch of the Republic military, Navy personnel intertwined with Army as gray uniforms mixed with greens in the hallways.

The main building comprised several surgery, burn, and trauma departments with each of their wings spreading out like a compass in four directions. It had the necessary tools to tackle most injuries sustained in combat, but it could only do so much. For the more serious injuries, once stabilized, the wounded would be transported back to a medical ship in orbit above the planet.

During his tour, Moore walked each wing with his squad and took note of the procedures being laid out for them by the veteran staff. There was no controlled chaos that Moore could see, and everyone worked with a determined efficiency as they briskly walked from one room to another. Some of the admitted soldiers had been wounded in combat operations while others suffered from illnesses obtained on the planet. Captain Hideo Shinjo explained to the group that there were still a lot of unknown diseases that found their way into the soldiers during their deployments to the planet. Some resulted in mild discomfort, while others rendered the patient unfit for duty.

Plant life and animal life were big problems on New Eden. Ravagers were four-legged beasts with large fangs and spikes that rippled down the spine onto the tail. If attacked, one's chances of survival were very slim from the ferocity of the attack itself, but even a single bite from a ravager could be fatal. The fangs were tough but hollow and allowed a paralytic agent to be injected into its prey. Using blood coagulant gel was a routine procedure when dealing with snake bites on Earth. You could buy the affected individual time by slowing the flow of venom from the bite to the heart. For ravager bites, it was worse—

way worse. The venom injected from one of the beasts was at a high volume and moved fast through the bloodstream. Medics found out the hard way when trying to apply coagulant gel to stop the spread not to spend too much time on the bite and not enough time on getting them to a proper facility.

After the first eight deaths perpetrated by the ravagers, the Republic had finally changed the rules of engagement. Because the military was a reactionary force when it came to those sorts of things, tragedy always led to change.

****

When the tour had concluded, the medics of Apollo Company had been given their assignments. Moore was looking forward to heading back to his squad and running operations with them, but unit rotations had them pulling security for the forward operating base that month. That meant his time would be delegated to the needs of the medical facility, and those needs came in the form of shift work. He didn't mind it if he was being honest with himself. His goal was to become a doctor one day, and doing shift work would help when it came to that career later in life. He just wished someone had told him how boring it would be.

His shift had begun that same day at midnight, which gave him enough time to go to the chow hall and take a shower before changing into black medical scrubs with the Edwards Joint Troop Medical Facility logo stitched on the left breast pocket. When he'd arrived, he had been bright-eyed and bushy-tailed, ready to take on the chaos he was sure to experience. He'd quickly realized as the hours passed that he was most likely in for a long night. He looked at his watch before going back to stare blankly at his terminal screen behind the reception desk. The digital numbers read 0330 hours.

"Is it always this quiet?" he asked the nurse next to him.

She was a short woman of about forty years of age and was a contractor working for the Republic military, not an enlisted soldier or commissioned officer. She brushed a piece of lint off her pink scrubs and gave him a disapproving glare. "We like it quiet. It may seem boring to you now, but a quiet medical facility means that none of our men and women are being killed or maimed. Also, never use that word again. It has a way of biting you in the ass and soon we'll have several code blues hit us."

210

Moore's eyes went wide. "Oh, I didn't mean anything by it, ma'am." His eyes nervously looked at the floor. "I have a friend going out on patrol in the morning. I'm just trying to make small talk."

Her eyes softened. "You just got here, right?"

"Yes, ma'am," he replied.

"Well, then, you have all the time in the world to get into the thick of it. For now, just enjoy how quiet it is and count your blessings you aren't going out on patrol with your friend. I've seen what waits for them outside the wire, and I wouldn't be so eager to go experience it if I were you."

"Yes, ma'am."

"And please don't call me that, I already feel old enough. My name is Nancy."

"Oliver Moore." He reached out his hand and shook hers. "Pleasure to meet you."

"The pleasure is all mine, Moore. Now if you don't mind, can you please bring me some blood toner from the supply shop? It's down the hall to the left," Nancy said, pointing down the long hallway that led to the emergency stations.

He was quick to please and got up from his seat and began heading down the hall. "Blood toner?" he stopped and asked.

"Yes, sugar. Ask the supply sergeant for blood toner. He'll know what you're talking about."

As he made his way through the winding hallways, he realized he not only had no idea where the supply shop was, but he had never recalled ever learning about blood toner. Of course, he had a long way to go before knowing everything there was to know about medical supplies, but it sounded important—too important to know nothing about. He reached the end of the hall where it forked in opposite directions and looked up at the signs that showed which department was down which hall, but none said "supply shop."

"Lost?" came a voice from behind him.

Moore turned and delivered a crisp salute upon seeing that it was Captain Shinjo that was addressing him.

He laughed and waved his hands. "Don't worry about all that in here, Moore. We're professionals that need to be at our highest levels of readiness. No reason to muddy all that with rank formality. I don't need you saluting when we're trying to save a life."

The universe had a funny way of creating moments as if on verbal cue. The moment Moore dropped his salute, an alarm klaxon sounded in the building. Moore froze in place and looked to Captain Shinjo to see what he needed to do—if he needed to do anything—and without a word, Shinjo began running down the hall toward the emergency stations.

Moore followed close behind. He didn't know if he would be needed, but he'd hate to find out later that he was. They had been told during the briefing that if one of those alarms ever went off, it meant wounded were coming in. As his feet pounded down the hall, squeaking around the corners on the freshly polished floor, he wondered what would be waiting for him on the other side of the double red doors.

He had trained for this exact moment at Doss Station, and he'd finally have his chance to see if he could do it. The terrifying feeling he'd expected to be associated with this moment wasn't hitting him, though. The only thought on his mind was getting to the delivery bay and helping in whatever way he could.

The doors opened automatically, and Moore entered the emergency delivery station. What had been a quiet facility on the other side of that red door was controlled chaos on the other side. The two large doors leading outside were open, and outside, a torrent of rain was coming down on a gaggle of soldiers running every which way. He spotted Captain Shinjo heading into the rainy night and followed him without thinking twice.

A Puma IFV, or infantry fighting vehicle, was parked out front with its back ramp lowered, and a group of soldiers frantically tried to remove whoever had been injured. Moore stared wide-eyed at all the damage the large vehicle had sustained. Huge scorch marks covered the hull, and two of the tires were flat. Near the driver's seat, the armored plating looked to have been ripped apart like it was made of aluminum.

My God, what did that? he thought to himself. Some of the burn marks were still glowing red hot in the night, steam rising as the rain cooled the burning metal.

"Moore!" Captain Shinjo shouted over the sound of the rain on the steel building.

Moore turned his head and ran to where Captain Shinjo was climbing up the ramp of the Puma. A medic he knew from Fourth Platoon was activating the gravity stretcher and helped the captain navigate it down the ramp toward the building. The stretcher's underbelly glowed blue as it floated smoothly a meter above the ground with the slightest touch of the medic's hand.

"We took contact about twenty miles from here up—" the medic frantically tried to explain.

"Save the explanation for your report. All I need to know is what happened," Shinjo replied.

"Zodark grenade went off near him. He's taken shrapnel to his chest, left arm, and both legs. I was able to stop the bleeding for a while and gave him a cocktail of morphine about twenty minutes ago, but his chest wound opened back up and wouldn't seal."

Shinjo put his hands on the stretcher and pushed it out of the rain and into the medical facility. Moore ran to the other side and steered the stretcher toward one of the emergency stations as Shinjo continued to collect important information from the medic. Moore had to admit, the medic was performing very well for such a high-stress situation; he only hoped he'd be as calm, cool, and collected when his time came.

The soldier on the stretcher had had his helmet removed, his long blond hair sticking to his head near his eyes from a combination of blood and rain. The armor was worse for the wear—both armor plates on his legs were shattered in multiple places, he was missing the left triceps' armor plate completely, and a hole was gouged on the right side of his chest plate. As they wheeled into one of the emergency station's rooms, Moore began to remove the armor when Captain Shinjo slapped his hand.

"No time! Get him on the HALO," the officer ordered.

Moore lifted the soldier off the stretcher by his legs and placed him underneath the HALO, a large machine with two rotating arms that circled the bed when activated. It would read the patient on the bed beneath the machine and give a proper diagnostic to the highest level possible. If cancer had formed in the soldier the day prior, it would be picked up on the HALO.

The arms rotated around the bed four times, a blue light scanning over the wounded man's body. Moore watched the medical screen as the image of the soldier's body appeared on it. He gasped as numerous alerts popped up on the screen, one after another. The poor kid's liver, kidney, and left lung had been completely destroyed and no longer showed up on the scan. The shrapnel that still found itself embedded in the soldier's body showed up like dozens of silver streaks, which the machine tagged as foreign objects.

When the arms stopped rotating, Moore looked to Captain Shinjo, who gave him a nod. As quickly and delicately as he could, Moore removed the soldier's armor. As each shattered piece was removed, blood poured onto the white floors. Moore felt his boots slipping in the spreading pools and bile rose in his throat. For the moment, he kept his composure and placed the armor in the corner of the room before heading back to the captain's side.

"What now?" he asked, seeing Captain Shinjo standing idle behind the terminal.

"I've told the HALO to put Private Meeks into a medically induced coma while he undergoes his operation. The arms will now do everything for us—removing the shrapnel, cleaning and cauterizing the wounds, and they'll even take samples of his missing organs to be regrown. When the machine gets done with him, we will transport him to a stasis pod, where he'll remain in a coma for a few months while he grows his new organs."

Moore's voice caught in his throat for a moment as he tried to take in what the captain had just said. "So, that's it? He's going to survive?" Moore couldn't believe that it had been so easy.

"The hardest part of your job is in the field. A lot can go wrong, and you won't always be able to save someone who gets hit outside the wire. The medic who brought him in did a fantastic job stabilizing the patient and doing what he could out there. He bought us enough time to get him to the HALO." Shinjo tapped a few buttons on his terminal and the arms on the HALO came to life, switching out numerous blades and other tools built into the machine's arms as they went to work. Captain Shinjo continued, "Of course, regrowing organs has come a very long way with modern medicine, but it's never without risk. Regardless of the perfect DNA and blood match, the patient's body could still reject the flash-cloned replacements. If that happens, he'll die, and sadly he'll be awake to find out. See, your job out there beyond the wire is difficult in many more ways than mine, but I'll always envy it. Sometimes in here we must wake them up just to let them know they're gonna die. I wouldn't put the job on my worst enemy."

Moore gave a low whistle and wiped the sweat that trickled from his forehead and into his eyes. "I'm sorry to hear that, sir."

"I'm sorry to have to say it," Shinjo responded with a curt nod, "but I want to let you know that not only did that medic do a fantastic job, you did as well. You heard the alarm and came running to the emergency with me. That right there is the first hurdle to get over. It is our body's natural reaction to run away from an emergency, not toward it. You then helped me move the patient to this room and removed their armor properly to avoid causing more damage. You helped save this kid's life, Moore, and you should be proud of that. Good job."

Moore found himself smiling, regardless of the fact that a soldier was currently having a machine perform lifesaving surgery behind him with perfect execution. He felt like he had actually done something. He'd messed up and almost removed the armor too soon, but Captain Shinjo hadn't brought up that folly.

When the surgery was completed, he helped Nancy move the soldier into one of the stasis pods and closed the lid, activating the long freeze. "How long will he sleep?"

"Until the organs hold and his readings normalize. He has a long road ahead, but I've seen people come back from worse. He was lucky to have you and Captain Shinjo there," Nancy said as she patted him on the shoulder and left the room.

Moore looked through the glass of the stasis pod at the soldier's face, his blond hair still in his eyes, as the frost enveloped the view of the pod's occupant. In his first day at the joint troop medical facility, he had helped save someone's life—for now, anyway. He couldn't wait to tell Nova and Kodiak later that day if he saw them, but for the moment, he headed back to the reception desk to finish out his shift.

When he took his seat, he smacked his head with the palm of his hand and turned to Nancy. "I'm so sorry; I forgot the blood toner," he said.

Nancy let out a cackling laugh and slapped her knee. "Boy, I was just playing with you. I almost made your butt go back and find some, but you did good tonight, so I'll let you off easy."

Moore laughed and reclined back in the chair, looking up at the ceiling. "Good to know for the future, Nancy."

"Oh hell, honey, that one's for free. Get one of your friends with that trick—it's the oldest one in the Republic handbook."

Moore shook his head and smiled. "I think I will," he said, looking at his watch. It read 0430 hours. Only an hour had passed.

Chapter 31
Kodiak

Route Archangel, 10 Miles from FOB Edwards
ROCNE-South, New Eden

Harrison Kodiak had just returned from the chow hall that morning when his squad leader, Staff Sergeant Muleskin, ordered First Squad to kit up. A squad from Fourth Platoon had gone missing fifteen miles north of FOB Edwards during an early-morning presence patrol. In the northern parts of the region, Sumerians had begun building villages out of the slave quarters they were kept in at the mines. Kodiak hadn't seen one in person yet but was curious what they looked like. The rumor was they looked like normal humans, just not from Earth, a slave race for the Zodarks to prey on. If they did look human, Kodiak would be beyond disappointed. The Zodarks were another story. Those big blue bastards were exactly what he thought of when daydreaming about alien races—massive monsters with braided black hair, sharp, jagged teeth, and blue skin. Of course, the more alien species he met, the more dramatically his chances of dying increased.

After getting his armor, helmet, and weapon, Kodiak loaded up in one of the two Pumas his squad would be taking out to search for the lost squad. Sergeant Woods climbed into the vehicle commander's seat and plugged into the neural interface that projected important information and the route to his helmet's heads-up display. Private Alejandro Garza was up front idling the engine and waiting for the word to move out, while Private Gwendoline Morgan sat in the gunner's seat. The neural interface at the gunner's station projected the sight of the weapon on top of the Puma. It was a mini railgun that used magnets to fire heated tungsten rods at catastrophic speed. The railgun's bark and the signature sizzle it emitted between shots gave the already deadly weapon an even more wicked sound.

Some of the soldiers in Charlie Team had filled in the holes with Alpha Team as they did in the other vehicle with Bravo Team. Privates Gerald Sato and Lacy Brown sat across from Kodiak and Moreau. Kodiak knew both Sato and Brown—they had been in his basic training platoon, and he'd gotten along well enough with them. It was easier to

217

do with a guy like Skaggs taking all the heat from anyone else, but even so, they had conversed on several occasions and weren't strangers.

"How does a squad get lost?" Sato asked over the internal vehicle communication.

They had already traveled fourteen miles toward the last known location of the missing squad and were getting close. In basic, the drill sergeants had never let them talk on internal communication, and even in the sim, Sergeant Woods would yell at them to shut up when they struck up a conversation. Life was different outside the wire. When you left the safety net of FOB Edwards, you felt vulnerable. At any moment, a Zodark ambush could take you by surprise and you'd be fighting for your life.

"They're most likely not lost, *estúpido*," Garza responded from the driver's seat.

"Zodarks have been getting more ballsy with how much territory they encroach on," Sergeant Woods added. "This isn't an invasion force anymore, it's an occupation force, and the remaining Zodarks apparently don't like being occupied."

After the invasion of New Eden, the Republic had gained significant ground on all the planet's continents. Still, after more than a year of fighting, pockets of Zodark resistance had formed. At first, it was raiding parties attacking supply depots and small outposts, but soon, they had consolidated their forces under scraped-together leadership still alive after the invasion. The largest concentration of Zodark forces was on their continent, which also happened to be where the Republic Joint Ground Forces Command was located at the southernmost tip.

Fighting hadn't been intense for the last unit that had been deployed to the region, but in the last couple of months before Apollo had taken over, the fighting had intensified. Rumors spread through the company that the Zodarks were planning a massive push into the region that saw FOB Edwards in its direct path. When it came to the odds of such battles, Kodiak was indifferent and didn't want to think about it. He was sure for the commanders sitting in their luxurious headquarters penthouses, it was just a matter of numbers here and there. That was all soldiers like Kodiak were to them—numbers on a war map, sent to wherever they wanted.

"Well, OK, so if it's Zodarks and they wiped out an entire squad, what's the sense in sending another one to find 'em? Why not send in a platoon, or at least provide air support?" Sato continued.

"'Cause this is the Army, Sato. It's not supposed to make sense," Kodiak replied.

"Amen to that," Woods sighed into his comms. His voice became sterner as he quickly said, "We're arriving at dismount point Edinburgh."

The Puma slowed and Kodiak felt the vehicle swing to its right and come to a stop. The back ramp lowered, and the soldiers dismounted from their vehicles and moved to the edge of the road on either side. To their left was a wide-open field of grass, waving in the slight breeze. To their right was a dense and dark forest, illuminated by the plants in hues of blue and orange.

Just like the damn simulator. Kodiak shook his head.

"Charlie and Bravo Teams, get off the road and pull security. Alpha Team, check the vehicles for survivors," Staff Sergeant Muleskin ordered as he walked by Kodiak toward the rear of the Puma. He put on foot up on the ramp and keyed his mic. "Apollo One-Six, this is Apollo One-One. How copy?"

Kodiak remembered the call signs and what the numbers represented. The "One" in One-Six signified First Platoon and the "Six" meant he was talking to their platoon leader, Second Lieutenant Cooley. The first "One" in Muleskin's call sign again designated First Platoon and the second "One" was for First Squad.

"Apollo One-Six, we have located the vehicles of Four-One and are searching now. Over."

"Let's go." Sergeant Woods tapped Kodiak on the shoulder.

Sergeant Woods advanced toward the front of the Puma they had driven in on and Kodiak followed. He held his rifle at low ready and felt the movement of Moreau, Sato, and Brown behind him. Even though Sato and Brown were in Charlie Team, Garza and Morgan had to stay in the vehicle in case they needed to leave in a hurry and to provide overwatch.

Kodiak almost gasped as he rounded the Puma and was met with the sight of Fourth Platoon's vehicles. Two Puma IFVs were on their sides and smoking in the road. Woods made his way across the orange clay road towards the turned-over vehicles with Kodiak hot on his tail. Kodiak spread out from behind Woods, flanking the back ramp as they approached the first vehicle. Sato and Brown took a knee just behind them and pointed their rifles toward the forest, and Moreau did the same across the field, covering them from all angles.

Woods opened the scanner on the outside of the door and plugged in his data pad. Numbers scrolled across the screen before the device blinked green and the ramp lowered. Kodiak stepped back to avoid being hit by the door now opening sideways, and when he came to a stop, he activated his helmet's light and peered into the back of the Puma. The inside of the hull was dark, with only the light from their helmets and the occasional sparks lighting up the interior. Kodiak stepped inside and slowly made his way over the boxes and supplies that had been tossed around the unsecured cabin. The troop area in the back was empty save a few boxes of MREs and ammo boxes, but as he made his way to the gunner's seat, he paused.

A ghostly white hand shined brightly in Kodiak's helmet light. It was motionless, its fingers curled slightly, the pinky finger bent at an awkward angle. His brain told him what it was, but his body wouldn't respond and move forward. He knew it was going to be a dead Republic soldier, and it wasn't lost on him in the moment that this would be the first dead body he'd ever seen. Taking a deep breath, he stepped forward and knelt down beside the gunner's chair. The armored body of a Republic soldier lay crumpled in the corner where the feet would normally go when sitting at that station.

"I got a body," his voice croaked.

"What?" Sergeant Woods called from the back.

Kodiak cleared his throat and repeated, "I have a body here. Send in Doc."

Woods moved deeper into the vehicle to where Kodiak knelt. "Christ, they're alive?"

Kodiak's eyes fell. "I don't think so."

Woods looked from Kodiak to the mangled body shoved into the corner and sighed. He let his rifle hang on its three-point harness and placed his hand underneath the uniform where the neck was. Kodiak held his breath for a few moments, mistakenly letting hope seep into his brain.

Woods turned and shook his head. "His neck's broke. Go outside and report it to Sergeant Muleskin."

Kodiak just nodded and moved past Woods and out the back of the Puma. The fresh air instantly swept up his nose, replacing the damp, smoky odor inside the overturned Puma. Brown looked back at him with the same hope he had felt in her eyes. He just shook his head and continued down the road to where Sergeant Muleskin stood.

"At least one is KIA in the first Puma. No signs of the others," Kodiak reported to Muleskin.

The old veteran grimaced. "Yeah, I was afraid of that." He spat into the clay and ground his foot into it. "All right, check the other vehicle and I'll let the PL know."

"Sergeant Muleskin, I got a blood trail!" one of the soldiers in Bravo Team called.

Sergeant Muleskin went over to the soldier who'd called out as Sergeant Woods walked up beside Kodiak. "It's the same thing in the other vehicle," Woods said. "Gunner and driver are both dead."

"Where the hell's the rest of the squad?" Moreau asked, walking up.

"Someone from Bravo said they found a blood trail," Kodiak replied, still staring at the soldier who was pointing at something in the grass.

Sergeant Muleskin turned and waved his arm at them. "Sergeant Woods, come over here."

Sergeant Woods jogged over to Muleskin, and they began looking at whatever the private had found. Kodiak turned to look at the vast field of green on the other side of the road. He squinted to see if he could make out any movement but saw nothing out of the ordinary. He hated being so vulnerable in the exact same spot where an ambush had occurred.

"What are you thinking?" Moreau asked.

"I'm thinking we're really exposed," Kodiak replied.

She looked around. "Yeah, that pretty much sums it up."

"Alpha Team, on me," Woods shouted.

Kodiak, Moreau, Sato, and Brown jogged over to where Sergeant Woods and Muleskin stood. A dark red trail painted the disturbed grass up and into the forest. The blood was still shining, and some was dripping off the blades. Whoever it was, they were going to die with a bleed like that and no help.

"Alpha, you're gonna follow that trail with Bravo. Sergeant Woods, you'll be the lead element, but coordinate with Sergeant Casper if you find something, understood?"

Woods nodded to Muleskin and responded, "Too easy, boss."

Charlie Team stayed behind with the vehicles as Alpha and Bravo Teams spread out and moved into the dense forest. The leaves and branches in the canopy were so thick it created complete darkness. The plants and fungi had adapted on the planet to glow orange and blue, lighting up the otherwise pitch-black night.

Kodiak's visor adjusted to the low light, but the orange and blue lights still lit up the forest around him. It was hard not to become distracted by something so beautiful, but he wasn't the point man at the moment. He just hoped that whoever was would be paying closer attention to what was in front of them.

A tiny red dot blinked in the upper right corner of his visor's heads-up display, signaling that the advance had halted. He was too far behind and to the right to see what was happening up front, but most likely the point man had seen something. After a few moments, he went from a knee to lying prone in the underbrush, pointing his weapon to his front and looking for any movement.

Kodiak took a moment to look over his left shoulder toward the front of the line and saw Woods kneeling next to Sato, who must have been on point. Woods turned his head rather quickly to the right and grabbed Sato as an eruption of green laser fire burned the place where they had been seconds earlier. Kodiak turned back to his front but didn't see any movement coming in from their flank. Whatever was happening was at the front of the patrol.

"Alpha, get in line with me!" Woods yelled over the team's internal comm net.

Kodiak pushed himself to his feet and sprinted toward where he had last seen Woods kneeling with Sato. After a couple of seconds, he realized just how much of a target he'd made himself and panic hit him. His feet tripped into each other and he stumbled forward, hitting the ground. He felt hands grab his armor from behind and pull him back behind the cover of a moss-covered boulder grown into the side of a thick tree.

"Nice feet, ya big goof," Brown chuckled as she raised her rifle, angling her body around the tree trunk.

What sounded like a fist hitting a pillow popped over his head, and he watched Brown lose her footing and fall onto her backside. He smiled for a minute and was about to send a funny insult back her way when he noticed her breathing was irregular. Her back was to him, but he saw her shoulders moving up and down in violent, deep breaths. He scrambled to his knees and crawled to where she was sitting up straight. All around them, green lasers illuminated the area, clashing with the blue and orange of the plants.

He reached up and pulled himself around, looking at Brown's face. Her helmet looked intact, but he could still see her shoulders rising and falling rapidly. He looked down and saw what was wrong. A fist-sized hole was glowing red in the center of Brown's chest plate.

"Oh, shit! No!" he cried as he slowly lowered her body to the ground. "Medic!" Kodiak screamed onto the comm net.

This can't be happening...this can't be happening.

He activated the medic beacon on Brown's armor and grabbed his rifle. Using the rock to protect his lower half, he poked his head and weapon above the rock and tried to locate the fighting. Thirty meters ahead of him, Woods, Sato, and Moreau were firing from behind cover to their front. He didn't see any Zodark movement, but the green glow from their laser fire illuminated their general vicinity.

Sergeant Andrews, the squad's medic, slid behind cover next to Kodiak and looked over Brown's body. He turned to Kodiak and shouted over the chaos, "Get to Woods. They need help. I got this."

Kodiak didn't know what else to do but nod and run toward another boulder to Sergeant Woods's right. The run wasn't long, but every time his foot hit the ground and pushed him closer to safety, he felt more exposed. At any moment, he expected a flash of green and that would be the end of it, but death never came, and he slid into cover.

"Nice of you to join us, Kodiak," Woods grunted as he slapped another battery pack into his rifle.

"Brown's hit. Doc is with her, but I don't know—it was bad," Kodiak said, breaking the news that someone he, Sato, and Moreau knew personally from basic might be dead.

"You can't do anything about it now. I need you in the fight," Woods responded as he turned and let loose another volley from his rifle.

Kodiak knelt and raised his body above his cover and fired a burst toward where a green bolt had just come from. He switched his visor to thermal vision, but the range was too far to get a proper view of wherever the Zodarks were hiding. He fired off another burst and ducked back down. He didn't want to give them a nice target to shoot at.

"Apollo One-Six, this is Apollo One-One, over," Woods called into his radio. There was a momentary pause and he responded to the platoon leader, "Apollo One-Six, fire mission. Stand by for grid."

Kodiak went over how to call for fire in his head as he listened to Woods. He knew the grid coordinates for the fire mission were being sent to the TOC from Woods's scan and he would then ask for whatever ordnance he thought they needed. He hoped he was calling for high-explosive rounds.

"Six rounds, smoke, fire when ready, over," Woods called over the net and then switched to the internal comms. "We have mortars dropping some smoke rounds on their position. Be ready—when they hit, I want you to switch to thermals and we're gonna push through the ambush. Bravo Team is flanking around now and will meet us there."

A pit formed in the bottom of his stomach. As soon as the mortar rounds impacted, Alpha Team was going to charge through the cloud and take the fight to the Zodarks. He had fought up close with Zodarks before in the simulation—he eventually died every single time. He stood again and fired another burst into the darkness ahead and knelt back down. His knees shook, and he gave his leg a smack in frustration at his body's response to the stress.

Chapter 32
Hall

Forward Operating Base Edwards
ROCNE-South, New Eden

Hall's morning routine had become simple with the first month of deployment under his belt. When he wasn't going on patrol with a platoon-sized element, he would wake up, get breakfast at the mess hall, make sure "the pit" was prepared for any fire missions that day, and then relax. He was now enjoying his newfound love of "hurry up and wait" as he lay out on the couch in the rec room.

Life was easier when you manned the mortar tubes on a forward operating base. You were too important to relegate out to meaningless tasks with the high rate of patrols they sent out every day. He understood that his job was important, but he also wasn't going to complain or sit around feeling sorry for himself that others were on patrol and he wasn't. Hall had played that game before and didn't particularly want to go looking for an opportunity to go through it again.

He had gone on his first patrol a week after arriving on planet. Second and Third Squads were tasked with clearing out a mine that a clan of Zodarks had recently occupied and the mortars were asked to tag along. Their mission was straightforward—go to the dismount point and provide indirect fire for the assaulting element. They drove in Puma MFVs, or mortar firing vehicles, and followed the main convoy until they reached the dismount point.

Everything had gone relatively smoothly until Second and Third Squads made contact at the mouth of the mine. They were over six hundred meters away from the mortars' positions, but between the radio communications and the distant sounds of battle, Hall could tell they were in one hell of a fight. Just as quickly as the battle began, they received their first call for fire.

They fired six rounds of HE, high-explosive, in five different fire missions over the course of forty-five minutes. Both gun teams were recording solid hits, but with the protection of the mine shafts, the bulk of the Zodark force remained safe. The attack couldn't sustain the firefight after taking numerous casualties and began to fall back. What remained of the two squads came barreling out of the forest toward their parked vehicles. The burst of running and fighting soldiers from the tree line spooked Hall. He hadn't been expecting them to fall back so soon or so haphazardly.

By the time his teams were able to close the roof hatches and secure the still-scorching-hot gun, they were under direct fire from Zodark lasers. The vehicle's armor was able to withstand a certain amount of laser bolts, but too much would melt their only means of protection. The enemy fire faded as the convoy had made its escape back to the FOB, but a stray laser bolt had pierced the softened armor and bounced into the troop compartment. Hall had stared wide-eyed at the hole it melted between his and Jackson's heads. Jackson had gotten the worst of it and spent five days getting the burned skin on his face skin regrown. What was left was some nasty scars, but Jackson was alive.

A Zodark's weapon fired a laser that formed plasma made from hollow atoms. The result was a superheated bolt of plasma, shaped like a tiny missile. The farther and faster it traveled, the more defined the bolt became until it reached its highest volatility. A single bolt hitting one of the thick trees in the New Eden forests would cause major damage but wouldn't knock down the tree, but enough bolts into that trunk and it would melt the wood away like acid.

Hall's eyes shot open, his nightmare a distant memory, as alarm klaxons rang inside the mortar's barracks building. He jumped to his feet and ran down the hall toward the exit. By now, their platoon leader, Lieutenant Kincade, was receiving the grid coordinates and coming up with a firing solution to send to the pit. Hall's job was to get down there and feed the data into the mortar.

His feet skipped across the grass and rocks as he slid down the embankment into the pit below. Red was already there, stabilizing the bipod and making sure the gun was up and ready to fire. As Hall knelt next to the sight terminal, Jackson came from around the corner with rounds in his arms.

"Make sure you set the correct mode on the round, Jacks. I want the smoke to blanket the area, not land on one of our own," Hall said as he manipulated the terminal to level out the gun.

"When have I ever set it to the wrong mode?" Jackson snapped back as he removed a smoke round from its packaging.

Hall shrugged. "First time for everything, bud."

Numbers appeared on the terminal as Sergeant McHenry came around the corner, shouting, "Fire mission, troops in contact, six rounds at ten-meter intervals, smoke, charge two, fire for effect!"

Hall and his team repeated the info as he brought the gun on target. The markers for his deflection and elevation data flashed a steady green light and he yelled, "Hang it!"

Fitzgerald held the smoke round in her hand, Jackson behind her with another in his hands, ready to give it to her. She inserted the round halfway into the tube and held it in place, waiting for the order.

Hall checked the lights one more time and yelled, "Fire!"

Fitzgerald dropped the round, sweeping her arms out and downward with her body as she ducked below the tube. The round spiraled down the barrel and hit the firing pin at the bottom sending it into the air towards its target.

They repeated the fire mission five more times, and each time, Hall would manipulate the gun to fire left and right of the first round in ten-meter intervals. That way, when the rounds impacted and began to conceal the area, the troops in contact would have a thick wall of smoke between them and the enemy.

Hall sat back on his heels and breathed out slowly, letting the sun shine on his face. From the moment he'd run out of the barracks to the last round fired, his entire body was tense as he methodically went to work. It wasn't until now that he relaxed.

"Rounds complete. Good effect on target. Job well done, squad," Sergeant McHenry said before turning and walking back up towards the barracks.

"Told ya I wouldn't flub the mode," Jackson laughed as he patted Hall on the shoulder and followed McHenry.

Hall looked up and smiled as he passed. "Yeah, good job, brotha." He turned his head to look at Fitzgerald as she sat on her heels across the gun from him. "You too, Red, good job on the rounds."

She smiled and pinched his cheek teasingly. "Aw, thanks, Dad."

Chapter 33
Kodiak

Troops in Contact
ROCNE-South, New Eden

A bolt from a Zodark weapon zipped through the dark forest and crashed into the rock above Kodiak's head. He watched as it sparked and blackened the corner of the boulder with molten plasma. They were in way over their heads, and if the fire mission Sergeant Woods called didn't come soon, the stalemate they currently found themselves in would quickly turn.

Kodiak peered around his cover to try and spot any movement at all. He switched back and forth between vision modes on his helmet's visor, but it didn't seem any were helping until he spotted something. The unmistakable silhouette of a towering Zodark was bouncing back and forth between tree trunks, firing his rifle as it moved. Kodiak dropped to a prone position, aimed towards the gap between the trees and watched. He wished it would come down to skill but knew the probability of hitting the enemy as it moved in and out of such a small window of opportunity was low. The key was to time it perfectly.

Kodiak controlled his breathing and squeezed the trigger at his natural respiratory pause. The bolts of energy arched across the forest floor, illuminating the plants along their travels before finding their home in the target. The Zodark leapt between trees and was hit in the side by Kodiak's fire. The beast lost its footing at the sudden impact and tried to get to its feet and behind cover, but Kodiak let loose another salvo of rounds into the stumbling figure and watched it fall out of sight.

He had been in firefights before, even ambushes like this, but it was very rare to witness what you were firing out. After a battle ended, they would secure the site and see Zodark bodies littered across the area, but this was the first time he had seen one of his rounds kill an enemy. He'd thought he would feel a certain weight at extinguishing a life, but all he felt was a surge of adrenaline.

"Holy shit, I got one!" he shouted.

"Great work. Now shut up and keep firing," Woods yelled back as he rose to his feet and fired toward the enemy position. He ducked back down behind the rock and stared at the ground as if listening intently. He nodded and looked over to Kodiak. "Ten seconds till rounds impact, brace!"

Kodiak rolled behind the cover and buried his face in the dirt. With modern technology, it was almost impossible to hit your own soldiers with indirect fire, but "almost impossible" wasn't impossible. He counted down from ten in his head, wondering if at any moment a smoke round would land on top of him.

That would be some luck, he thought, *my own guys take me out while I'm in the middle of a firefight with Zodarks.*

Something that sounded like a bullet train screaming through the station passed overhead and the ground shook with anger. Kodiak's body lifted a centimeter off the ground, and he looked up toward his front. Large explosions pounded the ground in front of them, leaving a thick white cloud in its place.

"Splash over. Good effect on target. End of mission," Woods called into his headset. He once again looked to the team around him. "Get on line and switch to thermals on your visors. Remember, Zodarks emit heat differently. Look for the green and yellow discoloration of their feet and hands."

Kodiak flicked his eyes and selected the thermal imaging setting on his visor. The world faded from its natural glow to blues and blacks. The smoke screen that had once been in front of him was no longer blocking his vision, and he watched as the Zodarks slowly backed up. He knew Alpha Team had to take advantage of their momentary confusion, but Woods wasn't firing his rifle yet as they cautiously advanced into the cloud.

The outlines of the trees and plants were easy to identify, but he couldn't see the textures and features. He also saw heat emanating from bugs that darted across his vision, causing his body to tense. He knew where the Zodarks were in relation to him, but they were disciplined and rarely moved. Even when they did, it was with the deliberate, fluid motions of expert hunters.

Kodiak looked to his left, wondering why Woods wasn't firing, but his team leader just continued advancing forward, his weapon raised toward the enemy position. Kodiak's finger slowly moved from outside the trigger well and hovered over the trigger. If Woods didn't fire soon, they would be out of the cloud and exposed. He felt his finger press against the trigger and applied soft pressure. They were getting close. Too close.

The yellow-and-green glow of a Zodark's hand came into view only twenty meters in front of Kodiak, and soon he made out the features of the beast that towered over him. They were too close. The Zodark turned and seemed to be looking directly at Kodiak but didn't fire, most likely because he was still obscured by the smoke screen. The Zodark then turned its head to the sky and took in a deep breath before its head snapped back and it looked directly at Kodiak. They were too close.

Kodiak squeezed the trigger and a burst of fire leapt from his rifle and slammed into the Zodark who'd just been looking at him. The beast fell backwards, but despite being hit numerous times in the chest, it scrambled to its feet. Someone yelled next to him, but he no longer focused on what was happening around him, only on the Zodark.

Kodiak fired again into the dazed enemy, and it stumbled backwards at the force of more rounds hitting it. Kodiak flipped his weapon to the 5.56 railgun and fired on semiautomatic. With each squeeze of the trigger, a tungsten slug slammed into the flesh of the Zodark, and he didn't stop pulling the trigger until the Zodark stopped moving.

He saw movement to his left and jumped back just in time as a huge curved blade swung past him and into the ground. He removed his visor's thermal imaging and was greeted with no smoke obscuring his view, a gamble that paid off when he saw the Zodark swing its blade accurately.

Kodiak raised his rifle, knowing he wouldn't get it up in time to fire, and instead blocked an incoming blow from the sword. The impact rattled his arms so bad that it felt like his wrists snapped. He tried to step back and put some distance between him and the Zodark, but some roots got wrapped around his feet, and he fell on his back. Kicking his feet, he watched in horror as the Zodark raised its blade above its head to bring crashing down on him.

"No!" was all Kodiak managed to yell as the Zodark's head split in half and the beast fell to the ground.

Rolling from his back onto his feet, he raised his rifle and pointed it around him. He was panicking; he knew he was panicking. His heart was racing, his helmet's HUD was screaming at him to slow his breathing, and his suit injected him with calming agents until his heart rate slowed. A cool sensation raced up his body through his femoral artery, and he sighed.

A fist grabbed him and pulled him around. Sergeant Woods had his helmet off and his teeth were clenched in a snarl. "Who told you to fire?" he screamed in Kodiak's face. "No one! You wait for my command, damn it!"

Kodiak looked at him wide-eyed. He had at least four inches on the sergeant, but at the moment, he felt very small. "I'm sorry," was all he managed to say.

Sergeant Woods's face softened for a moment. "Don't be sorry. Be better." He released Kodiak from his grip and walked off.

Those words cut deeper than any "I'm disappointed in you" line his father had ever used on him. Looking around, he noticed there was no more gunfire. Smoke still lingered in long wisps on the forest floor, which was now littered with Zodark bodies. He couldn't believe they were all still standing.

Bravo Team had pushed into the objective after Kodiak had fired his weapon, and together with Alpha Team, they had been able to assault through. Sergeant Woods was talking with Sergeant Casper over a couple of dead Zodarks, Moreau had her helmet removed and was smoking a thin cigarette, and Sato was sitting against a tree. The only person he didn't see was—

"Brown," he said suddenly and turned to run back to where he'd left her and Doc Andrews.

He felt a hand grab him from behind and he turned to see Sergeant Woods. "Brown's KIA, Kodiak."

He felt his knees go weak but caught himself. Kodiak turned to look back where Brown had been and felt tears form in his eyes. He closed them, trying to force the water away, but all he saw was the image of her dropping to her backside and the hole in her chest. He had thought she'd fallen; she'd hit the ground so hard but was still sitting upright. The last thing she had done was crack a joke with him.

They weren't even a quarter of a way through a deployment; they'd only been on five missions, and he'd only been in seven firefights. Now someone he knew very well, someone he'd known for more than a year, was dead.

"Look at me," Sergeant Woods said forcefully.

Despite having his helmet on, Kodiak looked at him through the visor. "What?"

Woods sighed. "It sucks." He gripped Kodiak's shoulders tight. "But we got a lot of fight left and this is going to happen. It's inevitable. Right now, I need your head in the game. When we get back to the FOB tonight, we can drink, talk, fight, whatever you want, but until then, I need you one hundred percent focused on right here, right now!"

Kodiak breathed in deeply and his quivering breaths almost made him begin to cry again, but he composed himself. "Yes, Sergeant."

Woods squeezed his shoulders and smiled before putting his helmet back on. "Good man, Bear."

"Hey, Sarge, we got something over here," Sergeant Casper said.

Woods turned and jogged over to Casper. Kodiak didn't want to stay behind and continue thinking about Brown, or worse, get the bright idea to go over to where her body was, so he took off after his team leader. The two walked up to an unnatural break in the trees that led to a very bright section of the forest.

The circle was surrounded by thick trees but was covered in grass, with no other plant life. The entire area was about ten feet around and was bathed in the light of the sun that came through the circular opening in the canopies. In the middle was a Zodark-built structure that was secured at unnatural, jagged points into the air.

Kodiak's stomach churned at the sight in front of him. On the wooden structure were fourteen naked humans hanging upside down. Their arms, legs, feet, and hands were nailed to the structure, and they had all been cut open from their stomachs to their throats.

They had found the missing squad.

Chapter 34
Moore

Forward Operating Base Edwards
ROCNE-South, New Eden

Oliver Moore hadn't known Brown as well as Kodiak had. He knew her from basic training, but after that, they'd split off and he'd left for medical training on Doss Station. Still, the ceremony was sad, and as he stood in formation with the rest of the company, he stared at the lone rifle sticking straight up behind Brown's boots with her helmet rested on the buttstock. A picture of Brown smiling in her dress uniform, flanked on both sides by the flag of her country of origin and the official flag of the Republic, stood next to the display.

He looked down the line toward Kodiak, who stood with his team. His back was ramrod straight and his face was stoic, without a hint of emotion. He was a tough kid, and Moore couldn't imagine what was going through the young man's mind. He had to keep reminding himself that Kodiak was only nineteen years old because he carried himself better than most of the older adults in the platoon.

Death was not a new concept to the men and women of Apollo Company. They had experienced death from other platoons and even other companies, but this was his platoon's first casualty. Moore turned back to the picture of Brown and took a deep breath. Her smile in the picture was like daggers through his heart.

Their platoon leader, company executive officer, and company commander stood next to the picture of Brown, and Second Lieutenant Samantha Cooley stepped to the front. She glanced over at the picture of Brown momentarily and cleared her throat. "When you're an officer in the Republic military, you learn to accept casualties when they come—it's part of the job. But when you lose a soldier directly under your command, you can't help but feel the pain that comes with the loss. Private Lacy Brown was a fantastic soldier who never once complained about following the orders given and carried them out to perfection. Her team leader, Sergeant Nelson, told me she was on the fast track to become a team leader herself one day, and Sergeant Casper said he would take her on his team any day. She is the personification of what it means to be a Republic soldier, and just by looking at the faces of all of you out there who knew her, I know she will forever leave a mark on you. Although Private Lacy Brown will no longer grace us with her smile and spitfire attitude, the memories each of you made with her will last a lifetime. That is what we all strive for, and she did it in spades." Lieutenant Cooley stepped back from the podium and raised her fist in the air. "For the lost!" she shouted across the parade grounds.

Moore raised his fist in the air along with the entire company and shouted, "For the lost!"

The ceremony was followed by a twenty-one-gun salute before they were dismissed. The soldiers leaving the parade ground spoke in hushed tones with somber faces as they all found their ways back to the barracks. Moore wanted nothing more than to go back and get some sleep since his shift had only ended an hour ago, but he knew he had to check in on Kodiak. He found the man they called "Bear" sitting outside his barracks building in the shade of the poncho liners the soldiers had rigged between buildings. Across from him at the table were Hall and Moreau, and as Moore approached, he gave a soft smile and took a seat next to Kodiak.

He didn't know what to say. "Sorry for your loss" seemed too clichéd and most likely would've been insulting. He wouldn't want to hear that after losing someone like Kodiak or Hall, so why would he subject his friend to that nonsense? Instead, they all sat in silence, taking in the ceremony that had just passed and listening to the songbirds sing in the wind as they flew above.

Finally, Moreau spoke. "Remember that time Brown was running toward that stupid building during a field op in basic?" she laughed as she remembered. "She was so excited to get inside and capture the flag that she didn't see the ambush set up by Second Platoon."

Hall also laughed and added, "Yeah, and then she got hit by like every single rifle in the area. She hit the ground so hard her pants got tangled in the weeds and were pulled down."

A small smile came across Kodiak's lips. "Then when I tried to grab her and drag her out of the way, she said, 'Forget about me, just grab my damn pants.'"

They all laughed, remembering the encounter.

Moore took the opportunity to chime in. "She had an awesome sense of humor. What was it she called Skaggs?"

"Oh, it was so stupid." Moreau tried to remember. "What was it?"

234

"Squiggly Skaggs," Kodiak said solemnly.

"Squiggly Skaggs," Hall laughed, "that was it."

"That was a dumb name, but, man, he got so mad about that," Moreau added with a laugh.

"That guy could find an insult in a dozen roses," Kodiak said, and silence fell across them once more. Moore noticed a tear forming in the corner of Kodiak's eyes, but the man didn't bother wiping it away and instead let it trail down his cheek. "I ended up tripping over my own feet out there. The last thing she said to me was, 'Nice feet, ya big goof.'" He smiled. "She always knew what to say when something bad was happening, like cracking a joke made the desperation of a situation fade away."

"She said everything is the mission, the rest is just noise," Moreau added.

"She was a damn good soldier," replied Kodiak as he nodded in agreement.

Moore sighed and reached across the table to squeeze Kodiak's arm. "She always will be."

They sat together for the next hour, sharing more stories of Brown's antics from basic, and Moore got to hear a few more from their training on the RNS *Currahee*. It was a time for laughs, and even though tears fell from all their faces, by the end, they weren't tears of grief but of happiness.

As the sun began to fade on another day on New Eden, the group gave each other hugs before they were to head off for the night. Moore squeezed Kodiak one last time and turned to leave when he saw Staff Sergeant Muleskin walking toward them down the sidewalk.

Moore nodded to Sergeant Muleskin, who nodded in return and said, "Stick around for this, Private Moore. You'll get briefed when you head back to your hooch, but you might as well not be taken by surprise." This got the attention of the others, who'd also stayed to hear what their old drill sergeant had to say. He heaved a long sigh and continued, "First and Fourth Platoons have been ordered to head out in the morning to Combat Outpost Legion, which overlooks the river crossing just north of here. That's where they believe the Zodark offensive will begin. They don't have time to wait any longer as the rivers will become impassable with the high tides. That river is the only place they can cross within a hundred miles, and it's the only gap that apparently makes sense to the brass. We'll be accompanied by the mortars as well," he said, looking at Hall, "so you'll be joining us too."

The four friends all looked at one another and back to Muleskin, who continued, "It's not the news you wanted, and if I'm being frank, it's not the news I wanted to give, but those are our orders. So go back to your billets, pack up for a long stay and get your affairs in order. We most likely won't be coming back to FOB Edwards anytime soon."

Muleskin turned and walked into his own building across the sidewalk, leaving the four to stand there in stunned silence. Moore was Fourth Platoon's medic, so he knew when he got back to the barracks building, he would be told to get his things in order as well. It was bittersweet that all four of them would be together on the side of a mountain to hold off a Zodark offensive. The rumors had been bouncing around for a while that the combat outpost would be the company's next destination, but just like the rumors that had spun across the *Boxer*, it was all taken with a grain of salt. Now it was coming to fruition, and Moore didn't know how to take it.

Kodiak broke the silence and held out his fist to the others. "Well, that's that, y'all. Time to earn our pay."

Moore bumped fists with the others and watched Kodiak turn and walk into his building. That was a leader if Moore had ever seen one, still green behind the ears compared to the other NCOs, but he knew he'd get there eventually. He had watched one of his friends die less than twenty-four hours ago and was now transforming from a grieving comrade to a determined warrior, and Moore didn't understand how he was able to do it so fast. He was impressed and happy that Kodiak was on his side.

Chapter 35
Kodiak

Combat Outpost Legion
ROCNE-South, New Eden

Combat Outpost Legion sat at the top of a large hill that overlooked an open valley of green below. The valley was flanked on both sides by thick forests and ran from the base of the hill five miles north until it hit a wide river that the Republic called the "Peratis." The outpost was large enough to house two platoons and the headquarters of Apollo Company, which Captain Striker had requested be the case since he insisted on commanding from the front.

COP Legion also housed a makeshift mess hall, field hospital, armory, TOC, a gym and a rec room building. Because of its location five hundred feet above the valley and because it was the highest point in the area, the Puma IFVs were placed at the edge of the perimeter with their weapons pointed downward toward the valley. There were also several machine-gun bunkers that lined the perimeter, and the mortar section was at the highest point of the hill, surrounded by sandbags and high metal walls.

Fourth Platoon was the first to occupy the Pumas and bunkers while Second Platoon took part in operations like presence patrols and reconnaissance missions to the river. ROCNE command had received reports that a large Zodark force was gathering on the northern side of the Peratis River, and they feared the group was making ready to assault across the river pass. It was a logical conclusion, given that monsoon season was fast approaching and the crossing that COP Legion overlooked was the narrowest pass for more than a hundred miles.

Private First Class Harrison Kodiak had already been on a few patrols since arriving, but they had run into zero resistance, and it seemed that whichever Zodark forces had been in the area had pulled out. It was an ominous fact his unit had taken note of after their sixth patrol had turned up no enemy contacts.

He had just returned from his seventh patrol when Staff Sergeant Muleskin pulled him and some others aside. "I need six volunteers to go with me on a recon mission to the river's edge. One of the ships in orbit is saying the Zodark force massing on the other side of the river has grown over the past couple of weeks, but because they're using cloaking methods, they can't get a good read on just how many. We're gonna need to bivouac for a couple of days and send a drone over to check it out. It's voluntary, but just know if I don't get eight names you'll be voluntold."

Kodiak was sick of the monotonous patrols they had been going on, and with their rotation of manning the perimeter coming up, he saw his chance to do something a little more interesting. He stepped forward and raised his hand. "I'll come."

Sergeant Woods raised his hand as well and said, "Me too."

Muleskin hesitated for a moment and then said, "Casper can funnel whoever is left from Alpha Team into Bravo, then. That means I'm gonna need at least one more from Alpha."

Private Morgan stepped forward and said, "I'm the best damn drone pilot we got, so I guess I'm in."

Muleskin nodded. "All right, Moreau, you will be in charge of Alpha until we get back."

Moreau looked dejected at having to stay behind but nodded in acknowledgment before turning and heading to the barracks building. Some soldiers from Bravo and Charlie Teams had volunteered to come along as well. Sato, Sims, and Mendoza raised their hands and fell in line.

Sims turned to Kodiak, gave him a nudge, and said in his smooth Irish accent, "Guess we're getting the band back together, bruh."

He was right.

Kodiak looked at the soldiers who had volunteered to come along on the recon mission, and he noticed they were all from his basic training platoon. The roster made him feel confident in the operation since they had all worked together before, and most importantly because their old drill sergeant was going to be the team leader.

"Get your gear in place and make sure you're fully kitted for the next two days. You should already be good to go since we didn't do anything on this last patrol, but all the same, give it a once-over. We're pulling out in thirty minutes," Muleskin announced.

****

The recon team commandeered the last remaining Puma that wasn't being used for perimeter control and set off precisely thirty minutes after Muleskin had gotten done briefing them on the mission. Sims was up in the driver seat, bouncing the vehicle across the difficult terrain as it transitioned from the rocks of the hill to the valley grass. Sato was in the gunner's seat, and across from him was Staff Sergeant Muleskin behind the vehicle commander terminal.

"So what if we *do* see a large force across the river?" Mendoza asked.

"Well, you aren't gonna take them all on, I can tell you that much, Private," Sergeant Woods chimed in.

Mendoza grunted in annoyance.

"We'll report back to Apollo Six and wait for further instructions," Muleskin responded.

"He'll probably say something witty, like 'Attack the blue bastards, son. We are Apollo's Arrows.'" Mendoza mocked Captain Striker's gruff voice.

Kodiak laughed.

"You're on command net, idiot!" Morgan shouted, pointing to her ear.

Mendoza's face turned scarlet in embarrassment and he stammered, "Um, oh, man, I'm sorry—"

"Relax, Private, she's messing with you," Sergeant Andrews said as he laughed with them.

Mendoza stared daggers at Morgan from across the vehicle as her laughter turned into giddy cackles. "You should've seen your bloody face," she said in between laughs.

"Someone's face will be bloody, all right," Mendoza snapped back through clenched teeth.

"Calm down, Doza, the Welsh are particularly bad at telling jokes," Sims said from the driver's seat.

"Almost as bad as the Irish are at fu—" Morgan began.

Muleskin cut her off. "That'll be all, you two. Sims, get us into the trees to the left over there. You see that clearing?"

"Yes, Sergeant," Sims responded.

Kodiak felt the vehicle turn to the left and slow down. The sound of tree limbs scratching the armor of the Puma screeched along the sides as the vehicle came to a stop.

"Thank you for riding the Puma Express. Please watch your step as you exit into the wondrous forests of New Eden," Sims said over the internal comms.

239

Kodiak smirked and shook his head as he removed the seat harness and stood, crouching slightly to avoid hitting his head. He exited the vehicle with the others and spread out into the trees to provide security. When you'd seen one forest on New Eden, you'd apparently seen them all, at least on this continent. It was dimly lit from the thick canopies, and the area glowed in blue and orange bioluminescent fungi.

Muleskin's voice crackled over Kodiak's helmet comms. "OK, let's form up in a line. Keep your spacing, and follow me. We'll set up camp on the forest edge overlooking the river."

No sooner had Kodiak's knee hit the ground to pull security than he was standing back up and falling in line behind Morgan. When she had disappeared ten meters ahead of him through the brush, he stepped off and followed the soft green glow of her helmet's glow in the dark strip.

Despite being deep in enemy territory and a good distance from any quick reaction force, Kodiak felt freer. There wasn't any stress weighing him down, and by now, while the death of Brown was still present in his thoughts, it was only as a distant memory. He worried that it might be complacency slipping into his mind, but every time a tree limb snapped or a bird cried out, he would turn to find the source of the noise. For how relaxed he was, the slightest noise caused him to tense up, the sign of a soldier always on alert.

"Moreau seemed pissed she couldn't come along," Morgan said in Kodiak's left ear.

He had customized his internal communication settings to direct someone's comm traffic to one ear or the other. All personal internal comms only came through his left ear, and any traffic meant for the entire team came through both ears. That way he knew what was private and what wasn't. Sergeant Woods had shown him that trick after only a week on planet, and he found it very helpful. Woods had always been a hard-ass to Kodiak and the others on his team when they were aboard the *Boxer*, but once they were planetside, he had relaxed a lot more. That wasn't to say he wouldn't chew you out if you got out of line, but overall, he was more pleasant to be around.

"Can you blame her?" Kodiak responded. "I'd be pissed too if I finally had a chance to head outside the wire to do recon but instead got held back to provide security."

"Very true, but we both know that's not why she's mad," Morgan responded.

Kodiak thought about what she meant but then shook his head and said, "I'm not trackin'."

"You'd think after years of generational evolution, men would finally be able to take a hint," she responded.

Kodiak knew where she was headed and rolled his eyes. "It's not like that," he said.

"You keep telling yourself that," Morgan replied. "I think everyone in the platoon has already pegged you both as a couple except for you."

"Morgan, I'm stumbling through an alien forest, on an alien planet, fighting blue freakin' aliens. Why on Eden would you ever assume I'd have time for a relationship?"

"Moore has one."

"Yeah, who's all the way back on Earth," Kodiak replied.

"No one forced him into that dumb decision," she scoffed. "I'm just saying, if you have a chance to relieve stress in a safer way than shooting at the enemy, why wouldn't you?"

"It's not smart, Morgan. We're in a war zone, people die. I think it's much crueler to make such a commitment knowing you could be dead the next day."

Morgan didn't reply.

Just because a decision was difficult didn't mean it wasn't the right one, and Kodiak knew that. Of course, he found Moreau attractive, and her French accent was exotic and nice to listen to, but he remembered the pain he'd felt when Brown had died. Now he was expected to amplify that grief by becoming more than just friends with another soldier? He couldn't put two and two together on why that was a smart idea.

"Well, I'd rather die happy than miserable," Morgan finally said.

"Who says I'm miserable?" Kodiak shot back.

"Wasn't talking about you, dear," Morgan replied.

The recon team arrived at the edge of the forest after an hour's walk from the vehicle and pulled security just inside the tree line. The team spent the next hour digging foxholes deep enough to lie down in and fire over the lip if they got in contact. They looked like shallow graves lining the area.

Sims, Sato, and Mendoza pulled security first as the sun reached its apex above them and began to suffocate the forest floor with humidity.

Kodiak's helmet adjusted to the rising outside temperature to reduce the chances of his visor fogging up as he emerged from his foxhole and made his way to the center of the patrol base.

Sergeant Muleskin knelt in the middle, surrounded by Morgan, Andrews, and Woods. "OK, first thing I want is that drone in the air. Patrol the other side of the river and follow the tree line in a mile radius. You see anything of note, I want you to tag it and send it to my console. Woods and Kodiak will provide security for you."

They all replied in unison as Morgan removed the drone from her rucksack. She extended the four wings with rotary blades to their fullest length and attached the video lens to the underside. It was a heavy machine, but Morgan was aided by her armor in lifting the drone and carrying it to the trees' edge.

Kodiak crawled through the underbrush toward the very edge of the forest and pushed some of the vines out of his way to get a clear view. A hundred meters of open field separated the tree line with the river, but Morgan only needed to get clearance from the treetops before deploying the drone. Sergeant Woods dragged the XMD-7 sniper rifle he'd brought along, unfolded its bipod, and deployed the weapon so it pointed towards the other side.

Morgan set the machine down and ran back into the tree line, where she lay down between Kodiak and Woods and opened her own terminal. She really was the best drone pilot Kodiak had ever seen. Even now, when he looked at the terminal, it made little sense to him. Yet there she was, pushing buttons and toggling settings like she had been doing it all her life.

The drone lifted off the ground and hovered for a moment before shooting into the air with lightning speed and disappearing into the sky. Everything was quiet as she flew the machine across the river toward its starting point. Once it linked up with the designed flight path Morgan had created, it would begin to automatically patrol. Her hands left the terminal and she propped herself on her elbows and stared intently at the video feed.

Kodiak's attention turned to the river ahead of him. He wanted to watch what she was doing on the drone, maybe learn a few things himself, but he knew his job was to watch the water.

"When's the last time you've been swimming?" Woods asked in their internal comms.

"Years ago. I went with a few buddies after we won state and floated the Brazos River," Kodiak replied.

"Won state? What sport did you play?"

"Football."

"Shoot, boy—I played football in high school too. What position?"

"Linebacker," Kodiak replied.

"Well, now, that makes sense. I played quarterback. We didn't win any state championships, but it was fun. Were you any good?" Woods asked.

"I had a scholarship to play in college but chose this instead," Kodiak replied but then immediately regretted it. Not a lot of people understood his choice. Sometimes even *he* didn't understand his choice.

"Why the hell'd you do that?" Woods asked.

"It seemed like everyone in my life, parents included, wanted me to go on and play in the pros. I don't know, when I finally sat back and thought about it, I wanted to make my own path. Football was everyone else's dream for me, not mine."

"Yeah, but join the Army?"

"Well, when you say it out loud it sounds pretty dumb," Kodiak replied.

"Hell yeah, it does. I mean, you could be at a frat house right now humpin' sorority girls like a rabbit but instead—"

"I'm here looking at a river with you," Kodiak finished his sentence.

Woods laughed in disbelief. "Well, yeah."

"Trust me, Sergeant, I've thought about that every day since getting here."

"Well, I wouldn't. You made your bed, so you might as well lie in it for a while. Plus, you're a pretty good soldier, Kodiak. Maybe this was the right choice."

"Thanks, Sarge," Kodiak replied.

"Well, don't thank me just yet. You still got a lot of time left."

"Contact, bearing one-eight-two-seven by six-four-five northeast," Morgan broke in over their comms. "Looks like three Zodarks with a mobile gun platform heading toward the river."

Woods's voice grew serious. "Are there any others near them?"

"Doesn't appear to be. Could be a patrol or something," Morgan replied.

Kodiak placed his rifle steadily on the ground and amplified the optics in his visor as he searched the riverbank on the other side but saw nothing. If it was a larger force, the entire recon mission could be in serious jeopardy. Even three Zodarks with an MGP could wreak havoc on their position. If they had any more in reserve, contact could prove fatal.

"Apollo One-One, this is Apollo One-One Alpha, over," Woods said into the team net.

"Go for Apollo One-One," came Muleskin's reply.

"We have a three-Zodark patrol with mobile gun platform heading to the river's edge. Please advise."

There were a few moments of silence before Muleskin replied. "Just observe and report for the time being. If they try to cross the river, then engage. Apollo One-One out."

Woods looked over to Kodiak and tapped his helmet to make sure he was listening. Kodiak nodded and turned his attention back to the river. He had never seen one of the Zodarks' mobile gun platforms before but had seen video of them during training. They hovered about two meters off the ground and had a large gun turret on the top that could rotate 360 degrees. He knew the weak spots on the MGP were around the hover ports as well as the base of the weapon itself, but it took a lot of firepower to knock it out of commission.

"Ten meters from the tree line, you should be able to see them in a moment," Morgan reported as she left the drone in auto-hover mode and grabbed her own rifle.

Kodiak scanned the trees on the far side of the river and watched as three Zodarks emerged along with the MGP. They didn't look like they were on high alert. Their weapons were at the low ready and they walked slowly next to the hovering platform, talking amongst themselves. Every time he'd seen a Zodark, it had been in the heat of battle when they were trying to kill each other. It was a fascinating turn of events to get to watch them behave as if they weren't in any danger.

His fascination quickly turned to worry as the patrol neared the water's edge. He had heard the order from Muleskin saying they were to engage if they attempted to cross the river. He didn't think such a small unit would try and do so, but as they continued to make their way toward the coursing water, he began to have doubts about that initial assessment.

Woods's voice popped into Kodiak's ear. "If we have to engage, wait for me to fire first. I want them to be halfway across the river before we open up."

He emphasized the word *wait* and Kodiak knew it was for him more than Morgan. When they had been ambushed in the forest earlier in the deployment, he hadn't waited for Woods's signal and had fired first. It had worked out that time, but he knew he needed to trust Woods this time around. Confidence and cockiness could quickly lead to a bullet in the head on New Eden.

The Zodarks stopped at the bank of the river and stared across. Kodiak instinctively shrank himself lower in the brush and hoped they didn't possess some unbelievable eyesight. He knew he was in pretty good cover but also didn't want to be the first one shot because his arm was unknowingly exposed.

They didn't react like they knew anything was wrong, and under the barrels of three Republic soldiers, the Zodarks stepped into the rushing water and began to cross. The fast-flowing crystal-blue water came up to their waists as they waded toward the other side, and Kodiak slowly slipped his finger into the trigger well of his rifle.

"Hold your fire," Woods said.

Chapter 36
Hall

Combat Outpost Legion
ROCNE-South, New Eden

"What's got you all boo-boo-faced?" Red asked Hall.

The mortars had been placed just above the main section of the combat outpost. The only way to reach them was up narrow man-made stairs carved out of the hill's rocky face. Aiden Hall didn't mind it. He liked the seclusion, and it limited the chances of running into the company commander. Captain Striker had made it his daily duty to check on all the battle positions around the combat outpost, a gesture Hall could appreciate but still wanted to refrain from participating in. Usually, Striker's appearance was followed by an hourlong story about "the good old days" followed by a list of things they needed to change. The last time he had taken a trip up the "stairway to hell," as the mortars so affectionately called it, he had rolled his ankles on the wet stone, and they had never seen him since.

Hall looked up from the ground and turned to Red, who sat beside him. "Oh, I was just thinking," he replied.

"Do you always look so depressed when you think?" she asked.

"Depends on what I'm thinking about," Hall replied honestly. "But, no, not this time. I was just thinking how happy I was not to be getting daily visits from Captain Striker anymore."

Red nodded as she took a bite of a PowerBar and said, "Well, you're not wrong about that one. Poor guy almost broke his legs trying to get up those damn stairs."

"The product of not doing PT after hitting a certain rank," Hall replied.

"Oh, be nice," she said, punching his arm teasingly.

"I didn't say I didn't like the guy—just happy he isn't poking around here anymore." Hall punched her back playfully.

"Yeah, it was getting annoying having to hide my guitar every hour," Sergeant Richards replied.

Hall pressed his back against a sandbag and closed his eyes. His helmet lay on the ground next to him, like the others, and he let the sun warm his face, mixing with the cool wind that came over the top of the

246

hill and into the mortars' area. Life at COP Legion was easier and less noisy than on FOB Edwards. The barracks were smaller and more spread out to protect from indirect fire and where the mortars were was quiet and peaceful. Even from their barracks building on Edwards, they could still hear the singing and laughter and yelling coming from the infantry's barracks across the base. The noise that traveled up the hill from their barracks on COP Legion was lost in the windy air.

Of course, with the peaceful seclusion came monotonous boredom. You could only clean and reclean a mortar tube so many times before concluding that there wasn't a whole lot else to do. None of the patrols that had gone out needed fire support because they had never come across the enemy. Which was a good thing—if the mortars had to do their jobs, it was because the infantry was in trouble. Peace might be boring, but your friends weren't out there getting slaughtered. Hall also couldn't help but feel that this peacefulness was only the calm before the storm. Command seemed pretty sure that a Zodark offensive was on the way; they just didn't know when.

Sergeant Richards removed his guitar from his rucksack, unfolded the neck, and began tightening the strings. He plucked each string until he found the perfect pitch and then picked through the notes until something that resembled a song came out. Hall had to admit, the sergeant could play the instrument very well and could actually hold a tune for the most part.

He began to sing:
Maybe I'll just watch the sun go down
While I sit and wonder what's around the bend
Circles in the sky
As the bird flies south on their way home
Leave me peacefully there
Laying in fields of grass and among my friends
The silent trend of what's in store for us and them
Though paths among the dust may cross
I'll just sit here and pretend I knew of what love was lost...

"Lord, would it kill you to play something happier?" Red said as she threw the rest of her protein bar toward Richards.

Richards blocked the bar with his guitar and laughed. "The happiest of songs can be found in the saddest of sounds."

"What the hell does that mean?" Red asked.

Richards folded his guitar in his lap. "You ever fall in love, Red?"

She scoffed. "Love is for idiots."

Richards smiled. "That'd be a yes. Who broke your heart?"

Red scowled at Richards and ignored him.

Hall thought for a moment and said, "I was in love once, or at least I think I was. There was this girl who lived in the same low-income apartments as me. She had red hair, green eyes, and the cutest freckles. She was a madwoman in bed but, man, was she mean."

"You sure your neighbor wasn't Red?" Richards asked with a wry smile.

"Get bent," she responded.

"Her name was Juniper Lawson," Hall remembered. "She'd always come by my place at night when my roommate wasn't home, and we'd be in every room, wearing out all the furniture in it. She was wild."

"What happened to her?" Richards asked.

"Oh, I don't know. She just stopped coming around and I moved on. It is what it is," Hall responded, shrugging.

Richards contorted his face in confusion. "Hall, that ain't love; that's lust."

Hall didn't understand the difference between the two. What was love but a manifestation of lust? He'd thought he loved her. He had enjoyed her company well enough, but only when they were on top of one another.

"Shoot, I loved it. Ain't that enough?" Hall asked.

"Well, of course you loved what you were doing, who wouldn't? I'm just saying you can bang someone without being in love with 'em. I do it all the time," Richards responded, laughing.

Sergeant Wells walked out of the ammo pit and yawned. "Richards hasn't been in love either, Hall. Don't let him tell you anything of the sort. Love is different than just knockin' boots all the time. You gotta enjoy their company, take 'em on dates, and make 'em feel special. You must have stuff in common and make each other laugh and cry. That's the secret of any relationship. If you aren't ready to die for that person, then you don't love 'em."

"I'd die for you, Sergeant. Doesn't mean I want to go out back with ya," Hall responded.

Wells laughed. "Well, that's good to know, Hall, but that's what's expected of you. There are different types of love. Love for your family and love of another. We, for all intents and purposes, are family."

Hall stared blankly at her. Now she was saying there were different types of love, and the confusion mounted. Maybe he didn't want to be in love—it certainly was less complicated to just find someone to spend the night with and forget the next morning.

"See, Wells? You hurt his brain," Richards said, laughing.

The sound of footsteps echoed off the rocky hill face, and they turned to see who was coming around the bend. Staff Sergeant McHenry turned the corner from the stairs with Jackson, Green, and Giovanni, holding paper trays of food from the mess hall.

"Merry Christmas, y'all," McHenry said as he began to hand out trays with the others.

Richards scrambled to look at his watch. "What?" he blurted out.

"Calm down, Richards, it's just a phrase. It's not actually Christmas," McHenry said with a chuckle. He handed Hall one of the trays. "Mess hall had turkey, mashed potatoes with gravy, Belter red beans, and Luna split carrots."

Hall mixed the mashed potatoes with his spork and took a bite. His eyes went wide. "Holy hell. These are real potatoes," he exclaimed.

Richards took a bite of his as well and then put the tray down. "Damn," he sighed.

"What?" Hall asked, taking another bite.

"Only time command feeds you with real food from Sol is when something big is going to happen. Can't have their soldiers dying on an empty, unfulfilled stomach," Richards explained.

Hall looked down at his tray again and lost his appetite. Richards was right—he couldn't remember the last time he had been given something to eat that wasn't freeze-dried or out of an MRE. The steaming food was inviting, but he didn't want to touch it again, almost like if he took another bite, the rumors of an offensive would come true.

McHenry sat down on the dirt next to him. "Listen, Hall, eat up. Richards might be right, but that's no reason to let it go to waste. Might be the last good meal we have for a while." He pointed over to the sandbags with his own spork and continued, "If they're coming, not eating isn't gonna stop 'em. So, eat."

It was like Staff Sergeant McHenry was inside his head. Then again, someone with as much time in the military as McHenry knew what they were talking about. He had been there before, no doubt, and his words made sense. Taking another spoonful of potatoes, he shoveled it into his mouth and savored the taste.

"Attaboy," McHenry said between bites with a smile.

"By the way, someone's here to see ya, Hall," Giovanni said as he sat across from him.

Chapter 37
Kodiak

Peratis River
ROCNE-South, New Eden

Although Kodiak's finger remained on the trigger, he let it hang loosely within the trigger well. Woods had yet to give the order to open fire, and Kodiak was hesitant to disobey his orders again. The Zodark team was still wading across the river in a close gaggle, and at different points they grabbed on to the sides of the hovering platform to steady their advance through the rapids. They had made it just past the halfway point when Kodiak watched Woods tuck the sniper rifle deeper into his shoulder and place his cheek on the buttstock. It looked as if his team leader was about to take the shot.

"I'll hit the MGP, I want you two to concentrate your fire on the Zodarks wading across," Woods ordered.

Kodiak sent back an inaudible confirmation through his team leader's HUD and tucked his own rifle deep into his shoulder. He placed his finger firmly on the trigger and steadied his rifle's sight on the Zodark farthest to the left. Taking his thumb, he toggled the selector switch on his rifle from its railgun selector to the laser-powered designator.

Woods's rifle barked loud as its .50-caliber slug slammed into the MGP's front-left hover port, spinning the platform on its axis as it tried to automatically correct itself. The three Zodarks stopped moving, confused as to where the gunfire was coming from. It was a fatal decision.

Kodiak pulled the trigger on his rifle, sending a bolt of laser fire across the water into the beast he had his sight picture locked on. He watched as the water popped and splashed around the enemy soldiers as they struggled to gain any sort of traction. The Zodark he had been aiming at forgot all about holding on to anything and raised its rifle out of the water in a last-ditch effort to try and find whoever was shooting at it. He watched as his rounds slammed into the Zodark's upper body, and finally its head snapped back and to the left. The body went limp and sank below the waterline.

With his target no longer a threat, he positioned his rifle's sight on the next target. The two other Zodarks were using the MGP as cover while also trying to steady themselves. He watched as Morgan's laser fire sparked across the platform's black body, leaving behind scars on the metal but doing little more. The turret on the MGP turned on its axis, no doubt searching for their heat signatures, and if they didn't get the platform destroyed, it would find their positions soon.

Kodiak changed his target from the Zodark to the platform and aimed for the turret. He couldn't tell if the lasers were doing any damage to the machine—and the only time he knew where he was hitting the thing was when a larger explosion from Woods's sniper would make impact.

"Use your lasers on the organics and use your railguns on the turret, guys," Woods shouted over the net as he fired another shot.

That order made so much sense to Kodiak that he was amazed he hadn't thought of it. The railguns would be able to smash through the heavy armor of the MGP and with a high volume of fire could probably take it out of action through sheer force. The lasers could then be used to mop up the Zodarks struggling through the water and hopefully leave them good and charred at the bottom of the river.

He flipped his selector switch from the laser fire to the railgun setting and reacquired the target he had been aiming at. The first round from his rifle went wild as he watched it disappear below the blue waters. He steadied his aim and fired another round, this time watching the 5.56 tungsten projectile slam into the platform around the turret.

The turret turned towards their position. Kodiak's eyes went wide in surprise. Up until that point, the MGP had been having trouble pinpointing the enemy fire. It turned out Kodiak and Morgan's plasma bolts were like little beacons for the platform, leading it right to their position.

Another bark from Sergeant Woods's rifle went off to Kodiak's right. The round slammed into the other hover port on the front right of the platform. The turret fired a volley of large plasma bolts towards their position as its hover ports sizzled and failed. Kodiak tucked his head into the ground and tried to make himself as small as possible as the turret's shots splashed through the trees and underbrush around them. He could hear the crackling of oxygen being cooked around them, and the noticeable smell of burnt ozone hung in the air.

He opened his eyes and waited for a moment to see if any pain would rush up. He didn't feel like he was hit, but he had never been wounded before and had zero reference. He was still alive, that was for sure. He took a deep breath, rolled onto his back and patted himself down but couldn't find any wounds, superficial or fatal. As he stared above him, he saw several trees burnt black and splintered, their remains littering the forest floor around his position.

A cough broke the silence in his ears as he heard Morgan's voice croak, "I'm good. Are you guys all right?"

"Yeah, I'm all good somehow," Kodiak replied as he turned back onto his stomach and crawled to his rifle, which was lying in the debris. He grabbed it, tucked it into his shoulder, and aimed back toward the water where the Zodarks had been. A feeling of elation came over him when he saw the MGP struggling to stay afloat with its two front hover ports off-line. The platform was falling forward into the water as the turret struggled to readjust its aim back toward the tree line. The other two Zodarks were still clinging to the platform but seemed to be navigating themselves to the front to push the hulking machine level.

"Morgan, aim for the Zodarks—they're trying to level out the MGP!" Kodiak yelled into the comms.

"What about Woods? He's not answering," Morgan asked, worried.

"We need to take care of the threat first. Use your lasers to take them out," Kodiak called back.

He was worried about Woods not answering as well, but if he was injured, they wouldn't be able to help him if they were dead. He heard Morgan's rifle firing relentlessly towards the water from down the line as he switched his helmet's comms to the team net.

"Apollo One-One, this is Apollo—" He paused, unable to think of his call sign in the heat of the moment. "This is Kodiak. We've taken heavy fire from a Zodark MGP, and Sergeant Woods is not responding to us."

He flipped his selector fire and let loose a volley of laser bolts at one of the Zodarks clambering to the front of the machine. The rounds sparked across the metal, and the Zodark spun in pain and sank below the waves.

"We're sending Doc up to you, Kodiak. Hang tight," Muleskin's voice came back to him over the net.

It was good enough for now. He watched the other Zodark bend over, grabbing its stomach, and float off down the rushing river. The platform continued to struggle, but its turret couldn't fully extend itself level to attack them; however, it continued to push forward toward the river's edge. If the MGP was able to get on land, it could shut down its hover ports and traverse freely from a deployed position. Kodiak knew what he had to do.

With the Zodarks dead and the platform struggling, he stole his chance and jumped to his feet. He rushed through the forest toward Woods's position, hoping that when he arrived, he would see Woods, at the worst unconscious but alive.

When he arrived, it was a much worse scene than he could have imagined. Sergeant Woods was lying on his back twenty meters away from the sniper rifle, which was still deployed in its original position. Kodiak slowly approached the downed soldier, knowing already what he would find by the way Woods's body was contorted and bent in an unnatural position.

The sergeant's helmet was split in two and the exposed flesh was charred and disfigured. Five red-hot molten holes littered his chest armor, and his left arm was dangling by only a couple of untorn ligaments. Kodiak sighed and felt a sudden wave of sadness come over him like he hadn't felt since Brown's death. Unlike that first time, though, he pushed the feeling aside and turned to the unattended rifle.

He went prone and looked down the magnified scope of the rifle towards the MGP, which was still struggling to find the sandy embankment on their side of the river. He aimed the reticle at the base of the turret and fired. The round punched through the armor, and he watched the impact spray water into the air behind the machine. The recoil was tougher than he'd remembered from basic training but nothing he couldn't handle, especially with the recoil dampener in his armor. He reacquired the target and pulled the trigger again, but the rifle didn't fire. Instead, he heard the click of an empty magazine.

"Shit," he muttered in frustration and looked around for more magazines of the .50-caliber rounds, but he saw none.

He turned back toward the mangled body of Sergeant Woods and pushed off the ground. He ran as fast as he could, slid on his knees next to his former team leader and grabbed for the pouches on his armor. Two of the pouches were destroyed, the metal of the rounds and magazine melted to Woods's armor and skin.

The rustling of leaves perked his ears up and he lifted his rifle with panicked speed until he saw the flash of Republic armor weaving in and out from behind the tree trunks. Sergeant Andrews, their medic, was bounding through the forest with Mendoza following close behind.

"Where's Woods?" Andrews asked as he made it to the clearing where Kodiak knelt and stopped in his tracks. "Oh my God," he muttered, looking at the carnage.

"You can't do anything for him, but you can still help us," Kodiak said as he threw his rifle into Andrews's arms. "There's an enemy MGP trying to crawl its way out of the river and we need to stop that thing before it gets to shore. Mendoza, find Morgan. She's that way"—he pointed to his right—"and give her some help. Doc, I need you with me. Grab as many magazines as possible from Woods's pouches and bring them to me."

Kodiak didn't have time to wait for a reply. He had to get back to the rifle and stop the MGP from getting to the shore. He watched as Mendoza took off in the direction of Morgan before turning himself and heading back to the rifle. He went prone again and was happy to see two magazines of .50-caliber ammunition drop next to him. He looked to his left and saw Doc Andrews going prone with Kodiak's rifle.

"Here, I'll trade ya," Kodiak said, throwing a battery pack toward Andrews and placing a fresh magazine into the sniper rifle.

He pulled back on the charging handle and felt a fresh round seat itself into the chamber. He watched as railgun fire leapt from the woods to his right from Morgan and Mendoza and saw the rounds slam against the metal, causing more critical damage, yet the MGP continued to push forward.

"Fire at the base of the turret," Kodiak said as he trained his own reticle on the weak spot below the platform's gun.

He fired the rifle as fast as he could while still trying to be as accurate as possible. The combined fire from the four of them was causing the platform to stumble and sink lower into the water. He replaced the empty magazine in his rifle and pulled the charging handle again. The platform was now rising out of the water as its back propulsion systems found the shallow floor below and it crept onto the shore.

The moment it could, the platform's hover ports shut down and the MGP slammed into the dirt embankment. It was now level, and the turret traversed toward the biggest threat—Kodiak's position.

"Get down!" Kodiak yelled as he tried to reach up and grab Andrews before the volley of MGP fire hit them. Luckily, Andrews flattened himself out as plasma slammed into their position. Kodiak didn't want to end up like Woods, and he didn't want the last thing he did to be nothing. Grabbing the large rifle, he rolled his entire body to the right and continued to roll for five meters until his back hit a tree trunk. His muscles were aching from the weight of the rifle he'd spun with him, which by some miracle hadn't gotten caught in any of the weeds.

The plasma fire continued, and he heard the crack and sizzle of the rounds destroying the vegetation around him, but he paid it no mind. He had to block all the chaos around him out of his thoughts. His life and the team's lives depended on it. He reacquired the target through the scope and watched more 5.56 tungsten rounds smash against the turret's base from Morgan and Mendoza.

They're still in the fight, he thought with a smile.

Steadying his aim, he fired another shot into the base of the turret and watched blue fire spew from the hole the round had made. He aimed for the same spot and fired again, watching the turret begin to separate from its base. He fired a third and fourth time and the machine sputtered. The turret stopped firing and dropped its barrel towards the ground as it shook, smoked, and spewed more of the same blue fire. He fired a fifth round and an explosion ripped through the valley as the MGP detonated and sent pieces of machinery flying in every direction.

A calm fell across the area as thick, acrid smoke filled the sky over the river and drifted north with the winds. Kodiak slowly pushed himself to his knees and removed his helmet as all the stress and adrenaline dumped itself from his body, replaced with drained energy. He sucked in the fresh air and wiped the sweat from his forehead. Even with his armor's climate control settings, a soldier still sweated inside the helmet, the body's involuntary response to a stressful situation.

"You good?" Andrews asked.

"Yeah, I'm good. You?" Kodiak replied.

Andrews looked over himself for a moment, patting down his legs and arms in disbelief as his hands came away clean. "Yeah, I think I'm good." He let out a low whistle and looked around at the devastation. "How the hell did we manage that?"

Kodiak turned to see Morgan and Mendoza making their way through the forest toward their position. He waved them over as he keyed his mic. "Apollo One-One, this is Apollo One-One Alpha, over," he said. Now that the chaos around him was over, his new call sign came to him easily. With Sergeant Woods dead, he had become the acting team leader of Alpha Team, and until told otherwise, that was what he was.

"Go for Apollo One-One," Muleskin responded.

"Zodark team and MG platform have been eliminated. Sergeant Woods is KIA, but the rest of us are uninjured, how copy?"

"Solid copy, Kodiak." Muleskin would've never used his name over the command frequency, but on their own side channel they could be informal. He continued, "Use the drone to recon the area across the river for any more activity. If none is imminent, beat feet back to our position. Apollo One-One out."

Kodiak looked up towards Mendoza and Morgan. "You guys hurt?" he asked.

"I'm good, Bear," Morgan replied.

"Solid, boss," Mendoza replied.

"OK, Morgan, I need you to link back up with the drone and see if those explosions attracted any more attention to us."

Morgan's shoulders sank. "I already tried. Something took out the drone while we were in the fight," she said.

"Was it the turret or one of the Zodarks we were shooting at?" Kodiak asked.

"I don't think so. I didn't see the turret traverse to the sky, and the others were too busy trying not to drown, let alone finding a drone and shooting it out of the sky."

She was right, but that was what worried Kodiak. If the ones they had ambushed hadn't shot the drone down, who had? Not only that, it had been their only drone, and now they were effectively blind for what was to come. Thinking that far ahead was not Kodiak's job, however. His job was now to secure Sergeant Woods for transport and link back up with his team at the patrol base.

Kodiak keyed his mic. "Apollo One-One, we're returning to the patrol base. We lost signal with the drone during the firefight."

****

The sun was beginning to make its arch toward the horizon, cooling the forest floor underneath the canopy. Kodiak had kept his helmet off and attached it to a carabiner on his chest's armor to allow the cooling air to wash over him on the walk back. Doc Andrews, Mendoza, Morgan, and himself carried the body of Sergeant Mark Woods to the patrol base and set him down gingerly in the center.

Staff Sergeant Muleskin approached, looked down at the mangled body of Alpha Team's expired leader and grunted. He then knelt next to the half-zipped body bag and closed it the rest of the way. He stood and looked over towards Kodiak. "How'd the drone go down?"

"We don't have any idea. When we got in contact with the team crossing the river, Morgan let it continue its flight vector while we engaged. After the fight, there was no signal coming from the drone," Kodiak replied.

"OK." Muleskin sounded resigned to the situation at hand. "I'll contact Apollo Six and see where this all stands."

As the sun set on New Eden, the remaining members of the recon team pulled security around the patrol base. Sato and Sims were ordered back to the tree line overlooking the river as an advance scout team to warn the others if Zodarks crossed. Kodiak was fine with that—he'd had his fill of combat for the moment and was much more comfortable lying in the shallow grave of his foxhole.

Staff Sergeant Muleskin had talked to Captain Striker on COP Legion but had been told to wait until the morning to pull out in case of any Zodark activity throughout the night. They were all uneasy with that order but knew complaining about it to one another was about the only thing they could do. The order made sense from a command point of view. They no longer had eyes over the valley, and across the river, something had taken out those eyes, so all the evidence suggested that the odds that Zodarks were camped there were high.

Around 0300 hours, Muleskin slowly slid into the foxhole beside Kodiak and rested his back against the dirt. "Can't sleep?" he asked.

"Not really," Kodiak replied.

"Yeah, me either," he said as he looked over at Kodiak. "You did good today, Kodiak. You did your job and then some with how you improvised and used Woods's rifle."

Kodiak shrugged and thought about it for a moment. "It doesn't feel like I did."

"That's good. There are two types of leaders when you really break it down: those that strive to do what's best for their team, and ego-driven promotion chasers that do what's best for themselves. It's easy to know which is which if you just sit back and observe. When Woods wasn't responding to your comms, what did you do?"

Kodiak remembered back to the firefight and his hands began to sweat. "I didn't know he was dead at the time—thought he was maybe just incapacitated or his comms were knocked out," he said. "I told Morgan to keep the fire up on the Zodarks that were still alive."

"Why?" Muleskin asked. It wasn't accusatory but more out of curiosity at his decision.

"Woods had taken out the front two hover ports on the underside of the turret, so it was essentially dead in the water until it got on land and was able to set down. The Zodarks, however—man, they were smart. They tried to swim to the front and lift it level so it could continue firing. We eventually took them out, and that's when I moved to Woods's position and found him."

"Why did you decide to leave your position at that moment?"

"The turret couldn't do anything until it got on land, and Morgan and I alone wouldn't be able to take it down in time with just our rifles. I wanted to see if Woods was OK and could get back on his rifle, but when I got to him—" Kodiak paused and fought back the choking rising in his chest. He cleared his throat and continued, "When I got to him, he was dead. I checked his rifle and that's when Doc and Mendoza rolled up."

"Doc Andrews told me you took charge from there. Why didn't you hand over that duty to Andrews? He is a sergeant, after all."

"He wasn't there when the battle started, and I didn't have time to fill him in on all the details. I felt like I had a better understanding of the situation than he did at the time. I knew Mendoza needed to get over to Morgan and I needed to get on that rifle before the turret got to shore. Doc didn't have a rifle, so I gave him mine."

Muleskin smiled. "You did very well, Kodiak. I'm proud of you," he said in a hushed tone as he stood and began to move to the next foxhole. "You've come a long way since basic, I'll say that."

Kodiak took a deep breath and let himself smile. It felt good knowing he was at least making someone proud, and it was nice to know he wasn't out there messing it all up. He didn't quite understand what exactly he had done that was special, though. All his choices that day had come naturally, as if each one was the obvious next step toward the end goal. He looked up into the glowing blue and orange of the canopy above and slowly drifted to sleep.

Chapter 38
Moore

Combat Outpost Legion
ROCNE-South, New Eden

If the joint troop medical facility on FOB Edwards was the penthouse, the field hospital on COP Legion was the outhouse. The four-room medical building sat in the center of the combat outpost, surrounded by sandbags and armored shielding. Inside was an office for Captain Shinjo and Lieutenant Hodges, while the other three rooms acted as makeshift operating rooms. In the back corner of each operating room stood a refrigerated containment safe that housed every type of blood and plasma. It was a long way from the pearly-white tile floors of the JTMF, but so far, they'd made it work.

Private Oliver Moore was the primary medic for Fourth Platoon, so when they got spun up to go to COP Legion, he was going with them. He didn't mind getting off the FOB for a while. Late shifts at the medical facility were becoming painfully slow and repetitive. It also helped that Sergeant Alexander, Corporal Martin, and Nova came out too. Medics from Belus Company filled in the holes for Second and Third Platoons, who had stayed back on the FOB to pull security detail.

Moore stepped outside the field hospital, squinting as his eyes adjusted to the natural light. With the building being surrounded by armor sheeting, there was barely any light inside except for that produced by the lights hanging from the ceiling. The air was so much nicer outside, though, that he couldn't argue. He took a deep breath of the fresh air and began making his way up to "Mortarville," which was the clever name given to the quiet little alcove the mortars had set themselves up with on the top of the hill.

After the rain the previous night, the climb was annoying as his feet slipped on every other step on the way up, but Moore had nothing else to do at that moment. Sergeant Martin and Nova had bonded over a new NeuroNet game that had recently come out on gaming headsets. Moore didn't understand the fad of the NeuroNet, but it was rather popular in the Belt according to Nova, so the fact that an Earther like Martin was into it probably fascinated her. So that eliminated Nova as someone to hold a conversation with.

Kodiak had gone out with Staff Sergeant Muleskin on a recon operation to the river, so Moore couldn't stop by his billet for a chat. Moreau was an option, but if Moore was being honest with himself, she scared him without Kodiak around. Nope, nobody but Hall was available to listen to how his day had gone, so he was the unlucky bastard to be stuck with him.

Halfway up the steps, he came up to a slower-moving group of soldiers. He recognized them as some of the other mortars, and they were carrying plates of food from the DFAC. He had forgotten to go to the mess hall for chow, but he didn't really have an appetite at the moment, so the smell of the fresh food didn't bother him too much.

The staff sergeant turned and looked at Moore. "Where ya headed, Doc?" he asked.

Moore took a few more steps up to them and stopped. "Just wanted to come see Hall, Sergeant," he replied.

"Well, come on up, then. He should be up there jawing it up with some of the others. You get yourself any chow?"

"No, Sergeant," Moore replied, shaking his head. "Not really hungry if I'm being honest."

"Well, all right, Doc, but if you get hungry, you let me know. We can't have one of our medics trying to save us on an empty stomach."

Moore smiled. "Well, let's hope it doesn't come to that, shall we?"

They made it to the top and he waited just outside the sandbag entrance so as not to get in anyone's way. The mortars were meticulous about their things and territorial when outsiders came up. If it was an officer, they'd play nice, and they tended to treat the medics friendlier than usual, but if a stray grunt found their way up the stairway to hell, they'd get a good reminder why it was called that.

"By the way, someone's here to see you, Hall," came a man's voice from beyond the sandbag.

Hall came around the corner and smiled. "Well, damn, Moore, you could've come in and said hello," he said.

"It's all right, mate. Just wanted to know if you wanted to have a chat?"

"Yeah, man, sounds good," Hall said as he came around and they began walking down the steps.

They got about halfway before stopping and looking out over the valley below. Moore still couldn't understand how somewhere so beautiful could be scarred by so much devastation. It put into perspective just how quickly life could change. If the Republic had chosen to go to another planet in a Goldilocks zone, this war might not have ever happened. Of course, rumors were spreading that this war was not only being fought on this planet and its moons but in other entire solar systems. He didn't want to think about that.

"What's on your mind?" Hall asked.

"Have you heard anything from Kodiak?" Moore asked.

"Naw, man, I haven't heard a peep. You ask Moreau?"

"She's, umm—well, a little bit intimidating if I'm being honest."

"Angie? She's harmless, Moore. You should know that."

"Oh, I know. I can't help it, been like that since basic."

"Well, then, you know as much as I do. We don't really get a lot of info fed our way up in Mortarville."

Moore watched a pack of wild animals run across the valley and into the forests. "You think that offensive is gonna actually happen?" he asked.

"Well, they gave us real potatoes if that says anything for ya. The team thinks it's a bad omen."

"What do you think?"

"I think I'm still a little too wet behind the ears to know anything about it. If they come, then they come, not much we can do about it. If they do come, they better come hard. The valley is just open fields. Even if they try to use the forests, it'll only get them concealed so far. Command was smart and put Legion on the highest point in this area."

Moore thought about that and tried to envision a battle taking place in front of him, how it might look, the good and the bad. "I guess you're right," he finally said. "If it's gonna happen, though, I'd like to get it over with."

Hall chuckled and slapped his hand on Moore's shoulder. "You and me both, buddy, you and me both."

Silence fell between the two for a moment as they both looked out across the valley, its glow fading with the sun as it set. Moore again tried to picture the battle in front of him, but even he thought his imagination couldn't conceive of an attack's full might. In his time on New Eden, he had only seen the aftermath of such fights and had never been in active combat. When they'd first arrived at COP Legion, they'd been given compact versions of the infantry's main rifle. He had fired one in the simulator on the *Boxer* but never in the real world. Even now, as the rifle hung loose on its three-point harness, it felt alien to him.

"Have you gotten any vids from Lilliana?" Hall broke the silence.

"She received the one I sent just before we left to come out here—I got her reply a couple days ago. I'm finding it hard to explain exactly where we are and what this place is. On FOB Edwards, it was easy to make it sound safe, but here? I'm trying not to scare her by simply explaining our circumstances."

"You don't need to go into detail. She knows what your job is, and she knows what you're doing. The last thing on her mind is finding ways to stress you out about meaningless crap at home you can't help. You should do the same. Don't make her stress out any more than she probably already is. At the end of the day, she can't do anything about it. Make the videos about her, not about what you're doing."

Moore had always known Hall to be the more practical of the group, and the words he had just spoken were exactly what Moore needed to hear. When Moore had met Hall in basic training, he had been quiet and tried to go unnoticed as much as possible. It wasn't until they were in transit to New Eden aboard the *Boxer* that he'd become more outgoing. The new side of Hall was a welcome as he transitioned from introvert to the class clown.

Hall also played dumb a lot, especially when being naive came in handy during conversation. Moore knew Hall had been a criminal before being enlisted by the state to serve his sentence in the Army—he had known since basic training, and he didn't care. But he also knew Hall had a way with words, slippery at times, although he'd never done that to him. He was grateful for that, beyond grateful. That was why his words meant so much—they came from the heart. Maybe it was because of Hall's past that he had chosen to stay closed off in the beginning, only showing his true colors once he trusted those around him. Whatever it was that made the once-isolated kid become the life of the party, Moore was thankful.

"Wise words from an otherwise indifferent individual," Moore teased.

"You could learn a thing or two by just sitting back and listening to what everyone else says. Sometimes it's better to sit back than to show your hand. Plus, you're my friend and you needed advice. If I were in your shoes, I wouldn't listen to it, but I'm also a stubborn moron who thinks he knows better than everyone else."

"Well, it meant a lot. You're right about it all—I can't put any more stress on her. It's hard enough."

"A broken clock is right twice a day, my friend," Hall teased, tapping his head.

"Well, like I said, I appreciate it."

"I tell you what," Hall replied, "when this deployment is over, and the next time we get leave somewhere halfway decent, I'll take you, Kodiak, Moreau, all of us out for dinner. We'll make it a thing. After every deployment, we go and remember the fallen and drink to the memories."

Moore thought about it and grew a little sadder. If he was lucky enough to survive more than one deployment, how many faces would he see disappear from the dinner over time? How many more of his friends would he lose before the war was over? How many more of his friends would die at this very combat outpost? He tried to shake the thought from his head.

"You all right?" Hall asked.

"Yeah, just thinking about stuff I don't really want to think about," Moore replied truthfully.

"Get some sleep, Moore. You're gonna need it if our dinner was any indication."

Hall was correct again. Moore's sleep cycle had been all messed up because of his late shifts at the JTMF on FOB Edwards. Ever since getting out to Legion, he hadn't really taken time for himself to lie down and try to get some sleep.

"Yeah, mate, I think I will," Moore said as he patted Hall on the back. "I'll see you in the morning, yeah?"

"I'll see you in the mess hall," Hall replied.

****

Moore made it back to his sleeping quarters just as the blue sky turned to the deep purple of dusk. The barracks he shared with the other medics was a one-room open floor that had two-person bunks stacked against the walls. Unlike the forward operating base, COP Legion had more than half of its occupants working at some capacity day and night. Because of this, more than half the beds were empty at any one time. The barracks on a combat outpost were meant for sleeping and that was about it.

The dimly lit interior and stale air were a kind of welcome to Moore as he opened the door and walked toward his bunk. He saw the silhouette of Cara Nova on the top bunk. The slow, rhythmic rise and fall of her shoulders told him she was sleeping. Just the sight of Nova peacefully counting sheep caused Moore to yawn as he sat down on the bunk and lowered his head. Clothes be damned, he no longer had the strength to take them off. It was as if his body was realizing that it had the opportunity to finally get sleep and it wasn't going to wait for him to get comfortable. He groaned in pleasure when the bunk's mattress creaked at his body settling in, within moments, he too was fast asleep.

Chapter 39
Kodiak

Patrol Base by the Peratis River
ROCNE-South, New Eden

Kodiak sat upright as he was shaken awake by Mendoza. Wide-eyed, he looked up at the man and tried to blink the sleep from his vision. There were a lot of things going on around him, and his senses were beginning to overload. One minute he was peacefully asleep, and the next, the world was in chaos.

"What's going on?" Kodiak asked in the hushed tones he had used earlier with Sergeant Woods.

Mendoza discarded the whispers and said, "Sims and Sato said there's a regimental-sized Zodark unit pushing to the river's edge now. They're pulling back and we're getting the hell out of here—let's go!"

Mendoza grabbed Kodiak by his armor and yanked him to his feet. He gathered himself, grabbed his rifle, put his helmet over his head and turned on his visor's HUD. "Does COP Legion know?" he asked as they ran toward the center of the patrol base.

"Oh yeah, they see it. They're preparing defenses now," Mendoza replied.

Just as they stopped in the center near Sergeant Muleskin, Sims and Sato came sprinting into the area. Sims put his hands on his knees and ripped off his helmet, gulping for air. "They're bringing across numerous MGPs, tanks, and a lot of infantry," he croaked through gasps for air.

Sergeant Muleskin stared at Sims for a moment as if calculating his next move. "Put your helmet on, Sims." He turned to look at the rest of them huddled around. "We need to get back to the Puma and get back to the COP. Sims, you'll drive. Sato, you're the gunner. Now let's move!"

The recon team began sprinting in an unorganized mad dash to get to the Puma as it was the only thing that would get them to the COP. Depending on how fast the enemy moved, it might be tight getting back to the base before the battle started. Those damn Zodarks could move quick once they got going. Even as they ran towards where they'd left the vehicle, Kodiak could feel the ground tremble under his feet. It was like an earthquake was striking the continent, but instead of tectonic plates being the cause, it was thousands of Zodark warriors bearing down on their position.

As the patrol base faded from their sight, he felt a twinge of guilt at leaving Sergeant Woods's body behind. He understood the reasoning—there was no way they could carry the body bag to the Puma without using up precious time they just didn't have. It still made him feel like a bad soldier. It had been drilled into his head in basic training and beyond never to leave a soldier behind. Woods was dead, but he was still one of their soldiers. Kodiak didn't know how, but he promised himself that if he survived that day, he would go back and retrieve Woods's body.

Kodiak and the team found the Puma exactly where they'd left it and wasted no time at all climbing on board. Sims started up the engine and raised the ramp after the team had climbed inside and strapped up. He gunned the vehicle in reverse, and Kodiak's body pulled to the side from the g-force as he spun the tires and turned the vehicle around 180 degrees.

"Don't crash the damn Puma, Sims," Muleskin growled into the vehicle comms.

Kodiak sat right behind the vehicle commander's seat and watched Muleskin's terminal as it tracked the vehicle's location and showed the gun's camera in the top right corner. The ride was not a smooth and pleasant one as Sims continuously turned the vehicle sharply from left to right, changing its direction with sporadic movements to avoid getting locked on by a Zodark missile launcher. It was a maneuver they had all trained for in the simulator, and Sims, for the time being, was executing it to perfection.

"Keep that up, Sims, you're doing good," said Muleskin. "Sato, I don't want you firing on them unless they start shooting at us. If they think we're small potatoes compared to the COP, they might just let us get there."

"You know what they say about wishful thinking, Mule," Doc Andrews said from his jump seat.

"Yeah, shit in one hand and wish in the other and see which one fills up first," Muleskin responded.

Kodiak looked across the troop compartment to Morgan, who was facing him. "You good, Morgan?" he asked.

"Oh, just peachy," she responded through gritted teeth.

They had three more miles to cross before reaching the gates to COP Legion, but it might as well have been a hundred miles. For the first time in a long time, Kodiak felt helpless. Outside, he could move to cover, react to contact, and if need be assault through an ambush as a last-ditch effort to live. Inside a Puma, his life rested in the hands of Sims, and even then, Sims could do the best driving in the solar system—none of that mattered if a Zodark missile hit them. One minute he'd be sitting there staring at Morgan, and the next, he'd be vaporized atoms.

"Sergeant, have you heard from the other patrol that was out by the Lalibok River?" Mendoza shouted over the noise in the cabin.

Kodiak turned to pay attention to the answer. He had been aware that another patrol with Sergeant Antonis had gone out with them, but they had taken another route to cover where the river forked into the murky Lalibok. If Kodiak's patrol had been hit, there was no doubt Antonis and his team had gone through the same.

"They were overrun. No one survived," Muleskin replied flatly as he continued working at the station.

Mendoza turned and faced Kodiak, who shook his head. The way their day had been going, it seemed it was going to get a lot worse before it was over.

Chapter 40
Hall

Mortarville, Combat Outpost Legion
ROCNE-South, New Eden

"Get your asses up!" someone yelled.

Aiden Hall slowly rolled over in his camouflage woobie and tried to ignore whoever was shouting so early in the morning, but the hollering continued. He withdrew his head from under the sheet and looked around the mortar pit. Staff Sergeant McHenry was now screaming at the top of his lungs and kicking soldiers still in their sleeping bags like Hall was. Hall had never seen his section leader so angry in the whole time he'd been under him.

He scrambled out of the warm woobie and got to his feet. "What's going on?" he asked groggily.

"Get on the gun, Hall. The blue bastards are coming!" McHenry said as he continued to get the others awake.

The words chilled Hall to the bone, so he grabbed his rifle and headed to the sandbags that faced north. The sun was above the horizon and bathed the valley in golden light as the dew twinkled in the grass below. When his gaze turned toward the river, his jaw dropped and his eyes went wide. A massive column of Zodark soldiers and machines were marching across the river and entering the forests and valley.

Oh my God, it's happening, he thought.

Running to gun one's mortar pit, he began loading up the system, checking the battery, and leveling out the tube. Red knelt at the bipod of the system and helped level the bubbles while Jackson and Green went scrambling into the ammo pit to retrieve rounds for their respective guns.

Hall looked back toward his team leader, Sergeant Richards, and waited for some sort of signal from the TOC. Before moving away from the sandbags, he saw the rest of the outpost coming alive. The soldiers moving below looked like ants pouring out of a kicked anthill. None of the guns were firing yet, and he wondered if they, like him, were waiting for some type of signal.

Richards nodded at something Hall couldn't hear and turned to them. "Fire missions incoming to your terminals!" he shouted.

Hall looked down at his terminal, where several fire missions spilled over the screen. He counted over fifteen targets so far and more were coming in. It was going to be a very long day. He selected the first fire mission and cycled the list so they would come one after another. The first called for eight HE rounds.

He called out the information and adjusted the tube using his deflection and elevation knobs until the terminal blinked green, telling him he was aligned with the coordinates. "Hang it!" he shouted. He checked the terminal one more time and said, "Fire!"

Red dropped the round into the tube, but instead of following through and pushing her body low beneath the barrel, she turned her body and retrieved the next round from Jackson. She repeated the same motion and dropped the second round down the tube.

When the first mission was complete, Hall toggled the next and shouted over his shoulder, "We're gonna need a helluva lot more rounds if these are the types of missions I'm gonna be running!"

He laid in the tube again and Red began dropping more HE rounds on the enemy in the valley below. He wished for a moment he could stand and look at the view below to get some idea of how the battle was going, but the fire missions kept coming.

On the seventh fire mission, the first mishap occurred. Red hung the round and dropped it down the tube, this time flowing downward of the barrel with her arms to the side. The usual thumping sound that would accompany the round exiting the tube was more subdued, a bad sign that everyone noticed immediately as they looked into the sky.

"Short round!" Hall screamed as he stood and ran to the sandbags.

Luckily, he watched the misfire land in the valley, well short of the advancing Zodarks but far enough away not to hurt any of the Republic soldiers. A short round was an indirect-fire soldier's worst nightmare. It happened very rarely, but when it did, the usual culprit was a low battery.

Hall looked down and groaned as he saw the red light blinking on the battery pack, showing that it was empty. It was a really bad mistake and one he shouldn't have made. Warning signs always flashed on the terminal to let the gunner know when the battery was running low, but Hall had been so wrapped up in the battle that he hadn't kept an eye on it like he should have.

Staff Sergeant McHenry came storming around the corner. "What's happened with gun one?"

"The damn battery pack is fried, Sergeant. Our last round fell short," Hall answered.

"Then get another damn battery—gun two has to pick up your missions until you're back online. Get to it!"

Hall knew gun two couldn't sustain that type of fire for very long before their gun's battery ran dry as well.

Nobody was moving and Hall looked around to the others in frustration. "Get me another battery!" Hall shouted frantically to Jackson and Red. He needed to calm down.

Chapter 41
Moore

Field Hospital, Combat Outpost Legion
ROCNE-South, New Eden

Oliver Moore had been checking in at the field hospital that morning to do sick call when word of the Zodark offensive had gone out. Staff Sergeant Bernard Hamilton, Fourth Squad's squad leader, had come by the field hospital to grab Moore and bring him to their position by the northern wall. Moore didn't protest—it was his job to be with Fourth Squad, but he still felt bad about leaving the tent without letting Captain Shinjo know.

When they had arrived at the wall, Hall's mortars were already booming above them, pounding the enemy lines as they approached. Moore stole a glance at the hilltop the mortars were on and smiled as he watched the tubes recoil from another shot.

"Doc, we have three battle positions along this line," Hamilton bellowed over the mortar tubes firing. "BP Six and BP Seven are Puma IFVs, BP Eight is a machine-gun bunker. Stick with me, and if I get a call for a medic, I'll send you to them. I'm on frequency six-five."

They were standing at a small section of the COP where the sand and rock that had been brought in by the wind and storms was brushed aside to show the metal floor of the outpost underneath. In this section, you could see where the metal floor connected with the high metal walls lined with sandbags. In other parts of the outpost, it looked as if these gigantic black metal walls had sprouted from rocks of New Eden like natural armored castles.

Moore walked over to the machine-gun bunker and ducked inside the doorway. The bunker was in the shape of a bulbous half-moon, with three windows that pointed down toward the valley. At each window, a soldier from Fourth Squad stood with their machine guns ready to fire. He moved to the first window and noticed the gunner was a man he'd talked to during their many times in the simulator.

"Blackmon, how ya doing, mate?" Moore asked.

Blackmon, a thin-faced young man with freckles all over his dark face, smiled. "Oh, hey, Doc," he said. "Sergeant Hamilton drag ya out of bed for this?"

"Wouldn't miss it for the world, mate," Moore replied.

He looked out the window, and his smile quickly faded. The lines of Zodarks that continued to march through the valley began to separate as a few dozen MGPs raced through the line and took the lead. Standing on each platform were five Zodarks, holding their rifles in the air and screaming.

The platforms began to gain speed as they raced towards the COP, but something in the formation stuck out. Ahead of the others was another vehicle speeding across the open field toward them. He tapped Blackmon on the shoulder and pointed at the object.

"Hey, can you magnify that?" Moore asked. "What is that ahead of the MGPs?"

Blackmon turned and aimed down the sight of his machine gun. "Holy hell—that's one of ours!" he blurted out.

Moore turned and ran for the exit. Someone had to tell Staff Sergeant Hamilton that the recon team was being chased by the machine-gun platforms. He ran up the ramp until he got to the ground level and jogged over to where he'd left the squad leader.

"Sergeant, I was just in BP Eight and we saw one of our recon Pumas being chased by Zodark MGPs!" Moore exclaimed as soon as he saw Hamilton.

The sergeant turned. "What are you going on about, Doc?" he asked but then turned his head as if listening to something in his ear. "Copy, BP Six, Seven, and Eight. You are cleared hot on those MGPs attacking the Puma," he replied to whoever it was he was talking to, then looked back to Moore. "Good job, Doc. Now stick close to me and hope you don't have to leave again."

The guns opened up at the battle positions and up on the wall as Fourth Squad engaged the MGPs hovering across the valley toward their position and closing in on the recon Puma. Moore didn't want to think about the Puma because he knew it was the recon team that Kodiak was on. He had a job to do and couldn't worry about the things he wasn't in control of.

The Zodark platforms returned fire on Fourth Squad, which in a way was a good sign because it meant Fourth Squad had been making a dent in the advancing platforms. The battle positions' machine guns were still hammering away, but the volume of fire from on the wall had died down noticeably. Moore looked over at the wall just in time to see four plasma bolts streak a few meters above the top. A Republic soldier's body crumpled and then slid off the wall and onto the ground below.

Moore didn't need to go over to know the soldier was already dead. He had grown accustomed to how the body reacted when life was suddenly snuffed out. Whoever had fallen had been dead before they'd hit the ground. When he turned the corner, he saw the soldier's body on its side against the wall. He approached and knelt next to the body to retrieve the dog tag around the neck, but there was little left of the area.

At least it was quick, he thought.

He instead took his MD14 medical device and inserted the cable into the soldier's helmet port.

Private Jacob Nimitz

Nimitz was from Bravo Team in Second Squad; Moore remembered that much about him. He downloaded the service record onto his terminal and recorded the death and its cause before turning and heading back to where he'd been with Hamilton.

"Doc, I was just about to call you. They need you in BP Eight." Hamilton gestured down the path to where Blackmon and his team were.

Moore didn't reply and instead sprinted as fast as he could toward the bunker. He ducked his head once more into the battle position and saw a large hole melted into one of the windows. A soldier was lying on his back, writhing in pain and grabbing his face as another stooped over them.

Moore approached and knelt beside the wounded woman. "What happened?" he asked the soldier next to him. His armor's nameplate said "Richwalski."

"Dawes was standing in front of the window when it blew. It'd taken so many rounds, it just gave out. I don't think the bolt hit her, but her face is jacked up something fierce."

Moore grabbed her hands and slowly lowered them. "Hey, it's Doc Moore. Dawes, can you hear me?" he asked.

Dawes could barely get above a whisper. "Yes," she croaked.

"OK, I'm gonna help you out, all right? Just stay with me and try to control your breathing—you're in good hands." He tried to use a reassuring tone to calm her down as he plugged into her armor. The diagnostic scan showed fourth-degree burns on the left side of her face, and her heart rate was skyrocketing. He approved a painkiller to be administered through Dawes's armor, and she stopped struggling with her arms.

He was able to move her arms to the side and get a closer look at her face. The helmet was still on, and even though he wanted to remove it, something told him not to. He gripped the chin and rolled her head to the side and gasped. The left side of her helmet was melted to her skin. He reached into his medical pack, removed a burn mask and opened the packaging. He stretched the cool material and formed a similar shape to the scar left by the helmet, placing it onto the exposed area. The gel-like mask stretched and filled the remaining spaces and sealed tightly like the air was being sucked out.

He then unbuckled the hover stretcher from his pack and unfolded it. He looked to Blackmon. "You gonna be good if I leave?" he asked.

"Do what you gotta do, Doc. Get Dawes out of here," Blackmon responded.

With the help of Richwalski, Moore loaded Dawes onto the stretcher and activated the pod underneath. The stretcher rose into the air and hovered, allowing Moore to grab hold and push it along as fast as he needed to over any terrain.

Dawes's vitals stabilized on the way to the field hospital, and Moore pushed the stretcher inside. Captain Shinjo was behind his desk when Moore ran in. The man didn't miss a beat as he dropped his cup of tea and raced over. "What do we got?" he asked.

Moore sent the data to Shinjo's terminal and updated him on Dawes's wounds. "I applied the burn mask five minutes ago, and I gave a standard painkiller twelve minutes ago. I didn't want to remove the helmet because of the burns. Her vitals are stabilized at the moment, but that could change. It said she has fourth-degree burns."

"Very good. Help me transfer her to our stretcher and then get yours and get back out there. Today's the day, Moore."

Chapter 42
Kodiak

En Route to Combat Outpost Legion
ROCNE-South, New Eden

An explosion buffeted the infantry fighting vehicle as it violently swerved to its right to avoid whatever Sims had seen in the driver's seat. Kodiak felt helpless as he watched the vehicle's progress on the vehicle commander's terminal over his right shoulder. They were only a mile away from the combat outpost, but every second that passed was another second they were exposed in the open valley.

Kodiak had gone to church on Sundays with his family growing up but stopped when he had entered high school. He still believed in the Christian God but wasn't as devout as his parents were about going to service every week or to confession or any of the other things required by the church. Now, more than ever, he'd wished he'd done a little more in that respect. It was a saying as old as time—there were no atheists in foxholes, and he was getting a taste of why that was true.

"Multiple MGPs bearing down on us!" Sato shouted over the roar of the engine. The railgun turret on top of the Puma was chattering away at the unseen enemy.

Kodiak wished he could link up his helmet to the gun terminal's camera as he watched Sato manipulate the controls and shift in his chair as he continued to hammer away with the gun system.

The ground shook beneath the Puma as it continued to bounce along the road toward their destination. He could feel the tremors rattle the wheels and travel up the armored body until they vibrated his seat.

"What's going on out there, Sergeant?" Morgan asked with worry in her voice.

"Our mortars are hammering the Zodark columns as best they can. That's what the rumbling is," Muleskin replied calmly, but there was a certain tenseness in his voice.

"Oh, so we aren't being shot at?" she asked.

Almost like some bad twisted joke, her question was answered by an explosion that rocked the side of the vehicle. Kodiak had been looking over at Sato behind the gun controls when sparks and flame punched through the armor above his head and enveloped the gunner's station.

Sato let out a horrific scream as the Puma turned violently one way and then the other before all noise ceased inside the troop compartment.

Kodiak felt his body rise in his seat and strain against the belt straps. He knew exactly what was happening. "Rollover, rollov—" he tried to call out before a heavy object smashed into the side of his head, plunging him into darkness.

****

Something was grabbing at Kodiak when he woke. His head was pounding, and he felt something warm running down his face. He grabbed at whatever had its hands on him and struggled to push them away. All the noise inside the Puma was muffled, and a horrible ringing blared in his right ear. He was struck again in the face, and his eyes shot open in pain. Kodiak was looking up at Mendoza, who had his open palm raised to deliver another blow.

"All right, all right!" Kodiak shouted with his hands raised in surrender.

Mendoza smiled. "Snap out of your slumber, Sleeping Beauty. We gotta move," he said.

Kodiak looked around the Puma, suddenly remembering where he had been and what had transpired before the vehicle had flipped. The Puma was lying on its side, engine still rumbling as if Sims's foot was still pressed down on the accelerator. Kodiak hit his restraints' release and stood up, grabbing his rifle, which remained in the magnetic strip next to where he sat. Mendoza was across from him, helping Morgan out of her jump seat while Doc Andrews and Muleskin knelt next to the half-open back ramp, their only escape route.

Kodiak didn't see the others and began to walk back to where the gunner's terminal was before Mendoza grabbed him by his armor. "Sims and Sato are gone, brotha," he said. "We need to get moving. Help us with the door."

Everything was happening so fast, and Kodiak felt that he'd missed a lot. He must have been unconscious for only a minute or two, but it seemed like so much had transpired in that time. He still looked over to the gunner's terminal. The last thing he had seen was flame shooting into the compartment over top of Sato. Light poured in from a melted hole where the top of the Puma was, and below it was the charred corpse of Sato, his hands still clutching the gunner's joystick. Mendoza had said

Sims was also gone—he had to have meant that he was dead as well, which was probably why the vehicle was still roaring.

He turned and made his way to the back of the Puma, where the ramp was slowly lowering as Staff Sergeant Muleskin pulled the emergency release lever next to the ramp. The lever released all the tension on the motor that held the ramp in place, but the armored door was too heavy for one man to push open. Kodiak joined the others, placing his shoulder against the ramp and pushing with his legs. With all five of them pushing against the ramp, it began to move; then gravity did the rest and dropped the ramp out to the side.

As the light poured into the dark compartment, Kodiak's eyes adjusted to the scene outside. He saw the black metal walls of the combat outpost protruding out of the sand and rock in front of them, and relief flooded over him. If they had flipped farther away, they would've been sitting ducks, but he saw Republic soldiers on top of the walls, firing over their vehicle toward the unseen enemy. He didn't have any idea how close they had gotten since the vehicle had flipped.

"Mendoza, pop smoke and cover us while we cross. Doc, you'll be the first to go, OK?" Muleskin ordered as he leaned against the compartment to make a hole for the others.

Kodiak removed a silver smoke grenade from his chest rig and tossed it up to Mendoza, who caught the cylinder with one hand. In the same fluid motion, he pulled the pin and tossed the grenade underhand between the Puma and the front gates of the outpost.

"OK, wait for—" Muleskin began, but Doc Andrews had started across the open ground before the smoke even billowed. "Doc, wait!" Muleskin tried to warn.

Mendoza reached out to grab the medic's armor and pull him back but missed as Andrews continued to run across the unconcealed open ground. Mendoza and Muleskin turned around opposite corners of the downed vehicle and fired at the enemy that was no doubt bearing down on them, hoping to provide some sort of covering fire for the medic.

Andrews was halfway to the gate, smoke just now starting to billow at his feet, when a bright blue bolt of plasma entered his left side and exited out the right. His legs gave way and his body hit the ground with a sickening thud, coming to a stop just before the outpost's gate.

Kodiak shook his head as the smoke filled the area. He wasn't mad and he wasn't frustrated—he was just disappointed with the outcome.

All Andrews had to do was wait for the smoke to finish filling the area and it would've been safe to move, yet panic had set in, and he'd made a dumb decision that had cost him his life.

"Now, go!" Muleskin yelled in frustration.

Kodiak turned to Mendoza. "I got this covered—get across with Morgan."

Mendoza looked at him for a moment, unsure of what to do, but relented and grabbed Morgan. Kodiak turned the corner with his rifle and immediately pulled the trigger. A Zodark warrior had come around the front of the overturned Puma and was charging with a sword high in the air. The sudden movement alone scared the hell out of Kodiak as he held down the trigger, releasing a deadly spray of 5.56 tungsten rounds at his attacker. The Zodark's body shuddered under the intense fire and fell to the ground in a heap.

"Control your rate of fire, Kodiak!" Muleskin yelled behind him.

He was right—Kodiak needed to be smarter with his ammunition, at least until he was able to resupply what he'd lost inside the COP. He checked to see if the front was clear before turning to see Morgan and Mendoza make it across. Muleskin nodded to him, letting him know it was his time to cross.

For the hell of it, Kodiak removed a grenade from its pouch and depressed the activation button before throwing it over the Puma. He crossed to Muleskin and felt the grenade detonate on the other side, accompanied by howls of pain and anger from unseen enemies. Using the detonation as his signal, he ran across the open ground toward the front gate of the outpost and dove for cover as he neared the other side. Mendoza caught him and set him up straight.

"You good?" he asked.

Kodiak nodded. "Yeah, buddy," he replied as he took a knee and aimed his rifle through the smoke. "I got you covered!" he yelled toward Muleskin.

His squad leader didn't wait for another invitation and sprinted across the fading smoke toward Kodiak and the others, who were firing relentlessly into the smoke to provide as much cover as possible. Zodark bolts sizzled through the smoke and splashed across the ground at Muleskin's feet as he continued to run through the fire to safety. He was within ten meters of the gate when a plasma bolt found its mark. It slammed into Muleskin's knee, ripping the lower half of his leg clean off, and the grizzled veteran hit the ground hard.

"Oh God, cover me!" Kodiak shouted in surprise.

Without thinking, he dropped his rifle—it was only going to get in his way—and sprinted into the hail of Zodark fire toward his downed squad leader. Mendoza had taken his place at the lip of the entrance and was providing covering fire as Kodiak reached Muleskin.

"What are you doing? Get out of here," Muleskin growled.

Kodiak ignored him and grabbed the big man, heaving him over his shoulder. His legs were aching at the added weight, but Kodiak used every ounce of strength left in him to push himself to the safety of the front gate. He reached it successfully, and with the help of Mendoza and Morgan, he was able to get Muleskin behind the doors, which slammed shut behind them.

The battle raged on around them, but for the moment, Kodiak and the others were safe within the walls of Combat Outpost Legion. He readjusted Muleskin on his back and started off at a trot up the hill toward the field hospital.

"You should've left me," Muleskin groaned, his voice wavering.

"Yeah, well, chapter my ass after the battle," Kodiak hissed through gritted teeth.

Chapter 43
Hall

Mortarville, Combat Outpost Legion
ROCNE-South, New Eden

    Aiden Hall's mortar had a fresh battery connected at the base, the coils were cleared, and they had started their fourth fire mission since the weapon had come back online. Staff Sergeant McHenry continued to yell words of confidence up and down the gun lines, running the fifty meters between the two to check on their status. The times Hall was able to look up at the section sergeant, he felt pride swell up in him. Through all the chaos that was happening around him, his section sergeant was doing his best to motivate the teams—the sign of a true leader.

    The last round flew from his tube, and he shouted over his shoulder, "Rounds complete!" He looked over at Jackson, who didn't have a round in his hand. "Come on, we need the next HE!" he shouted.

    Jackson shrugged. "We're out!"

    "Out?" Hall asked in surprise. "Didn't you go down and get more with Green?"

    "Yeah, we grabbed everything we could before—" He was cut off by an immense explosion.

    The concussive blast threw Hall's body through the air, and he slammed into a sandbag behind him as dust and smoke covered the entire area. He tried to blink the grit from his eyes as he coughed uncontrollably at the loss of oxygen around him.

    What is happening? What the hell is happening? He began to panic.

    In the cloud of dust, he saw some figures darting back and forth, and another on their hands and knees, crawling through the debris. Hall got to his feet. He didn't feel any bones breaking or grinding underneath him as he straightened himself out.

    The shouting was muffled as his ears rang from the explosion that had hit their position, but he didn't know where the blast had come from. In the faint glow of the sun trying to break through the dust, he saw his mortar tube, still smoking but standing erect. Red was the one on her knees, and Hall grabbed her by her armor and hauled her to her feet.

    "What happened?" he shouted.

"I have no idea," she sputtered in response, spitting sand from her mouth.

"Medic!" someone screamed from their left.

Hall and Red took off running for the source of the yell, which took them around the corner, fifty meters to their left. The sight they came upon was gut-wrenching.

"Oh no," was all Red managed to say, her arms dropping to her side.

Gun two had experienced a critical failure during its last fire mission and the round had detonated in the tube. A charred crater now stood where the mortar system had been, black smoke billowing from the wreckage. Its gunner, Private Smart, was nowhere to be seen and had been most likely vaporized in the explosion. The bodies of Green and Giovanni lay heaped in ribbons against the sandbags, and Bravo Team's leader, Sergeant Wells, sat with her back against the far wall.

Blood dripped from her mouth as Wells screamed hysterically for a medic. Hall approached her mangled body, and his heart broke into pieces. Her legs were gone, and a large piece of shrapnel had embedded itself in her chest armor. Tears rolled down her cheeks as she looked up at Hall, gulping for any air her body could find, and he grabbed her shaking hand.

"Where's my team?" she asked softly.

He didn't see the harm in lying to her. "They're OK, Sergeant. We're looking after them."

Her eyes softened and she gripped his hand harder. "Thank you," she whispered before her hand relaxed and her eyes closed for a final time.

Staff Sergeant McHenry limped around the corner, a trail of blood dripping from his leg. "We need to get our gun back in action. Did any of their rounds survive the blast?" he asked.

"Sergeant, your leg," Red replied, pointing to the blood trail.

"I'll be fine. Does their gun have any rounds left?" he asked again.

"Negative, Sergeant. That was their last round," Hall said, looking down at the ground.

Sergeant McHenry sighed. "Jackson, get down to the ammunition supply point and try to get us some more rounds for gun one," he ordered. Jackson took off down the stairway to head towards the ammunition supply point. McHenry turned and saw Sergeant Richards from gun one approaching. "Richards," McHenry said urgently, "make sure gun one's battery wasn't damaged by the blast and have it ready to go before we start our next fire mission."

"Will do, but tell me the captain's gettin' us some fire support before we get overrun?" Richards asked, a look of concern on his face.

"Hell yeah, he is. An orbital strike is apparently not an option, so Captain Striker got a request for some close-air support approved. Until the fighters get on station, we've got the 155mm howitzers out of FOB Edwards gearing up to lay some hurt on the bastards. Now go check on gun one and make sure we're ready."

Richards smiled approvingly as he turned and ran back to his team's gun to do what McHenry had asked of him. Red followed and Hall turned to go as well but stopped at the sandbags in front of him to look over at the battle.

Smoke was rising in hundreds of spots across the valley from where their rounds had struck, leaving behind countless Zodark bodies in their wake. What had seemed before the battle to be an insurmountable number of enemies had diminished considerably, but they continued pushing forward. They used their still-standing machine-gun platforms as cover and deployed personal shields into the ground along the way for the ones behind them to use. The Zodarks were good at taking ground, and what seemed like a lack of emotion helped fuel their ability to push forward even under the worst conditions.

The soldiers on the walls below kept hammering away and the battle positions around the walls were still active as the combined firepower slowed but didn't stop the advance. The Zodarks seemed to be making a dent as well as there were far fewer soldiers on the walls defending the position than there had been earlier in the fight. The possibility of being overrun had crossed Hall's mind at the beginning of the fight, when the enemy had been crossing the river in large columns of soldiers, but now that the armada had gotten across, he could see an end to their lines. They could be defeated, but as he looked around at what was left of gun two, he wondered at what cost victory would be achieved.

A shrieking scream pierced the air above his head as Republic fighters broke through the sound barrier towards the Zodark positions. A roar of cheers erupted from the soldiers on the ground as they watched Republic air assets join the fight to relieve some of the pressure they were under. In the distance, long, thin Zodark fighters soared through the clouds to meet their Republic counterparts. They spun unnaturally fast as they dodged Republic missiles and raced past the formations before arching high into the air and firing laser bolts into the Republic ships. One of the friendly fighters sputtered flame and smoke before spiraling into the ground, igniting a terrifying fireball.

Hall left the sandbag wall, unwilling to watch the dance of fighters any longer, and walked back to gun one, where Sergeant Richards and Red were cleaning off the exposed coils. Hall took his mortar tool from his vest and attached it to the bottom of the tube, twisting until he heard it unlock. Removing the firing pin, he went to work cleaning it with water, a rag, and some lubricant. It took several minutes before he was able to chip away the metal that had been melted to the pin, but he was finally making progress. The magnetized shot was a lot cleaner for the mortar system than the old nitroglycerin accelerant used before Hall's time, but the tube still needed cleaning. The harder the mortar system worked, the faster the batteries drained.

"How's the battle going?" Richards asked as he pulled the swab from the tube.

Hall looked up at him as he applied the lubricant to the pin. "The wall's holding. Republic fighters have joined the fight, but the Zodarks have fighter craft dogfighting them. The good news is you can actually see where the Zodark column ends, but their front lines are only about a hundred meters from the outpost," he replied.

Richards spat onto the ground. "Well, at least we're holding," he replied.

Hall recognized that he needed to have that sort of confidence at moments like this one. When everything seemed to be crashing around him and he felt that he was in an impossible situation, he needed to find the brighter side of things. It seemed inconsequential for meaningless day-to-day things, but in the heat of combat, he'd take anything he could.

"We're good, right?" Red asked, worry in her eyes.

Hall looked over at her and tried to give her a smile. "Yeah. We're good, Red," he said.

Chapter 44
Moore

Field Hospital, Combat Outpost Legion
ROCNE-South, New Eden

Moore had strapped the hover stretcher back to his medical pack and hefted the heavy bag onto his back. More wounded began to flood inside the field hospital—some already dead, and some that they just couldn't help. He felt for those soldiers who were still aware of where they had been taken—so close to those that could help them, but not enough hands to get to them all. Moore could stay and try to help, but others like Nova were already doing so and they needed more medics out on the outpost to grab the wounded and bring them back.

He ran out the front flap of the building just in time to see a massive explosion rock the mortar pit above them. The concussion of the blast shook the area, and he watched in horror as fire, smoke, and debris shot into the air hundreds of feet above Mortarville. He dug his feet into the ground and took off towards the stairs, but a shout stopped him in his tracks. He turned to see who had yelled his name and saw Kodiak with someone on his shoulders.

"Moore, we need help!" Kodiak yelled from across the road.

Moore looked back at the mortar pits and then turned toward his other friend. He pointed to the field hospital and ran back to the door, meeting Kodiak and the wounded soldier inside.

Kodiak dropped Sergeant Muleskin onto a stretcher and Moore looked him over. One of his legs was missing below the knee and blood was coming out of the mangled stump. He looked up at Kodiak angrily. "Why didn't you apply a tourniquet, Bear?" he growled.

He removed one from his kit and slipped it over the stump. When the light on the outside of the black band glowed green to show he was over the main artery, he pressed the button and it tightened down on the leg. Sergeant Muleskin let out a bloodcurdling cry as the tourniquet cut off the blood flow and stopped the bleeding.

Moore then removed a coagulant gel sleeve from his kit and slipped it over the stump, letting it seal over the wound. He then inserted his medical device into Muleskin's helmet port and approved a single painkiller into his bloodstream.

"What do you need us to do, Moore?" Kodiak asked as he looked over Sergeant Muleskin.

"Something happened up at Mortarville—they're gonna need your help," Moore replied, not taking his eyes off Muleskin as he went through his vitals.

Kodiak slapped the guy next to him and they ran out of the field hospital and into the chaos outside. Moore looked back down at the vital readings and saw that they were stabilizing. He took his white marking pen and wrote M for morphine on Muleskin's armor along with the time he'd administered it.

"I gotta go, Sergeant. You're in good hands," Moore said. He didn't wait for a reply as he heaved his pack onto his back and ran out onto the outpost.

The ground trembled below his feet as more explosions rocked the area, but he had to continue moving toward where Fourth Squad had been—that was his primary objective. When he arrived at the spot where he'd been with Staff Sergeant Hamilton earlier in the fight, Hamilton was no longer there.

The rumbling continued as the sky darkened above him, and for a moment Moore feared the worst—a Zodark ship entering orbit above the outpost. But when he looked up, he saw black storm clouds quickly spiraling above the outpost and valley below. Thunder was shaking the outpost as each crash was brought on by streaks of lightning.

When he moved down the line toward one of the Pumas, rain began to fall. The dust and dirt of the outpost turned to red mud, and tiny rivers of muddied water ran down the stairs and floors of the outpost and its buildings. Moore's feet slipped on the mud and his backside hit the ground. He cursed in anger at the turn of events.

If it's not the damn Zodarks, it's the flipping rain, he thought as he picked himself off the ground and made his way toward battle position six.

When he neared the Puma, a horrible shriek pierced the air above as an incoming Zodark banshee shell began its descent into the outpost. Moore looked around and tried to find anything close that could provide cover from any shrapnel, but he saw nothing significant. An indirect-fire bunker was only twenty meters ahead of him, but it was too far to make it in time, so he did what his training had taught him to do—he dove for the closest low ground and curled himself up in a ball as the world exploded around him. The blast lifted his body off the ground and slammed him back down as a rush of wind and rain washed over him. He knew he hadn't been hit, and he quickly scrambled to his feet. To his dismay, he watched parts of the northern wall crumble under the direct hit it had sustained.

"Medic!" someone yelled in front of him.

Without thinking, Moore ran toward the cry for help, which led him to the indirect-fire bunker he had seen moments before the blast. The outside appeared heavily beaten up by shrapnel, but it remained structurally sound. He entered the dark, cramped space and saw the body of a soldier illuminated by the headlamp of the one who'd called for him.

He moved past the man and knelt next to the body. The soldier was lying facedown in the mud, blood flowing from a hole in the small of his back.

"Do you need me for anything, Doc?" the man behind him asked.

He looked up and saw it was his company commander, Captain Striker.

What the hell is he doing out here? Moore wondered. "No, sir, I'm getting him stabilized," he replied. "Sir, it's getting pretty bad out there. I'd feel much more comfortable if you went back to the TOC." It was bad enough having to worry about his friends out in the chaos—to have to worry about their company commander getting schwacked also was too much for him.

The captain smirked grimly before walking out of the bunker and back into the torrential downpour. "We are Apollo's Arrows, son. This is what we train for."

Moore rolled his eyes and went back to work on the wounded soldier at his feet. He inserted his medical device into the port and saw that Private Shugart was breathing but his pulse and blood pressure were way too high. His lower spine had been severed by the piece of shrapnel, and moving him before he was stabilized would be fatal.

He removed a tube of coagulant gel and inserted the tip into the wound until he saw the gel push out of the hole. His pack was becoming considerably lighter again as he removed a spinal disk from its pouch and placed it onto the armor in the middle of the wounded soldier's back. The disk lit up green and the soldier's body went rigid as the disk locked the soldier's armor and stabilized the spine in place. Moore could now place the body on the hover stretcher and transport him to the aid station to be treated.

He rolled the body onto the hover stretcher and activated the lift, and it rose off the ground to about waist height. Lowering his head, Moore walked out of the bunker and into the rain. It was coming down even harder than it had before. Moore turned the corner and ran up the hill toward the aid station. Another blast rocked the ground and he lost his footing and fell to his knees.

When Moore stood and looked over his shoulder, he saw the company commander on his back outside of a Puma that was now twisted and on fire. A soldier called out, "Hey, get over here!" The lone soldier turned and ran toward Moore. "I need you to take this guy to the aid station. Captain Striker is down, and I need to get to him."

Moore sprinted back down toward where his CO was lying. He grimaced at the sight. A large piece of shrapnel had embedded itself in the company commander's head, but he was still awake and alert. *Tough bastard*, he thought.

"How bad is it, Doc? My vision is fading, so shoot me straight," Striker said through sharp breaths.

Moore plugged his medical device into the helmet port and sighed. He wanted to lie to the commander—it was what he did for the others in his situation, but he felt if anyone deserved to know the truth, it was him. "It's fatal, sir. Even if I try to take you to the aid station, you'll die along the way. I just have no way of stopping it."

Captain Striker closed his eyes and took a deep, ragged breath. "I need you to do something for me, then, son. Get to the TOC and tell Lieutenant Gallagher that she's in charge now. Also tell her these specific words: 'broken arrow.' She'll know what to do."

The words held weight to Moore, but he had no idea what they meant. Regardless, he nodded and replied, "Yes, sir."

As he turned and ran up the embankment toward the tactical operations center, Zodark plasma bolts slammed the ground around him, sizzling in the mud and turning it to glass. Moore wanted to steal a glance behind him as cries of "enemy in the wire" echoed across the outpost, but he didn't want to know if certain death was going to leap from the darkness and take him out.

He somehow reached the top of the hill and turned towards the TOC, its door open as some soldiers flooded in. He joined them and looked around for the company's executive officer when a corporal stood and put out her hand. "Where are you going?" she demanded.

"I need to see the XO," he panted. "I need to see her right now!"

"What's going on?" a blond-haired officer asked as she stood up from her station. Her nameplate read "Gallagher."

"Ma'am, Captain Striker is dead," Moore announced. "He told me to tell you that you're in charge, and 'broken arrow,' ma'am."

Her face dropped in horror, and she didn't move. "What?" she asked, astonished.

"Broken arrow, ma'am, broken arrow!" he screamed in her face. Captain Striker had said it was important, and he was getting frustrated that she'd asked him to repeat himself.

The company's acting commander nodded slowly and turned towards the terminal on her desk. She flashed her fingers across the screen, and a transparent blue image of the valley appeared above a table used to plan out operations. No one was hurrying Moore out of the room, so he stood in the corner and lingered for a moment. Several enemy unit designators were located across the tactical map, or tac-map, and moved slowly as it updated their position every three-tenths of a nanosecond. The telescopes on Republic ships orbiting in space above New Eden were able to capture the data and send it to the tac-map in real time, allowing soldiers on the ground to make accurate command decisions.

She highlighted the rear section of the advancing Zodark column and compiled whatever data she had retrieved and sent it over to her terminal with a flick of the wrist. The tac-map disappeared as she left the table and took her seat.

"Republic Navy Ship *Concordia*, this is Apollo Six. Broken arrow. I repeat, broken arrow. Sending coordinates to you now, authorization code Orion Epsilon Delta 382-22."

"Apollo Six, this is the RNS *Concordia*, confirm your coordinates for orbital strike," came the disembodied voice over the terminal.

A hushed murmur fell over the TOC as explosions continued to detonate outside. Moore couldn't believe the words he'd heard. An orbital strike was always used in a last-ditch effort when a base was being overrun. He couldn't remember reading about the Republic using the strategy any time in his studies, but he knew its theoretical effects.

The *Concordia* would fire a solid shot of tungsten from the railgun mounted on its hull towards the coordinates Lieutenant Gallagher had given them and they'd only have a few minutes to hunker down in place and hope the round landed far enough away. Even then, the shockwave would be devastating, and although the walls of the outpost were buried deep within the New Eden soil, he wondered if they'd withstand the force of such an impact.

The earpiece in his helmet crackled and he looked over to see the acting company commander key her mic. "All Apollo units, I've declared broken arrow. An orbital strike has been called in on the following coordinates: Golf Papa one-niner-two-eight, tree-niner-two-one."

He turned to run out the door but was stopped by the company first sergeant, Desmond Kirk. "You're not going anywhere, Doc. Find somewhere to hold on and wait it out. There's nothing else you can do."

Moore's heart dropped.

Chapter 45
Hall

Mortarville, Combat Outpost Legion
ROCNE-South, New Eden

Hall, Richards, and Red had finished cleaning the tube and got it back up and ready to fire when an explosion below reverberated under their feet. They looked at each other with the same worried eyes before checking to see if the system was level.

"Hall, check to see where Jackson is with our rounds," Richards ordered.

Aiden Hall left the gun system and ran over to the sandbag wall that protected them from incoming fire from below, looking down into the outpost. Smoke rose from several sections of the outpost's walls, and Zodark soldiers were forcing their way into the gap. The fighting had now spread into the outpost and Republic soldiers were forming new lines within its walls to try and repel the attackers.

He looked to the far side of the outpost where the ASP was and saw soldiers running in and out of the building, but he couldn't make out if any of them were Jackson. Hellish screams from what Hall knew was Zodark indirect fire streaked across the sky, the rounds hitting targets within the walls. A barracks building exploded outward as one of the rounds made contact. Blue electricity mixed with the fire that erupted.

He watched as several more rounds impacted until one landed a direct hit on top of the ASP. The explosion was blinding, and Hall had to shield his eyes as a monstrous fireball roared into the sky. Everything around the ammunition supply point had been flattened and was now on fire as thick black smoke rose into the air. He had no idea if Jackson was still inside the ASP when it was hit, but if he was, then he wasn't coming with any more mortar rounds.

Hall slowly turned and walked back to his gun. For the first time in the battle, he didn't know what to do. His mission was to provide indirect fire for COP Legion, but now he had no way to do so. As he joined the others around the gun, he shook his head at Richards. "The ASP is gone," he said.

"Whatya mean, gone?" Richards shot back.

"It just got blown to hell. The entire building is gone," Hall replied.

"Did you see Jackson?" Red asked, concerned.

Hall could only shake his head.

"What the hell is happening?" Richards muttered. He sat back against the sandbag wall and put his head in his hands.

"I got more rounds!" came a shout from their left as Jackson came around the corner with three ammo cans under his arms.

Richards jumped to his feet and grabbed one of the cans. "You beautiful bastard!" he shouted.

"Good job, Jacks!" Hall added as he knelt next to the gun terminal and began to set up the last fire mission they'd received before running dry. He adjusted the coordinates on the tac-map to find a new firing solution and make up for the time lost as the Zodarks advanced. "Hang it!" he yelled.

Red took one of the new rounds, placed it into the tube and dropped it when Hall gave the order. Hall looked up and watched Red turn her body to grab another round when a guttural roar erupted from above the hilltop just past the sandbags.

They had all heard that roar before, both in the simulator and while on patrol. Somehow, the Zodarks had scaled the cliffs on the other side of the hill and maneuvered to flank the outpost.

"We got Zodarks incoming!" Staff Sergeant McHenry shouted as he came around the corner with his rifle and began firing at the rocks on the hilltop.

Hall looked over and saw his section sergeant running toward them, not knowing where he had come from moments before. He went to grab his rifle, but Red, Jackson, and Richards had already grabbed theirs. He wasn't going to continue on with the fire mission—although he could have if he needed to. Instead, he did what no mortarman ever wanted to do but all had trained to do at one point. He spun the deflection and elevation knobs until the mortar tube was sticking straight up in the air.

As the others fired at the incoming Zodarks, he grabbed the rounds that Jackson had delivered only moments before and started laying them out around him. If the Zodarks were able to break their lines, he would have no choice but to turn the guns on themselves.

Once that was done, he grabbed his rifle and ran to the sandbags to help repel the assault. The Zodarks were using the rocks at the top of the hill as cover as they poked their heads up and fired for a few moments before dropping out of sight. If they were being cautious with their approach, they must not have a lot with them.

Sergeant McHenry must have thought the same as he fired his rifle and yelled, "Keep pouring it on 'em, mortars. Don't stop!"

Plasma bolts sizzled over top of his head as he tried to ignore the ever-present danger and return fire, but the volume that was coming down on them was heavy. Zodark weapons could fire at a higher rate of speed than Republic guns, and the enemy was using that fact to their full advantage.

Richards knelt back behind the sandbags and replaced a magazine of 5.56 railgun rounds into his rifle. "I think we need to try and flank, Mac," he shouted.

Sergeant McHenry nodded as he returned fire over the sandbags. "Do it," was all he said.

"Jackson, on me," Richards said as he stood and took off over the sandbags and out of sight with Jackson close behind.

"Keep hitting them, guys. We need to keep up the fire so Richards can—" Sergeant McHenry began but his voice cut off.

Hall looked to his left and saw his section sergeant fall backwards and hit the ground. Blood poured from a large hole in the center of his helmet, and Hall knew he couldn't do anything for him.

He keyed his mic. "Any Apollo units, this is Mortarville. We are being overrun—we need assistance!" was all he managed to say. "Damn radio etiquette," he cursed.

Chapter 46
Kodiak

Combat Outpost Legion
ROCNE-South, New Eden

Another battle position had just gone up in flames on the north end of the outpost as Zodarks poured into the perimeter. Harrison Kodiak could feel the heat radiating on the back of his neck despite being on the other side of the area. The enemy had managed to breach the eastern wall, which sat below the mortar pit where Hall and his crew's guns had fallen silent earlier in the battle. That was where Kodiak's team was headed.

With Sergeant Muleskin at the aid station and Sergeant Woods's body in the forest beyond the walls, Kodiak had taken control as team leader. As they crossed the outpost, which had now fallen into absolute chaos, he grabbed other soldiers from his squad that he had come across in the confusion and formed a little more than a team's worth of bodies.

Garza, Moreau, Griffin, and Redner had joined Kodiak, Morgan, and Mendoza as they made their way to the steps that led up to Mortarville. The stairway to hell was now undoubtedly slick with the rain that poured down from the heavens.

In the heat of the day, all one had to worry about was the occasional loose rock that resulted in a sprained ankle. In the monsoon months, the stairs became a ramp of slick mud and rivers of water. With how bad the rains had been the past few days, Kodiak knew it would be hell getting up the stairs to support Hall and the mortars, but it had to be done.

When Hall had come over the radio asking for assistance, he'd said they were being overrun. Kodiak had no idea how the Zodarks had scaled the cliffs to get up there, but that was irrelevant. They were there now, and Kodiak had heeded the call of his friend.

Kodiak swept his hand forward. "Follow me," he said as he led the team around the mess hall toward the stairway. Last time he'd checked, Sergeant Casper of Bravo Team was taking her team around to the gate entrance to secure the hole that had been made, but he hadn't heard from Sergeant Nelson of Charlie Team. Kodiak's team was on their own.

Turning another corner, they came to a forked intersection. One path led towards a section of the wall that had been destroyed and the other up to Mortarville. The radio traffic from the mortar pit was becoming more panicked. They had already suffered several casualties, and the enemy fire was overwhelming them.

Three plasma bolts streaked past and slammed into the concrete barrier in front of them, and the team came to a halt.

Kodiak motioned back to Morgan. "Pop smoke so we can cross," he said.

Morgan nodded and removed a smoke grenade from a pouch on her armor. Pulling the pin, she tossed the device into the street, and in a flash, eight explosions unleashed a thick white smoke screen that enveloped the area. Kodiak tapped Garza on the helmet and sent him across first. Garza slid behind a steel barrier that marked the halfway point across the street and took up position with his rifle. Kodiak then nodded to Morgan, who began her trek to the middle. Passing Garza, she continued across the road, reaching the entrance to the stairs.

"You're up, kid," Kodiak said, giving Moreau a nudge forward.

She gripped his shoulder and tried to smile. "See ya on the other side," she replied.

Kodiak watched as Moreau passed Garza and continued until coming to a stop beside Morgan. She then lifted her rifle and provided overwatch, looking up towards the mortar pit. Kodiak, Griffin, Redner, and Mendoza were all that was left on their side of the road. Kodiak wanted to get to the other side and start figuring out what his next plan of attack was going to be. He turned to Mendoza. "I'll go next, you come after me, and so on," he said.

Planting his feet into the mud, Kodiak kicked off and ran as fast as he could across the open area, passing Garza and sliding in next to Moreau and Morgan. The smoke was dissipating, and he held up his hand for Mendoza not to cross, but it was too late—much too late. Mendoza had already made it to Garza's position and was in the process of bounding over to Kodiak when he was struck. It happened in slow motion, something Kodiak thought only happened in the movies, but he saw everything. He watched as the beam of blue plasma streaked across the opening, out of the fading white smoke, and into the back of Private Mendoza. The beam of deadly blue light then exited his chest and splashed across the ground.

His body slammed down between Garza and Kodiak's position, and soon, more enemy fire came in their direction. Kodiak stared at the lifeless corpse of the man that had been with him for the past two days, the man who'd had his back both in the forest and in that stupid overturned Puma, as his blood leaked onto the mud. Shock had its grip on Harrison Kodiak for a moment, until Moreau smacked the back of his head.

"What the hell do we do now?" she shouted.

Kodiak looked over to Moreau and then back across to Garza, who was huddled underneath the concrete barrier that separated him from the Zodark fire. "Throw more smoke," he ordered.

Morgan took her last smoke grenade, pulled the pin, and tossed it into the middle of the road. Eight explosions blasted into the air, basking the area with thick white smoke, concealing Garza and the others from the incoming fire. The Zodarks had become wise to the smoke as bolts of blue plasma continued to punch through it, and Garza kept his head down.

"Can you get to us?" Kodiak shouted over to the trapped soldier.

"I don't know, man, I don't know!" Garza shouted back.

Kodiak turned to Morgan and Moreau. "I need covering fire. Switch to the laser setting and pour it into the smoke, and don't let up until Garza is here with us."

He echoed the same orders over to Redner and Griffin, who had yet to cross, and they nodded in acknowledgment. Kodiak stood from behind the barrier and sprayed the smoke with automatic fire, lighting up the smoke in hues of blue. The sustained fire was immense from all five guns on both sides of the road as Garza got to his feet and sprinted to the safety of the stairway.

Whether it was out of fear of being left behind or not understanding the orders that Kodiak had given, Griffin got to his feet and bolted across the road, firing his weapon wildly through the smoke as he ran. He had almost made it to them before a stray plasma bolt slammed into him, spiraling his body into the ground, where it lay still. Redner was smarter as he stayed where he was.

"Don't cross," Kodiak shouted to him. "Try and link up with Sergeant Casper or Nelson—we got this."

"You sure?" Redner called back.

Kodiak held a thumbs-up and turned to head up the stairs. He keyed his mic. "Hall, this is Apollo One-One Alpha. We're coming to you."

Chapter 47
Hall

Mortarville, Combat Outpost Legion
ROCNE-South, New Eden

Kodiak's voice in Hall's ear was all he needed to hear. He turned to Red. "Some guys I know from First Platoon are coming up to help out. We just gotta keep holding on till then," he reassured her.

Red was gripping her side after a plasma bolt had taken her in the flank last time she'd poked her head up from the sandbags. She was alive but in severe pain. Gunfire erupted from behind the rocks as Jackson and Richards got in contact with the Zodarks who had them pinned down. He had no idea how the fight was going, and the volume of fire was no indication of who was coming out on top.

"All Apollo units, I've declared broken arrow. An orbital strike has been called in on the following coordinates: Golf Papa one-niner-two-eight, tree-niner-two-one," a female voice announced in his ear.

"Good copy, out."

He looked over to Red. "Is that the XO?" Hall asked in disbelief.

"Captain Striker must be doing as bad as I am," she laughed through coughs.

Hall ran over to his mortar terminal and found the coordinates of the drop. It was being angled toward the far side of the river, where the Zodarks had come from. He had to hand it to the XO—she was doing everything in her power to avoid wiping out the entire outpost in one strike.

"We have a really big round coming in thirty seconds, Red. Just stay down and hold on."

Hall lifted his head over the lip again and saw a Zodark dashing from behind cover toward them. He raised his rifle and squeezed the trigger, and railgun rounds slammed into the beast and toppled it down the hill until it came to rest against the sandbags in front of him. He brought the rifle over the top and fired a burst into the top of the beast's skull before trying to find a new target.

The new target was another Zodark who was much closer than its partner. The beast leapt over the sandbag and swung its blade down toward Hall. He parried the strike with his rifle and tried to roll out of the attack, but the weight the Zodark was applying toppled him onto his back. He scrambled with his feet to try and get some distance before raising his rifle, but the Zodark was on him. It grabbed him by his armor and lifted him high in the air.

The Zodark's fist was clamped down hard on Hall's throat and he kicked his feet against the brute, gasping for any air he could get, but his windpipe was closed shut. His vision blurred and began to darken when a fine mist sprayed him in the face. His body hit the ground hard, and he scrambled to his feet.

The Zodark lay dead on the ground at his feet, a hole in the back of its head. He grabbed his rifle and looked over to Red, who was smiling at him, but Hall just looked on in dismay as a third Zodark climbed the wall and buried its sword deep into Red's chest.

Her cries of anguish mixed with his cries of rage as he emptied what was left inside the railgun magazine and only let go of the trigger when he heard the weapon run dry. His rifle fell to the ground, and he fell to his knees. That Zodark was dead, but so was Red, a smile still on her face as her head bent low toward the ground.

The gunfire above the hilltop was still going back and forth but was much more subdued than a few minutes before, and he had a feeling that, just like Red, Richards's and Jackson's time on this planet was ending. He grabbed his rifle one more time and inserted his last magazine into the magazine well. Three more Zodarks crested the hill and raced toward him. Hall stood on the sandbags and fired into the group, watching one spin to the ground in pain as the others continued pushing forward. The first raised a sword that it had in its hand and Hall fired a burst at close range into the monster's face. He turned to fire at the next, but that Zodark had been wise. They both fired their rifles at the same time, and both collapsed onto the ground.

Hall's back slammed into the mud, and he gasped for air. He tried to sit up, but every time he told his body to do something, it didn't respond. His neck still worked, and although blurry, his vision was still there. He looked down and saw a smoldering hole just below his chest. He was hit bad. It was weird, though; he didn't feel any pain. He was frustrated his body wasn't responding to what he was trying to do, which was to escape the hill. Strangely, no pain washed over him.

A loud roar broke through the storm clouds and a bright white light blinded Hall just before he was plunged into darkness.

Chapter 48
Kodiak

Mortarville, Combat Outpost Legion
ROCNE-South, New Eden

Kodiak and what was left of his team bounded up the stairs, slipping on every other stone as they tried to get to the top of the hill as fast as possible. More gunfire erupted overhead as the mortars continued to fight, but it was slowing, and he feared they were down to their last soldiers. The call had come over the net that an orbital strike was incoming on some location nearby, and he figured if it was right on top of him, he might as well save his friend first.

As they came around the final bend, a blinding white light flashed across the sky. Kodiak and the rest fell to their knees and threw themselves into the stairs and mud, hiding their faces in the ground, but the light continued to push through. It faded in seconds, but a tremendous heat swallowed him like he had been placed in an oven and left to cook. The heads-up display on his visor crackled and warnings flashed across it, but he ignored the ringing. The visor's HUD flickered and disappeared.

Just when the heat subsided and he thought the worst was over, the ground began to shake violently. Kodiak tried to hold on to the rocks he was next to, but the man-made earthquake threw him around the stairs. Garza tried to stand but lost his footing and fell. Kodiak tried to yell, tried to warn the rest to stay put, but he could barely hear himself think, let alone get the words out of his mouth. What Kodiak later realized was that the shockwave from the orbital strike had slammed into the outpost, and Garza, who'd tried to stand again, had been thrown into the air and over the edge.

Kodiak prayed. He prayed harder than he had ever prayed before in his life and promised whoever was listening that when the war was over, he would find a quiet little farm in Texas and live in peace the rest of his life. Almost as if a higher power had heard him, the ground settled, the shaking stopped, and the noise disappeared.

Without thinking, he got to his feet and shouted, "Follow me," to whoever was still with him.

They bounded the final couple of steps and entered Mortarville. To his right was a destroyed mortar gun with the bodies of its handlers strewn across the ground. None of them looked like Hall. He pushed past camo netting and found the other gun system tipped over on its side with rounds covering the floor. A staff sergeant lay dead over in the corner and a young woman with a blade in her chest was smiling but also dead. That was when his eyes fell on Hall.

He was lying on his back, eyes wide, with a plasma bolt wound to his chest. "Hall?" He heard his voice crack. "Hall?" he asked again, shaking his friend.

Hall's head just wobbled back and forth as Kodiak shook him, but he didn't move, didn't blink, and didn't breathe. Kodiak's heart broke in two at the sight. He hadn't made it up the hill in time, and the mortars had paid a heavy toll. He looked around at all the Zodark bodies scattered across the area and shook his head in disbelief.

"I'm so sorry, Bear," Moreau said as she touched his shoulder.

Kodiak's body went numb, and his shoulders sank. "Me too," he whispered, looking at Hall.

The sound of rocks rolling down the hilltop to his front spooked him and his team, and they all raised their weapons toward the noise. A Republic soldier bounded down the side with his hands raised, his rifle hanging on his chest. His nameplate read "Jackson."

"Whoa, I'm friendly," he called out to them.

Kodiak lowered his rifle. "Where the hell were you?" he screamed.

"Whatya mean? I was flanking with Sergeant Richards—didn't Hall tell…" His voice trailed off as he looked down at Hall's body.

Kodiak saw the pain in his eyes and softened his words. "Where's Sergeant Richards?"

Tears fell from Jackson's eyes as he knelt next to Hall and placed his hand on his chest. "We almost had them when the orbital strike hit. When the dust cleared, he was dead. So were the Zodarks." He looked up at Kodiak. "Did we win?"

For the first time since getting to the top of Mortarville, Kodiak thought about the orbital strike and ran to the sandbags overlooking the valley and outpost. The sight he was met with was devastating. The entire valley was blackened and on fire; the forests were flattened down to stumps, and the river no longer existed. Day had slowly turned to night as thick black smoke from the impact zone blacked out the sun.

Sporadic fire continued in the outpost below, but there were far more Republic guns going off than Zodark guns. Above them, Republic fighters screamed through the sky, strafing Zodark ground units that were trying to escape across the river. Some of them split off and engaged Zodark air units that had arrived much too late to the party, and they were shot down with ease. He watched one of the strange-looking vessels break apart and slam into the ground where the river had once been.

He turned back to Jackson and the others, and with as much confidence in his voice as he could muster, he said, "We need to head back down, find our platoon leader, and report in. They're mopping up the straggling units."

"Wait, that's it?" Moreau asked. "We won?"

Kodiak sighed, looking at Hall. A tear ran down his cheek. "The battle is over, but I'd hardly call this a win."

****

Forward Operating Base Edwards
ROCNE-South, New Eden
24 Hours Later

Reinforcements from Belus Company replaced the men and women of Apollo at what remained of Combat Outpost Legion shortly after the battle. Kodiak had gathered his gear and made sure all of the surviving members, his friends, had climbed on board the awaiting Osprey. He had taken one final glance at the outpost before the doors closed. Columns of acrid black smoke climbed into the sky, blocking out the sunlight. Soldiers from Belus Company were offloading from vehicles, some standing in shock at the destruction of the compound. Before the hatch closed, he thought he spotted a familiar but unwelcomed face.

Even as he stood in formation twenty-four hours later, he wondered if he had indeed seen Skaggs. Leaving the outpost was still a haze in his mind as his brain tried to compute what he'd been through just one day before. If it was Skaggs he'd seen stepping out of a Puma, that meant he'd sadly survived the Zodark offensive.

The nondenominational chaplain had said, "Death is a part of life, whether warm in your bed surrounded by family or alone on a battlefield in the heat of combat. What matters are the actions we take in between now and death that will define us and who we were forever."

The chaplain stood at the head of the formation as they said their final farewells to the fallen. On both sides of him stood rows of rifles, bayonets affixed, anchored into a stand with helmets on top of the buttstocks and a single dog tag hanging from each of the rifles' grips. Behind the rows of rifle memorials, pictures of the fallen members of Apollo Company faded in and out on a projection behind the chaplain.

The bodies were already aboard transport shuttles, headed to the ships that would take them home. With Captain Striker dead, First Lieutenant Gallagher, who'd survived the battle, had taken over as acting company commander. Standing next to her on the elevated platform with the chaplain was the company first sergeant, Kirk, who looked just as bloodied as the rest of them.

The picture of Aiden Hall flashed on the wall, staring back at Kodiak. It was a picture of a happier time. Then, as suddenly as Aiden appeared, he was gone, replaced with the image of another fallen soldier. It almost felt like a metaphor to Kodiak. *We're here for but a moment in time...and then we're gone*, he thought privately before another thought formed in his mind. *I may not be long for this world, but I assure you, the world will know who Kodiak Harrison was.*

When the ceremony was over, they broke formation and mingled amongst themselves. Out of the seventy soldiers in First Platoon that had landed on New Eden, only forty-two remained. That made it easier to find the ones he was closest with. Morgan, Moreau, Moore, and Redner were the only ones from Kodiak's basic that had survived.

He looked back up to the projection as another image of Hall appeared. The picture had been taken the first week they'd arrived on New Eden. All of the graduates from his basic training class that were put in Apollo Company had gotten together for a party. Garza and Mendoza had grilled steaks, Moreau and Hall had somehow managed to find a stash of liquor, and Sims had found a radio to play music. When the party had died down and everyone had started to head back to their barracks, Kodiak and some of the others had gathered around a fire. Moreau had taken a picture of Hall staring into the flames, a grin on his face. Hall had changed since basic—he smiled more.

"War's not fair," Moreau said, standing next to him as she stared at the picture of Hall.

Kodiak looked at her. "And it never will be."

He didn't know what else to say. It was all still very raw.

Moreau grabbed his arm softly. "We're gonna lose a lot more before this is all over."

Kodiak put his hand over hers and tried to smile. "You're correct. Doesn't mean it'll be us. We'll keep our heads down and drive on—and, hey, if we somehow make it out the other side, drinks are on me."

"Bear, if we ever make it out of this war alive, I'd probably just marry your ass because we'll be old by then." Moreau laughed and squeezed his arm lightly.

"You've got yourself a deal," Kodiak replied.

When the memorial ended, the two of them walked a short distance away from the others. Standing near an empty field used for physical training, Kodiak held her hand.

She interlaced her fingers with his and squeezed tightly. Together they stood as the sun set behind the forest-covered mountain and they looked into the approaching night sky. A dark moon covered in veins of pulsating lava glowed in the waning light of dusk.

"I heard a rumor that we're headed there next," Moreau said, pointing to the moon with her free hand.

"You mean the glowing ball of death?"

She laughed before saying, "I was told the Zodarks have a resistance force on New Eden's moons. Someone's gotta snuff 'em out."

Kodiak took a deep breath and closed his eyes. The sunset displayed an array of deep blues, violets, and orange across the sky. The clouds looked like they were bewitched by purple fire. It was beautiful, and the dark moon in the sky was the opposite. He wanted to try and capture that little bit of beauty to erase some of the scars that had been left behind.

He looked back down to Moreau, who looked at him. Their eyes locked and he kissed her forehead. "I reckon we'll find out soon enough."

Epilogue

RNS *Boxer*
In Orbit Above New Eden

It had been a couple of weeks since the battle of COP Legion. The soldiers of Apollo Company along with the rest of their regiment had been relieved of combat operations and brought to FOB Edwards to rest and recover. When the *Boxer* reappeared in orbit, they relocated to what would now become their home ship. As the shipyards completed more assault transports, some of the regiments were being permanently assigned to them.

Kodiak was glad to return to the *Boxer*. It held a lot of fond memories he'd made with friends on their way to New Eden. Walking the halls of the ship, working out at the gym, or eating in the mess hall also reminded him of the friends who weren't with them any longer. The ones left behind on the strange alien planet below, never to return. Their bodies would be buried in war memorial cemeteries like the ones that exist all over Europe from World War II.

Recovering from the physical wounds of war was much easier nowadays. Processing the images and the terrors of fighting the horrifying Zodark hordes proved harder to deal with. Kodiak did his best to focus his mind and efforts on the ones who had survived. The friends he still had. Together, they'd learn to deal with the pain he'd felt at Hall's memorial and prepare themselves for whatever might come next.

As Kodiak returned from the gym one morning, he received a message from Staff Sergeant Muleskin, asking Kodiak to come see him. When Kodiak found him still recovering in the med bay, he was told to take a seat.

"Kodiak, I wanted to speak with you and give you a heads-up. Tomorrow, some transports are going to arrive on the *Boxer*. They're going to deliver enough replacement soldiers to bring the regiment back up to one hundred percent strength. That means our platoon and our squad are going to get a few new faces," Muleskin explained.

Kodiak wasn't sure how he felt about that. He knew the reality of it—you had to replace the soldiers lost. But each new face also represented a friend he'd lost.

Muleskin must have read his thoughts. "I know what you must be thinking, Kodiak. But here's the deal. Replacements are a part of war. No one likes it or wants it, but we all have to deal with it and accept it. I want to explain something to you. Something my grandfather told me when I first joined the military. Something each Muleskin has passed down from one generation to the other when it was our time to serve. He told me when his grandfather had fought in a war way back in the 1960s, most of the soldiers who fought in it were draftees. They were sent to fighting units in Vietnam as individual soldiers to backfill the combat losses a unit had taken. There was little to no unit cohesion as soldiers who served their tour would rotate back and new ones filled their places.

"My granddad told me what made it harder for the guys who fought in that war, and ultimately led to higher casualties, was that when a new guy showed up, no one really wanted to be their friend. To take them under their wing. They treated them as outsiders until they got a little time under their belt and they survived a few missions or patrols. My granddad told me if I ever found myself in a war, I should never view a replacement like an outsider. He told me if I wanted to live, if I wanted the rest of my friends to live, then I needed to make sure that replacement knew he was part of the team and we got him as trained up as we could.

"The reason I'm telling you this, Kodiak, is that we're going to get replacements tomorrow. We'll continue to keep getting them for as long as this war goes on. And I won't tolerate any weak links in my squad or platoon. Don't create a weak link I'll need to handle later, got me?"

Kodiak thought about what Muleskin had said. There was only one response he could give. "Roger, Sergeant, I'll make sure they're squared away and part of the team."

"Good, now here's your new corporal stripes—you're being promoted. Now don't let me down. I'm counting on you, Kodiak," Muleskin replied as he handed him his new rank insignia.

Kodiak smiled for the first time in weeks as he took the new rank. He wasn't sure why or what had changed, but somehow, he felt like a strange weight he didn't know he'd been carrying had just been lifted.

Before he left, he asked, "By the way, with all the replacements we're getting, any ideas on what we're doing next or headed to?"

"As a matter of fact, a day after our replacements arrive we're supposed to receive some new orders. Don't hold me to it, but I hear we may be supporting some kind of operation near one of New Eden's moons."

Grunting at the news, Kodiak responded, "Sounds fun."

"Don't get too excited. We'll have to train some of the more fresh-faced privates on New Eden to get them acclimated to what we're doing here. I see a few humanitarian missions and a couple of patrols in your future, Corporal. Once that acclimation period is over, you'll join the rest of us on the *Boxer*. In the meantime, look at this as an opportunity to hone those superior team leader skills I know are buried deep inside."

Kodiak didn't necessarily like the sound of that if he was being honest. Playing babysitter while the rest of Apollo Company kicked it up the well wasn't exactly what he had in mind. It could be worse, though. He shrugged. "Well, nothing can be as bad as COP Legion, I suppose," he replied.

"Damn, Kodiak, we make you a corporal and in sixty seconds you go and jinx the whole regiment with a comment like that. Get the hell out of my room," Muleskin half joked as he motioned for Kodiak to leave.

As Corporal Harrison Kodiak walked to his room, he racked his brain for any info they'd been given about the moons above New Eden. He knew there were two. One appeared to be like New Eden in that it had water and vegetation growing on it, but it didn't have an atmosphere that was breathable to humans. The other did have a breathable atmosphere and looked terrifying from space. Deep red veins of flowing lava ran in rivers through cracks of broken black rock. As he opened the door to his room, he wasn't sure which one would be better.

As he lay on his bunk, looking at the empty one he knew would be occupied with a replacement tomorrow, a sickening feeling settled in his gut. Given how hard these Zodark bastards had fought, he was left with the feeling that this was going to be a long, brutal war of survival. Muleskin was right—if he and his friends were going to make it through this, they couldn't have any weak links. If they did, the Zodarks would tear them apart.

Taking a couple of breaths, Kodiak drifted off to sleep. Tomorrow would be a new day. Tomorrow he'd welcome their new replacements and they'd get ready for this new mission, whatever it might be.

From James Rosone

I hope you have enjoyed the first book of our Rise of the Republic spin-off series. Our goal was to give you, our readers, the opportunity to see the world we had created in the main series from a new angle, a new point of view. In contrast to the main series, T.C. Manning is showing us this world through the eyes of the young men and women who joined the military for adventure, a new future, an escape, or a second chance. Both T.C. and I served in the military. We have that soldierly bond all military members have. Apollo's Arrows is about that bond developed through shared sacrifice for something greater than oneself.

Cherubim's Call is the first book Miranda and I have published through our veteran mentorship program. I want to thank all of you who have joined us in supporting our effort to help military veterans learn how to become self-published authors. We couldn't have done it without your help and support.

If you enjoyed this book and you want to find out what happens to the men and women of Apollo's Company next, the pre-order link to the second book, *Malevolent Inferno*, is now available for preorder as well as the third book in this series, *The Zealot*. We hope you will keep following Apollo Company through the war until this timeline eventually links to the Rise of the Republic in the battle for Alfheim, which we saw unfold in *Into the Chaos* and *Info the Fire*. If you haven't had a chance to read the original series, we hope you will jump into the action by picking up a copy of *Into the Stars*.

To join the Front Line Publishing, Inc. newsletter, please visit frontlinepublishinginc.com and scroll to the bottom to subscribe.

The Rise of the Republic has a Facebook page for you to visit: https://www.facebook.com/FriendsoftheRepublic. From there, you can also join the private reader group for the Rise of the Republic world, or the Apollo's Arrows reader group, where we will talk about everything related to the Apollo Company. We offer opportunities to name characters, read scenes before they are released and provide feedback on what you want to see in the next book.

If you enjoyed this book, we would love it if you would take the take to write up a review on Amazon and Goodreads. Your continued support of our mentees' books and our mentorship program means a lot to Miranda and me, and to T.C. and his family.

From T.C. Manning

Apollo Company came to life in the Rise of the Republic Series with *Into the Chaos* and *Into the Fire*. The men and women of Apollo Company fought one of their toughest battles yet on the frozen tundra of Alfheim, but this was not where their story began. The more I continued to write about their experiences, the more I wanted to experience their past. In this series, we went back to the beginning, before the Republic ruled over all of Earth and before humanity knew of Zodarks or Orbots. You experienced the origin stories of those familiar to you, like Harrison Kodiak and Oliver Moore, while meeting new faces with unknown fates.

Science fiction is one of my favorite genres to write as it gives you endless possibilities to create whatever you'd like. Coming from a military background, I always wanted to write about the grunts on the ground. I've read, and enjoyed, so many series that follow the bigger picture, but not enough show you what it's like to go through the future's version of basic training. You don't normally get to experience what first contact with an alien race looks like in the trenches.

My hope with this series is to explore humanity's fight against an alien threat while bringing memorable characters to life—characters that will stick with you long after the series concludes. We will all experience loss and triumph, heartache and happiness. War is hard, dirty, bloody, and horrific, but it can also lead to stories of great heroism like those that still echo in our history today. You will see a soldier's life in a future where soldiers are not stationed on Earth. You will experience new planets' ecosystems and the perils that await those who visit.

If you have ever served, currently serve, or hope to serve in your nation's military, thank you. To all the fallen in wars past and present, thank you for your sacrifice and your family's sacrifice. We are forever in your debt.

To my amazing wife, Amanda, my sons, Patrick and Grayson, and my little Lilly, thank you for dealing with the long nights and days where I locked myself away in pursuit of my dreams. Without you, those dreams would never have come true.

To sign up for T.C. Manning's email list, please visit the following website: http://eepurl.com/hY2JVP. If you would like to keep up to date with T.C. Manning and the future of the Apollo's Arrows series, please visit his author Facebook Page at: https://www.facebook.com/AuthorTCManning

Abbreviation Key

AAR	After Action Report
AIT	Advanced Individual Training
AO	Area of Operations
ASP	Ammunition Supply Point
BP	Battle Position
CO	Commanding Officer
COP	Combat Outpost
DFAC	Dining Facility
DS	Drill Sergeant
EOD	Explosive Ordnance Disposal
EKG	Electrocardiogram
FOB	Forward Operating Base
HALO	An advanced autonomous surgical system
HE	High-Explosive
HUD	Heads-Up Display
IFV	Infantry Fighting Vehicle
IP	Insertion Point
JTMF	Joint Troop Medical Facility
KIA	Killed in Action
LAS	Light Atmospheric Shuttle
MFV	Mortar Firing Vehicles
MGP	Machine-Gun Platform
MOS	Military Occupational Specialty
MP	Military Police
MRE	Meals-Ready-to-Eat
NCO	Noncommissioned Officer
ODT	Orbital Drop Training
PAC	Personal Access Code
PDC	Point Defense Cannon
PL	Platoon Leader
PLANRO	Planetside Rotation
R&R	Rest and Recreation
RA	Republic Army
RNS	Republic Naval Ship
RP	Rally Point
ROCNE	Republic Operational Command of New Eden

SET	Space Exploration Treaty
SOP	Standard Operating Procedure
TOC	Tactical Operations Center
UCMJ	Uniform Code of Military Justice
XO	Executive Officer

Printed in Great Britain
by Amazon